Praise for *The River of Kings*

"A literary achievement: a complex, character-driven story that's powerful in concept and execution."   —*Kirkus Reviews* (starred review)

"Drawing comparisons to James Dickey's *Deliverance* and Charles Frazier's *Cold Mountain,* Brown's impressive second novel is an intense, solidly written story of family loyalty, Southern traditions, and haunting historic landscapes."   —*Library Journal* (starred review)

"Captures the essence of an enchanting place with a story combining adventure, family drama, and local history."   —*Publishers Weekly*

"There is enough adventure, mystery, and historical references in this polished, tightly controlled narrative to fill two novels, all richly and lovingly evoked in Brown's sure hands."   —*Booklist*

"*The River of Kings* is almost impossibly visual—cinematic in the best sense. Like Cormac McCarthy and Annie Proulx, Brown possesses rare and wild gifts, writing with the arresting precision and unremitting intensity that can keep a reader's jaw clenched for books at a time."   —*Paste* magazine

"Scorchingly vivid . . . [Brown's] ability to thrill is ever present, and the mastery of craft that made his first novel so compelling comes flooding back."
                    —*The Atlanta Journal-Constitution*

"*The River of Kings* is a masterful, mature work that again marks its author as a talent to watch."   —*StarNews* (Wilmington)

"The main characters of each era are vivid, complex, and deeply conflicted about their environment. The novel deftly reels its readers into a world where life and death are intimately entwined with the river's ebb and flow."
                    —*Atlanta* magazine

Also by Taylor Brown

Gods of Howl Mountain

Fallen Land

In the Season of Blood & Gold

THE
RIVER OF KINGS

TAYLOR BROWN

ST. MARTIN'S GRIFFIN
NEW YORK

THE RIVER OF KINGS. Copyright © 2017 by Taylor Brown. All rights reserved. Printed in the United States of America. For information, address St. Martin's Publishing Group, 120 Broadway, New York, NY 10271.

www.stmartins.com

Maps by Environmental Protection Division, Georgia DNR

Cartographers: Tara Muenz and Taylor Brown

Interior reproductions of Jacques Le Moyne's sixteenth-century illustrations courtesy of Special & Digital Collections, Tampa Library, University of South Florida

Title page photograph courtesy of Freeimages.com/Chris Winfield

Designed by Kathryn Parise

THE LIBRARY OF CONGRESS HAS CATALOGED THE HARDCOVER EDITION AS FOLLOWS:

Names: Brown, Taylor, 1982– author.
Title: The river of kings : a novel / Taylor Brown.
Description: First Edition. | New York : St. Martin's Press, 2017.
Identifiers: LCCN 2016044294 | ISBN 9781250111753 (hardcover) |
   ISBN 9781250111760 (ebook)
Subjects: | BISAC: FICTION / Literary. | FICTION / Historical.
Classification: LCC PS3602.R722894 R58 2017 | DDC 813/.6—dc23
LC record available at https://lccn.loc.gov/2016044294

ISBN 978-1-250-16551-0 (trade paperback)

Our books may be purchased in bulk for promotional, educational, or business use. Please contact your local bookseller or the Macmillan Corporate and Premium Sales Department at 1-800-221-7945, extension 5442, or by email at MacmillanSpecialMarkets@macmillan.com.

First St. Martin's Griffin Edition: March 2018

D 10 9 8 7 6 5 4 3 2

To Whit and Ben, who always led me to the river.

You are my brothers, and I love you.

To L.G., who has my highest respect, and all those who serve.

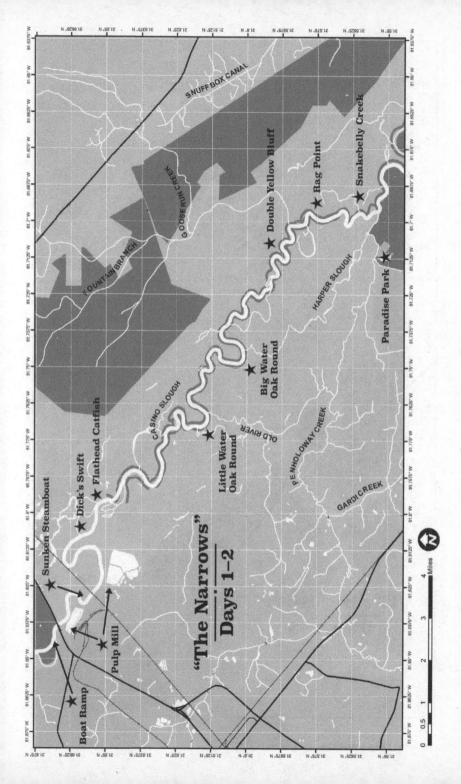

"The Narrows"
Days 1-2

Boat Ramp

Sunken Steamboat

Pulp Mill

Dick's Swift

Flathead Catfish

CASINO SLOUGH

SNUFFBOX CANAL

GOOSE RUN CREEK

FOUNTAIN BRANCH

Little Water Oak Round

Big Water Oak Round

OLD RIVER

Double Yellow Bluff

Rag Point

Snakebelly Creek

HARPER SLOUGH

PENHOLOWAY CREEK

GARDI CREEK

Paradise Park

N

Miles

0   0.5   1   2   3   4

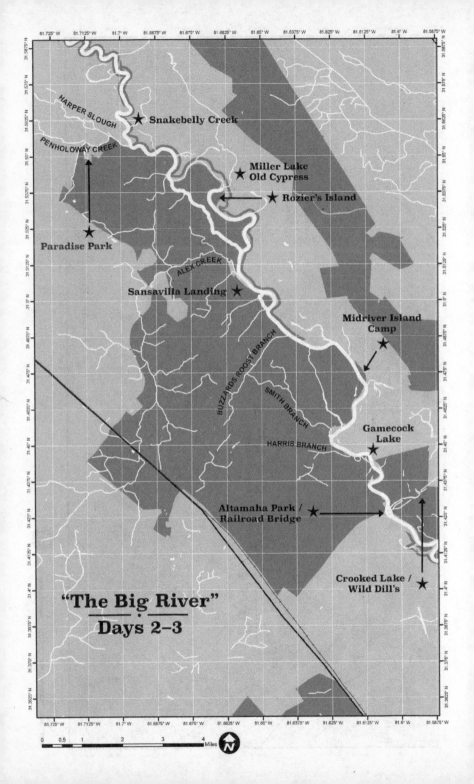

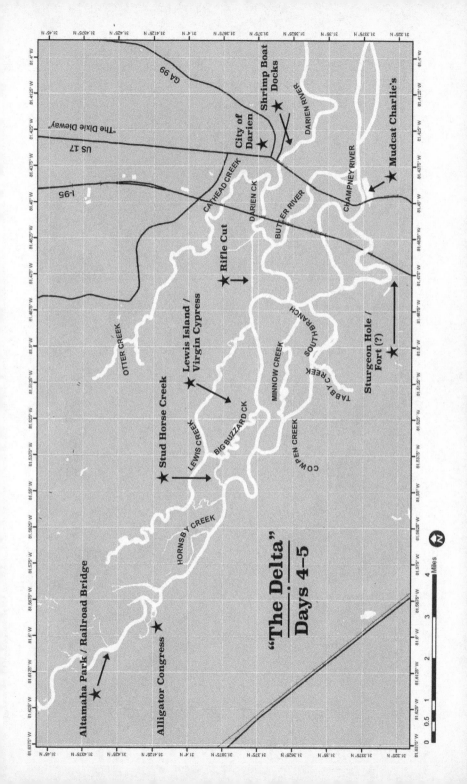

"The Delta"
Days 4-5

Altamaha Park / Railroad Bridge

Alligator Congress

Stud Horse Creek

Lewis Island / Virgin Cypress

Rifle Cut

Shrimp Boat Docks

City of Darien

Mudcat Charlie's

Sturgeon Hole / Fort (?)

OTTER CREEK

HORNSBY CREEK

LEWIS CREEK

BIG BUZZARD CK

MINNOW CREEK

COW PEN CREEK

TABBY CREEK

SOUTH BRANCH

CAT HEAD CREEK

DARIEN CK

BUTTER RIVER

DARIEN RIVER

CHAMPNEY RIVER

GA 99

"The Dixie Dieway"

US 17

I-95

0 0.5 1   2   3   4
Miles

N

The uncertainty of things imagined becomes an assurance by
beholding with the eye things as marvelous as prodigious land
and sea monsters long ago seen and known
in that land of Florida.

—Captain Giles de Pysière, 1565

BOOK I

An old man stands tall against the rise of sun, balanced upon a river of shattered glass. His boat thumps gently in the current. His shadow is cast long down the surface, crossed by the beam of the weapon balanced upon his shoulder. A harpoon. His hair is white, wild as a mane. His eyes are strange worlds, storm-clouded. They seek a myth beneath the river's surface. A water-serpent, toothed and armored like the monsters of prehistory, the saurian progeny of the God he once worshiped. He fears the monster will rise again into the light of history, and all the earth will be as it was in the days before Adam. A world of yellow eyes and red teeth, in constant war. A savage kingdom.

BOOK I

1

Altamaha River, Day 1

The river, storm-swollen and heavy, gleams like a long dark muscle in the earth, a serpent sliding mindless through the yet-bare arcade of river birch and cypress that lines its banks. The two brothers stand motionless over the waters, silent, then haul their kayaks onto their shoulders, bearing them bloodred and blue down the old boat ramp, the concrete scarred beneath them like ancient stone. A pair of fractured gullies, parallel, marks the hard decades of boat trailers and trucks, and the traces shine wet and broken in the early light. The ramp runs like a dagger into the shallows, vanishing into the tea-dark current.

The brothers wear short-torso paddling vests, each with a silver dive knife affixed in an over-heart sheath. Their spray skirts hang from their waists like floppy tutus. They carry sufficient provisions for five nights on the river: canned beans and freeze-dried fruit, mixed nuts and combat rations and a flask of Kentucky bourbon. They carry eight gallons of fresh water stored in bottles and plastic bladders, along with sleeping bags and insect repellent and a tent they'll use only if it rains. On one of the boats, lashed aft of the cockpit, they carry five pounds of ash in a black nylon dry bag.

Their father.

Hunter, the younger, steps knee-deep into the current, and he can feel the weight of it pulling at his calves and ankles, the dark pull that is like an ambition. The spring rains charge down the dark swales of the Appalachian foothills, rumbling in wider and deeper confluence, birthing rivers that slither for the sea. Midway, they tumble and crash over the Fall Line, the belt of shoals and waterfalls and hydroelectric dams that marks the lost edge of the continent, past which the state of Georgia was once the bottom of a prehistoric sea. The fossils of ancient corals and mollusks are found far up-country, and the land is full of sharks' teeth.

Hunter wears one on a string around his neck. It's the size of an arrowhead, with a jet-black root and blue-gray enamel, the edges slightly serrated. He found it digging for baitworms as a boy, several miles inland of the coast. It is from Megalodon, the fifty-ton shark of the Cenozoic era. He and his brother are putting in deep below the Fall Line, down in the ancient seabed of slash pine and cypress and gum, while above them roam heavy gray monsters of cloud.

Lawton sits erect in his boat, waiting.

"Boy, you planning to lollygag all day or what?"

Hunter looks down at him. His older brother has a bushy red beard, fire-hued, that he grew in-country. In some of his pictures, the other men have black ovals instead of faces, and the mountains and vehicles and buildings are of a color: sand.

"I'm coming," says Hunter. "Jesus, your horses run off?"

"I want to make the house before dark."

"So you said. You keep badgering me, you'll get an ass-whipping before we even get there."

Lawton, forty pounds heavier, grins. His eyes a vicious, merry blue.

"I'd like to see that."

"Keep it up, big boy, you'll have a front-row seat."

Hunter settles himself into the cockpit, checking the ashes are secure at his back. The eight-liter bag is waterproof, held down by crisscrosses of elastic deck rigging. He wanted to store the bag under one of the hatches for safekeeping, but Lawton wouldn't have it.

"The old man ought to see his last ride down the river, don't you think?"

Hunter hadn't said what he was thinking: the old man was long past seeing.

They push off, letting the river ease them out into its flow. The ramp recedes behind them, the pickups and trailers grown toylike, and the river stretches itself through the trees. They are outside the mill town of Jesup, Georgia, some fifty miles to the coast by crow flight, but their journey seaward will be twice that long, the river winding its way through the lowcountry before them, curling nearly back onto itself again and again, growing ever more brackish and tidal before it empties its mouth into the sea.

Half a mile downriver stands the old Doctortown Railroad Trestle, the iron trussworks red-rusting over pilings of wet stone. This is the Altamaha Bridge, where state militia armed with two cannon and a rail-mounted siege gun held off a brigade of Union cavalry—one of the only stumbles in Sherman's long march to the sea. Hunter squints, searching the woods for men on horseback, earthworks bristling with bayonets or gun barrels, purple plumes of gun smoke. The world alive from his history books. But the riverbanks are quiet, the ghosts asleep in the shade.

He looks to the bridge. Two boys who should be at school sit hunched on the edge of the tracks, bare feet dangling. They are watching wads of their spit swirl down into the current, comparing whose is fastest. One of them looks up, seeing the kayakers. He squints an eye, aiming, and shoots them the bird. He elbows his buddy, and now they're both doing it, both-handed, grinning like fat-cheeked little devils.

Lawton's neck swells like a pony keg.

"Them little sons of bitches."

"Same as we would of done, that age."

Lawton isn't listening. He lays his paddle flat across his lap and gives them the bird in kind, pumping his arm up and down like a trucker on his air horn, his middle finger slightly bent from some old fistfight or doorjamb or car hood. On the belly of his forearm, there is a tattoo the size of a postage stamp, the tiny skeleton of a frog.

"Boy, get you some of *that*!" He slaps his arm for emphasis. "Get you some!"

"Bad idea."

They have to paddle hard for the cover of the bridge, passing through a hail of spittle and curse. They slide white-flecked into the shadowed hollows of the span, the pilings graffitied like cave art on either side of them. Above them the thump of bare feet, the enemy repositioning for a second barrage. Lawton lifts a hand from his paddle, two sharp chops.

"Spread out. Don't let them concentrate their fire."

His face bristles with flame. He shows his teeth to the coming light.

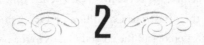

2

New France, June 1564

Jacques Le Moyne stands on the quarterdeck of the three-hundred-ton man-of-war, the *Ysabeau*, the hull timbers groaning beneath his boots. A pair of brigantines trail in the flagship's wake, their towering mainsails challenging the tall trees that line the riverbanks like sentinels of this new world. Le Moyne has his sketchbook out to capture them—*les cyprès*—before darkness falls. They are as tall as the topmasts, soaring giants with green ledges of leaves, their branches trailing gray mosses that sway in the wind like the long beards of indigents. Some stand from cutbanks white as sugar, the gray skeletons of their roots clutched for purchase, their lowest reaches blacked with tide.

He draws them.

They sailed from Le Havre on April 22, a three-ship fleet with three hundred colonists, Huguenots mainly, soldiers and sailors and noblemen in flight from Catholic swords. A few musicians, with pipes and ditties to entertain the garrison, and one artist: he, Jacques Le Moyne de Morgue, commissioned by the King of France to map the coastline, the rivers and bays, and to catalogue the beasts and foliage that reveal themselves in this new land. The Spanish call the territory La Florida, but Le Moyne's king would have it La Nouvelle-France.

New France.

The expedition's leader, René de Laudonnière, stands near the helm. His hands are clasped behind his back, his chest swelled full. He was second-in-command during the disastrous expedition of 1562, which established the outpost of Charlesfort on one of the coastal islands to the north. Latrines were dug, walls raised, a twenty-five-man garrison left while the ships returned to France for supplies.

Only after accepting his commission did Le Moyne learn the fate of that settlement. Resupply was delayed, the men of the garrison soon starving and diseased. There was mutiny, the ranking officer murdered, and some of the men fled into the wilds to live like beasts among *les hommes sauvages*. Still others, desperate to escape, constructed a ship of their own, caulked with pine pitch and rigged with sails of stitched bedclothes, an open vessel in which they attempted to cross the ocean. They were picked up off the English coast, half-dead and sun-blistered like the victims of some new plague. A ship of lepers, they looked, cast out to sea. They had eaten their meager store of corn, their shoes and belts and own dry-burned skin. In the end they had subsisted on the blood and flesh of their own brothers, men sacrificed so that the rest might live. They had not simply eaten their dead. They had killed them first, by vote and dagger.

These stories, whispered after dark as the sea-wind skirled in the sails, became commonplace on the voyage across, the tellers bright-eyed with power, with the dread and fear they instilled. Le Moyne, try as he might, could not help but listen. He had been trained from an early age as a painter of flowers and fruits, tubers and leafy plants, the stuff of tamed gardens and somnolent drawing rooms. Now he was sailing to a land far over the edge of the earth, a savage Eden, to hear it told, where one could be eaten as easily by man as by beast.

There were the Carib Indians of the islands, rumored to have the heads of wild dogs, who butchered and ate the flesh of their own kind, and men of northern kingdoms with long wings and vests of golden fur. There were stories of headless tribes whose faces were embedded in their breasts, like some outward growth of the heart, and giantesses said to pleasure themselves with the stiffened bodies of the men they killed.

Some of these wonders had been rendered in ink or lead and distributed throughout the cities of Europe, though none by an artist who drew on more than hearsay. Le Moyne would be the first. During the long sea-nights of storytelling, when his heart raced like a rabbit in his chest, he recalled that he was chosen for this task, by God and by king. Over the long voyage, his hand itched for something to draw besides the men hauling at halyards and wielding marlinspikes, clinging spiderlike to ratlines as the ship rocked them through the endless troughs. He wanted only to begin.

In early June, there were cries and hurrahs from the men, the thunder of boots across the deck. Le Moyne scampered topside in time to see the whistling cloud of swallows that heralded land. La Florida hove into view. The coast was unlike any Le Moyne had seen. The sea penetrated the land in a maze of thrusting arms, inlets and sounds and rivers and creeks that shattered the coast into a multitude of sea islands, every spit of high ground protected by waving swords of marsh reeds. They sailed into a wide river furrowed by the gleaming backs of dolphins, and Le Moyne bent over the capstan with paper and stylus, trying to trace the coast as they'd taught him in the cartography school at Dieppe. He looked up to find figures swarming the riverbank like ants, the white blade of beach soon blacked with bonfires.

Laudonnière assembled a landing party. He looked at Le Moyne.

"You, Le Roux."

"Le Moyne, monsieur."

"Le Moyne. Can you handle a gun?"

Le Moyne could only nod. His uncle had insisted he learn firearms before going abroad.

They waded ashore to greet the natives, the iron barrels of their arquebuses arrayed like organ pipes, their swords banging against their legs. The surf exploded against their knees. The natives waited on the beach with round eyes, white as bone, and Le Moyne could smell them as he neared: an animal musk, smoky and wild. They surrounded the white men in twitching rings, their limbs long and powerful, their skin queered with inks and mazelike designs. They had long fingernails, sharpened into claws, their ears yoked with inflated fish bladders. Their eyes darted about, quick as baitfish. Like children they reached out, shyly, their brown fingers seeking the godlike torsos of the landing party's armor, the long black beards that pointed their chins.

All the while they chattered in their strange tongue, the words skittering too fleetly to catch. Le Moyne could decipher only one word, said again and again like a chant: *Saturiwa*. Now there were more of the savages, a brown sea of flesh on the beach, and suddenly they parted. A chieftain strode forth through the throng. He was dark as stained wood, his body knotted, swelled with oak-like burls.

"Saturiwa," they said. "Saturiwa."

In the man's hand lay an ingot of silver, like a brick cut from the moon.

Le Moyne watched the eyes of his countrymen widen, spark.

The native bowed and presented the offering to Laudonnière—the French chief—and Laudonnière bowed in turn, drawing the ingot against his chest. The chieftain beckoned them: *Follow me into the woods.* His warriors mimicked the gesture.

This way, they gestured. *This way.*

Wary, the landing party followed the chieftain into a wood of sandy pine, the flesh of his warriors swimming through the trees on every side, shadowing them. Before long the pines broke onto a small clearing, and there Le Moyne saw the first scene he would record of this new land: a six-sided pillar of stone thrust white from the earth, one facet carved with the fleur-de-lis, the royal arms of France. The head of the stone was crowned in wreaths and flowers. At its foot lay baskets of fruit and roots, yellow gourds and discs of gleaming oil, quivers of arrows and scarred war clubs. Offerings, they looked, to some savage god. Natives lay crumpled before the idol, gape-mouthed, like grievers under the cross. This was the marker erected by the ill-fated expedition of 1562, pronouncing dominion over the land.

La Nouvelle-France.

The chieftain stood before the French. His black hair was knotted high atop his head, like the limbs of a trussed fowl, and from this topknot sprang a pair of banded tails that arched each to a side, bouncing on his shoulders. He was nearly naked, his manhood curled against a flap of animal skin that covered his loins. His nose and forehead were of a plane, flat as a ram's. He kept waving at the column with his claws, chattering in his unknown tongue. Laudonnière looked to their interpreter, one of the officers from the Charles-fort catastrophe.

"What does he say?"

"He says we are his brothers. His friends." The interpreter licked his lips. "He says you are brother to Soleil, the sun-god, sent to defeat his enemies."

Le Moyne nearly gasped—such idolatry. But Laudonnière stood unfazed, cradling the ingot of silver closer against his heart. He nodded, as if speaking the pillar's meaning.

"*Camarades. Frères*. Yes, tell him that."

They have come north since then, looking for a river deep enough to accommodate their fleet. Today it seems they have found it, sailing upstream into this unknown land. Le Moyne squints through the failing light. The sun is down, the river like polished black marble. It is the hour between the dog and the wolf, when the world grows smoky with night falling, when you cannot tell whether the beast from the woods is friend to you or enemy. Le Moyne sighs and closes his notebook on the tower of cypress he has been sketching. Beneath it, just visible, the ghostly outline of pillar and chief.

A cry goes up from the bow, now others, and men race toward the fore-deck. Le Moyne dashes among them, elbowing his way to the rail. He looks past the bowsprit, seeing the reason for their cries, and the stick of charcoal slips from his hand, crushed underfoot as he staggers back from the sight.

"*Serpent de mer!*" cry the men.

"*Monstre!*"

It is thrice-humped from the water, this monster, its spine armored like the giant lizards that sun themselves on the riverbanks. But it makes newt of such creatures, a serpent the size of a cypress tree mounding its way through the water, a string of stony dark islands. For long seconds the creature swims upriver before their bow, as if leading them, only to slide beneath the surface, swallowed in black glass.

Le Moyne can hardly breathe. His heart sounds wildly against his ribs. He has been tasked on this journey to fill the white spaces on the map, the places that warn of dragons, and now it seems he must fill those oceans of white with blacker terrors still.

3

Altamaha River, Day 1

The brothers round a bend and the Rayonier pulp mill rises smoking on the bank, a towering industrial fortress of silos and catwalks and smokestacks whose upper rims blink all hours to warn away low-flying aircraft. Long convoys of logging trucks deliver forty-ton quivers of slash pine day and night, the arrow-straight trees chipped and fed into steel digesters the size of space rockets. The mill produces bleached cellulose fibers used in cigarette filters and diapers. Bark and sawdust are burned for power, the smokestacks launching endless fleets of yellow-edged clouds. The plant's wastewater rumbles into the river just downstream, the current foaming cauldronlike where the discharge pipes empty out, a mysterious black effluent that stains the river for miles on. People say the river used to be green, the bars white as flour.

Lawton's nose twitches in the red profusion of his beard.

"Smell never gets no better."

It smells like rotten eggs, or cabbage. An odor common in this part of the state, emitted by the pulp and paper mills sprung like mean little cities from the pines.

Hunter spits. "You just ain't used to it no more. Been sniffing officers' asses too long. I can't even hardly smell it."

Lawton arches an eyebrow. "The hell you can't."

They pass the rusted wreck of an old paddle-wheeler downstream of the mill. The *Gulfmist*. It's wedged against the far bank, half-submerged, a relic of the 1950s that once ran lumber to feed the mills. As boys, they scrambled across the slanted, rust-eaten decks, staring into the gaping holes they found, the iron-enclosed ponds accrued in the hull's interior. Who knew what creatures were hiding under the scum? They touched the big paddle gear that stood from the water like an iron wagon-wheel and looked into the glassless windows from which river pilots once commanded these dark waters. Upstream, anglers floated their skiffs over a twenty-five-foot eddy hole, storied for sixty-pound catfish.

Lawton sees Hunter looking at the wreck.

"Nope. Waste of time we don't got."

Hunter spits. "You really got the trains running on time these days, huh?"

Lawton shrugs.

The wreck slips past them, and soon the trees are all there is. A kingdom of cypress and tupelo, of water oak and river birch and black willow from which moccasins might hang like scaled question marks. Roads will cross the river only twice, and ancient swamps and sloughs and oxbows insulate its snaking path from the high ground of men, harboring beds and roosts of the rare and endangered.

The Little Amazon.

Their father was born on this river, in one of the shantyboats that float on the water like flood-borne houses. The place is downriver from here, a day's long paddle, and they plan to reach the house by dusk. They will over-night there, then push on for four more days, delivering their father's ashes to the river's mouth, a long last ride down the waters that birthed him.

They themselves were raised in Darien, the port town perched at the end of the river, but their father kept the old floathouse in the family, using it as a retreat from the ocean he had come to hate. River-raised, he worked at sea. A shrimper. A failed one, really, by most definitions of success. Probably the old man was biased, though. A childhood of river cat and gar, of long days on smooth water that reflected the sky—those were days of glory. And later, dredging up empty nets for weeks on end, that was anything but.

When they were boys he would bring them upriver for weekends away from the world they knew. He allowed them nothing from civilization, no juice boxes or Pop-Tarts or G.I. Joes. They ate only what they caught on their trotlines. Hunter remembered the man sitting on the porch, staring at the river, smoking a cigarette through his mustache while his boys ate fried fish balls with their hands.

"The ocean, you cain't trust it. It's got nothing to contain it. No direction nor purpose, not like a river's got." He pointed his cigarette at them. "Don't neither of you take to the sea for a life. Ain't nothing in it for you but what you can see. No riches nor treasures to bring up from the deep. Just water, the kind you cain't even drink, flat boring or big-swelled enough to make you sick."

He nodded, telling these things to himself as much as to them.

"This river'd always feed you if you needed. People been living on its banks since always. Altamaha himself, he was a river king, and there was tribes long before him, hunting deer and alligator with arrows made from fish teeth. They say there was forts down here, Spanish and French, more'n half a century before all that *Mayflower* shit up north." Here he pulled a six-pack of Michelobs from the water on a length of string, cracking one in a white lump of foam. "You ever in trouble, this is the place you come."

He looked at them, but they had their heads down, intent on their food.

"Hey. You listening to me?"

They both looked up. Lawton was closest.

"You listening?"

Lawton nodded.

Their father struck the plate from his hands. It shattered on the pine planks. Lawton lifted his chin, swallowed his food.

"Yes, sir."

"Good."

In the end, it was the river that killed him, or something from it. They found his boat first. A couple of fishermen did. A thirteen-foot Gheenoe, narrow-hulled with a tiller throttle and poling deck. It was tangled up in a sedge at a kink in the river. He wasn't in it. Two days later, his body washed up on a mudflat just downriver of the old coastal highway.

Hunter was at the ramp when the sheriffs brought him in. They let him unzip the bag. The old man was shirtless, his skin white as something from a horror film. Hunter hadn't realized how much age and time had damaged the old man's tattoos. Muddled them. They covered him like old bruises.

There was the old *River Assault* tattoo from his time in the brown-water navy, a devil's head with downturned trident. Mark of the Delta Devils, Terror of the Mekong. The insignia lay bleary now upon his shoulder, made as if by a bully's fist. On his left chest the inscription *SAT CONG—Death to Communists*—tattooed as tribute to the Biet Hai sea commandos who wore it there, a death sentence if they were captured. There were the swooping swallows, one on each shoulder, to carry him to heaven if he died at sea, and the North Star to help him find his way home, its points dulled over his heart. All these signs and wonders inked upon his skin, symbols of power and luck, and a new one among them they couldn't stop. Square in his chest was a depression, a sunken wound the size of a man's fist, the color of storm. Burst veins fractured it, jagged and red. Hunter touched two fingers to the place, his father's heart softer now than it had ever been.

Broken.

Sturgeon strike, they said. It was September, and the sturgeon had jumped all summer.

No one knew why they did it, these remainders of prehistory. They inhabited the deepest holes of the river, the lightless benthic regions, each clad in a bronzelike armor of bony plates. Brother to the dinosaur, they'd survived cataclysm, extinction, coming upriver for eons in spring to spawn. In summer they rested in their dark places, watery caverns protected from the river's pull. In the fall they returned to the sea. Near the interstate bridge lay a ninety-foot hole where the real leviathans were rumored to gather, armored and silent, like a fleet of submarines. Fishes a century old, some weighing seven hundred pounds.

In June, without fail, they started jumping.

God help the man running thirty knots when one of the beasts torqued itself from the water, its bone-shield bright and deadly in the sunlight.

Artillery. That's what the old-timers called it.

Some said they did it for joy. Others, reasons darker. They said it was a defense mechanism, an evolutionary protection against humans, against their boats and dams, their wastewater discharge and industrial runoff. The only weapon for a fish with no teeth.

Some wanted them eradicated. Finish what the world-killing meteor couldn't, what the caviar craze of the late 1800s almost did. No more prehistoric beasts. No more broken limbs, shattered faces, collapsed lungs. Kill them off. Convenience, revenge.

Legend had the great monster of the river living among them. The Altamaha-ha. A survivor of the Mesozoic era, a cryptid of the first order. At least twenty feet in length, and black, with the toothed snout of a crocodile, the bony plate-armor of a sturgeon or gar. A creature trapped here, perhaps, when the prehistoric seas receded. Probably just a line of sturgeon surfacing—only that—but their father believed it something more. He believed the stories of the old-time timbermen, who described a thing darker, more sinister.

"Ridge-backed," he said, his broke-knuckled hand cruising before their boyhood eyes. "Got a head like a Tyrannosaur, teeth like one, too. Flippers the size of ship's oars. Swims like a dolphin, up and down. Got a body round and strong as them cypress trunks they sent streaming down the canals."

Hunter looks at the trees along the riverbanks. There is hardly any of that old-growth timber left now, a few ancient survivors that pose for photographs, a centuries-old myth trolling the waters they once guarded.

"Hunter."

He looks up, seeing Lawton some ways ahead, his boat turned slightly sideways so he can look back over his shoulder.

"What?"

"What you doing back there?"

"Paddling."

"Skylarking, more like it." Lawton looks at his watch and the river and the sun, triangulating. "We got to make better time than this."

"You just go as fast as you want, big boy. I'll keep up."

Lawton makes a noise in his chest and goes back to paddling. He is short but cruelly built, with yokelike shoulders and a barrel chest. His body rises V-shaped from the cockpit, a brutal form that makes his boat look almost delicate beneath him, the red shoe of a fairy or elf. In high school he was a fullback, a human wrecking ball that crashed through defensive formations, blasting holes for Hunter, the tailback, to dart through untouched. Lawton was too short for a career at a big state school, but his bruising style caught the eye of Annapolis scouts, always in need of fullbacks for the triple option. He was offered an appointment. He would attend the Naval Academy, the stone forge of midshipmen.

A dream.

Hunter harbored his own hopes back then. He was light and quick, his body roped in veins. He ran one of the fastest forties in the state. Tacklers crumpled before him as if spell-struck, their bearings lost. In the open field he couldn't be caught. He started two seasons, playing behind Lawton until a middle linebacker's helmet cannonballed his left knee, kinking it wrong-angled like a dog's leg.

You saw it happen all the time on television, the tragedy of a blown knee. Feeling it was wholly different, the sudden-struck knowledge that you were not invincible. That the endless hours of up-downs and sprints and tackling drills couldn't help you, the thousand mornings of ringing steel plates. Your dreams could be ruptured in an instant, your body wrecked. Your chance lost to face those armored boys alone, with no brother to pummel and daze them first.

When the whistle blew, Lawton knelt alongside him, looking at the ruined knee. He touched Hunter's forehead, and Hunter could still remember the softness coming into his brother's eyes, the watery light, and he reached up to stop Lawton too late. His brother had already bolted upright, ripping off his helmet.

"Who hit him?" His gold helmet swung from the end of his bowling-pin arm, the facemask hooked in two knuckles. "Who was the son of a bitch that hit him?"

The Brunswick High linebacker, still helmeted, stepped forward. They stood chest to chest. He was half a foot taller than Lawton, his arms long and white and lean.

"Me, motherfucker. What you gonna do?"

The referee was scurrying to part them when Lawton's helmet came swinging on the end of his arm like a mace. He cracked the defenseman, helmet to helmet, then punched him straight under the facemask. A fury of blows followed, and Hunter could still remember the cage-eyed fear of the linebacker when they were pulled apart. Lawton's bared face hungry for more, as if his own blood were only war paint. He was ejected from the game for using his equipment as a weapon. His appointment to play for the Midshipmen was withdrawn. He stood over Hunter's hospital bed a week later, bright-eyed, tucking a smuggled issue of *Playboy* under the blanket.

"Yeah, but you seen the look on that big fucker's face?"

He enlisted straight into the Navy after graduation, a mere seaman recruit, determined to be a frogman. He survived the hundreds of miles of beach runs and ocean swims, the surf torture and agony on the asphalt courtyard, the week of hell when candidates staggered weeping to ring the brass bell and lay down their helmets before the hardened sadists of the cadre, veteran operators who whispered endlessly to men gone witless and hypothermic of hot coffee and blankets and *shit-for-brains why are you even here?* Then combat diving and land warfare, jump school, and six months of tactical training before he earned his Trident. After that he was mostly overseas, in one place or another—often he couldn't say where.

Hunter watches him. He is paddling in perfect cadence, his head on a swivel, a hard look on his face. It isn't often that he comes back. It has to be something big enough, mean enough, to draw him home. The ashes seem too light, too little of the man who left them. Lawton's eyes hunt the river, the banks.

There must be something else.

4

Sapelo Sound, March 1975

Hiram Loggins stands at the helm of his shrimp trawler, the *Amelia-Jo*. He has a sweetheart at home and two tons of marijuana belowdecks. He hasn't been this awake since the Cua Lon River with the turret guns charged, waiting to scream hot tracer fire into the jungle. The moon is high tonight, full, the coast a dark animal crouched on the tin roof of the sea.

Waiting.

The drop went off as planned, which worries him. Nothing ever goes right. They anchored off the three-mile buoy at midnight and waited until a hum rose from the southern horizon, a black cross climbing against the navy sky. They flashed their signal lights as arranged, two quick flashes and a long third. The aircraft flashed its landing lights in answer, the same pattern in reverse. It circled them once, a bomber-sized machine with twin radial engines. It looked too big and slow to fly, floating instead on its own engine thunder. Then the cargo door slid open and the bales began to fall out, big cubes splashing into the sea.

"Square grouper," they call it, tongue in cheek. Marijuana wrapped in plastic and burlap, product of Colombia. It took them more than an hour to haul in the catch, Hiram chugging from one drop to the next on the shifting swells. The sea kept playing hide-and-seek with him, tucking the bales in its valleys.

Pissing him off, like it usually does. He's never been comfortable offshore. A world too unsteady under his rubber boots, nothing to hold to if you go overboard. He's always ready to get back within swimming distance of land. He watches the deckhands retrieve the bales with long gaffs, stowing them in the hold. It's the same crew as always, moonlighting for more pay than they might make in a month working the nets. His first mate scans the swells with a pair of starlight binoculars.

"Starboard bow, boss. Fifty yards."

Hiram nods, spins the wheel to the right.

They enter the sound just north of Blackbeard Island, rumored to hide the pirate's old treasure. Hiram went hunting buried chests as a boy, as did most of the other river people. A lot of them too old for such delusions, shuffling along with half-empty vodka bottles and pawnshop metal detectors. They found nothing save the brick ruin of an old crematory built to burn the bodies of the yellow fever victims once quarantined on the island.

Soon the creeks and inlets and rivers of the coast spread weblike before the bow, and Hiram feels his boat enveloped, protected, a white beast slipping into the marsh. Here is a world he knows inside and out, backward and frontward. It can hide outlaws like them. It has already, for centuries.

Sheriff Poppell will be there with his deputies to assist in the offload. They call him the Last of the High Sheriffs, men who run their counties from end to end. He doesn't mind getting the moon on his back to keep county business in the black, Hiram has to give him that. There are the clip joints and jukes to manage, the whorehouse at the S&S Truckstop, the liquor stills and drug-running fleet. All that couldn't be overseen by a lazy man. Even if, thinks Hiram, the Sheriff wears his suit-britches too bright and belled out at the bottom, his collars too wide, a man spiffy-dressed and potbellied like a little king.

Hiram's first mate comes in from the bow, binoculars draped around his neck.

"Looks clear."

Hiram nods.

They enter the Sapelo River, the spiked banks narrowing around them. Up the coast is Harris Neck, the old WWII airbase where the Civil Air Patrol launched their antisubmarine flights. Its runways are all green-clumped and fissured, though rumor has low-fliers out of the south landing there now and again under cover of darkness. Down the coast is the town of Darien, set nearly at the mouth of the river that raised him. His cinderblock house is crouched down there, battling climbing vines and falling moss, families of dust-backed roaches, the green-boiling heat. Before him, in the distance, race the high-speed cars of the coastal highway, 17, shooting like tracers across the marsh. The Dixie Dieway, so called for the wrecks in dead of night. Too often Florida-bound vacationers, sleepy-eyed to make the state line, drift into the oncoming lane, semis full of citrus or pulpwood or fertilizer to greet them.

To keep the voting poor happy, the Sheriff calls them from their shanties to scavenge the highway wrecks for whatever they can gather up. You might see them juiced up on oranges for the next week, juggling them or rolling them in the dust like toys, sucking the rinds against their teeth like mouth guards, or all of them tromping around in squeaky white shoes meant for some hospital up north. The whole town might be eating Mars bars for a month, sugar-happy as Pooh Bear, boys black and white dangling yo-yos two from a hand like carnival men.

But Interstate 95 is newly completed, crossing the county like a long white bridge in the west, sleek and clean, and soon this place will shrivel yet smaller on the map, a point forgotten at the edge of everything green. The Sheriff saw it coming. He reckoned if the shrimp boats couldn't fill the bellies of Yankee tourists, they could fill the lungs of the long-hairs now running the country.

Hiram agreed. There was never enough of anything since he'd come home from the war: money, food, time. Shrimp, especially, which might have provided all that. Meanwhile the price of diesel kept climbing, Jimmy Carter no match for those sheikhs sitting atop their oceans of black gold, and the Russians just itching to hit the big red button that would sprout mile-high mushrooms across the globe.

He pulls back the throttles, the diesels burbling down. The rendezvous point is coming up, a nameless point covered in scrubby pines and high brush. He sees the boxy shape of the offload truck hidden in the trees. His men are already in the bow, ready with throw-ropes. The bank nears. He can almost feel the river bottom rising beneath his keel, heavy with his ocean haul, and something else: a stillness in the trees, like a held breath, even the wind afraid to speak. The symbols on his skin turn to fire, like they always did before Charlie opened up.

Too late, Hiram's man throws the rope.

Shadows flood through the trees, converging at the truck, and the night shatters with light, a staccato cracking of small-arms fire, the bushes pulsing like thunderclouds. Among all this, voices screaming:

"DEA!"

"Jackers!"

"Sheriff's Department!"

"Shit," says Hiram.

He leaves the wheelhouse and goes to the rail. Men are locked together on the ground, rolling in the dirt, some in uniform, others with long beards and gold badges on chains around their necks. DEA and sheriffs, duking it out.

Situation Normal, he thinks. *All Fucked Up.*

There is nowhere to go. Hiram runs to the far rail and jumps.

5

Altamaha River, Day 1

At Knee Buckle Island, the river winds back on itself, nearly reversing direction, and Lawton points them through Dick's Swift, the channel that shortcuts the loop. Soon the first of the old navigational dikes appears, a row of hundred-year wood pilings that jut from the water like broken teeth. They are a stony gray, as if petrified. Once they held a bulwark of brush and rocks and mud intended to control the river's flow. The Corps of Engineers tried to tame the river here, to force a deeper, straighter channel for streamers and timber rafts, but the spring freshets tore through the man-made jaws unchecked.

Lawton points his boat between two of the old pilings. They are objects of lore. For more than a century, flatwoods loggers assembled their harvest of longleaf pine into sharpshooters, two-hundred-ton rafts with fifty-foot oars, the bows pointed for shooting the river's snags and bars. Rafthands black and white floated the pinewood colossi some hundred miles downriver to the port of Darien, a trip of two weeks. They broke up the timber at the docks and spent the night reeling through the portside taverns and whorehouses, stumbling at dawn beneath the forest of shipmasts that sailed heavy bellies of pine lumber to shipyards in Maine and Boston and Belfast. Darien boomed until the timber ran out, a whole state of old-growth pine cut to stumps.

Lawton watches the teeth pass by.

"I figure them old raftsmen had it pretty good, out on the river for maybe weeks at a time. What you think?"

"I think they didn't do the trip but twice a year, during the freshets and snowmelts. They had to spend the rest of the year cutting timber by hand."

Lawton shrugs. "Seems like a pretty good life to me. Simple."

"You ever really took down a big tree with saw and ax?"

Their boats are nearly parallel now. Lawton eyes him.

"What, they got you doing a lot of timber-cutting in college?"

They do, actually. Georgia Southern has a timber sports team, and Hunter has been going to practices. It seems a good balance to what he is learning indoors, the piles of history books with their flat-printed words piled layer on layer like the blandest cake. They practice the springboard and the stock saw, the underhand chop and the single buck and the standing block chop, severing all that white pine with gleaming saw-teeth and ax-bits. On the first day, they sent him off into the woods with a five-pound felling ax, telling him to take down a hardwood at least one foot in diameter and bring back a twelve-inch block of it as evidence. He threw up twice in the process but emerged from the woods in under an hour to the surprise of the boys sitting on the tailgates of their trucks, drinking canned beer and talking about their race-saws. No one had ever done it that fast the first time.

Sometimes he feels bad hacking into all that timber, down into the hard white flesh of it, and it seems he might loose a jet of the wildest red as he strikes into the heartwood. But this is nothing, he knows, compared to what Lawton has seen and done. So he keeps his mouth shut. He says nothing to his brother of his place on the timber sports team, the only underclassman with a chance at first string, beating out ham-fed country boys who outweigh him by sixty pounds.

"You might be surprised what they got me doing."

They are just past the first dike when the sound of an outboard rises behind them. They look back to see an olive johnboat turn the bend. It blasts past them at full throttle, a blur of pale faces over the streak of hull, the bow cutting a white arrow through the river. The wake comes sliding toward them, dark and ominous as a tail, and they nearly capsize, their boats rolling on the swell. Hunter reaches back to keep the ashes from breaking loose as the second wave hits, the third, the shark's tooth flopping at his neck.

"Son of a *bitch*!" Lawton rams his paddle into the river like a staff, fighting to stay upright on the swells.

The boat rounds out of sight, the river slowly settling, the white wrapper of a candy bar left like a postcard. Lawton fishes it in with his paddle, crinkling the plastic in his hand. He is looking downriver, as if he can reel in the boat with his eyes. A vein throbs in his neck like a fork.

"People. No fucking respect."

Hunter grins. "I know what your spirit animal is."

"What's that?"

"Curmudgeon. You need one of those hats with a warship on it, goldleaf on the bill."

"River didn't used to have all these sons of bitches on it, Hunter."

"It had Daddy."

"Hey now, you know what I mean."

"I know every generation thinks they got the record share of assholes."

Lawton growls. "I don't know, brother. Shit I been seeing, home and away, we got a real strong team right about now."

The sun is climbing, the day warming. A wind comes up, scaling the surface of the water. The river slides black through the trees, like something birthed from the mill upstream, great strings of the blind roaming its belly. Hunter watches the current bend before them, revealing a pale bluff on the left bank, the site of a Confederate gun battery that once defended the railroad bridge upstream. During the Second World War, a detachment of state defense forces was stationed there to prevent German U-boats from sneaking upriver like giant sturgeon, sabotaging bridges or spilling black-faced commandos into the backyards of sawhands and cotton farmers. The submarines cruised the coastal waters instead, once sinking two oil tankers in the span of an hour. Rumors abounded. Nazis submariners were coming ashore to buy bread and cigarettes, to meet spies, to watch the picture shows.

Below the bluff, Hunter sees a steel research boat outfitted with a bow-boom, two men in uniforms and sunglasses working the waters with long-poled nets. They're with the Department of Natural Resources. Lawton steers his boat in their direction.

"Let's go see what they're up to," he says.

"What happened to all your shit about no time to stop?"

Lawton shrugs. "You sped up, like you said you would."

He sounds surprised. Hunter wishes he was close enough to hit him with his paddle.

Around the DNR boat, the river is speckled with floating catfish, bodies mottled olive and brown and black, like camouflage. Some are upturned, showing yellow-white bellies. Their heads are hammered flat between the eyes, their mouths wide and underbit, their whiskers hanging down like the Fu Manchu of old Chinamen. Flatheads, people call them, or Appaloosas or shovel cats. They're an invasive species, introduced illegally in the 1970s as a sport fish.

The DNR men straighten as the brothers paddle up. One of the officers is big, with a stout belly that could take body blows like a heavy bag. The other is smaller, strung with tendons and sinew. They say their hellos, and Lawton lays his paddle flat.

"Electro-fishing?"

The big officer nods. "Flathead populations been exploding. Decimating the redbreast and bullhead populations. They got us out mopping up."

Hunter looks at the electroshock contraption. The boom at the front of the boat holds a silver ball just below the surface. It sends an electric pulse through the water, stunning the fish to the surface, where they can be netted and counted and killed.

"How many y'all getting a hour?" asks Lawton.

His accent seems thicker to Hunter, dialed up.

"Been averaging sixty-one."

Lawton whistles and squints at the stunned fish. He might be doing his own count.

"Hell, I don't doubt it. I seen the *Wanted* signs at the landing."

"People been getting sixty-pounders on bank hooks."

"Some say they're the tastiest cats," says Lawton.

"Course, you're eating cancer from the mill," says Hunter.

Everyone is silent a moment, thinking of their own cells multiplying like so many flatheads under the skin. Some of the stunned fish are beginning to wiggle, the shock wearing off.

Lawton rubs his chin. "Say, how 'bout the sturgeon. They jumping over-normal last summer?"

The big DNR officer tilts his net upright and leans his elbow on it like a shovel. "The population's been hurting, near as we can tell. But a boater did get killed last year. September. Poor son of a bitch caught one square in the chest."

Lawton's lips disappear inside his beard, sucked against his teeth.

"Yeah. We heard about that. Ain't September a little late for the sturgeon to be jumping?"

"Not for this one, apparently."

"Must of been a big'un, all right."

"Big enough," says the smaller officer. "We tell people to keep their speed down in summer. Don't none of them listen. Guess somebody got what was coming."

Hunter watches his brother's body react, the nations of strength beneath his vest contracting into a single ball-like mass, marshaled as before some burst of power. But the moment passes, his body relaxing into its old shape, his knuckles coloring again on his paddle.

"I guess so." He licks his lips. "Y'all seen anything else strange on the river of late?"

The big officer's head is stock-still, his eyes surely roaming their boats behind his sunglasses. "A couple researchers from the university went missing a few months back. Left the dock and never come back. They were studying the sturgeon population. Probably they got struck by one, too." He pauses. "Course, people got other theories."

"What kind of theories?"

"There's been a camera crew hunting around. Say they're looking for the Altamaha-ha."

"We told them they might as well be looking for Bigfoot," says the smaller officer. He shrugs. "Said they already had."

The big officer sets the handle of his net before him, his hands gripping it one atop the other. "You boys sure ask a lot of questions. Where y'all headed, anyway?"

Hunter speaks up. "To a creek—"

"*Downriver*," says Lawton, cutting him off.

The big officer's face hardens.

"Downriver, huh?" He juts his chin toward Hunter's boat. "Mind telling me what you got in the sack?"

Lawton cocks his head; his teeth show.

"Oh, that? That's just our daddy's ashes, Officer. Seems he was killed by a sturgeon strike last summer."

The DNR men seem to waver in place.

"Oh, I'm sorry for your loss."

"Lawton ain't been able to do the trip," says Hunter. "Seeing as he was deployed."

Lawton cuts him a look.

"They ain't asked for my service history, brother. Or my name." He looks back at the officers. "Or have you?"

"No." The big officer raises a hand to settle him. "No need for all that."

Lawton looks back at the stunned fish, bulbed like tumors on the river. He prods one with his paddle, like it might wake up. Everyone is watching him. When he raises his head, his face looks young, unlined.

"You said this camera crew already went hunting Bigfoot?"

"So they said."

"Say they found him?"

The big officer shrugs.

"Shadow and rumor, like what everybody finds."

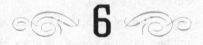

6

Fort Caroline, 1564

They have found no secret trade-river to the Orient as yet, nor any cities of gold as the Spaniard Cortés discovered, sailing home heavy-hulled with his ingots of melted treasure. But they have found a wide bend of river to build their fortress. It is to be called La Caroline, Laudonnière announces, a triangular fort of three earthen walls, each a thousand king's-feet in length. There will be a storehouse for grain and munitions, a set of thatch-roofed barracks built low to survive the coastal winds, and a gate that can withstand the natives, should they become unfriendly, or the Spanish, who already are. And it will have a house for him, their commander, in which he and his handmaiden will reside.

This handmaiden, she is one of only four women in the colony, and already there is speculation that the woman is inordinate in her duties to him.

One of the men leans on his mattock.

"She is naught but a cock-scabbard, Le Moyne. Would that our commander was a sharing man, no?"

Such a prospect disgusts Le Moyne, who sings his Psalms in the afternoons, who tries so hard in the nights not to take his own sprouted flesh in hand, loosing his seed into this foreign ground. Le Moyne, whose very name means "the Monk." In the mornings he works among the tradesmen and soldiers, the heat thick and wet as bath steam. They cut trees, planing them for use as framing timbers and rafters, and they dig endless ditches for latrines, moats. The spoil they use for earthworks. The backs of the men have taken on a hard brown luster, like burnished wood. Their teeth seem whiter in the sun. There is already talk of baking bricks for a bread oven. Le Moyne allows himself to take direction. He has no patience with the soft-palmed noblemen in the colony, men who puff their tunics with cotton bombast and spend their days hunting winemaking grapes in the forest, never deigning to dirty their hands in labor.

His father is a royal embroiderer, a man who earned his position instead of inheriting it, and this commission is his way of expelling his son from France. Le Moyne is *le brebis galeuse*, after all. The mangy sheep. The sole Lutheran in a family that serves the Catholic crown. In France, there are riots in the streets, massacres, open combat between the factions, these sects that profess faith in the same God. His father claims the voyage will save his son from more bloodshed sure to come, though Le Moyne suspects the old man has other hopes. Perhaps his son's exploits in the New World will repair the family name, rid him of the mange of Luther and Calvin. No matter, Le Moyne was exhausted by the insufferable nuance of court life, the sectarian gossip. He thirsted for adventure, purpose. A new world, heavy with promise, lay beyond the gray swell of the sea.

In the evenings he often accompanies the hunting parties, honing his skill with the arquebus—the hook-gun that fires a shot the size of a grape. They take deer and rodents rooting through the wilds, the occasional feral pig fugitive from Spanish pens. They even try shooting the great toothed reptiles that lie still as gargoyles along the riverbanks. Here is the beast the Spanish call *el lagarto*—the lizard. Its back is a map of power, risen in armored ridges that can thwart arrows and shot. Sometimes the lizards bellow over the water, a sound like stones being rolled across a cobbled street. Others join in, a chorus that brings the river to a thunder, and Le Moyne watches the dark-moving current for the giant sea monster to rise again. This monster that haunts his dreams, perhaps they call it forth. Their king. It does not rise, though sometimes great bony fishes leap from the river in arcs of spray, their bodies gleaming as if bronzed.

Des esturgeons.

One evening Le Moyne and his hunting companions discover a throng of deer poised motionless in the wood. Only when the animals rise manlike upon their hind legs do they realize these are not deer but men cloaked in the gutted and dried carcasses of deer, crowned in the antlered heads of stags. Le Moyne cannot but recall *The Transformation of Actaeon*, the etching by his country- man Jean Mignon, which depicts the fate of the mortal hunter Actaeon, who stumbles upon Diana, virgin goddess of the hunt, as she bathes naked with her nymph maids in some woodland spring. The goddess, embarrassed, splashes water on the mortal's chest, the streams beamed arrow-straight from the tips of her fingers, and poor Actaeon's head is transformed into that of a stag, a beastly prison that robs him of human speech. In the background of the etching, Ac- taeon's fate: his own pack of hounds, no longer recognizing him, chase him through the woods. They tear him to pieces.

But these warriors have transformed of their own volition, moving among their prey without the slightest suspicion. They raise their hooves to the French in salutation, and Le Moyne feels like unto some beast of the earth, raising his own strange hand to echo theirs.

Their king, Saturiwa, emerged from the forest during the first days of the fort's construction, his subjects building for him a shelter of palms and saplings on a little bluff overlooking the scene. A party of pipers heralded his arrival that day, their cheeks puffed with effort, a shrill and wild discordance from the trees. He was accompanied by what looked a war party of some several hundred men, armed with clubs and bows and spears, their bodies adorned with feathers and pearls, strings of fish-teeth and shells that rattled upon their necks and wrists as they walked. The men of the fort were alarmed by this display until the chief ordered his warriors to assist in the labor, the raising of works and structures and thatching of roofs. Laudonnière and he proceeded to exchange more gifts, a ritual forging of alliance against the tribe's enemies in the west. A hasty accord, thought Le Moyne, rash to make in an unknown land, but politics are not his duty.

On another evening hunt, he comes face-to-face with the Indian king, who is enjoying a leisurely walk down the trails of his realm, accompanied by one of his wives and their retinue. Le Moyne's duty is to record that which he witnesses, drawings and paintings for his king across the sea. This he does, sketching the scene of Saturiwa's evening walk. There is the great war-chief adorned in his own cloak of deerskin, his long hair trussed atop his head, his every step attended by two servants with palm-frond fans, a third who holds the tail of his cloak so that it might not be sullied upon the earth. There is the wife trailing just behind, she and her maidservants long-haired and strong-legged, draped only in silky green moss that does little to hide their womanly features, their heavy-swollen breasts and the dark wedge of their nethers.

The chief nods his head to the white men respectfully, and they return the gesture. There is no translator among their party this evening, but the chief make signs to congratulate them on the deer they have felled. The women stand back from the men, their eyes dark and shining, their lips dusky and plump as wine grapes. On the walk back to the fort, one of Le Moyne's companions elbows him in the ribs.

"You saw the fruit of the land, Le Moyne, yes? Heavy-swelled and ripe, I say, over hips so wide they might birth a corsair's crew."

"You are in error, Francois," says another of the party. "A navy, I say, those hips could."

"And with such handholds," says a third, "one might accomplish the task *par-derrière*, as any good sailor should."

"What say you, *monk*? Would you partake of the dark fruit?"

Le Moyne looks from one grinning face to another, hard men who have journeyed long months at sea, under leathering sun and cold winds, where a sharp tongue is more prized than any good knife.

He shrugs. "*Bien sûr.* It is fruit of an equal color once pierced, no?"

The men fall to laughing on every side of him—truly fall—rolling around in the black dirt and leaves, holding their bellies, tears streaming from their faces. Their sharp-pointed mustaches are nearly upturned in delight. Le Moyne knows he will have to kneel this night and pray for forgiveness, for glorifying such sins of the flesh, but he is happy for closer friends than only his God high above.

7

Darien, Georgia, 1975

Annabelle Mackintosh sits on her porch watching the moon shadows stir in the yard. She is nursing a final highball, unable to sleep, her pale skin glistening with whiskey sweat. At least the stinging film keeps the bugs at bay. The porch screen was torn earlier in the night, the work of the careless men with whom her careless husband drinks, who leer and stumble and grope her at will. He is passed out facedown in bed now, snoring wetly, and she can think of worse things than him not waking up.

This is McIntosh County, Georgia, and she is born of the Direct Descendants, the families who can trace their ancestry in unbroken blood to the Scottish Highlanders who founded the town in 1736. These families are the keepers of tradition in the county, the elite who carry the same surnames as the Highland warriors chosen by the founder of Georgia, General James Oglethorpe, to hold this outpost against Spanish Florida. He chose them for their hardiness, their fierceness in battle. They fought in the Battle of Bloody Marsh, so named for what they made of a Spanish invasion force, and they survived decades of disease and hurricanes and musket balls to keep the town of Darien alive at the river's mouth.

Annabelle had been groomed for success—her father a doctor, her mother a socialite—and she had the striking looks that were needed, too. The long slender limbs, milk-pale and shapely, and the fiery red curls that crouched halolike on her shoulders, red-gold in the sun. Big eyes, clear and blue, and freckles like blood-flecked bone. She looked a warrior princess, which frightened and buckled softer men, and she had a weakness that perhaps the women in her clan once had, too: hard and rough men, mean-made with callused hands, who might have held swords in centuries past. Men who more often hold wrenches or tire irons in this day, or guns or hammers or heavy-equipment controls. Not the gold-nib fountain pens her mother had hoped for, for contract signings or prescriptions. Certainly not those.

Barlow Pegram, dead-drunk in their marriage bed, got her pregnant at nineteen, doing it with her debutante dress hiked up in the back of his '71 Chevy Chevelle SS. She wanted it that night, every panicked thrust, no thought of diminished dreams or what might come. The baby didn't survive but she did, married already to a man who loved only Chevrolet muscle and Evan Williams and Waylon Jennings and his own lost red-diamond glory, centerfield for the state winners in times long ago. He liked what she had red-bushed between her legs, too, but only, it seemed, when his own body could not rise to meet it.

So fat is he now, bloated on bourbon and hush puppies, she wonders when he last saw that whiskey-weak disappointment between his legs. She is trapped here, she thinks, marooned on a tin-roofed island set on the edge of the continent, lording her legion of roaches and swamp rats and drunks. The porch screen might as well be iron-knit. She leans her head against the rocker, wondering how she might claw her way out of this place, to Atlanta or Charlotte or New York, her checkerboard past swiped clean, her life made equal to her name.

She drifts, hearing what must be the crackle-pop of lightning in the distance, a coming storm. She is nearly asleep when she hears a snap in the yard. She opens her eyes to see a bent figure slinking across the grass before her. She is up in an instant, the single-barrel shotgun snagged from the corner where it leans, the porch door kicked wide as she comes down the steps, cocking the rabbit-ear back.

"You're hell-bound in half a second," she says. "What you doing on my property?"

The man freezes, eyeing her over his shoulder. Slowly he turns around. He is shirtless, his torso dark-inked and mud-slick, and there is not an ounce of anything wasted in his body. Hard little muscles push right up against his skin like they might bust out. Annabelle has to lower the barrel slightly, just for a better look.

"I was just out for a walk is all." He clears his throat. "Got lost."

"You must think I got nothing in my head but red moss, same as out."

"I know what it is you got in that scattergun."

"What's that?"

"Birdshot. It ain't but a four-ten snake-gun. A pest-shooter."

"But it'll make a mess of you at this range, now won't it?"

He scratches his chin, looking down the barrel of the gun.

"It might."

"What kind of trouble is it you're in?"

"The personal kind."

"And here I was thinking I might could help you out. Be a good Christian and that."

"It ain't nothing you want to know about," he says. "I just need to get along."

He starts to go. She calls after him.

"They're going to catch you pretty easy, looking like you do. You'd stand a better chance cleaned up."

He stops and eyes her again, suspicious.

"You offering?"

Annabelle lowers the shotgun.

"Maybe." She licks her lips. "You got something in it for me?"

8

Altamaha River, Day 1

They don't stop for lunch, letting the river float them as they eat peanut butter and banana sandwiches. From now on, their meals will be from pouches or cans. Hunter tilts his head back, chewing, and closes his eyes. The sun feels good on his face, a cure for the glaring fluorescents of campus. Sometimes he sits in the classroom, listening as the lecturer drones on, and wonders where Lawton is at that very moment, shawled in some mountain cave or black-finned in a jungle river, streaking down-arrowed through the sky, breathing the purest oxygen through a hose, his salvation a silken sheet folded on his back.

He wondered the same when his father was still alive, whether the man's nets were swallowing up anything as he dragged them those long days through the darkness, if they would bring him anything that might make him unharden a moment, a smile breaking the hard cast of his face. He'd lost his first boat before they were ever born. No one knew quite how, though there were whispers of him trawling the open waters for things he shouldn't have sought.

Square grouper.

According to their mother, he never fully recovered from that. He went upriver, disappeared for weeks, and came back a different man—a man who'd commanded a patrol boat in the brown waters of the Mekong Delta, now forced to swab the decks of others' boats. A man hard-made, full of shadow and thunder. They never knew him any other way.

Hunter feels something cross his face—a shadow—and opens his eyes. A flight of white ibises low against the sky, wading birds with long-curved bills and ink-tipped wings, their reddish feet pointed like divers'. Now more of them, white wedges crossing like bombers overhead. Cold dark forms race across the river, curling over him, his brother. Shadows. And Hunter feels a strange urge to dart and hide, like prey, like the crabs and crawfish that surely scuttle for shelter beneath his boat. He feels spotted—by what he isn't sure. They are far from paved roads and shopping marts, from the steel and glass and brick that pronounces their species' dominion over the land.

They pass Cole Eddy and Doe Eddy, little inlets cut upstream in the river's bends, and they enter the Narrows, the treacherous section where the river races between funneled banks, wheeling through tight rounds and sharp kinks that smashed timber rafts in years past. The logs splitting between the raftmen's feet, the dark vents swallowing them up. Their broken bodies found down-river, crushed soft as meal sacks. Dead trees—snags—reach clawlike from the river here, waving white-daggered in the current, and there are hidden shoals at every bend. Ahead is Hannah's Island, where their father would never stop. There is a large bald cypress on the island's bank, lightning-scarred, a pale gash scorched black at its heart.

"Found out what Daddy had against the place," says Hunter.

Lawton slows his paddling. He's put on a pair of angular sunglasses, like a centerfielder might wear. One eyebrow lifts over the wings of lens.

"You planning to spill this information, or sit on it like a hen?"

"I didn't know if you'd care."

"It's about Daddy, isn't it?"

"Back in the Civil War, a group of Confederate militia was camping out there. They'd brought a woman with them. Some say she was a prostitute, others say a homesteader forced to the job. Either way, they had her again and again, all night. It was so many of them, so many times, it killed her. Some people say she's still out there, pink-skinned like a scalded pig, smoke pouring out her wounds. They say bad shit happens to anybody who stops there."

"Motherfuckers," says Lawton. He shakes his head. "What I could of done with a single platoon back then. Where'd you hear this?"

"Book I read."

"For class or on your own?"

"My own. Been reading up on the river."

"Look at you. What about the Altamaha-ha? You learn anything on that?"

Hunter nods. "Some. Indians told the early explorers about a giant snake-like creature in the river. Said it bellowed and hissed. That's the earliest we know of anything that sounds like it."

"That's long back."

Hunter nods. "Schooner captain in the 1830s reported seeing a creature seventy feet long, big around as a sugar hogshead, mouth like a crocodile. Then sightings all the way up through the eighties, nineties."

Lawton pulls on his beard.

"Huh."

"You know, the Highlanders that founded Darien were from the shores of Loch Ness. The county's putting up a new billboard by the interstate with a picture on it, a smiling sea serpent, to draw in tourists. They're rebranding, calling it 'Altie.'"

"Bull-fucking-shit they are."

"Like Nessie." Hunter shrugs. "It's probably just a monster sturgeon, or else a line of river otters surfacing."

"Daddy always thought it was real."

"He thought a lot of things."

"Sure he did. But tell me this, you wanna stop on Hannah's Island?"

Hunter looks at the dark banks sweeping past, the bare cypresses with their tangled crowns and bony knees. He thinks it would be a brave thing to stop, to defy somehow the powers their father believed in. The ones that didn't save him. Still, he shakes his head.

"Hell no, I don't."

"I didn't think so." Lawton shivers. "They pay me to jump out airplanes for a living, but you couldn't get me onto that island with a cherry-picker."

"I never knew you to scare easy."

The sun shines in Lawton's sunglasses, a white star at the very bridge of his nose.

"That's just because I was dumb. I didn't know what was out there. And I never been too big on bad guys don't respond to a double-tap."

They continue on, the river accelerating yet faster beneath them, channeled as if through a sluice. The bends become sharp and unexpected, switchbacking like a mountain road, the current swirling over hidden shoals. Hunter can hardly imagine how men navigated rafts the size of basketball courts down these kinking, curling narrows. The pilots calling out *bow white* or *bow injun* to direct the sweep-hands, a harkening back to the days when whites only lived on the north side of the river, and it was all Indian land to the south.

It was blacks, mainly, who worked the rafts. At dusk their wordless hollers jumped from raft to raft, plaintive cries falling between the trees. Hunter read the adventures of Snake Sutton as a boy, the mythic raft-pilot of the Altamaha, white but raised by freed slaves, who tried to break into the Darien timber merchant society—a door heavy-barred even for a man so good with the maul and peavey and ax.

They paddle on, looping Little Water Oak Round as upon a giant carousel, the banks wheeling past, a heavy green alligator sunning itself like a prehistoric tank. They say you can never step into the same river twice, and Hunter knows the adage means that the waters you touch once you never will again. They're gone, part of the sea or the clouds or the blood of beasts or men. But it isn't just that, he knows. The shape of the river itself is in flux, the cycles of freeze and flood, erosion and deposition, reshaping its very course.

He once saw time-lapse footage of a river in Europe, taken as a satellite overflew it year after year. Over the course of a decade, it looked like nothing so much as a whisper of smoke, the bends swelling and curling and merging, the plume of an idle-held cigarette. Soon they will be to the bluff where you can stand and see Bug Suck Lake to the north, an oxbow where the river once ran, orphaned now like a scar in the earth, forgotten in the river's new course. And yet so many things do remain, he thinks, such that they can be named and returned to—points and signs recognizable, even after so many years. Centuries. The bights and rounds, the sloughs and swifts, the river wriggling like a miles-long serpent in the earth, ever restless, the same as it always was.

Hunter looks at his brother. He is coasting, his paddle stilled, his thumb prodding the inside of his arm, pushing on the tattoo there.

"New ink?"

"What?"

"Frog on your forearm. It wasn't there last Easter."

Lawton looks down, as if seeing the tattoo for the first time.

"Yeah. Bone frog. Got it before my last deployment."

"What's it mean?"

"Mean?" Lawton looks at it, the tiny skeleton printed on the flesh of his arm. He clenches his fist and the frog jumps against the belly of muscle. "It's just a brotherhood thing. Like I haven't forgot all the ones before me. That didn't make it. Some of the boys don't like it. Think it's bad luck." Lawton shrugs. "The dead get under everybody's skin. You're full of shit you say they don't."

9

Fort Caroline, 1564

A*palatci.* The word is upon every man's lips, whispered like the name of a god. *Apalatci.* It haunts the fort, in the night-dreams of men like a fever, a summons to rise and go west until the land rises up against the sky, jagged as wolf teeth.

"Is it true?" they ask. Always in the hours after nightfall, when truth can walk freely among them, swelled under the moon.

Le Moyne cannot but nod. It seems it is.

In the west is gold.

He was chosen to accompany a small-boat expedition sent upriver once the fort walls were raised. Three days ago he stood before the greatest tree of the land, a giant cypress that marked the boundary between the lands of Saturiwa, king of the coast, and the lands of Utina, king in the west. Rivals. Le Moyne and the others could only stare at the giant cypress, their jaws agape.

"Mon Dieu."

It stood upon a broad knuckling of roots, each the size of a lesser tree. The trunk itself was as broad as the mortared turrets of the Loire Valley, towers built to keep watch over baileys and keeps, but the tree was so much taller than those works of stone. It raced skyward, the crown swirling high against the blue, like one of the helical flying machines of da Vinci, the Italian genius Le Moyne studied as a boy. Strange formations surrounded the tree, roots thrust from the earth like daggers or teeth. The French joined hands around the base. It took eight of them to encircle the tree. When the chain of arms fell away, the soldier next to Le Moyne stepped back, tugging on his beard.

"What a table it would make, no? Broad enough to feed *l'entourage* of our king."

"Aye," said another. "But how would we sail home such a gift, it is so big?"

Le Moyne looked at them.

"You would cut down such a tree *pour une table*?"

"Not just any table, man. *Une Table Ronde*, like that of Arthur or Charlemagne."

"If not a table, what then?" asked another. "*Un dais*, fit for King Charles's throne?"

Le Moyne rolled his eyes and skulked off into the woods.

"What?" they cried.

They continued upstream, and the trees soon pressed close, the ribbon of river kinking and whirling between narrowed banks, rounding bights and eddies that Le Moyne struggled to mark for later mapping. In his notes he wrote: *Le Goulet.*

The Narrows.

Upstream, they were received by one of Utina's river chiefs. He fed them bread and fish, telling them of his enemies in the foothills to the west, men who adorned themselves in plates of gold and silver that scattered his people's fish-tooth arrows like thrown pebbles. Captain Vasseur, leader of the excursion, thought the chief must be speaking of Spaniards, so armored. But no, the chief assured him, these were men who lived at the foot of the Apalatci, mountains rich with many bright metals, heated and hammered to fit a man's body like a second skin.

He said Saturiwa, king of the coast, merely collected what metals he could from the shipwrecks. His own people sifted the silt at the confluence of the streams that formed the river. But the Apalatci range, this was the true source of these wonderful and unusual things, these fine stones and metals the French desired. So plentiful were the mountains with riches, they could be dug free by hand and floated down the river by canoe or barque.

Captain Vasseur, so inspired, assured the chief that the French of La Caroline would ally themselves with Utina, king in the west, helping him to achieve victory against his enemies at the foot of the mountains. Le Moyne said nothing. It was not his place to question diplomacy, the wisdom of pledging themselves to the great enemy of their ally, the coastal king. A man who brought them corn and thatched their roofs, whose warriors moved fleet-footed and silent through the woods, disguised in the hollowed-out hides of deer. Le Moyne was only to record what he saw, and so he did.

He sketched the natives knee-deep in the current, sifting the silt for bright nuggets carried down from the mountains in the river's flow. They urged him to come in, to try it himself. He removed his boots and stockings and rolled up his culottes. He was wading in the current among them, learning their movements, when he cut his foot on something buried in the riverbed. He bent, found the object, and washed away the mud, holding it to the light.

His heart jumped.

A stone the shape of a dart. A glossopetra. A tongue stone. The petrified tongue of a dragon or giant serpent. Royals carried them as amulets to protect against poison and plague, or wore them about their necks like charms. They were found high in the cliffs of Malta, where Saint Paul turned the vipers to stone, and in mountainsides storied for ancient dragons. He tucked it quickly into the pocket of his tunic, worried the natives might not wish it disturbed, and he was thinking all the while of the great serpent risen from the river on the day of their arrival. Here was further evidence, a treasure more prized to him than any golden nugget.

They departed for home at daybreak, and the onset of night forced the expedition to stop upstream of the fort. Here they were welcomed by one of the coastal chiefs, eager to hear of the enemy blood they'd shed upriver. After all, he assumed this to be their excursion's purpose. Le Moyne watched as some of the men leapt up to demonstrate how they'd struck down a pair of enemy warriors, a complete fabrication.

Captain Vasseur took up the lie.

"Had not the rest flown before our swords, surely our victory would have been great."

The chief was well pleased at this. He called for a feast in the Frenchmen's honor, seating them in his hall above even his sons. Partway through the feast, jolly with food and triumph, the chief asked to see the captain's sword. His face darkened as he held the blade to the firelight. It was stainless.

Vasseur held out his hands.

"It carried such enemy blood, I was forced to wash it clean in the river."

"Ah." The chief smiled, pleased with this excuse, and handed back the sword.

A little later he asked to see their scalps.

Again, Vasseur held out his hands.

"It is not the custom of my warriors to avail themselves of such trophies."

Again the chief smiled, accepting the captain's explanation.

Le Moyne watched the chief's sons, their torsos wide and slatted as carved sandstone. Their faces showed nothing, solemn as masks. Perhaps they believed the lies. Then came a gibbering through the hall, a thumping of the floor, and a holy man entered with a bowl held high and steaming above his head. It was the black drink, *cassena*, consumed at rituals. The chief and his sons and warriors each drank from the bowl. Soon their faces shone, their eyes round with new mania. White blisters of sweat quivered on their noses and chins. The priest dislodged a dagger embedded in the central beam of the hall and began dancing among them, skipping and stomping and chanting, the blade winking in the torchlight.

Le Moyne and his companions cut eyes at one another, their hands creeping toward their swords. Meanwhile Vasseur, their leader, sat fixed in his seat of honor, a pained smile upon his face. The priest whirled around the table, striking strange heraldic attitudes, first rampant with arms outflung, now embowed like a leaping dolphin, toeing his way across the floor. He hovered behind each of the chief's sons, chanting, his gaze locked even as his limbs hurled and spun, and none of the sons turned to look. He came to the last of them, the most boyish of the line, and the dagger fell in two quick whips of light—*"hyou, hyou!"*—plunged hilt-deep between the boy's ribs.

A stifled scream bloated the boy's face, his neck webbed and veined. He stared only at the far wall, refusing to look upon the wounds in his side, twinned like the bite of a great fanged serpent. Soon he began shaking, seizing, and his eyes rolled white in his skull. He collapsed, his limbs splayed, his blood coiling in the dirt. Now the other sons rushed to kneel about him, groaning through their teeth, as if to voice his pain. The women were let into the hall, mothers and wives and daughters who prostrated themselves at his feet, keening, their eyes rounding balefully to the sky.

The French sat immobile, wide-eyed, hands on the pommels of their swords. The natives would not speak now save for the names of their enemies, vicious utterances that crowded the hall. When the boy was taken away, Le Moyne went with the interpreter—a man called La Caille, from the previous expedition—to try and learn what had happened. They found the wounded son on a woven mat in a nearby hut. The air was ragged with smoke; a clutch of women knelt at his side. They were placing poultices of fire-warmed moss on his wounds, weeping as they did. He looked but a child now, his face ashen, a white paste gumming the corners of his mouth. His breath came fast and shallow, fugitive. Le Moyne and La Caille looked at one another.

"Ask them why he was struck."

The women responded with open palms, their faces pleading.

"No trophies," translated La Caille. "No weapon-blood."

"I don't understand."

The women slapped their sides where the boy had been struck.

"The wounds," said La Caille. "The wounds must be remembered."

"Whose wounds?"

Back at the boats, the men pressed them for an explanation. Le Moyne looked from face to face, each awed and expectant.

"If warriors return from battle with no evidence of shedding enemy blood, the chief must order his most-beloved son struck by the blade that killed his ancestors. The wounds of the dead are renewed, their deaths newly lamented." Le Moyne held out his hands. "It is like a penance, I think."

The men looked at one another, their eyes wide.

"*Des sauvages,*" they whispered. "*Des barbares.*"

Savages.

Captain Vasseur decided it was not too dark to navigate the river after all. They cast quickly from shore. Le Moyne stood in the bow of the vessel, thumbing the tongue stone in his pocket. The moon trembled like a silver platter on the river, the same as it did on the quay-waters of Dieppe. He wondered at the blood ritual he had witnessed, at how strange and strangely familiar it seemed.

But back at the fort, in the days that follow, the story of the chief's son is soon forgotten. For it is not of bloodletting the men want told. It is of the Apalatci. The mountains.

"Apalatci," they whisper. "Apalatci."

Gold.

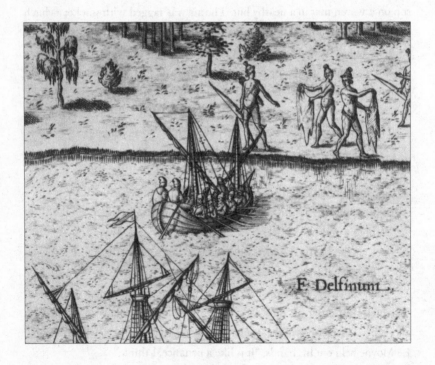

F. Delfinum.

10

Altamaha River, 1975

Hiram Loggins pushes upriver through the swirling dawn mist, his hand on the twist-grip throttle of an outboard motor. The two-cycle din sets river birds to flight, rails and storks and ibises trailing their long, stiltlike legs. He is wearing another man's coveralls, fresh from the drawer with the fold-lines still in them, the name *Barlow* stitched on the patch over the heart. He is wearing another man's boots as well, size twelves—a size too big—and he has the taste of another man's woman in his mouth. A taste he can't get out.

It's that red hair, maybe, that sets him on fire, those blues eyes that might cool him. He'd had her there on the porch, on the rail, with her husband snoring just inside the house.

"Dead to the world," she said. "Take a load of buckshot to wake him up."

Then a second time, in the hull of this very boat, Barlow's, too, as he slipped it into the creek. He'd never been with a woman like that, that moved like she did, that forced him so deep, looking like he was killing her with every thrust. And still she wanted more, her white legs climbing him yet higher, her heels digging into his kidneys, her toes kinked. She was well made beyond anything he'd seen, like another species almost, so wet-hot he thought his thing might come out pinked.

After the second time, he stood in the boat, his new coveralls on but unzipped, and watched her step back into her panties on the creek bank. The ink under his skin was still burning, as if danger were yet near, in the trees or wiregrass or water.

"Come with me," he said.

"Where?"

"I got a floathouse. Upriver. Just you and me."

She tried not to laugh.

"You were good, I'll give you that. But you want to take me out of here, it won't be to no shantyboat."

He could take a punch, always could. In the chin or ribs or tight-made belly. A skill learned early on the river. It didn't matter if you bled or fell, as long as you didn't cry. He set his jaw, stubborn and underbit, and ripped the starter cord on the outboard, waking the thing in a blue puff of oil smoke. He pointed the bow upriver, into the dark kinks he sought when the straighter world went crooked.

Now he can feel the dawning sun on his back, clearing the trees, and he twists the throttle to the stop. He is racing daylight. They are both headed upstream, the sun burning off the white river of mist that conceals him. No witnesses but the tree birds and alligators, the wild hogs rooting in the bushes along the shore. Even to them he might seem the ghost of something skating upriver, a shadow in the mist.

The *Amelia-Jo* is gone, he knows—seized by the DEA, surely, laced now with official tape and writs—and he doesn't know how many of his men got away. He heard splashes in the night, other men jumping ship, but he didn't see any of his crew as he made his escape. Sheriff Poppell turned on them, acting as if he and his deputies were out to bust the shipment, not protect it. Hiram, floating on the far side of the boat, one hand on the hull, heard the drawl come sliding from the lawman's mouth.

"Thank God y'all shown up. We could use the reinforcements intercepting these here grouper-catchers. Didn't see you was DEA in all this dark."

Hiram reported the boat stolen early this morning, calling from a payphone at one of the dark little marinas on his way up the river. The DEA will know it was him, but they will have a tough time proving it. Still, he figures it will be a long time before he sees his boat again, if he ever does. *Evidence*, they'll say, *part of an ongoing investigation. Apologies,* they'll say, *somebody dropped a wrench on the gauges* or *ripped open the upholstery looking for contraband. Somebody cut a hole in the hold, looking for secret compartments,* or *broke off the rudder putting it in storage.*

This is the sixty-foot trawler it took him ten years to save for, finding a bank to finance the part he couldn't. In the span of a night he's traded it for a ten-foot johnboat, trading also the arms of a good home-woman for the legs of another man's wife. All this, and little to look forward to now but the decks of other men's boats.

He spits and wipes his mouth with the back of his arm.

He motors upstream of the floathouses that jumble the riverbanks, entering the Narrows, finding the bend where a line of willows grows along the bank. Rag Point. He runs the bow into the reeds and steps onto shore. He has his jeans from earlier with him, a crusty ball wadded under his arm. He snaps them flat, disbursing flakes of dried mud in every direction, then ties them around the trunk of a willow that stands along the shore, knotting them leg to leg. An offering. A few of the other trees bear rags or torn shirttails like rotten neckties, old talismans long forgotten, the faith in such powers mostly lost. Done, he curls his boat in the river and heads for the creek of his birth, passing the city of shantyboats watching dim-windowed from the river's banks.

11

Altamaha River, Day 1

The sun burns low behind them, a fiery peach that casts their shadows long, a pair of black lances on the river. They pass the entry to Steamboat Slough, the site of an old freight landing, and soon Double Yellow Bluff rises before them, shouldered high from the water like a yellow clay beach. It's empty but for a single alligator, four feet long.

Hunter scratches his nose.

"Spring break, and no girls in string bikinis to welcome us."

"You come to the wrong beach for that," says Lawton. He squints at the alligator. "Though you got one there might indulge. Love that little pecker of yours clean off."

"Know what I heard, Lawton?"

"No."

"Too much muscle, it's bad for your dick. Not enough blood to go around. You might ought to keep that in mind."

"Bullshit."

"How come you think Arnold quit bodybuilding? Dick like a rubber band." Hunter droops his index finger, frowning.

Lawton sniffs. "It was his heart made him stop."

"Well, what else would he say? Conan the Barbarian can't have a limp dick."

Lawton growls.

"Where'd all the college kids go for spring break? Panama City, some bullshit?"

"Lot of them. Few down to Mexico."

"You wanted to go?"

"I don't have the money for that. Not much my scene, anyway."

"That's because you're smart." Lawton places his paddle across his lap and reaches into his vest for his can of dip. "Bunch of horny, spoiled-ass college kids drinking neon shit and humping in the street. It's a damn disgrace is what it is. No wonder there's countries want to blow us off the map." He tucks a wad of tobacco under his lip, screws closed the lid, and looks at Hunter. "Still, though, you got to put your dick in more than a tube sock sometime."

Hunter feels his face redden.

"Big talk from you. For all you know I'm knee-deep in it, beating ladies off with a stick."

Lawton lifts his sunglasses and looks him up, down, his blue eyes big as little oceans.

"Nope. You ain't been getting any."

"Least I don't have to be fed saltpeter to keep me from soiling the sheets."

Lawton grins. "If that's what they're doing, brother, it ain't working. I been on ships it's a factory of fist-pistons under the hatches. You'd think they were hand-powered."

They paddle on past the beach, and Hunter is thinking of the girls at school. They're so golden, their calves and shoulders and necks; their teeth and toes gleam. They aren't the same species as him, seems like. They can't be. Their language isn't even the same.

He fingers the shark's tooth at his neck.

"Seriously, though. When you guys are deployed, living in a hooch or out in the field or whatever, how is it you deal with, you know . . ."

"The threat of vasocongestion?"

"Vaso-what?"

"Blue balls, brother. Serious business there. We handle it the same as everybody else, just takes more creativity. You ain't really jacked off till you done it kneeling in a hole you dug, hunched in full kit, trying to see a six-month-old copy of *Maxim* with your night-vision goggles."

"Damn."

Before long they're in sight of Rag Point, where the low-hanging willows along the bank once fluttered with hundreds of makeshift pennants, torn shirttails and sleeves and bandannas. Their father said it was a sacrifice to the river. A man who failed to "treat" the point could expect a world of hurt to come down on him before he saw the mills of Darien, if he ever did.

Lawton noses his boat into the bank and jumps out. He hitches his bowline to a snag and turns around, fists jammed on his hips.

"You coming?"

Hunter is still maneuvering toward shore.

"Jesus Christ."

Lawton already has his dive-knife out, luminous in the purpling light. He's cutting the tail from his shirt.

Hunter shores his boat and steps past him.

"I got to piss."

He walks into the trees. It's dark under the drooping willows, a world dappled gunmetal and gray. There are no rags he can see. He wonders how many old shirttails are buried in the ground beneath his feet, their magic dwindling as they rot away. He picks a bush and unzips his shorts and looses himself, a yellow-bright beam. He's thinking he needs to hydrate when he feels his shirt yanked taut, slashed, and he whirls to find Lawton standing behind him, grinning, holding a strip of his shirttail like a cut-out tongue. In his other fist, the knife gleams.

"All that college pussy making you slow or what?"

"Tell me you didn't just scalp my fucking T-shirt."

"Hell, boy, it ain't but some cotton. What about your *life*?" Lawton shakes his fist, the shirttail with it. "What about . . . your *destiny*?" He's grinning, his teeth stacked and clenched like the grill of a semi truck.

"I don't figure tying my shirttail to a willow tree is gonna alter my destiny much."

"I'm just looking out for you is all. Didn't figure you'd treat the point yourself." Lawton looks down at Hunter's crotch. "Now, you gonna put that piece of tackle away or keep me looking at it?"

Hunter looks down, feeling the sting of all that pressure wanting out.

"Actually, big boy, I ain't done just yet."

Lawton's eyes bulb out. He leaps as Hunter shoots a stream at his feet. He lands and runs whooping through the woods, trophy aloft, while Hunter pursues him, shooting piss in his wake.

They leave the trees rag-tied behind them, and soon they're floating out into the river, paddling downstream of the falling sun. In less than a mile, the river will begin to widen, the Narrows spilling into a broader flow. Here where the river fattens, the banks were once lined with shantyboats of every kind: shacks hand-built on scows or pontoons, floathouses raised on airtight drums, old houseboats covered in green scum. A whole floating city, the river like a giant flooded street.

People started coming out here during the Depression, families in flight from the dry world with its towns and taxes, its debts and warrants. They became river rats. To hear it told, they lived on the very edges of the law, eating only what they killed or caught, sleeping with whatever warm bodies were nearest in the night. Living however they would. There were stories of grand drunkenness on the river, men whose wives forced them into life jackets the instant they opened the second jelly jar of shine, so many times had they fallen overboard. More than one man had been found miles downstream at dawn, fished from the river before he even woke from his whiskey-stupor. There were stories of cross-river duels between rival fishermen, each firing at the other from the comfort of a lawn chair or La-Z-Boy dragged to the porch, the river too wide for an accurate pistol shot. And rumors of drug-running, too, and murder-for-hire, and floating brothels that didn't care your age.

In the early nineties the state government outlawed floathouses on the river, citing their lack of marine toilets, their menace to navigation, but many of the owners simply towed their homes up into the creeks and sloughs exempt from the law. Their father's house had always been on such a hidden backwater, Snakebelly Creek.

They follow the bank closely and still they almost miss it. Willows drape the entrance like camouflage netting. They pass in file through the trees, and soon the narrow creek swells like a rat in the belly of a snake. Here are the shanties, dark-windowed, most of them, sinking slowly back into the waters that float them. The creek is nearly stagnant, littered with the hulls of beer cans and cigarette cartons, coupon vouchers and spent shot shells, condoms tied off into little sacs. Hunter passes a toilet paper roll trailing a ten-foot tail of tissue like a giant tapeworm.

"I don't remember it this bad," he says.

"Me neither, brother."

"You'd need an army of pool boys with skimmers to clean this shit up."

Lawton points with his paddle. "There's your problem."

They come upon a floundered shanty, sunk to the porch, the trash of the place vomited forth into the creek. It takes them a moment to realize it's their father's.

12

Le Moyne sits on a cypress stump watching the barques being built. There are two of them, ribbed like the beached carcasses of whales. These vessels are to carry them upriver, to the storied riches of the Apalatci mountains, from which all good things come. There is an energy in the shipbuilding work, the men swarming over the frames like white ants, working with a shirtless vigor not seen in the planting of crops or setting of traps or baits.

Beyond the barques stands a palisade of sharpened timber—one wall of the triangular fort—and beyond that is the dark bend of river from which the river monster rose at dusk those weeks ago. The sturgeon are no longer jumping, not like they did in June and July. Le Moyne has tried to arrest them in his mind's eye, the way they gleam silver in the sun, shuddering with fleck-shot power, their bodies ridged like the gate-rams of a sieging army. Somehow, he cannot translate the image to paper. He has burned wad after wad in the fire.

Le Moyne sets aside his sketch and removes the tongue stone from the pocket of his tunic. It is half the size of his palm, iron gray with a black root. The point is sharp enough to cut, to kill, and the edges have tiny serrations. He is running his thumbnail along the edge, as if to saw a groove, when he hears shouts from the landward side of the fort. He turns to see men climbing parapet ladders and knotting at the gate, a bristling forest of spades and halberds and guns. He hurries toward that side of the fort, hearing the name Saturiwa whispered again and again.

King of the coast.

"How many are they?"

"Hundreds! Armed!"

Laudonnière appears at the gate. He is straight-backed, ordering men left and right with bladed hand, jutted chin.

"The chief wishes to enter," says the interpreter atop the gate.

"Tell him I will admit but him and twenty of his men."

The interpreter speaks over the far side of the gate, gesturing with his hands.

Le Moyne stands well away as they slide the oak beams from the gate locks. He can see what reception their commander has ordered. The gate groans and in walks Saturiwa, striding prideful atop his burled legs, each thigh vented with power. His shoulders hang wide over his narrow waist. The dark planes of his chest are adorned with mazes of hammered ink, and he wears from his buttocks the striped tail of some unknown beast, as if to show himself its killer or kin. Upon his head is a spiked crown of palm fronds, freshly cut and weaved.

He is flanked by twenty of his most powerful warriors, their spines straight as the spears they carry in hand. Laudonnière waits to receive them, smiling. The gate has only just closed behind the native retinue when Laudonnière opens his arms, as if in welcome.

His signal.

Trumpets blare and cannon boom, drums thunder in might, the fort barking its full power to the wilds. The Indians drop low to the ground, tensed in battle crouches, eyes darting for the danger sure to come. Meanwhile, Laudonnière stands open-armed, unmoved, beaming godlike while powder smoke tumbles over his boots.

Seeing him, Saturiwa rises, flipping his hand for his men to do the same. They do, white-eyed like spooked beasts, spears pale-knuckled in their hands. Saturiwa strides forward, chin high, as if unwounded by the display. Here is a man of no small spirit, thinks Le Moyne, who can withstand such alien thunder—heathen though he is.

The talk is of war. Saturiwa has gathered his warriors to strike Utina, his enemy in the west, and he has come for the Frenchmen and guns promised him. Laudonnière put off his emissaries some days ago. Now the chief has come in person.

"Tell him my barques are not ready." Laudonnière points to the ribbed keels upon their cradles. "Tell him it will take two months for them to be ready."

"He wants to know what happened to our other ships, the ones that brought us here."

"Tell him they departed last week for France, to resupply. I told his emissaries this already. Tell him we must build others to take upriver, and these take much time to build. Tell him I would like to assist him, but I have not the means at this moment."

"He says his vassal chiefs have assembled already, his foodstuffs are in order, he must strike at once. He says all has been ordered on the strength of your promise."

"Tell him to wait two months," says Laudonnière. "Then I will consider our agreement."

Saturiwa looks about the fort, seeing perhaps the thatch-roofed barracks his men helped to raise, the storehouse and guardhouse, the commander's court lined with covered galleries. The scant cookfires here or there, the heavy armor and hook-shaped guns that require such strength to carry.

"He says he does not see much cultivation within the fort or without," says the interpreter. "He wonders what a lot of corn it must take to feed such strong men once the season grows cold, the woods empty of game."

"Tell him not to worry," says Laudonnière. "Tell him we will be fine."

Saturiwa cannot delay, such are his preparations, and so he departs grimly through the gates, assembling his warriors on the riverbanks upstream of the fort. Le Moyne and a party of officers go to watch the native army prepare for battle. The natives bear longbows, sinew-strung with arrows of fire-hardened cane, each tipped with buckhorn or fish-teeth. Others carry war clubs of various shapes, fat-headed or double-edged, and many of them have spears not so different from French spades, yet darted with fishbone or flint. They wear the plumes of various animals, the hooked blades of talons or claws through their ears. The French officers have brought along their arquebuses, the heavy barrels resting on their shoulders, the curved stocks cupped in their palms. They know not how indiscriminately these savages might make war.

Saturiwa stands before a bonfire. His army encircles him, a ring of blazing flesh. He lashes his arms this way and that, screaming and cursing, as if angry spirits might burst free from his throat. He hops here and there, his eyes bulged with hate, his mouth wet, his striped tail whipping about his legs. In response to certain screams, his warriors thump their weapons against their thighs, a war-drum of pummeled flesh. Saturiwa holds a bowl of water high above his head, speaking to the sun, asking for some blessing, it seems, and then he casts the water upon the heads and shoulders of his warriors.

"What's he saying?" someone asks.

Their interpreter is bent forward, listening.

"He is comparing the water to blood, I think. That they may spill it like water. 'Do, do as I have done, with the blood of your enemies.'"

Finished, Saturiwa dumps water on the fire. It explodes in steam, curdling the air at his feet, and the warriors march upstream to make blood of the water that covers them.

II.

R. Saturiova

13

Altamaha River, Day 1

It's an eighteen-foot houseboat built from a set of plans mail-ordered from *Popular Mechanics* in 1950. Their father's childhood home. The rafters are sawed from hard pine, the roof covered in tar-papered tongue-and-groove, the house sheeted in one-by-eight shiplap. There's a ten-gallon tank on the roof, fresh water hand-pumped from a shallow well dug ten feet up the creek bank, and the windows are screened instead of glassed. The doors have round glass portholes in them, glazier-cut, the only indulgence. There are double bunks; the children slept above the parents in the same room. There's a chemical toilet on the rear porch. The house floats on a wooden scow, caulked with oakum and tar, the waterproofing no longer perfect. The place lists like a doomed ship, one corner of the porch submerged, water slipping under the door.

"It didn't get this bad overnight," says Hunter.

"Not in a year either."

"I don't believe this is his trash."

"Squatters, likely." Lawton shakes his head, looking at the litter. "I don't believe the old man wore a rubber once in his life."

They tie their boats to the porch railing. Hunter steps aboard first, slowly, as if onto some new shore. The once-familiar planks are strange beneath his feet, slanted and water-warped. Lawton follows, the deck shifting under his weight. More water swells across its surface, running up around Hunter's ankles. He starts to step inside but Lawton stays him, going first. He pushes open the door with one hand, his opposite thumb hooked high on his vest, not far from his knife. He steps inside and stops.

"Who the fuck are you?"

Hunter steps into the cavelike darkness, and in the dim light he thinks for a moment that he is looking upon his risen father sitting Indian-style on the bed, his hair grown long and wild in the months since the miracle that raised him. But no, he sees, this cannot be his father, for the man bears unfamiliar symbols on his skin, tattoos of crosses and serpents and scrolled words, the canvas of his torso weathered like shed snakeskin.

"Bless ye," says the old man. "Bless ye."

He is giving them the sign of the cross with a flat hand, like a karate chop.

"Get your ass off that bed," says Lawton.

When the man doesn't move, Lawton grabs him by the elbow and drags him up. Hunter grimaces at the treatment. Lawton produces a flashlight from the vast recesses of his vest and shines it here and there, this corner and that, in precise jabs of light. The floor is trash, the walls covered in mold and animal skins, the sink piled with dishes and small bones. Lawton stabs the light into the old man's face. His beard burns white in the beam; his yellow teeth are polished clean. Over his heart, there is the tattoo of a slim foot, womanly almost, crushing the neck of a serpent. Below this, an inscription: *The dragon shalt thou trample under feet.*

"Who are you?" asks Lawton.

"A friend. I am a friend."

Lawton spits a bullet of tobacco juice into the nearby sink. The dishes clink.

"Friend to somebody, maybe. You ain't friend to me."

"I mean ye no harm."

"What's your name?"

"Uncle."

"Your name is Uncle?"

The man nods. "Yea, a name fit for kings."

Lawton looks at Hunter, one eyebrow arched. Hunter shrugs: *Hell if I know.*

"What is it you're doing here?"

"The waters are rising."

Lawton nods. "Springs rains will do that."

"No," says the old man. "The seas, too. The ice caps are melting, the heat of hell unbound. A coming flood. Whosoever is unprepared shall be drownt."

"Oh." Lawton cuts his eyes toward Hunter. "It's like that, is it?"

He starts leading the man toward the back door.

"There is a beast in this river," says the old man. "Such as what will rule in the days ahead, its kingdom risen again in tide."

Lawton stops. "Beast?"

"Yea, a monster of old time."

"You meaning the Altamaha-ha?"

"It has waited so long to rise," says the old man. "I hunt it."

He steps onto the rear porch and points at a canoe tied between the bank and the house. It's fitted with a small outboard motor, and a harpoon lies across the thwarts, long as a man laid flat. The wooden pole holds an iron shaft, the killing barb single-flued like a shark's fin. In the bottom of the boat, a coil of rope.

"How come you want to kill it?" asks Hunter.

The man looks at them confusedly, as if he doesn't understand the question.

They sit atop the slanted roof of the house, enclosed by the low railing that crowns the place, and eat their dinners from cans. It's cooling with dark, and they have their sleeping bags zipped up to the chest. The trees are mostly bare above them, stars bounding through their clutches.

"Whack-job. Hunting the Altamaha-ha with a spear." Lawton jabs his fork in his can of pork and beans.

"Like hunting it with something else is saner."

"You know what I mean."

They can hear the old man down there, some few feet below them, snoring. They've decided to leave him be, giving him the wide berth you give the touched.

Hunter chews his dinner. "You think he's the one trashed the place?"

Lawton shakes his head. "I don't know. He don't seem like the packaged food and cigarettes type. I'm thinking people been squatting here for years. Daddy ain't been up here in half a decade, I bet. Maybe longer."

"So where's he been going?"

"Good question."

They sit chewing, their forks scraping. Hunter brought the bag of ashes up to their rooftop camp. Now it sits at the foot of their sleeping bags, the nylon slouched beneath the rolled and buckled top. He looks at it.

"'Cremains.' Sounds like a bad pun or something, don't it?"

Lawton quits chewing. Hunter can see the food in his mouth.

"What?"

"It's just a funny word is all. *Cre*-mains?"

Lawton rearranges the food in his mouth.

"Nothing funny about it, you ask me." He juts his chin toward the bag. "You ask him, neither."

Hunter forks a sausage from his can.

"He never could take a joke."

Lawton stiffens. He swallows and points his fork at Hunter.

"He was a hard man, but me and you was lucky he was. He hadn't been, who knows how we would of turned out." He is jabbing his fork at Hunter now, the red bean stuff dripping onto Hunter's sleeping bag. "I wouldn't be where I am today if he hadn't of hammered the right way of things into me."

Hammered, thinks Hunter. *That's the word*. More than once, marveling at his brother's brutal form, he has wondered if Lawton's body simply hardened itself against the blows and lashes of their father. Evolved. The old man a powerful stimulus for adaptation: his belts and switches and paddles. His fists.

They chew for a while. Finally Lawton sticks his fork in his can and looks up.

"You really think it was a sturgeon done that to him?"

Hunter shrugs. "That's what they said."

"I can't believe he'd let it happen."

Hunter swirls his fork in the can. "He didn't have to let it. It just did."

Lawton's mouth disappears inside his beard, his lips pressed tight against that statement, like he doesn't want to breathe it in.

"You know he was into something."

"What's that supposed to mean?"

"Mama wrote me last year, right after he got that new Gheenoe boat. She said she didn't know where he got the money for it. That he was all funny about it. She was afraid he was *into something*."

"Like drugs?"

"You know the shrimpers used to bring it in. Airdrops. Square grouper and all that. People say that's what happened to his first boat. It was that Great Sapelo Bust."

"Well, she never said nothing to me."

Lawton sniffs. "Maybe she was just trying to protect you."

Hunter feels a cruel urge rise up in him then. He wants to throw his meal in his brother's face, to coat his beard and eyebrows with a red explosion of kidney beans and meat. He wants to bloody him. He turns and hurls the can far off into the creek.

Lawton looks at him. "The hell you do that for?"

"Everybody else does."

Lawton grunts. That's about the last reason he'd do anything.

Hunter wakes in the night. He is standing on an island, alone, in the middle of a great dark river that rumbles like storm. It is the river he knows but wider, darker, with trees set like giants along its banks. Before him stands a pillar of gray wood, straight-struck as a ship's mast into a leaden sky. He finds in his hands a heavy felling ax, double-bit, and on his back a quiver of springboards such as the old-time axmen once used to elevate themselves over the splayed feet of old-growth timber, cutting the softer wood higher up.

He feels something tickle his feet and looks down to see that water is tumbling over them. Around him the little island gleams like a giant river stone, the current racing across its surface, swirling and tripping and rolling as it goes. It pulls hard at his ankles, rising every second, carrying away brush and fallen branches and loose debris, crushed cans and old bottles and dead leaves, whole anthills wisped away like smoke.

He must climb.

He chokes up on the hickory handle, like the boys taught him at practice, and begins slinging the ax into the tree at belly height, hard, whipping his body like a ballplayer. He torques his wrist to free the blade after each strike. He lets the ax fall from the cut, wheeling down past his feet and up again in a big arc, hovering a moment motionless behind him before he hurls it again into the hardwood. He cuts a deep wound in the tree, a pocket of white flesh.

The water is tearing at his shins.

He sinks the ax into the trunk above his head and jams the metal shoe of one of the boards he carries into the notch. He leaps onto the narrow plank, the wood groaning beneath his feet, bending, as if it might pop free of the tree. He unsticks the ax and starts again, cutting a second pocket three feet above the first. The river is rising beneath him, the plank shuddering with every strike. The current breaks around the tree's base, bubbling, whirling downriver in long snakes and folds.

It takes him six strikes to make the second pocket. He jams home a new board and climbs onto it, then begins chopping again. He ascends in a maddened spiral of planks, the tree crazy-limbed with his progress. His arms are swollen, filled with acid, his lungs throbbing like an engine. His mouth is wet, his body floating high over the water on these sprouted limbs. He stands finally upon the sawn top of the tree, balanced as upon the mast of a sinking ship, and the river swirls beneath him, ripping away the lower boards, and he sees he is not alone. There is a creature in the river, circling, slow-moving in the surety of its dominion. The hide is treaded like a truck tire, the tail long, and Hunter remembers sketches he has seen by the early explorers, rumored to have a fort on the river. In one drawing, six naked Indians ram a spear the size of a tree down the throat of an enormous toothed reptile come out of the river, like an alligator but with the beaklike face of a dinosaur, though they couldn't have known about those then.

Hunter looks at the ax in his hands, twin-bladed like a weapon, and he wonders how long until the monster reaches him.

14

Darien, Georgia, 1982

Annabelle waits on her porch, the moon hidden from sight, the night dark and starless as an enormous cave. She is waiting for him to slink again from the water like the very first man, the way he always does on such nights. Shirtless, as he was the first time, and sweat-slick like she likes him, his body badged with ink, his mission secret as a commando's. He will come. They will do it wherever they can. In the boat shed or against the side of the house. On the creek bank or bald-bodied in the yard, her husband dead to the world with drink.

Her blood is up, her toes splayed flat against the porch planks, kneading them. Here he is. The bow of her husband's old johnboat, painted camouflage now, slides through the reeds at the edge of the creek. She stands and straightens the dress she wears, belted tight around her narrow waist, and slips on her white heels. Then she sits and lights a cigarette, letting one shoe dangle idly from her big toe. She looks away, opposite his direction, as if there is something more important in the pines and oaks.

"Pssst."

He's at the door. Slowly, she looks his way.

"I thought you weren't coming."

He looks her up, down.

"The fuck you did."

He lights a cigarette, still on the stoop, then turns and looks over his shoulder at her husband's old Chevelle in the yard. He steps off the stoop and walks toward it. He toes one of the tires with his white rubber boot, then bends to run his hand along the body just back of the front wheel well.

"Ain't keeping it up like he used to. Rust's gonna chew up them rockers."

He looks over his shoulder at her, enjoying himself. She knows what he's doing.

She stands, clicking across the porch, the door groaning wide before her. She kicks off her heels at the bottom of the stoop, throws down her cigarette. She shoves him down hard on the hood her husband likes to rub so much, like it was a woman's thigh. There are two black racing stripes. She positions Hiram between them and climbs up on the bumper. She unbuckles and un- zips him and yanks down his pants. Once freed, he pops up like one of those blow-up punching bags they sell at the dollar store.

"I thought so," she says.

Afterward she stays on him, and his fingers find the slick groove of sweat down her back, sliding up and down. She knows what he will say.

"Leave him," he says. "Come with me."

She rises up on one elbow and tries to get the hair out of her face, the red curls pasted across her nose and forehead.

"Jesus Christ," she says. "I got hair in my mouth even."

"It could be this good all the time."

She sets both palms flat on the hood and looks down at him.

"It wouldn't," she says. "Before long it wouldn't be any different than with him." She cocks her head toward the house.

His face darkens. "What you want is a big white house with fancy columns, ain't it? Decorated by some queer you brung in, with furniture you can stand around and talk about like it's accomplished something besides being old as Sherman's horseshit. Maybe get you some seersuckered dentist to bankroll it all, some poor son of a bitch you can make shave every night before bed so his whiskers won't scratch your precious pussy. Take you to nice dinners down at the country club, shopping trips to Atlanta. And all the while you'll be fucking me every night that's moonless, or wanting to."

She starts to push off from him but he grips the back of her neck, firmly, holding her close. "That's what you want, ain't it?"

She twists her head away, but he pulls her closer, still inside her.

"Say it ain't." He is almost pleading. "Say it."

She looks him dead in the eye. She doesn't say anything.

15

Le Moyne swirls his daily ration of wine in his wooden cup. It is dusk. The fireflies are out, tiny stars winking in the gray. His countrymen sit on stumps and logs, heads gathered close over their wine. Their voices hiss: *Apalatci, Apalatci.* Gold. Like a glow in the west. A yellow sickness. Le Moyne sighs and looks at La Caille, the translator, now his bunkmate.

"That I could multiply this cup, man, a flood of wine to sate our brothers."

La Caille pulls on the point of his beard, black as jet, and the white blade of his smile pricks the dark.

"That you were Christ, you mean."

"I would not dare such blasphemy, La Caille."

La Caille's smile widens, good-natured.

"No, my friend, you would not. But wine is poor stuff to sate a man. It fills only his head and sneaks between his legs at dawn."

"And gold?"

"Gold heavies a man's pockets, man, and sometimes his cock as well. Who would not choose it over your flood of wine, be it the very blood of Christ?"

Le Moyne only grunts. La Caille leans toward him, elbows on his knees.

"Why do you think these men left the world they knew? To be rich. Surely you did not cross the ocean only for the sake of art?"

Le Moyne swirls the wine, a purple eddy in his cup. He shakes his head.

"No, I cannot say that."

"Then for what?"

"Glory."

"Ah, my friend, and what is the color of glory but gold?"

"I fear this gold will brick our path to hell."

La Caille shrugs, raises his cup. "Perhaps, my friend. And whether it is paradise we have found here or hell, who might say?"

The words ring in Le Moyne's ears. He drains his cup and stands.

"So little wine, and already I have to go."

He walks along the duckboard paths, making for a latrine at the edge of the woods. It is not gold that fills his mind these nights. On his mattress of corn husks, he thinks often of the dark-skinned maidens striding through the forest, the wives of Saturiwa. The ampleness of their bodies, how savage they might be in the exercise of their desires. He has known women, certainly. Cousins first, those bumbling explorations in dark closets on Sunday afternoons, with the rest of the house asleep. And court trysts after that, skirts lifted breathless to the white thighs, the black-furred pockets of sin. The dark vault of guilt always to follow, the prayers for forgiveness. But the native women seem so free in their flesh, as if to desire them is no sin.

He empties his bladder in the latrine, looking to the woods beyond. They beckon him. Finished, he steps across the pit and into the trees. The world is cooler beneath them, darker, full of places he might hide from the eyes that watch him. Man's, God's. He finds a bare spot and kneels on the earth, his head against a tree, and frees himself from his pants, spitting in the palm of his hand.

This terrible ritual in the wilds.

When he rises his breath is ragged. The golden light of the west has turned; the sun runs red over the western cloudbanks, like spilt wine. He thinks of the Indian king beseeching the sun for victory a day ago. The upheld bowl, the wish to spill the enemy's blood like so much water. He wonders whether the chief's prayers have been answered, and by whom, and he wonders will his own prayers be heard. Will glory crown him or blood?

_____

The following day he stands with La Caille above a cleared field in the heart of Saturiwa's country. They've been sent to record the chief's victory rites. In the field stand seven tall trunks of sharpened pine, each bearing high the trophies of battle: the scalps of the enemy, with long twists of hair and white patches of skull, and a coterie of severed limbs, red-stumped arms and legs that dangle like gruesome pennants from their stakes. The August sun is high already and angry and the flesh is turning, the smell of death curling under the Frenchmen's noses. Le Moyne is breathing through his mouth so as not to retch.

"They cut around the bone with cane knives," says La Caille. "Then sever the joints with wooden cleavers. They march home with the prizes impaled on their spears, careful not to let them touch the ground."

Before the stakes, a priest dances low to the ground, back hunched, knees to chest, creeping here and there like a spider in the grass. He mutters and curses in the savage fashion, spewing incantations. Three men kneel before him. One of them holds a club, which he slams both-handed upon a flat stone, as if to give thunder to certain of the sorcerer's words, while the other two men shake gourds of pebbles or broken shells, a sound like the rattling of snakes.

Saturiwa's people sit in a circle before the stakes. The warriors have removed their war-plumes and paint, their earrings of talon and claw. They have set aside their bows, their bloodied clubs and spears, and they sit solemn-faced before the spectacle, as if in church. Le Moyne watches the priest leap and tremble, speaking thunder, the people bobbing their heads before him.

"What do they believe of life after death?" he asks.

La Caille's hands are clasped behind him. He thumbs the handle of the dagger strapped across the small of his back.

"The widows of the battle-fallen leave their husbands' weapons upon their graves, those used to war and to hunt, and they leave the shells from which they were accustomed to drink."

"As if the men might use these in a world that comes?"

La Caille nods.

Le Moyne finds a fallen log and sits, bent forward, eyes squinted, as if he might interpret the foreign sounds quaking from the holy man's throat. They are brutal words, he knows, words of blood and triumph, of the will of the white-hot god to award victory, and they are curses, too. Death, it seems, is insufficient for their enemies. Their bodies must be hexed and mutilated, their relics thrown down, the bones of their ancestors scattered and smashed underfoot. Here is the difference, he thinks, watching as if from on high.

"They have not the mercy of Christ in them, La Caille."

La Caille looks sideways at him, eyes clear over the sharp point of his beard. *"Et nous?"*

Saturiwa's village is housed within a spiraling wall of wooden palings, twice the height of a man, the entrance blind and narrow as that of a conch. His house is circular, timber-built with a roof of palm thatch, shaggy and yellowed like the hair of a squire boy. Before it is a covered piazza furnished with benches where men may lie shielded from the sun. Inside are shadowy lofts full of skins and cloaks, clubs and spears, the careless glimmer of trinkets and treasures scavenged from the shore wrecks. At the center is a giant hearth, a fire that always burns. Above this is a clay-rimmed hole in the thatch, blacked from smoke.

Saturiwa sits upon an oaken chair at the end of a long table, his once-flat stomach rounded with feast. Le Moyne stands by as La Caille speaks with the chief. The dark man keeps gesturing at them, wagging his finger and showing them his palm, and Le Moyne needs no interpreter to understand what he might be saying.

They have not upheld their end of the alliance.

They have not supported him in battle.

They have deceived him.

All around are the eyes of his warriors, hard as chipped stone.

The Frenchmen depart the village, hardly able to walk abreast through the blind corridor of palings. The eyes of the chief float yet in Le Moyne's mind, bulbed with fury, as if they might burst along the red veins that fault them.

La Caille shakes his head. "I believe we are in a bad position, Le Moyne."

"He wasn't happy."

"What do you expect? Our commander promised him men and guns against his enemies. I have traveled much of the known world, my friend. There is but one thing universally denounced: breaking one's word."

16

Dawn, a pale blade over the trees. They are already under way, sliding along the black glass in echelon, like warships on patrol. The sun breaks on the river, and there is mist. It curls slowly from the surface, rising skyward, as if in thrall to the light. Hunter puts out his hand to touch it, grasp it, but it eludes him, fugitive as spirit. He looks up into the sun, closes his eyes, lets his thoughts drift away like so much paling smoke.

"*Hunter.*"

His eyes snap open. "What?"

"You going to sleep on me? We just woke up."

"I'm meditating."

"*Meditating?*" Lawton's eyes buzz, amused. "How 'bout you *meditate* on how the fuck that old man disappeared like that?"

The old man was already gone when they rose that morning, the sun no more than a hint through the snarled branches of the trees. Not only that, they found the creek clean of the trash floating there the night before. It was a mirror of the overarching trees, untouched but for fallen leaves and sticks and the tiny indentions of jesus bugs skating along its surface. Hunter had to wipe his eyes to make sure he wasn't seeing things.

"Tide flush it out, you think?"

Lawton shook his head. "Tide ain't strong enough this far upriver."

"What then, that old man?"

"Who else?"

A grin quivered along Hunter's mouth.

"All that, and a bad mother like you didn't miss a wink of sleep?"

Lawton stared at the creek, brow furrowed. He was tugging on his beard. "Huh," he said. "I ain't the lightest sleeper, but still."

They pass Penholoway Creek, banked with yet more floathouses towed up out of the main river. At the mouth of the creek is Sturgeon Hole, one of the cold-water refuges where sturgeon once congregated, maybe still do. In the old days, locals catching big sturgeon would ice them down, then ship them on the daily passenger train to New York, where they sold for fifty cents a pound—big money at the time. An RV park sits in the woods above the creek now, boxy homes painted with howling wolves and sunsets.

Soon the Narrows end, the river widens. The current is slower here, heavier, more like the river of Hunter's dream. Bald cypress rise round and gray from the banks on roots splayed like the feet of elephants, their gnarled toes marked by dark lines of old flood. Their limbs spread horizontally, edged high over the water like rotors, each draped with long beards of moss. They are no more than two hundred years old, these trees, dwarfed by the towering ghosts of ancestors logged nearly to extinction. In one, a colony of great egrets has alighted, scattered white as spring blooms in the branches.

"Bald eagle," says Lawton, pointing.

It perches high in a leafless cypress, a white raptor in a dark frock. It watches them with glowering yellow eyes, head spiked like a Mohawk's.

"He don't look real approving of us," says Hunter.

"Trying to decide if we're too heavy to carry off."

"You know Ben Franklin thought the national bird should of been the turkey."

"Shit," says Lawton. "Turkey's for eating."

"He said the turkey was a courageous bird. Said a turkey wouldn't hesitate attacking a grenadier of the British Guards, he came into your farmyard with a red coat on."

Lawton sniffs. "Maybe so. But I don't see whistle-dicked Hitler or the Emperor of Japan being much afraid of boys with turkeys on their sleeves."

"You got a point there."

Lawton shakes his head. "Turkeys, shit. Sometimes I think I need to get you on some kind of federal watchlist."

"You could do that?"

Lawton shrugs. "Hell, I don't know. When they call us in, it ain't usually to put somebody on a list, you know? It's to cross them off of one."

They paddle on, the sun now big before them. It glares down like the eye of a hawk. Hunter can feel its power rising as it climbs. He thinks of the river it sees, the river it saw, the scrolled language of its becoming laid bare from on high. He wonders if it sees ice melting under its gaze, rivers swelling, the tide of the world risen darkly like the old man believes. Man has made for himself such perches, he knows. His airplanes first, like brutal birds in the sky, and now his satellites that float endlessly, invisibly, through the heavens, watching the Earth like gods. The world unsuspecting from that angle, its secrets revealed. The houses of bad men hidden in jungles and mountains, map-pinned for men like Lawton to visit in the night. The tracts of timber cut away by this company or that, never to regrow, the wetlands that shrink year on year. The mysterious wedge of terrain that Hunter found in a satellite photo of the river while looking for the place his father's boat was found. The old French fort, perhaps, rumored to lurk upon the river's banks, peopled with the ghosts of colonists and conquerors.

How he would like to find it.

But there are so many places the satellites cannot find. Depths unpierced by even the sun, that reflect only its white-fired eye. He dips his paddle in the current, as if he might swirl clarity out of its darkness, but the river closes quickly around the blade, like blood into a wound.

They pass Old Hell Bight, the deadly kink that ended many a timber raft, and they curl through Sister Pine Round and on past Sister Pine Drift. The mist has burned off the river, and the earth ticks with heat. Up ahead is Miller

Lake, a narrow slough. A large johnboat is plowing upriver, olive-hulled, riding on a white mustache of wake. There are four men hunched on the thwarts, the boat mounded with gear. Hunter sees Lawton straighten out of the corner of his eye. The boat cuts hard into the mouth of the slough, bow high, casting a high angle of spray as it turns.

Lawton starts toward that side of the river.

"What are you doing?"

The boat disappears into the trees.

"Teaching some manners," says Lawton.

17

Fort Caroline, August 1564

The men are hungry, the mountains far, and Le Moyne hears more whispering in the nights now. Men huddling at their fires, speaking only of far-off places, escape. In daylight many have taken to wearing their swords wherever they go, toting their arquebuses to the most menial of tasks. Saturiwa's ambassadors emerge from the woods less and less often, it seems. They bear turkey and deer and weir-caught fish, gifts that look pretty upon their shoulders but do little to fill the bellies of so many men. They say their stores of corn are mostly used up, traded already for French knives and sickles and trinkets. Saturiwa sends his apologies.

The previous month, Le Moyne and La Caille returned from Saturiwa's village with nothing but tales of the savage king's fury, his bulbed eyes and bared teeth. His anger at the French. Their mission, in fact, had been to secure some of Saturiwa's prisoners as a bridge of good faith with Utina, king in the west, who might lead the French to the treasures of the Apalatci mountains.

At word of Saturiwa's denial, Laudonnière swelled up red, his chest puffed like a cockerel's. He ordered a company of twenty of his best arquebusiers to march behind him to the village. They sat themselves in the chief's great hall, the tapers of their guns fuming in the room of skins and horns. The chief surrendered his prisoners to them, having but little choice.

The day they returned, Le Moyne was on the riverbank, sketching, hoping as always for the river beast to show itself. A raptor slashed and wheeled overhead, whirling and sighting for prey, whipping its black fork of tail back and forth across the river. Le Moyne was watching, trying to decipher what message the inked blades of wing might be scrawling against the sky, when the cloudy dome exploded, slashed in silver light, and the earth shook as if struck.

Le Moyne leapt to his feet, running with gun throttled and satchel flapping. Surely it was a Spanish attack, the thunder of enemy cannon. Instead, he found his countrymen amassed on the walls without armor or guns, slack-jawed as a fire rose along the seaward horizon. It was the marsh burning, the green-brown plains and islands of brush. The flames spread so fast that birds burst from their roosts in ragged parabola, tumbling scorched and blackened from the air, and white clouds of egrets churned under dark boulders of smoke. Deer leapt from burning islands of scrub, darting in panic, some flinging themselves into the river. An alligator pulled under a splashing fawn.

It burned for three days, a smoke so rich it stung the eyes. They wore rags and strips of fabric tied over their faces like brigands, yet many fell ill, hacking and coughing a black filth from their lungs. Those who ventured downriver found the waters strewn with thousands of dead fish, their bellies risen like boils upon the river's skin, and the alligators cruised in the middle of the channels where it was coolest. A stench fell over everything, that of death proceeding in the sun. It reeked like an evil in the land, and Le Moyne saw fear in the eyes of many, such as he had not seen in this new country.

On the third day, La Caille stood beside him on a small hill above the fort, staring down at the blackened waste to the east.

"What do you think, Le Moyne, a stroke of lightning as our leader believes?"

Le Moyne shook his head. "I have heard of a bolt striking when there is no storm, but not to cause such devastation. It is almost as if a part of the heavens came down, one of the stars fallen from its perch."

La Caille pulled on the sharp point of his beard.

"A good theory, I suppose, except that it fell during the day."

Le Moyne looked in the direction of Saturiwa's village.

"Then perhaps a piece of the sun."

At the beginning of September, a sail in the river, flying upon its topmast the standard of France. It is a corsair captained by a man called Bourdet, fresh from raiding merchant vessels in the Antilles. His men are of ruddy complexion, well fed and quick to laugh, and they bring ashore casks of wine and loaves of good hard bread. They wear crossed short swords, and golden trophies are draped from their napes and wrists, even the lowliest of them so adorned. Their faces burn demonlike over the night fires, their red tongues loosing stories of profit among the green jewels of the Caribbean islands, the words falling into the open mouths of their countrymen like food to the hungry.

Le Moyne and La Caille lie awake in their hut, in this fortress of whispers.

"Do you think Utina will lead us to the Apalatci, in truth?"

La Caille sighs. "I know he wishes our arquebuses to speak against his enemies, whoever they may be."

"Perhaps it will not matter." Le Moyne juts his head to the fort beyond the walls of their hut. "I fear the Apalatci have spread their glow to the sea. The men grow restless. All this talk of the islands."

La Caille nods. "Indeed. Perhaps it should not be a surprise. I have heard the islands of the Caribbean are but the peaks of great mountains born out of the depths."

Le Moyne rolls onto his elbow. "They do not float?"

"No, man. They are parts of ranges like those upon the land. This is why they appear to us in chains upon the sea. Who knows what treasures their peaks might hold?"

"*Merde.* You had best keep this to yourself, La Caille."

"I intend to."

18

Darien, Georgia, 1987

Hiram Loggins stands at the helm of a boat all his own, a sixty-five-foot shrimp trawler powered by a rebuilt 12-71 Detroit diesel. It has been nearly a decade since his last boat was seized. This one is slightly longer, steel-hulled instead of wood, with a hydraulic winch and twin screws. He's put everything he has into it, mortgaged to the hilt, his name on the paperwork even if the bank owns most of it. Before him are other boats, a long procession of them winding through the river. The Blessing of the Fleet. Their trawling booms are raised like drying wings, their white hulls glowing under the spring sun. They are passing beneath the gray hulk of the Darien bridge, their wakes bubbling, their names painted across their sterns: *Baby Girl* and *Miss Brenda Jane*, *Lady Ava* and *Melissa Lynn*. Women's names, mostly, to remind the captains of what they have at home, why they spend the long nights at sea. On Hiram's: *Amelia-Jo II*, named again after his mother.

He is married now—to Jo-Beth, the sweetheart he's been with since before the war.

She is good and loyal and strong.

She is not the name of his boat.

He squeezes his right hand. The knuckles are swollen, purple. He still can't make a fist. He was in the boatyard last week, the ship blocked for bottom-painting, when one of the crabbers stopped to let his eyes rove the white sweep of bow, like he might a woman's curves. Hiram knew him from nights at the blockhouse cut-and-shoot bar off Highway 99. The man scratched his chin, gray-whiskered, like Hiram's now is.

"Ain't after that square grouper again, are you?" He chuckled. "Maybe you ought not of named her after your mother."

It seemed too much a verdict, hailing a history he didn't want his future to be. The symbols beneath his skin burned, like brands newly made, and he lit into the man with both fists, knocking him over a sawhorse table and into a pile of rotten nets. He stood over the crabber, his knuckles split and bleeding, and found an iron turnbuckle in his hand, raised to strike. After a moment he dropped it, thinking to apologize, but the words came as a thick gob of spit that smacked the pavement between his boots.

He lifts the busted hand to his mouth now and tears off the scab with his teeth, spitting it on the wheelhouse floor. He sucks at the raw place, tasting the metallic tang of the sea inside him. They say blood is red for the same reason as Georgia clay: iron. He has one of the boys take the helm and steps out onto the deck. The bridge is nearing, set like an arch to the sea. On it stands a white holy man in a black cassock, wild-haired, his dog collar yellowed under the Georgia sun. Father Uncle King, flyweight champion of the interservice competition in Vietnam. A chaplain. Hiram and he were boys together on the river, brothers in ways he would rather forget.

The man has his arms spread wide, reciting Psalms and verses, blessing each boat that passes beneath the shadow of the bridge. People say he knows his Bible by rote. Every word. He looks down upon Hiram's boat as it nears, his voice booming:

"'What is man? For thou hast made him a little lower than the angels, and hast crowned him with glory and honor. Thou madest him to have dominion over the works of thy hands. Thou hast put all things under his feet. All sheep and oxen, yea, and the beasts of the field. The fowl of the air, and the fish of the sea, and whatsoever passeth through the paths of the seas.'"

Hiram doesn't kid himself at having dominion. He knows his little wood-decked island could be overturned easy as a plaything if the sea saw fit, dashed in gray mountains capped with foam. Down there is a whole universe not his own, full of dark giants and white ghosts, alien as anything from outer space. But he lets the holy man's words tumble over him, bless him, for he knows the power of this man's faith, and this is the tradition among Hiram's kind. He thinks of the glistening clouds of shrimp shooting through the depths, whole pulsing globes of them wild-caught in his nets. He thinks of his station rising atop those mounds of protein, his pockets heavied. His accounts paid. His prospects bright as the fresh coat of paint that covers his boat.

Uncle King is spread birdlike against the sun. Hiram closes his eyes and feels flecks of moisture dapple his face. Whether holy water or the man's wet-flecked words, he isn't sure.

"May God Almighty be upon this vessel, the *Amelia-Jo II*, in the name of the Father and of the Son and of the Holy Ghost. May she prosper in her voyages and bear home safely all those who work upon her decks. May she be consecrated to righteous work."

Hiram opens his eyes to see Uncle's palm hovering high over him in blessing. A white worm of scar, knife-made, crosses its deepest crease. Seeing this, Hiram's busted hand clenches closed despite the pain, a knot of fist he jams into the pocket of his overalls, hiding the boyhood scar that matches the holy man's own. Shame rocks him. The thought of what he did, what he was forced to do on a spring day long ago . . . Those are times long gone, he tells himself. Dead. He forces himself to think of the future, the white flame of what he might still become.

The boat passes into the cool hollows of the bridge, where the swallows keep their nests, and he feels the songbirds on his shoulders tingle. He can only hope the holy man's blessing is upon the boat and not its name. For what is painted along the stern is only that. Paint. It is not the boat's true name, the one Hiram says only to himself, again and again: *Annabelle.*

19

Miller Lake, Day 2

It's more slough than lake, narrow and straight as if man-dug. Hunter watches his brother work his paddle side to side, head bent, as if reading signs in the hull-cut surface. There is scarce sound but for the johnboat's wake still lapping at the banks. Lawton's sunglasses are pushed high on his head, his red-freckled arms bulged with pressure. The rudder of his boat yaws this way, that way, like the tail of a sea creature cruising the depths. He broadsides his kayak at the mouth of the small freshwater creek that feeds the slough. He looks back the way they came, then upstream, and nods for them to enter.

It's immediately cooler, darker, the creek roofed in a tunnel of cypress and tupelo. Shards of light lie shivering on the waters, tree-shattered, and the world seems older, taller, its younger self left shining in the sun. The knees of cypress rise bony from the water, some knotted with toads, and they seem to grow only higher as they press upstream. Soon they're as tall and twisted as blackthorn shillelaghs, gnarled and knobbed for clubbing skulls. The creek widens, and they paddle among cypress grown out of the water on every side, their bases furrowed like toe bones. These are virgin trees, Hunter realizes, a swamp of them hidden far up this creek, timber perhaps a thousand years old. He taps Lawton's boat with his paddle.

"This is old-growth timber. They might be deadheaders."

"Didn't see a winch on their boat."

"Could be using floats to pull them off the bottom."

Hunter thinks of the deadheads buried like the bones of giants, hardwood logs now coveted for their centuries-old patina. They're pulled out of the creek bottoms and sold for big money to custom furniture makers.

Lawton spits. "Last I known deadheading wasn't legal. That changed since I was gone?"

"No."

They find the johnboat beached on an island of molding leaves. It's twenty feet long with a side console, painted factory green. The hull is empty, just a couple of heavy nylon bags mounded between the thwarts.

Lawton noses into the bank, lifts himself from the cockpit, and pulls his boat ashore. He stands at the edge of the johnboat and leans over the side, peering into the hollows, his left thumb hooked high on his vest. He unzips one of the bags, sniffs.

"I don't like it."

Hunter shores his boat. "What is it?"

Lawton has already started into the trees, and Hunter only has time to catch a glimpse of tangled electrical cords in the bag. The wet ground muffles their steps; they are surrounded by towers of cypress. Lawton stops and kneels. He comes up with the silver foil of a discarded candy bar wrapper. *Three Musketeers.* He crinkles it quietly in his hand, slips it into his pocket.

"People," he says.

Other litter appears, a breadcrumb trail through the woods: an empty water bottle, a Tootsie Roll wrapper, a miniature comic from Bazooka gum. Lawton stoops to pick up each of these insults, silent, his neck swelled red. Soon they can hear voices sifting through the trees. They round a spiky thicket of palmetto and before them a stony colossus roars skyward from the earth, a cypress as giant-footed as a house, the root base knuckled and tapered like ten trunks grown all into a single primeval missile. Woody stalagmites, man-tall, stand like cloaked sentries on every side, and a dark cloud of vesper bats may or may not be hanging asleep in the tree's hollows.

Below stands a clutch of men in rumpled khaki shirts, like tourists on safari. Two of them bear shoulder-fired video cameras; one holds a sound boom topped with fuzz. The fourth is pointing here and there, red-faced, his shirt soaked in dark teeth of sweat. He wears a floppy hat and knee-high rubber boots, his pants thigh-bulged like the riding breeches of an old general. The chest pocket of his shirt is packed full—Hunter can almost hear the crinkle of candy wrappers.

"I want a low-angle here." He points to the base of the tree. "Show its enormity. I want close-ups of these spike-things. Good B-roll footage there. We'll add some menacing music."

One of the others hitches beneath the weight of his camera and scratches his unshaved neck.

"It won't look that impressive without a man in front to show its size."

The red-faced man turns and looks up at the tree. Sweat shames the seat of his pants.

"Well, I don't know just where our man is at the moment, now do I?"

At this, Lawton hooks his thumbs in his vest and strides into the clearing, chest-high like a banty rooster, his elbows flapping at his sides.

"You boys making a movie or what?"

The camera crew whirls, panning their lenses on him.

Lawton squints into the twin little shapes of himself, warped round.

"Don't you know it ain't polite to point a camera at a body ain't given you his permission?" His accent pours gravy-thick from his mouth. He cocks his head, his blue eyes bright as weapon-scopes. "I'd point them things somewhere else, I was you."

They do, lowering their cameras, and Hunter sees the producer man turn redder. He raises one finger and props up the brim of his floppy hat, then points the same finger at the ground, jabbing. "This is a shooting location, son. We're filming. I'm sure you'd like to see yourself on TV, but it isn't going to happen. It doesn't work like that."

Lawton ignores him. He sticks out his bottom lip and walks about, examining the scene with a large, theatrical eye. He looks over cameras, sound booms, shoes, leaning like a pecking chicken. He walks toward the tree, elbows flapping, and the man turns on his heel to glare at him.

"I'd appreciate it if you two'd clear out," he says.

"I bet you would," says Lawton. "But this ain't your property, now is it?"

He reaches out and touches the tree with the flat of his hand, then squints up at its heights. Hunter does, too. The topmost limbs catch their own winds, swaying like something at the bottom of the sea. What men have stood where he now stands, marveling? Men with spears or bows or muskets, drawn beneath the shadow of this crown. What beasts, giant themselves, have circled in times of flood?

Lawton looks at him. "How old you think she is, little brother?"

Hunter thumbs the shark's tooth at his neck. "Hard to say. They say there's ones a thousand years old out here, older, but I never seen one like this. Could be twice that."

"Old as Christ," says Lawton. "God damn." He looks at the camera crew. "Say, you them boys hunting the Altamaha-ha?"

The red-faced man straightens.

"Is there a problem with that?"

Lawton pats his vest, the wrappers crackling.

"Long's you don't trash the river, there ain't."

The producer man, holding his gaze, digs two fingers into his chest pocket and extracts a red jawbreaker in a cellophane wrapper. He pops the candy into his mouth, crinkling the plastic in hand.

"That mill upstream? They say it discharges fifty million gallons of wastewater a day. That's trash, son."

"I ain't asked for a definition, did I?"

The man sucks on the jawbreaker. "What is it you want?"

Lawton watches him. "I want to know whether you really think it exists, the creature you're hunting."

The man crosses his arms, candy bulging his cheek.

"I think it doesn't matter if it does or not."

"Because you can fill your show with a bunch of splashes and near misses, shit like that?"

"No. Because men *believe* it exists, and that's what's interesting."

"Men like your man that's missing?"

"Perhaps."

"His name Uncle, by any chance?"

"Perhaps," says the man. This time through his teeth.

"Seems a little off his rocker, that one. He know you're making some kind of a mockumentary out of him?"

The man smiles. His face is savage, blooded. "*Documentary*. The proper paperwork has been filed, son, I assure you."

"Oh, the paperwork. Thank God."

"It isn't really any of your business, now is it? Why don't you take your little brother here and get the hell out of my shooting location. I'm tired of hearing your banjos, son."

"Son," says Lawton.

"What?"

"*Son*. You keep calling me that." Lawton sucks his teeth. "Thing is, I had a daddy who called me that. He's ash now—bless him—but he wouldn't of liked some pompous little fly-tipper playing like he fucked my mother."

The man leans into Lawton's face. "This daddy of yours, too bad he didn't teach you some fucking manners." He opens his hand; the candy wrapper flutters down. "*Son*."

Lawton cuffs him in the face with an open palm. The man stumbles backward and trips, falling flat on his butt. He looks up, his face red-swelled like it might burst, tears silvering his eyes. The jawbreaker lies in the dirt, spit-gleamed, like a miniature of his face. Hunter leaps across the clearing and takes Lawton by the elbow, but his brother won't be moved. He is hard-cast in place, immovable as bronze. He leans over the man, pointing him down with a single rigid finger.

"Didn't he?"

Finally he yields, and Hunter tugs him from the clearing, away from the crew with their open mouths and forgotten cameras.

"The fuck you do that for?"

Lawton sniffs. "Talk shit, get hit."

"That ain't how it works, Lawton."

"That's funny, Hunter. It just did."

20

Fort Caroline, November 1564

Le Moyne hears the high-pitched shouts, like fearful dogs, of men upon the walls. He runs to the palisade, climbing one of the crude ladders. Two broad-shouldered deserters are raising sail in the river, stealing one of the newly built barques. Laudonnière rages atop the wall, having no way to give chase. The first barque disappeared just days ago, when the emerald charms of the Caribbean proved too strong. A dozen deserters stole it from the roadstead at the river's mouth, sailing away to make their fortunes.

These two new deserters are Flemish carpenters—*Flamands*—and they appear unhurried, floating beyond cannon range of the fort. They have cut the lines of the *Breton*'s small-boat, letting it twirl downriver on the falling tide. The 120-ton *Breton* itself, the fort's lone remaining vessel, could never be made ready in time to give chase. All along the wall, curses and shouts:

"Seed-swillers!"

"Sons of Satan!"

"A pox on your mothers' cunts!"

Le Moyne climbs down from the wall to find La Caille leaning on a barrel keg. He is facing the interior of the fort, arms crossed, as if oblivious to the spectacle without.

"The hopes of the men were in those barques, Le Moyne."

Le Moyne looks around at the men of the fort, red-burned under the alien sun. Their cheeks so sunken now, as if whatever once swelled them has dwindled. The curses are growing less frequent.

"Ass-thumbers!"

"Cock-swallowers!"

"Hie thee to Satan's door!"

The *Flamands* cannot even hear them. A hush falls over the fort.

"Other boats can be built," says Le Moyne.

La Caille stands from the keg.

"So I fear."

That afternoon Le Moyne sits upon a small bluff that overlooks the river. His sketch paper is blank, his stylus dangling idly between his fingers. He is watching for something to leap onto his page, the monster that might rise dreamlike to the surface, big as a ship that cruises through the long night of the river's depths. That he could seize it within the edges of his page, a prize to rival the greatest gifts of the Apalatci. A creature terrible and humbling, which might unite the men of the fort in awe of the God that shaped it.

This is what he seeks.

It does not rise this day, the river cold and quiet as slate between the browning trees of autumn. He walks home under the gray towers of cypress, the branches raftering the sky, the earth crackling firelike beneath his boots. It seems strange to him that so much in this new land is of such size, placed by God as if for a species of man or beast so much larger than any he knows. For a race of giants. He rubs the tongue stone in his tunic pocket, stepping over roots and crossing creeks. These woodland trails he knows as well as anyone now, exploring them daily with sketchbook and arquebus in tow. He flushes coveys of dove and other fowl from grassy thickets, their wings whistling to flight. Snakes scurry before him in riotous scrawls; fattened squirrels cling rigid to tree trunks, their tails snapping in furry plumes. Birds cross overhead on great sails of wing, like fleets aloft.

It is dusk by the time he reaches the fort. The men are huddled at their fires, smoking the plant they call *tabac* from long pipes, as the Indians have taught them. The pipes are fashioned from long shoots of cut cane, a small bowl affixed at one end. The dried cuttings of the plant are rolled into a ball and ignited with a burning reed, the smoke drawn cooling through the pipe into the man's chest and held there like a breath, expelled finally through the nose or mouth like a spirit going out. Some of the men claim the smoke carries away their hearts' burdens, light as air. Others say it satisfies hunger, sometimes for hours, an esteemed power in light of the tighter rations on bread and wine imposed with each passing week. The Indians inhale the smoke before going to war, marching long distances without meat or drink, though Le Moyne worries the smoke is more trickery than sustenance; as the weeks wear on, the men keep punching new holes in their tunic belts.

He sits on an empty stump, huddling before the fire of some noblemen he would avoid were he not in need of warmth against the autumn chill. They are Fourneaux and La Croix, grandees both of them, who sit beneath feathered hats and filigreed doublets. They swell excitedly at his arrival, like old hens at sight of the feeding pail.

"Le Moyne, my boy! *L'artiste du nouveau monde!* What say you?"

Le Moyne palms his eye a moment, squinting one-eyed into the fire.

"A long day, and I am tempted to damn the city of Flanders whole."

The noblemen lean forward.

"Truly," says one. "But can you blame them for wanting to escape *le pouce de Laudonnière?*"

"Perhaps not," says Le Moyne. "But it was our king who put the power in our commander's thumb, and we beneath it."

Fourneaux regards his own plump specimen.

"A thumb so fat, and yet our commander cannot keep even two barques beneath it."

"Perhaps our commander is too busy placing it elsewhere," says La Croix. His eyes gleam over the fire, and he tilts his head toward Laudonnière's residence, where he lives with his handmaiden. "*Indecent* places, Le Moyne, which make their owner squeal in the night."

Le Moyne shifts uneasily on his stump, blood tingling in parts of him he would rather it didn't. He has heard the sounds, like a woman dying, as he lay in bed.

Fourneaux leans forward, almost into the fire, opening his hands like a gift.

"Our king has much invested in this expedition, Le Moyne. If our leader is unfit, are we not duty-bound as our king's servants to make it a success ourselves?"

Le Moyne looks not at him but into the red heart of the fire.

"And how do you define success?"

The nobleman sits back from the fire, lacing his hands across his ample midsection.

"How does anyone, my boy? *Profit*."

21

Altamaha River, Day 2

Y ou didn't have to hit the son of a bitch."

A fresh dip lumps Lawton's bottom lip. He turns his head and spits.

"Hit him? I slapped him is all. Wasn't even no blood. You don't think he was asking for it?"

"You don't always have to give what's asked."

"No, little brother. But sometimes you do." The blades of Lawton's paddle skim the surface as he stows the can of Kodiak in his vest. "Anyhow, I got what I wanted."

"Which was what?"

"Make sure them boys was who they said they were."

"Who the hell else would they be?"

Lawton takes up his paddle again. He doesn't say.

They pass an island on their right, a forty-acre patch of high ground that splits the river like a wedge. Somewhere in the trees is the black carcass of an old house, burned before either of them was born.

"Rozier's Island," says Lawton.

"Not anymore. State's taking it from them."

"Taking it?"

"They can't produce a crown grant from the King of England."

"King of England? Jesus Christ. Don't they know we whipped the redcoats out of this country more than two hundred damn years ago?"

"I guess that doesn't matter in this case."

"Hell, I always heard they had some of the best hog-hunting on the river out there."

Hunter squints into the trees along the island's bank, looking for the army of barrel-like hulks that might be running the place, rooting through the understory and tusking the trees. Feral hogs are in season year-round, a scourge descended from the fugitive swine of conquistadors. Within a single generation, a barnyard pig loosed into the wild will grow a larger skull and sharper snout, its coat bristling like a mad dog's.

"You hear about Hogzilla?" he asks.

"I heard it was a hoax."

"Nope. Gang of scientists in yellow hazard suits dug up the remains for DNA testing. Confirmed it was a boar-pig hybrid, eight hundred pounds, eight and a half feet long. Our biology professor had us read an article on it."

"Fucking monster. Sounds like a cool professor, too."

"I've had a couple."

"That cypress was something itself."

"For real."

Lawton nods. "I seen some of the old-growth ones on Lewis Island, but nothing like that. Must of been forty feet around at the base."

"At least."

"You know they had one down in central Florida. Senator was his name. Pond cypress, biggest tree east of the Mississip'. Seminole used it as a landmark. Hundred sixty-five feet tall. Big as a water tower."

"Fucking A."

"Yup," says Lawton, "then some meth-head lit it on fire, lighting his pipe. They said it burned inside out, like a chimney, the top lit up like a big torch over the county. More than three thousand years old when it burned."

Hunter tries to picture a giant of that size, topping the forest like a king, crowned in a great ball of fire. He thinks of the cypress they left in the glade, a living tower from the age of sail and spear, improbable as a ghost in the woods. He looks out at the river that floats him on wind-cut shingles, hiding the world below.

"Makes me think of that old Shakespeare quote," he says. "What is it? 'There's more things in heaven and earth than dreamt of in your philosophy.'" He shrugs. "Something like that."

Lawton sniffs.

"Hamlet," he says. "What a dick."

They lunch at the powerline right-of-way above Sansavilla Bluff. The forest has been clear-cut in a channel perpendicular to the river, as for a railway. The lines are black-strung from metal tree to metal tree, five abreast like the strings of a guitar. Lawton constructs a teepee of twigs over a gray cloud of dryer lint he keeps in a pill bottle, then lights the structure with a weatherproof torch, blowing into the burning core. They sit their cans of pork 'n' beans in the fire and squat, waiting. Above them the high-voltage lines rumble and hiss, racing their power across the state. From one line hangs a pair of dark forms, black and shredded. Old boots, perhaps.

"Talk about hog-hunting," says Hunter. "You know what they found at a right-of-way outside Augusta?"

"What?"

"Two banks of Benelli shotguns mounted on remote aimers, hooked up to webcams, aimed to cross-fire under the powerlines. Utility contractor that found them thought they were a booby trap at first, like to protect a marijuana grow. They brought in Homeland Security."

"You'd be surprised the kind of setups the dope-growers got now."

"Turns out it was for hunting hogs. There was a food plot they were aimed at. This guy could sit at home and shoot them from the Internet as they came out into the cut. Hell, he could charge *other* people and let *them* shoot them."

"Ha," says Lawton. "Free enterprise for you."

"Don't seem real sporting, you ask me."

"Maybe not, little brother. But there's a few places I know could use a setup like that."

Hunter wants to ask what places but knows better. He knows his brother doesn't mean for hogs.

Lawton reaches his hand into the fire, turning his can.

"You still making them good grades?"

"Straight A's three semesters straight."

"Still majoring in history?"

"Yeah. And no, I don't know what I'm gonna do with that yet."

"Did I ask?"

"You were gonna."

Lawton rocks back on his heels.

"So?"

"So what?"

"What are you gonna do with that?"

"Dick." Hunter looks up at the powerlines that divide the sky, sighs. "I don't know. Teach, maybe. Entrepreneurship doesn't seem to run in the family."

Lawton grunts, snagging his can from the fire. He eyes the bubbling goo.

"God bless him, but I don't think Daddy could make four quarters from a dollar. Or at least couldn't keep it, anyway."

Hunter takes his own can from the flames, setting it between his legs to cool.

"You really think he was into something?"

Lawton polishes his fork on the torn tail of his shirt, eyeing the metal's shine.

"What else? I never known a man's luck to change that much." He shrugs. "Could be his did, I guess, there toward the end."

Hunter glances over at the bag of ashes still strapped to his boat.

"Didn't change much, I'd say."

Lawton glances in the same direction. He spits out his wad of dip.

"No. I reckon not."

22

Fort Caroline, November 1564

Le Moyne holds a plank in place while the sawyer cuts it to length, the teeth of his saw gnawing at the oak. Both of them are shirtless, glowing in a sheen of sweat despite the coolness of the fall sun. Le Moyne cannot but notice the veins jumping out against their skin, the bone-lines so much sharper than they used to be. Their bodies are like countries drying up, stony landscapes of ridge and hollow upon which a few purple creeks pulse. Saturiwa's gift-bearers come but scarcely now, and the woods are quiet. A muted landscape, leafless, that rattles in the wind. The deer have disappeared. The raccoons and squirrels.

The savages have hunted us out of game, whisper the men. *They wish us to starve.*

It is a plot. They wish to protect their gold.

Le Moyne says nothing, focusing only on his work. He sets the plank on a stack, squaring it with the others, then sets another upon the sawhorses.

"How many more?"

The sawyer shakes his head.

"Never count, Le Moyne. Look only to the next."

Laudonnière has ordered the construction of two barques to replace those stolen. Each is to be thirty-six feet at the keel with a single mast, shallops equipped with sails and oars for river navigation. He wants them completed in no more than a fortnight. All, without exception, are to apply themselves ceaselessly to the task.

These will convey them upstream—to the land of Utina, king in the west, and to the Apalatci beyond. But what a long and tiresome voyage that will be, snaking them ever deeper into this land that has failed already to feed them. That has yielded no gold as yet. Nothing but rumor. Again and again, Le Moyne looks up from his work to find men sitting at their stations, tools stilled. They stare longingly at the 120-ton brigantine, the *Breton*, floating idle upon the river. They imagine the ship's belly full of gold, plowing the ocean home.

In the afternoons, he goes out with the hunting parties. They are clumsy in their leather boots, crunching through the brittle woods, scaring their prey into trees and holes. He has better luck on his own, exploring with sketchbook and arquebus, a single man beneath the halls of cypress. Endless flights of birds pass overhead, flying south, and sometimes at dusk he glimpses great assemblies of stilt-legged wading birds, brown-plumed, that limp gently upon the lilied surfaces of lagoons.

In the bestiaries, the animal compendia of his youth, the world was the Word of God, spoken in stone and flesh, and each creature bore symbolic meaning. There was the mother pelican who stood in her piety, wings endorsed, vulning herself: spearing her breast with the point of beak, her young flocked beneath her, waiting to be revived by the blood of her wound. If she is the symbol of Christ, what are these birds that limp so humbly on water, like hobbled saints? They are endless; so many that, if startled, they could blot out the sun, thumping great winds from their thousand wings. He wonders whether future men will stand so small and infrequent in comparison, so shrunken and hungry—or will they rise in this land, swelled with faith and supper?

He prays for forgiveness, then aims his arquebus at the nearest bird and fires.

There are fewer fires now in the nights. Instead, the men huddle in their huts to whisper. The noblemen especially, their hands blistered and red-torn, unaccustomed to the common labor of shipbuilding. The nobles Fourneaux and La Croix come to Le Moyne one night, showing him by lamplight a list of those who have given their names for the cause of mutiny. There are many. He refuses to add his own.

"Our commander has set us between warring tribes, Le Moyne. He has broken his word to the man who would provide us food for winter, has kept all treasures to himself or favored subordinates. He has let our barques slip through his hands, and now the diligence he imposes for their replacement is immoderate."

Le Moyne says nothing.

"Do you believe these grievances invalid, Le Moyne?"

"It is your methods to which I will not consign myself."

"If you will not side with us, we cannot guarantee your safety when the day of reckoning comes."

"It is God to whom I will look for protection at such hour."

Fourneaux's bottom jaw juts out. He looks at the close walls of the little hut, as if searching for something.

"I fear the eyes of our God do not fall upon this land, Le Moyne."

"Then perhaps it is best you leave it."

Fourneaux smiles.

"Ah," he says. "Now you have the idea."

A Sunday morning, the air bright and crisp as old memories of the Lord's Day. Laudonnière stands, as requested, before the men of the fort. He wears a slashed leather jerkin, sleeveless, over a bloodred doublet, the white ruff of his collar hackling his neck like that of an angry dog. La Caille detaches himself from the assembled crowd.

"Sir, the men here gathered have requested that, as one friendly with all parties, I present to you their petition." He bows slightly. "I have agreed to do so."

"Present then, La Caille."

"Sir, they recognize you as the supreme lord of this province, the right and lawful lieutenant of His Majesty the King. They protest themselves ready to pour out their lives upon this foreign soil if necessity so dictates. However, they believe such a sacrifice contrary to the best interests of their nation and king."

Laudonnière grunts, unimpressed.

Là Caille goes on to remind Laudonnière that provisions for an entire year were promised upon their embarkation from France, and many men of noble position have set forth upon their own expense. But the fort's rations have dwindled to no more than a month's supply. He reminds the commander of the difficulties in trading with the Indians, their retreat from the land, the game following suit.

"The men here assembled believe some urgent action must be taken. Otherwise we shall starve. They beseech you, their commander, to make ready the *Breton* for sail. They will set forth into New Spain—Terra Florida—for obtainment of supplies." La Caille clears his throat. "By purchase or otherwise."

"Piracy," says Laudonnière. "It is this of which you speak."

The crowd shifts, wordless. Their commander looks upon them as if from a height, his hands clasped behind his back.

"You have not the authority to request any account of my actions. I am your commander, and it is in me alone that His Majesty's power resides. As for your worries of hunger, I have yet some provisions in my own personal stock that I will make available to you for trading with the Indians. When the shallops are ready, we will take these on short excursions upriver and along the coast, gathering sufficient provisions to stead us through the winter. As for sailing south into Spanish territory, I forbid it. No man here will abuse any subject of the King of Spain."

The crowd disassembles but slowly, amid groans and whispers. Le Moyne fears them a constellation of heated stars, their fate already set. Later that day he looks up from his work to see the nobleman Fourneaux sitting high upon the ribbed joinery of a barque. He smiles at Le Moyne and sets his thumb between his teeth, as if to bite it off.

23

Sapelo Sound, Georgia, 1992

Hiram Loggins watches the golden yolk of sun falling before him, the serrated edge of the coast waiting to sink in its teeth. The sky has grown smoky with dusk, and he is entering the sound that will lead him home. He can almost feel the treasure curled up in the holds beneath his feet: a boatload of famed Georgia white shrimp, soft-bodied and sweet-fleshed in their great bins of ice. The new boat has changed everything, who he is and what he might become. The possible paths of his life fork like the creeks before him, many-mouthed. Last year the government made the shrimping fleet install Sinkey Boone's turtle excluder devices on every net. A lot of the shrimpers blamed the TEDs for their poor catches. But Hiram has no grounds for complaint. Every time they winch up the nets, he can feel the boat foundering slightly at the great weights it pulls out of the depths, the balled hearts of sea-flesh that might make him a man of station and clout.

A catch.

He has two little ones crawling the rug at home now. Boys. He put that off as long as he could, but Jo-Beth wouldn't be denied. He was never much for children, and there was always the fear that Annabelle wouldn't want him if he went that far with his wife. But those little ones cause strange twists in his chest. A weakness, he thinks. He will make sure they grow up strong. Strong enough to survive the damage he knew as a boy. The darkness. And still, despite himself, he stares in the direction of the screen-porched house where Annabelle lives with her Chevy-lover, and he thinks what he always does: *one day.*

He slides the boat through shallow creeks, over hidden shoals, avoiding oyster beds that would shred the feet of men run aground, and on they chug toward the docks of Darien. Shrimp boats are tied all along the waterfront, a forest of trawling booms and green-woven nets. Before them stands the Darien bridge set like a concrete gateway between river and sea. From here, their blessings descend each year. He watches the waters curve out of sight, upstream into the Altamaha, and he squints as if he might see in the distance the mountains that feed the river. He sees none. The coast has bloodied the sun, swallowed it. A ruddy glow over the western horizon, the last red-burped bubble like from a dying man's mouth.

He shakes his head.

They dock and offload their catch and Hiram is paid in cash, an enormous sheaf of bills that he divvies up among the crew. A couple of them are new, former Soviets who came scrabbling up American shores when the Iron Curtain crumpled. Hiram doesn't like it, but they're old Black Sea fishermen who work for next to nothing. He just makes sure they keep their traps shut when the Coast Guard or DNR hails the boat, sniffing for permits or prohibited catch, perhaps the skunky odor of square grouper.

A man does what he has to.

Full dark now and he climbs into the cab of his old slant-six Dodge, battleship gray with a white camper top. The motor is small but purrs as if factory-new, not even a tick from the valves—the work of long hours under the hood. He rides up Fort King George Drive, paralleling the river until he meets the old coastal highway and turns through town. It's dead, no traffic but the prowl cars of the sheriff's department tucked like roaches in the shadows along the road. The old seafood restaurants are all closed now, kudzu climbing the walls and curses finger-written in the dust of their windows, hobos asleep out back. The fast food restaurants along I-95, lit up like football stadiums beneath their soaring arches and crowns, get all of the business now. It seems his luck runs counter to this place, his well rising even as the town dries up, left like an oxbow scar as the great river of steel and glass was redirected inland along the interstate.

He wheels the truck into a gas station and buys a six-pack of Michelob in the can. His money smells like fish but spends like any. Like always, he left the main portion in a lockbox hidden behind a bulkhead in the galley of the boat. His life savings. He dreams of it there. He dreams of taking that money one day to a jewelry store up in Savannah, watching the clerk snatch it up without even a flare of the nostrils, counting off the bills like a winning hand.

Annabelle.

This is what you missed.

He crushes his first can and throws it into the bed of the truck, hating himself for these dreams that drive him. He cracks open a new can. It's foamy and good, a golden brook that settles and numbs him. He drives past the fruit stands that once fleeced southbound Yankees with games of dice and chance, with bets on bottle pyramids that couldn't be struck down by a Nolan Ryan heater. The old joints are abandoned now, rotting, their slick-haired owners moved on.

He slows to turn off the highway onto the dirt drive that leads to his home, holding his breath as he passes the concrete-block church that lines the road, the sign lit up by flickering spotlamp:

HOLINESS CHURCH OF CHRIST THE KING WITH SIGNS FOLLOWING.

He doesn't know if the Catholics ousted Uncle King, or if it was the other way around. The man still wears his old dog collar but has two adopted children now, little coal-black orphans who squat barefoot day and night in the gravel lot of the old cut-and-shoot bar that's now his church.

Hiram ran into the man once last year, on a drunk night in July. The Fourth. He stumbled into the bar, looking for a drink under the bright-popping sky, only to find the man standing open-armed before the emptied shelves, as if waiting for him.

"Blood brother," he said.

Hiram stumbled backward out the door, the man's sea-gray eyes cutting through him like a sword. They saw the boyhood shame, the body buried in the black riverbed of their history. This man who saved him once, before they were even grown—the day they did grow up. Hiram turned away from him. He walked out into the darkness, his skin burning, his fist clutched tight against the scar that bound them.

If a man could give blessings, perhaps he could take them away.

24

Altamaha River, Day 2

Dusk is coming down on the river, deepening shadows and turning the water thicker, darker. The groan of the river deepens, the choral throat of it. Bats skitter across the purple gulf of sky, hunting. They pass Fort Barrington, a private landing, the site of a frontier fort from Revolutionary times. Nothing left now of its bastions or blockhouse.

A dark hump soon rises from the water, spined black, an island long and slender like an anchored ship. Lawton points and Hunter nods. They nose their boats through the shallows, working their way through a maze of half-drowned trees, the branches snarled like the guard-wires of a fort. They pull their boats onto the bank and open the deck hatches, retrieving the supplies they need for the night. There's an old campsite with a view downstream. Lawton unsheathes his machete, the blade gleaming in the falling dark like a giant tooth. He hacks through the vines that overgrow the place while Hunter hauls away the shed limbs that litter the ground, chopping them for firewood with his hand-ax. Before long they have the site cleared. They build a fire and eat their dinners from pouches, then sit staring into the flames, watching them shiver and crack. Lawton adds another log and squints, grim and intent, as if reading something in the swirl of embers set to flight. After a moment he reaches up for his paddling vest where it hangs drying from a branch. Down comes a silver flask, fire-glazed in his hand. He looks at Hunter.

"Tell you what, little brother. If a turkey was the national bird, this here would be the one."

"Wild Turkey?"

"One-oh-one."

Lawton has a pull and exhales through his teeth, then hands the whiskey to Hunter. Hunter sets the spigot to his lips and flips up the flask. Sweet fire, like burning oak, roars in his mouth, barrels down his throat. It's the color of the river but so much hotter, a brown flame that settles warmly over his dinner.

Lawton watches him.

"That's high-proof, boy. Careful now."

Hunter swallows doubly full, belching through his teeth.

"Careful your own damn self."

Lawton grins, taking the flask for a second pull.

"What are the college boys drinking these days?"

"Cheap beer mainly. Bourbon and Coke. Girls are into these flavored vodkas."

Lawton shudders.

"Jesus Christ, I seen those. Can't think of a better way to get sick."

"Or get a girl's clothes off."

Lawton flicks his trigger-finger free of the flask.

"There's a way to do it, brother, and that ain't it."

Hunter thinks Lawton might elaborate on what the way is, but he doesn't. He hands back the flask. It floats between them, back and forth, as if on a string. The bourbon sets the blood booming in their ears, the woods roaring. They belch hot, watching the fire-scrawled trees. Lawton clears his throat.

"Didn't mean to give you shit earlier, 'bout your major and that."

Hunter nods and looks down at his bare feet. A black ant is crawling between the furrows of his foot bones. He lets it walk onto his finger, sets it aside. He caps his knee with his hand.

"I know." He pauses. "It's just that sometimes I wish I could do what you do."

Lawton has been watching him. Now he looks out across the river, flask in hand.

"You don't, brother. You might think you do, but you don't."

"You don't know that."

"I know it ain't what it seems. Everybody wants to know *if* they could do it. Make it, I mean. Hell Week and that. But doing the thing itself, once you're in, that's another thing entirely. The shit I seen . . ." He shakes his head.

"Do you like it?"

"Like it?" Lawton stares into the red core of the fire, his beard lit like a fiery mane. "Like it," he says again, testing the words. He sets the spigot to his teeth. "I try not to, brother."

Hunter lies awake a long time in his sleeping bag, listening to a barred owl hoot through the trees. The cadence ancient: *Who cooks for you? Who cooks for all?* He can picture it out there somewhere, round eyes piercing the night. Hunting, hunting. He looks at his brother. Lawton's face is just visible in the withering firelight, his brow knit, his strength unbroken even in sleep. Hunter closes his eyes. He wonders what ghosts or beasts will visit him tonight, what giants or worlds aflood. The river croaks and groans, gurgles and whispers and plops. Sleep washes him, and soon he is drifting, edged on dream. He hears an echo on the river, the sound of a tiny motor muttering its way downstream. He sees a man standing tall against the moon, his weapon poised like a judgment over the silvery skin of the waters that float him.

Uncle King.

Now darkness.

25

Fort Caroline, November 1564

L e Moyne lies upon his corn-husk mattress, fully clothed, listening to the bedding crackle from the heavy swell of his breath. He tries to will them to silence, those husks, to quell the storm of his heart. Outside, whispers and the patter of boots, the rattling of armor and swords. This much he can hear over the roaring of his own blood. He closes his eyes and tries to pray:

Quand je marche dans la vallée de l'ombre de la mort . . .

Yea, though I walk through the valley of the shadow of death . . .

La Caille, friend and bunkmate, is gone, fled among the night-beasts of the woods. Earlier that evening, as Le Moyne stood at the latrine relieving himself, a Norman set himself alongside him, slightly too near for comfort. The man stared straight ahead, unbuttoning himself, then spoke in a voice none but the two of them might hear.

"It is to be tonight. You would do well to remove yourself from your quarters, Le Moyne." The man loosed his stream, speaking through gritted teeth, never once turning his head. "They have resolved to cut the throat of La Caille, believing him enemy now to their aims."

"But La Caille spoke for them."

"Not well enough. His heart was not in it, they say. Their plans for you, I cannot say."

Le Moyne finished, quickly.

"*Merci.*"

The Norman acknowledged his gratitude with but the slightest dip of his chin. Le Moyne walked hurriedly across the fort grounds in search of La Caille, willing himself not to dash. He found his friend in the hut they shared, rubbing oil into his boots.

"Tonight," he told him. "It will be tonight."

"How do you know?"

Le Moyne told him of the man at the latrine.

"And he is a true man, this Norman?"

"Yes, I believe so."

La Caille pulled on his boots, calmly, and fitted his belt and dagger. He took his arquebus from next to the door. He had known this night might come.

"Come with me into the forest, Le Moyne."

"No. I told them I would recommend myself to God at such an hour. It is this I will do."

La Caille placed a hand on his shoulder.

"You are a fool, my friend."

"*C'est possible.*"

"May God be with you."

"*Et toi, mon ami.*"

So here he lies, alone, wreathing himself in prayer, donning the old words of power like *maille* and armor. He tries to give them weight and consequence, his harried breath forming the very verses that deny his fear, that belt and strap him against the world to come. Outside, muted shouts and the pounding of fists upon doors. He hopes the nobleman Fourneaux was wrong, that their God might yet set his gaze upon this savage land, his will steered at least in part by the prayers of those here beset. Le Moyne prays and prays, the tongue stone held tightly in his palm.

The door is flung open and in bursts a storm of metal-clad men, mutineers in breastplates with weapons raised. Le Moyne can hear little of what they say over the loud silence of so many iron mouths, each waiting to speak its fury.

Dawn finds him on his bed, alive and unhurt. He's been confined to his quarters until the sun has fully risen. Rise it does, upon a world truly new. The whispers travel quickly, hut to hut. The nobleman Fourneaux, leader of the mutiny, led twenty arquebusiers into Laudonnière's chambers at midnight, setting his weapon against the commander's throat. He took the keys to the storehouse and armory, controlling thereby the flow of bread and blood through the fort, and Laudonnière was led in chains to the *Breton*, a prisoner now of the very ship that once marked his power. Other squads of armored mutineers snaked silver-backed across the grounds in dead of night, breaking into the quarters of all who had set themselves apart from the conspiracy. They stripped them of their weapons and confined them to quarters on pain of death.

"Where is La Caille?" they asked Le Moyne.

They'd encircled his bed, the fuses of their arquebuses smoldering like madness in the confined space.

"Fled into the wilds."

"The savages will dismember him," said one.

"If the beasts do not," said another.

"Perhaps," said Le Moyne.

The leader of the group stepped forward, dagger in hand.

"Perhaps we should kill you in his stead."

The words struck Le Moyne deep in the gut, fear erupting hot in his belly like an organ pierced. But he clutched the tongue stone yet harder in his hand, and a flight of black words burst from his throat without thought: "I wish you would, *pig-suckler*, and damn your own soul to hell."

A grin twisted the leader's face. He sheathed his dagger, and in the long night that followed, Le Moyne thanked God again and again for that curse, however vicious, protecting him as surely as any rote prayer.

In the days that follow, the mutineers, sixty-six in all, draft a warrant to sail into New Spain for the obtainment of provisions. They force Laudonnière, shackled within his floating prison, to endorse it as lieutenant of the King of France. The *Breton* is found to be in need of too much repair, so they outfit the two newly built shallops for their journey, taking a great store of bread and munitions and wine reserved only for the sick. They say they will make the Spanish Antilles by Christmas night and slaughter the Catholics during midnight mass, and if they meet any resistance upon their return to Fort Caroline, heavy with shot and plunder, they will tread the place underfoot.

They leave on the eighth of December, their masts crossed dark against the dawning sun.

BOOK II

The old man walks back and forth across the water, needing only the thin aluminum skin of his boat to perform this feat. He is wiggling his arms and lolling his neck. He is rolling his ankles and spreading his toes. The sun is rising, and he has been standing long dark hours under the stars, watching the eternal night that flows beneath his feet, like a world before God or light. He has been awaiting his prize, the riparian king of old.

In those hours, when the milky eye of the moon is hooded by cloud, he believes he can see into the creature's ken. He can see wrecked ships, double-masted or paddle-wheeled or bearing the steel blossoms of screws, and he can see the giant timber-bones of shattered rafts. He can see cypress dugouts foundered like coffins, home to giant catfish, and peaceful navies of sturgeon cruising through the depths. He can see men clad only in skins, gazing upward for the long-fallen sun, and men in strange billowy garb, hunting the bottoms for the golden twinkling of their god. He can see an evil man, sallow-faced, staggering drunkenly in the muck, looking for the pair of boys who sunk him. And he can see one of those boys grown old, his body bruised with ink, his hand unable to close for the tender white worm it holds.

Blood brother.

Some nights, in the blackest of hours, he can see his two children holding hands, chained to the black anchor of his guilt, planted like a crooked cross in the river's bottom, and above them all passes the creature he seeks, dark as storm, waiting to swallow them up.

26

Altamaha River, Day 3

The water lies shrouded in mist, like the ghost of a river, the trees but shades in the pre-dawn. The world is inchoate, dew-wet and not yet real, coming out of its own dream. They slide their boats into the water, finding the dark muscle that pulls them along, and Hunter watches his brother become a shadow of himself in the mist, amorphous as story or myth, a storm rolling slowly downstream. Hunter paddles faster, harder, to keep him blooded and fleshed, the brother he knows.

The sun scatters the mist, white traces lingering only along the banks, and soon the world springs brown-green under a blue dome of sky, the river written in a brown scrawl. Lawton turns toward him, his beard wilder with each day uncombed, his teeth straight-cut as if with a power tool. He's pointing to the left bank.

"Gamecock Lake. Back through them trees. You remember them limpkins we saw?"

Hunter nods. They were boys when their father pointed them out, a pair of wading birds high-stepping through the shallows on stiltlike legs, probing here or there with their long curved bills. They were fat-bodied, like baby ostriches, their brown feathers white-flecked as by snow.

"Hunted near extinct from the old days," said their father. "Ain't often you see one."

They sat a long time in the old man's johnboat, watching the birds stalk the shallows, their whole heads disappearing underwater, looking for hard prizes of snails and mollusks. Finding nothing, they would stilt forward, forward, to another spot, their knotty knees back-bent like elbows.

"See them long-toed feet, look like rakes? They can walk on lily pads with them feet." Their father's face slowly hardened as he watched the birds, his teeth grinding sideways in his mouth. "Course people 'bout killed them off, like most every damn thing else on the river. Overhunting." He turned to face his sons, their open faces. "People like to think the world ain't that bad. They assume there's Somebody up in the sky looking out. If you remember one thing, remember this: Assumption is the mother of fuckup."

He ripped the pull-cord on the outboard, the motor roaring to life beneath his hand. The birds crashed skyward on panicked wings.

Gone.

Lawton tilts his paddle to look at his watch.

"Let's go see if we see some. Like old times."

Hunter sets his paddle across his lap.

"What happened to the big hurry you were in day before last?"

"We got time today," says Lawton. He doesn't say why.

It's a backwater lake, deep, islanded with vast constellations of water lilies. Here or there a lone cypress rears itself umbrellalike from the middle of the lake, as if to shade anglers at their labor. But they see no boats tucked beneath the trees this morning, nor limpkins stilting through the shallows. Nothing, really, a lagoon seemingly deserted, like an abandoned movie set. Lawton slowly back-paddles, his boat rotating before the scene, his face grim.

"What?" asks Hunter.

Lawton tucks in a new dip, screwing the can closed with the palm of his hand.

"Nothing," he says. "I just thought we might find more of them birds here by now. Daddy'd said they might be making a comeback."

"I guess not."

Lawton's face tightens. Hunter looks out at the deadened place, wishing he could call up a flock of birds along the banks, a hobbling of limpkins for his brother.

"You really think they could walk on lily pads?" he asks. "On water?"

Lawton looks at him.

"You don't?"

They pass beneath the powerlines upstream of Altamaha Park, listening as thousands of volts thrum over the river, and a battleship-gray sheriff's boat rounds the bend before them. A single big deputy stands at the helm. He has on a ballcap and sunglasses, a low-profile PFD with a star stitched over the heart. Lawton brightens, wiggling upright in his cockpit.

The deputy slows his approach, dropping the craft into neutral as he slides alongside their boats. He looks down from the center console, his teeth bared in grin or menace.

"Loggins, you carrot-hair son of a bitch, I thought it might be you."

Lawton is grinning.

"Steve-a-rino, you luggy bastard. Where'd your belly go?"

"Snuck off with the carbohydrates." The deputy pats his trunk. "So the wife tells me."

"How's the Sheriff treating you?"

The deputy palms the wheel.

"Got me on river patrol now and then. Can't complain."

"Hunter," says Lawton. "You remember Steve Andino, played left guard?"

"By name," says Hunter. "I think you graduated when I wasn't but in eighth grade."

Andino nods, then straightens and removes his cap.

"Hey. I was real sorry to hear about y'all's daddy last year. That's some real bad luck."

Lawton nods grimly, his lower lip pouched. He looks out at the water, scratches his nose with his thumb.

"Yeah. Least it was this river he died on. Reckon the old man would of pre-ferred that, instead of bed."

The big man nods. "Sure."

Lawton spits and wipes his mouth with the back of his hand, then squints an eye up at the deputy.

"So lemme guess. You got a call from some angry little film man, saying a red-bearded maniac assaulted him up Miller Lake?"

Andino reseats his cap and chuckles, extracting a can of dip from his back pocket.

"Something like that." He looks up, as if reading a description pasted to the underside of his hat brim. "Suspect is a red-haired white male, approximately twenty-three years of age, built like a diesel bush-hog with an attitude to match."

"Sounds about right," says Lawton. "Though I hear your shit poetry there at the end."

Andino puts in a dip and screws closed the lid.

"So what happened, you hit some guy?"

"Hell, I didn't but cuff him for not having any manners. For saying Daddy never taught us none. We ran into his crew filming a big cypress up there, acting like they owned the place. Littering all over. If I assaulted him, he would of known it."

"He bleed?"

"Not even. But I'm happy to stand up, he wants to press charges."

Andino unscrews the cap of an empty water bottle and holds it under his mouth, loosing a black string of tobacco juice.

"I don't think that'll be necessary," he says. "Sounds like he was asking for it, besides which we got a no-blood-no-foul policy out in the county. Otherwise we wouldn't have any room in the jailhouse."

"Figured that might be the case." Lawton pulls on his beard, his eyes flicking across the surface of the river. "Say, while I got you here, you heard anything funny about Daddy's death?"

"You mean foul play, like?"

Lawton nods.

The big deputy crosses his arms, tapping the bottle against himself, working the wad of chew in his mouth. "Not specifically. Coroner said blunt-force trauma followed by drowning, consistent with a sturgeon strike." He squints out at the riverbanks. "But there's been some funny things going on down the river, that's true."

"Them couple researchers that went missing?"

Andino nods. "Never found hide nor hair of them. But it's a big river, been swallowing people up since the timber raft days."

Lawton scratches his chin. "How long was this after Daddy was killed?"

"Two, maybe three months. The fall."

"Anything else?"

"Not really. Somebody seen a boy throw a pair of stray cats over the powerlines up at Sansavilla, tails knotted to watch them claw each other to death. Said he had blond hair, a funny accent. Carried a rifle on his back. Other people seen a old man carries a spear in his boat, talks to himself. Seems harmless enough. The state's been upping their flyovers, looking for meth labs and marijuana grows. We had reports of boats at funny times of night, comings and goings. Nothing solid, though. You know how it is."

"These comings and goings, y'all investigated?"

Andino shrugs. "What's to investigate? Ain't been any crimes we know of." He thumbs the embroidered badge at his chest, one of the star-points slightly unstitched. "To be honest, Sheriff ain't seemed too interested in pursuing it." He drops his hand and spits again in the bottle. "If you know what I mean."

"You know anybody I should talk to, I wanted to hear something more?"

Andino rubs the back of his neck, grimacing, not wanting to uncage the words behind his teeth. "Well, you ain't heard it from me, understand? But there's a dude named Dillard Rollins has a stilt-house up Crooked Lake, just past where the old railroad crosses over."

"That's, what, a half mile up off the river?"

Andino nods. "People call him Wild Dill. Runs a baithouse, so he says. But we caught him selling all kinds of shit up there. Sugar whiskey and pre-rolled joints for the shad fishers, canned beer without a license. Illegal venison and alligator. Antler velvet, for the over-fifty crowd looking to harden up. If there's anything fishy going on, he's liable to stink."

"When's the last time y'all busted him?"

" 'Bout a year back. Parole violation, he hadn't been making his check-ins. We had to go up there three times before we got him." Andino spits in his bottle, his eyes flicking over the spout. "Makes a body wonder if he's got a camera at the mouth of that slough, sees everybody coming."

Lawton nods slowly, hearing him. "Somebody might could foot it in, though, down the old railroad tracks. What you think?"

The big deputy turns and spits the rest of his dip over the far side of his boat.

"I think I don't got any opinion on that."

Lawton is quiet, still thinking. Andino turns the key and the four-stroke outboard murmurs to life, chugging low.

"Tell me something, Loggins. You hit that guy just so they'd send me out?"

Lawton looks up at him.

"How would I know it'd be you?"

"You knew it would be somebody," says Andino. "But it ain't my job to block for you no more. Best you keep that in mind."

He drops the boat into gear and says his goodbyes, curling downriver before taking the boat up on plane. Hunter looks at Lawton. His arms are crossed high on his chest, as if after a good meal, and Hunter can almost see the words flaring behind his eyes: *actionable intelligence*.

27

New France, February 1565

The people of Utina dance at their arrival. They are red-painted, as if parboiled, a blood-colored throng that quivers along the riverbank. Le Moyne watches them from the boat, his weapon heavy against his shoulder. He wonders how to capture the brutal torquing of their forms on paper, the heavy thump of hammered thighs and chests. When he steps down the gangplank, first of a thirty-man force of arquebusiers, the natives come forward to touch the iron of his gun. It wrecks them. They tremble with glee. The sound of *l'arquebuse* has carried all through the land, from sea to mountain. Here is the great weapon that will speak fire against their enemies.

Lord d'Ottigni, leader of the detachment, yells from the boat.

"Mother-cunt of Christ, Le Moyne! Move it!"

Le Moyne pushes through the red sea of bodies, the flesh leaping back as if parted. Only their fingertips graze him, his cloak and gun. His body is angular now, sharp with hunger. The world has been growing quickly colder, browning and hardening under the paling sky. The woods are all but empty of game, the fish hidden in deeper holes. Even the alligators remain unfound. The mutineers took much of the remaining stores. The hard bread is nearly gone. Laudonnière assures them that reinforcements will arrive in April. Ships from France laden with provisions. They need only subsist until then.

Then came Utina, king in the west. Give him twenty guns, he said, and he would open the road to the Apalatci. They had only to defeat his enemies at the foot of the mountains. In that high country would be every good thing. Gold, of course, and silver and copper, too. Surely a man could not be hungry who was possessed of such riches. The scouts dispatched to the west sent back hunks of rock that twinkled with precious metals, plates of gold and silver the tribes of the foothills wore as armor in battle. *Les métaux précieux.* Here was dream annealed, become reality, the golden west that would sanctify their journey, their blood and hardship. They need only side with this man Utina, the western king. The mortal enemy of Saturiwa, their once-ally.

"Twenty guns," said Laudonnière. "I will give him thirty."

A new barque was completed in eighteen days. The artificers kept shrinking, it seemed, even as the boats grew before them, as if the vessels were caulked with their marrow, hammered fast with their very mettle. La Caille had returned from his weeks in the forest. He seemed older to Le Moyne, darker, more sharply made. A necklace of boar tusks hung from his throat. Together they watched the ships being built.

"Salvation is always upriver, eh, Le Moyne? A few leagues farther, just over the next horizon."

"Salvation is more than a full belly and purse of gold."

"Let us hope."

Le Moyne's gun continues sailing through the crowd of natives, his armor clanking. On his opposite shoulder he carries his bedding and kit. He feels a weight lifted and turns to find a giant of a man taking the burden under his own arm, bowing in deference. The man's body is devastating, slabbed and ribbed with power, though he wears the long hair and skirts of a woman. Le Moyne sees other such giants amid the crowd, she-men bearing the detachment's provisions under their arms like a race of overlarge footmen.

"Hermaphrodites," says one soldier, his voice a hiss. "I heard they have no balls. What do you think, Le Moyne?"

Le Moyne looks at the giant before him, sweet-faced and built like a mountain. He thinks of the paintings of angels hanging in the cathedrals of Europe, genderless beings whose long swords smite devils and serpents.

"No balls?" he says. "I heard they have four."

"And two dicks," says someone else. "So they can fuck you in the front and back, *simultanément*."

"How your mother likes it," says another.

That night they feast on corn and venison from Utina's stores, a plenty they have not experienced for weeks.

"If I am killed in battle tomorrow," says one man, "at least it will be with a full stomach." He laps the meat from a thighbone.

Another belches. "Unless you shit yourself empty in the night."

"A glorious shit, *mon ami*. I will hug that squat-tree like my wife."

"As if your wife is so skinny."

"Aye, she has an ass the size of a house. That's how I know I'm home."

"Laudonnière's chambermaid is skinny as a sapling," says another. "And flat as a plank. Would you not have her?"

"Have her? I would split her like an iron wedge, and she would beg me do it again."

As they sit cross-legged before their food, the she-men keep emerging from the village storehouse with baskets of fruit and meat, carrying them into the darkness. They dwarf even the largest warriors. Yet there is a gentleness to them. A monklike calm. They seem always at some ritual, a step beyond the world. They are called "two-spirits" in the native tongue.

Le Moyne's countrymen watch them with hooded eyes.

"Utina's people do not seem so hungry," says one, "hard as the season has been."

"*Oui*," says another, chewing. "You would think them more generous with their new friends downriver. What say you, Le Moyne?"

Le Moyne sets a bone in the communal bowl.

"I say friendship must be proven."

"Ah," says the first man. He pats the gun barrel set across his lap. "And what better way than this?"

Later they watch the two-spirits stuff a stag's hide with the bounty of their stores, swelling the hollowed-out beast with new innards: a giant fruit-heart and lungs of eared corn, bones of cut cane and muscles of smoked meat. They work slowly, with great care, as if they mean to resurrect the beast by such bounty. Le Moyne sketches them by firelight. He is the last of his countrymen to bed down, his head nodding over the page. The two-spirits are still working when he falls asleep.

Dawn finds the stag raised high above the plain, bounding as if into the rising sun. It is the greatest beast killed in the cold of the year, mounted upon a spear of the tallest pine, the tawny hide sewn up with the choicest fruits and nourishments of the land. Its neck is wreathed in leafy favors, its kingly antlers trailing garlands of plants and roots. The natives kneel naked at the foot of the stake, their arms thrown up to mimic the crown of antlers.

Le Moyne and the others gather on a hill overlooking the scene, and Chief Utina walks among them, pointing and patting their backs, his body red-striped over the exotic signs that ink his skin. He is even more powerful in body than Saturiwa, king of the coast, as if men grow only larger to accommodate the western lands. He tells them his people are offering this mighty stag to the sun, their god, who might make his kingdom plentiful in the spring of the year. They wish to be strong and fierce and able, he says, to kill their enemies and feed their children.

Le Moyne has produced his paper and stylus, and he crouches to one side, sketching the scene. The stag darkens, silhouetted against the rising sun. Soon the white orb of power perches boiling upon the spiked setting of antlers, fat as a jewel, and Le Moyne finds himself praying as he works, the words slashing quick as sketched lines through his mind.

Please God let us scatter our enemies like sheep before the wolf and none of us fail his frères d'armes. *Myself foremost Father God let me stand unquailed before my enemy's arrows and clubs. Give me the courage to stand and fight. Let us find what we seek in the west to our king's glory and yours. And let it sate us Father God that we may not starve for want of bread or blood. Let us water the earth with only a little of your creations' blood and that we spill be but the blood of our enemies. Please God let us not starve. Fill the woods with game, our guns with powder. Make our hands steady and eyes keen, our aims true. Let us be the instruments of your will in this land, the sharp tip of your power. Let us not fail you nor our-*

selves nor our dark brethren here at the end of the earth. Grant us victory now and in the days to come.

"Artist!"

Le Moyne jumps, looking up. There stands Lord d'Ottigni, lieutenant-confidant of Laudonnière, who bears upon his neck and jawline the years-old scar of a misfire. The flashpan of an arquebus ignited in his face, the once-melted flesh hardening into a gleaming terrain of ridges and valleys and veins, like a miniature of the high country for which they are bound.

"Artist, you have put a face on the sun."

Le Moyne, surprised, looks down at his sketch. There hangs a burning face in the upper corner of the scene, arched in power over the land, crowned in long arrows of light. He clears his throat.

"So I have."

A wicked half-grin twists d'Ottigni's face.

"You are an idolater, no?"

"I—I wish only for our king to know how these people imagine their deity."

D'Ottigni frowns, perhaps disappointed.

"Tell me, artist. What of its countenance, this Soleil? Pleased or angry with the world it sees?"

Le Moyne cocks his head, looking himself.

"Truly I cannot yet tell. Perhaps we must wait for what the season will bring."

"*Wait?*" D'Ottigni smiles, his face twisted and bright. "A lot of confidence you have, artist, when you might not survive the morrow."

Le Moyne stiffens.

"Not confidence," he says. "*La foi.*"

Faith.

But Lord d'Ottigni does not hear him. He has turned his ruined face to the sun. His weapons, the sharp edges of his armor, gleam.

28

Darien, Georgia, 1993

They're calling it the Storm of the Century, a cyclone that comes side-winding out of the Gulf in mid-March, a wheel of destruction the size of a continent. The squall line strikes the Big Bend of Florida. The storm-surge blasts across oceanfront streets, ripping palm trees from the ground and sending boats into dining rooms and shopping mall parking lots. The winds gust to one hundred miles per hour, unleashing a brood of tornadoes that turns the sky a sickly green. Debris crazes the air, roofs whirl like giant distraught birds through the sky. The spiky pines of the coast rip open the storm's belly like claws. Snow begins to fall on Florida, six inches on the Panhandle, and the storm wheels northward across Georgia, whiting the land, felling trees and killing power.

"Goddamn end of days," says Hiram, squinting through the windshield wipers.

He's at the wheel of his wife's Chrysler Town & Country, a station wagon with long slats of faux wood trim down the sides. They are plowing up the old coastal highway, the car rocking and shivering in the wind, lurching murderously toward the trees at every gust. The world is sideways, the big roadside oaks and pines heaving like an angry green sea. Clumps of moss tumble across the road like doomed opossums or raccoons—maybe some of them are. The tires of the Chrysler thump again and again over nameless wreckage the pavement feeds them, and Hiram keeps the accelerator down, his jaw slightly open, his breath coming through his teeth.

In the rearview mirror he can see his two slavering boys beating each other silly, each wearing a pair of overlarge white gloves. He looks at his wife riding shotgun.

"Those goddamn Mickey Mitts. One of them's gonna knock the other's tooth out before we even hit the county line. Twenty bucks for the damn things, another two hundred for the dentist." He shakes his head. "Shitfire."

"*Hiram!*"

He swerves around a fallen branch.

"I seen it."

They've been down in Orlando, the boys' once-in-a-lifetime trip to Disney World. For years, Jo-Beth has been after him to take them. He argued that everything was too overpriced down there.

"A kingdom of Yankees that don't know no better than to pay twenty dollars for a picture of their kid with some kiddie-diddler in a mouse suit full of trapped farts and lunchmeat-breath."

"It ain't that bad."

"Ain't bad? The got-damn place eats up money like a big hole in the ground. In *Florida* of all places, the drooping dick of America."

Jo-Beth is hard, though, always was. She has a square jaw like a man and big viselike hands, her hair shot through with iron. If Annabelle is the red dream of power and speed, of a world singing him *yes—yes* and *yes* and *yes—* Jo-Beth is his old battleship-gray truck churning through mired roads, never taking no for an answer. Her siege of the Magic Kingdom was deliberate, medieval. Mickey magnets on the refrigerator and Epcot brochures on the kitchen table. Disney movie nights and whispers before bed. It was a place every boy ought to experience, she said.

"Shit. I never did."

"And look how you turned out."

Finally he caved, throwing down his ballcap and stomping it flat.

"All right, *goddammit.*"

They left Orlando a day early to race the storm home. The radio man says roofs are collapsing all across the state of Georgia, homes and factories not built for the burden of snow, and airports are closed up and down the Eastern Seaboard. There are whiteouts in the mountains north of Atlanta. The National Guard is deploying in 6x6 trucks along the roads, aiding motorists trapped in their cars. A freighter has gone down in the Gulf and countless other vessels are missing at sea. There have been over thirty deaths reported in Florida already, another ten in Georgia so far. It's seven below freezing in Savannah; people are huddled in blankets in the powerless dark. Farther north, the snow is falling at three inches an hour, building record drifts. The weather people are calling it "thundersnow."

Hiram maneuvers around more limbs fallen across the road, grinding his teeth. Orange Asplundh chipper trucks have come out too early, parked lopsided on the shoulder. Ponchoed men cling to the machines in the screaming wind and rain and snow, trying not to be blown into the churning throats of their hoppers. Road signs shudder and twist; in front of a badly shingled house, a Silverado sits crushed under a fallen oak, the window glass blown out in icy blue pebbles. They pass the entrance to the old rice plantation, Hofwyl, which gives tours to schoolkids now, and the county line isn't but a mile ahead. The road turns a long bend and the trees open up, a paved causeway over the wide brown marsh flats of the Altamaha River Delta.

Hiram stomps the brakes with both feet.

There is no marsh. The delta is completely flooded over, the road skimming the very surface of a giant inland sea roiling and capping like a world aboil. Hiram's heart pummels his breastbone. Here is the sea risen up against him—the outgoing tide beaten inshore by cyclonic winds, the river crashing against it, the land overrun in high water. In places, dark rivers cross the road, who knows how deep, and the floodwaters swell and break against the shoulders of the causeway, spitting foam. The backseat is quiet, no more slapping of mitts to flesh. The punches no longer fly. The boys have smashed their faces against the cloudy windows, their mouths O-shaped with awe.

"We ought to wait it out," says Jo-Beth. "Turn around and get a hotel room."

Hiram can feel the signs on his skin tingling, making themselves known.

The swallows pinned fluttering to his shoulders, tugging at his spirit, the North Star pointing him on. There's something he needs to see.

"Fuck it," he says, "y'all wanted rides."

He pegs the accelerator to the floor. The tires skitter for traction, the rain slurring across the windshield, the little engine racketing under the hood.

29

Altamaha River, Day 3

Hunter looks up, watching his brother's feet on the rungs of the ladder. The rest of him disappears into the treed-over gloom of the old railroad bridge. It's dusk and tiny shapes flit in the lights of the park across the river, fliers drawn into the electric suns. The shrieks of children float over the water, and the heavy hawing of whiskey-throated men. Hunter looks down at the boats, hidden in a thicket along the bank, and then back at his brother, a cloud of shadow above him. He sighs and grips the steel rungs of the maintenance ladder, hauling himself off the ground.

Earlier that afternoon, they rounded a long bend, the sun high above them like a frying egg, and there it was: the old abandoned swing bridge at Altamaha Park. Big iron trestles stretched from the far bank, skeletal trapezoids bloodied with rust, and part of the bridge—a swing span—was turned parallel to the river's flow, allowing the passage of boats too tall to slip beneath the fixed trussworks. Thousands of freight cars once thundered across the river here, along with the *Silver Meteor* and *Orange Blossom Special,* the great passenger trains of the Seaboard lines. But this section of rail had been abandoned for nearly as long as they could remember, the trains diverted to newer tracks, the work of changing ownerships and accidents that occurred along such elevated stretches of line.

The park itself sat on the bank. There were two boat ramps, a man-made beach, a netted-off swimming area with Styrofoam floats to mark its limits. There were cabins for rent and campsites for RVs and tents, a kids' playground complete with slides and monkey bars, a lighted fishing pier and floating dock. A jumble of old river-houses lined the banks just downstream, each perched on thin, weak-seeming stilts. The floathouses here were all gone, hauled away or cut up by axes and chainsaws when the state ruled against them two decades ago.

They dragged their boats up the little beach, watched intently by two leathery women in beach chairs who twittered and giggled. They had crinkly cigarette faces and loud fingernails and koozied beers, their fleshy amplitudes hardly contained by stringy bikini ties. Their children splashed in the muddy water. Hunter watched one of the women dig her painted toes into the sand, staring right at him.

Lawton caught him looking.

"You don't want none of that. Rode hard and put up wet, them two."

Hunter felt his face burn.

"I wasn't looking like that."

Lawton looked at him: *Sure you wasn't.*

They tied off their boats and headed for the camp store set some ways back from the river itself. The door jingled as Hunter walked in, the cold blast of machine-air shocking him after two days without air-conditioning. He bought two hot dogs in yellow buns from the glassed rotisserie, each cradled in a paper tray of curlicue fries, and a bloodred can of Coke from the chipped ice of a display bucket. Lawton met him at a picnic table outside with a triple stack of hamburger patties set in a tray of near-colorless lettuce and tomato. A few purple onion circles were glopped in mayonnaise.

"The hell is that, Lawton?"

"Salad."

"That is the sorriest salad I have ever seen."

"Yeah, well."

Hunter bit into his hot dog, backing this with a handful of fries. "You worried you're getting fat or something?"

"No," said Lawton. He looked up. "Why, you think I am?"

"Getting fat?"

"Yeah."

"No."

Lawton shook his head. "Lot of the guys, they got eight-packs and shit. Veins in their fucking stomachs."

"I mean, you got a two-pack, at least. Not eight, but hell. I'm sure you can out-lift most of the guys."

Lawton shook his head, swallowed. "You'd be surprised, brother. I was always top dog in the gym. I'm still up there, but some of these guys, it's crazy. We got a guy can deadlift his mile time. Six-minute mile, six-hundred-pound dead lift. Speaks Dari, too."

"Jesus Christ."

"I figure I got enough shit to carry around as is. Don't need any extra fat on top of that." Lawton cut into his burger cake. "Besides, one of the Team docs said my blood pressure was a little high."

"How high?"

"I don't know, like one-thirty over ninety. Nothing serious."

"Huh." Hunter finished his first hot dog and licked the ketchup from his thumb, then leaned his elbows on the table. "Tell me something. You really hit that film guy just to turn up the sheriffs, like Andino said?"

Lawton looked up, chewing.

"What, I ain't crazy enough to do it just for fun?"

After lunch they walked over to where a group was assembling around the weigh-in stand of the South Altamaha Flathead Association. They had the tall hats and liver-spotted skin of men who spent too much time under the killing light of the sun. Mounted to the wall behind the stand was a plywood board painted with a rebel flag, a big river-cat curling over the white-starred X. Below this, in yellow, it said: FEED THE RUN.

The fish that had everyone's attention was a fat-bodied giant with a cartoon mouth. A whale of a cat big enough to swallow a man to the waist, halving him like a mermaid's tail. It took two of them to haul the monster onto the hanging scale. The man who'd brought it in had a goatee and camouflage ballcap, cut-off jean shorts and dirty white sneakers. He drove a log-truck for the mill, they said. His cap read: RAYONIER. He'd caught the flathead on a 50-pound mainline with a 3-ounce sinker, fishing a 15-foot hole. The old-timer who was refereeing the action squinted at the circular gauge of the scale, watching the red arrow quiver as the dead fish settled on the hook. Hanging there, it looked like a mutant tadpole, swollen on whatever scary chemicals flowed from the discharge pipes of the plant upstream.

"Seventy-eight point three," read the judge. "Five shy of the all-tackle record."

Everyone groaned.

Hunter turned toward Lawton, to say didn't it look bigger than that, but his brother wasn't there. He searched the crowd and saw him at the corner of the building, talking to a wiry little man with a ballcap and mustache, an unfiltered cigarette burning from his mouth. Hunter started toward them but Lawton held up his hand. He turned back to the man and said a few more words and shook his hand, then came toward Hunter.

"Good news," he said. "He ought to be up there tonight."

"Who ought to?"

"Wild Dill. Who you think?"

"Shit," said Hunter.

Hunter has reached the top of the ladder now. The last light of day slants through the high limbs, and the old rails run elevated into the woods, a long concrete bridge through the cypress. He expects to find a hard surface under his feet but doesn't. The rail-bed is buried beneath a deep layer of moldering leaves, soft underfoot, and the rest of the bridge is grown over with spidery roots and vines, a gray hulk drawn slowly back into the wild. In the failing light, it runs a straight shot into the distance, offering what seems an old wagon-road suspended amid the trees.

"Jesus." Lawton plants his fists on his hips. "It's like something you'd find in the jungle. Like from the Mayans or something. Don't take long, I guess."

"Nope," says Hunter. "You know they can't even find some of the early forts. They've been swallowed up. For years they thought the first European fort in the New World, Fort Caroline, was down in Florida. Jacksonville. Now they know it wasn't."

"Where was it?"

"Maybe here."

"Spanish?"

"French. People don't realize, if things turned out a little different, we might be speaking French right now."

"Or German or Japanese," said Lawton.

"Or Russian, to hear the old man talk growing up."

Lawton spits. "Come on, that's enough English for now."

He turns but Hunter doesn't move.

"Wait, Lawton. I want to know what it is we're doing, exactly."

Lawton looks at him. "We're going to have a conversation with the guy is all. Wild Dill."

"Bullshit. If that was the case, we'd just paddle up to his door."

"Thing is, Hunter, I don't know what *language* he speaks yet."

"What the hell language would he speak?"

Lawton shrugs, cracking his knuckles.

30

New France, March 1565

They depart Utina's village at first light. Le Moyne and the rest of the arquebusiers form the advance guard of a column three hundred warriors strong. The chief they are moving against is called Potano, king of the foothills, and he is detested by Utina and his people. His defeat will open the road to the mountains, the gold-rich streams they birth. Of this Utina has assured them.

It is said to be a single day's journey into the land of Potano, but the Indians have failed to anticipate the encumbrance of French guns and armor. The sun roars from on high, and Le Moyne and his companions cook inside their metal helmets and breastplates. They sweat pools into their boots, groaning and cursing, slogging over the swampy ground like ironwork facsimiles of men. In the end, the two-spirits must lift the French onto the great mountains of their shoulders, bearing them like sacks of feed.

At the end of the first day they have come but half the way, and they make camp near the shore of a lake. Utina beds down at the center of a burning ring, each campfire attended by a sixfold bristling of archers. The Indians hardly sleep. They have partaken of *la boisson noire*, the black drink that keeps them awake and alert on their battle marches, and they have inhaled the blue smoke of the *tabac* leaf as well.

Some of the French lie propped on their elbows, lifting the long pipes to their lips. The soldier nearest Le Moyne watches a long plume of smoke come curling from his mouth. He seems entranced, watching the smoke untangle itself into the night. He holds out the pipe.

"Le Moyne, you want some of this?"

"Not tonight."

The man shrugs and brings the pipe again to his mouth.

"Suit yourself."

Le Moyne rolls out his bedding on the night-dampened earth. Exhaustion weighs him down like a spell. His stockings are mired to the knees of his *culottes,* his skin raw in its creases and seams. His every joint sings its hurt, and he cares for nothing but sleep. He rests his head on his powder bag, his arquebus cradled beside him like a lover. Sleep infects his prayers. They meander down paths heretofore untraveled, carving new and glowing visions in the black lands of his mind. Thoughts rise riverlike, unwilled. He sees *thy kingdom come* upon these shores, great castles of metal and brass risen from the trees, their iron turrets smoking like gun barrels, and men who tramp upon their ringing parapets with tools instead of weapons.

Let us, Father God—

Bundles of trees are fed into the bowels of the place, whole forests consumed like fagots of kindling.

Let us, Father—

The lanterns shine on the walls like crystallized fire.

Let us—

He sleeps.

In the morning they start again, making better progress as the land firms beneath their boots. By midday they are three leagues from the enemy village. They are readying themselves, their swords and long-guns, when the forward scouts are spotted by three natives fishing from a cypress dugout. Cries sound through the woods, and soon the scouts return proud-chested, bearing an arrow-shot corpse. They busy themselves scalping and dismembering the body.

Meanwhile, Utina stands questioning them. Le Moyne has learned but little of the Indian language, yet he can interpret the blanching of the chief's face easily enough. The man is afraid of the two fishermen who escaped, surely to alert their king of the enemy await in the woods. Surprise, this was his great advantage.

Lord d'Ottigni stands watching the men butcher the corpse. He spits and looks at the interpreter.

"Tell him we must advance at once, before the enemy can organize a defense."

The chief shakes his head, refusing.

"*Jarua*," he says. "*Jarua*." He turns to his warriors. "*Jarua!*"

The natives part as an old man comes shuffling to the front of their ranks. His body is strangely young, his limbs rifled as by rope and fiber, his skin tight and unadorned.

"This man," whispers the interpreter. "Utina says he has the power to see the future, to read the outcome of future events."

"Blood of Christ," says d'Ottigni.

The old priest takes one of the French shields and sets it before his feet. Upon this dome he kneels, as upon an orb buried mostly in the ground, allowing no part of himself to touch the earth. With a sharpened stick, he draws a border around the shield, nearly perfect in its arc. He adds within this circle all manner of signs and symbols, stars and scrawls unreckonable. He is, Le Moyne realizes, dividing himself from the earth on which they stand. Now he begins to grunt and spasm upon his knees, his body torqued suddenly one way, his arms another, his form twisting into shapes inhuman, unnatural, struck as if by some unseen force. He is wrecked by it, his very joints popping and snapping out of place, their angles aberrant and sickening, like a corpse broken upon the rack. His lips peel back, showing his red gums, his bared teeth, his throat convulsing, erupting as if with the rumored war-screech of the ape. His sharp red tongue stabs the air like a dagger. His fingers are locked and clawed, his every vein evident, a figure tortured doll-like at the hands of some terrible god.

He suddenly quiets. The storm, it seems, has passed through him, and he is again an old man kneeling upon a shield in the woods. He rises and exits the circle to address Utina, who kneels in his war regalia to hear the man's tidings. The priest's eyes are glazed; his voice seems to come from a tiny demon buried in his breast, a chilling rasp rarely heard in the world of men.

"What does he say?" asks d'Ottigni.

The interpreter's head is cocked.

"He says Potano, king of the foothills, knows of our advance. Further, that he awaits it. He says the enemy king has two thousand of his warriors ready with cords to bind up the prisoners they will take."

"*C'est d'la merde*," mutters d'Ottigni. What shit.

Utina speaks to the interpreter, pleading with his hands.

"He says he does not wish to fight, sir."

The scar tightens on d'Ottigni's face.

"I did not slog for two days through this green hell of a land to turn back now. Tell him I thought he was a great warrior. A man. Tell him, if he turns back now, my men and I will be forced to regard him as a man *sans couilles*."

Without balls.

"He says he is a man with testicles."

"Oh?" says d'Ottigni. "Tell him to prove it."

31

Crooked Lake, Day 3

They march along the old rail line. Hunter's knee is throbbing, a pulsing ball of hurt, and his limp has become more pronounced. The pain is a song almost, hummed against the scar that zippers his kneecap, all the time threatening to wail. He grits his teeth to keep up with Lawton. The sun is fully down and moonlight is stalking through the roof of limbs, puddling on the old rail-bed set high through the trees. Crooked Lake looks more like a wide stream. He can see it gleaming through the trees, running parallel to the elevated rail line for half a mile before it begins rounding back and forth amid the concrete pillars, ducking through their shadows.

Lawton marches steadily on, his trophy-shaped calves quivering with each step, his feet grinding out hollows in the mulch. He has his chin tucked into his chest, his pair of black fins dangling from his vest. Hunter wants to ask him to slow down. The words are simple but won't come. They are rocks in his lungs, whole and unsaid. His mouth shuts only tighter, paled like a scar in his face.

He can't help but remember the night he blew his knee. It was a simple play: I Right 36 Power. He was lined up at tailback in the I. Lawton, at fullback, would kick out wide to the right, blocking the outside linebacker, and Hunter would accept the handoff as the backside guard pulled in front of him, leading him into the gap.

The November sky was black beyond the stadium lights, the players' breath pouring from their helmets like exhaust fumes. Lawton lowered himself into his three-point stance, the fingers of one hand spread out before him on the ground, his opposite forearm laid across his knee. His haunches were giant in their golden pants, his hamstrings lumped with power. The week before, Hunter had watched him squat 405 for five reps in the school weight room. High bar, ass-to-ankles, without even a belt.

Hunter set his hands on his knees, scanning the two lines of armored giants, trying to see what would happen before it did. On the other side of the ball, eleven boys in blue helmets who would hurt him if they could. He had never been afraid of being hit. It felt almost an honor to be the target of all that hate. In boyhood games of smear-the-queer, he would take up the ball again and again, tackled and beaten and kicked and gouged until he could taste the blood in his mouth, his knees and elbows badged red, his body absorbing the punishment that Lawton took at home. But as he listened for the snap-count, something didn't feel right. An acid burned in his throat, a warning waiting to be spoken. He felt almost weak.

"Hut!"

Helmets crashed, a wreckage of bodies, and the backfield choreography began. Lawton exploded to the right, sealing his man to the outside, and Hunter hovered a moment in the backfield, taking the ball as the guard pulled in front of him. He fell in just behind his blocker, hiding behind his bulk as they shot upfield, off the tackle and into the gap. Hunter watched a seam open in the storm of plastic and flesh, just wide enough for him to fit. He was about to burst into the open field when the pulling guard, Billings, dropped low to chop-block the inside linebacker, but the boy dove over the top of him, flattening in midair, 190 pounds of weaponized sophomore driving into the very point of Hunter's knee.

The next week, after watching the game film, Lawton broke Billings's nose in the school parking lot. Everyone watched the boy roll around in the gravel, holding his face in his hands. Hunter, recovering at home, only heard the story later. Lawton never said a word. Hunter figured he should have been thankful, but he wasn't. He didn't blame Billings for the missed block. It was simply a miscalculation, a mistake, a turn of bad luck—not ill will. He tried to tell Billings this later, but there was only fear and hate in the bigger boy's eyes.

He'd never quite forgiven Lawton for that.

Lawton kneels in the road, holding up a closed fist. His movements are silent, deliberate as a man in enemy country. He points over the side of the bridge.

Hunter looks. There below them, in a wing of moonlight, stands a stag the size of a thoroughbred horse, head motionless and erect, trees of bone-white antlers twinned crooked and perfect from the crown of his skull. He seems a revelation almost, the king of some nation long vanished, and Hunter finds himself wondering if the earth harbors the ghosts of beasts as well as men, if their majesty and torment echo through time. But there is the subtle swell of the chest, the wet blackness of the eyes, and he knows the big-hearted stag is alive beneath them, vigilant, breathing the power of his ten thousand generations.

Hunter's knee screams; he puts out a hand to steady himself, and the stag whirls back into the darkness, silent, silver as a wraith. No branches rattle in his wake, no leaves.

Lawton stands.

"Shit, boy. You see the rack on that? Twelve, fourteen point?"

Hunter is working the pain from his knee.

"Don't get your dick hard."

"Shame, though. That gash in his belly."

"Gash?"

"You saw it. Looked like he got caught on a fence or something."

"Huh," says Hunter. "I didn't notice."

Lawton points two fingers at his own eyes, clicks his tongue.

"Got to work on that situational awareness, boy."

Before Hunter can tell him where he can shove his situational awareness, Lawton turns and starts back down the road. Hunter follows, limping worse now. The ache has transformed. His knee is a ball of stone, cold and unyielding, that he bears through the tunneled trees. He thinks of the stag standing tall despite its wound, and he lets the pain remind him of who he is, what he can endure.

Ahead of him the long pair of fins, sleek and black, flop from Lawton's vest. Hunter watches them, so like trophies cut from a whale or seal. They will transform his brother, he knows. Turn him into an amphibian, a creature made to swim. A frogman. He always has them now.

The day they packed:

"What you got those for?"

"Mother Ocean. It gets too hot, we can always escape to sea. Don our fins and slip into the surf. Put a couple miles of ocean between us and the boogers."

"You figuring there's gonna be a lot of bad guys on the river?"

"There's boogs everywhere, little brother. You're living in a dream world, you don't think that. But Mother Ocean is always waiting."

"Hopefully she treats you better than she did Daddy."

"Hopefully. I figure having a nuclear submarine on your side helps."

They stand above the silvery waters of Crooked Lake, their moon-shadows pointed like a pair of horns against the surface. The stream wheels away, and in the far crook of the bend a mob of yellow lights hovers in the trees, flickering.

"That's it," says Lawton. "Wild Dill's." He leans over the bridge. "No ladder, we're gonna have to jump."

"All right."

Lawton sits on the edge and slips on his fins, hooking the straps behind his heels, then duckwalks toward Hunter. "Your vest cinched tight?"

"It's good."

"Come here." Lawton yanks on the buckles and straps of Hunter's vest, cinching it down like a corset. He slaps him on the chest. "There. I'm gonna jump first. When you hit, don't struggle or nothing. Just let the vest bring you back up."

"Got it."

Lawton grins. "Show you a little of what I do for a living." He sits on the edge of the bridge and spins to face the water, his legs long and tapered with the fins. He pushes off, a body used to falling through space, and smacks the water with a natural sound. Hunter follows, a twenty-foot drop. The water crashes under his feet, a black night that envelops him, and then he's up under the moon. They start swimming for the lights, making dark arrows in the current. Breaststroking.

They were water-babies growing up, so their mother called them. Always playing in the creeks or ponds or blue kiddie pools in the backyard, and Hunter took to the YMCA pool after his knee reconstruction, swimming laps until college and the timber sports club. He's light and fast in the water, unlamed, but this is no lap pool. There are alligators watching from the banks, he knows, and great catfish that comb the bottoms, big enough to swallow a man nearly whole. There are snakes that wriggle themselves across the river's surface, full of venom that can turn your blood to fire, and who knows what other monsters frozen in time and hungry. Still, he isn't afraid, and he wonders how much of this is due to Lawton, who seems above such worry, whose enemies have guns instead of teeth.

They edge toward the bank as they swim, the water laced with the shadows of overhanging cypress, and soon they can hear the drone of a generator through the trees. The place assembles itself out of the dark. There's a homemade floating dock, buoyed on plastic drums, and an airboat hitched to its cleats, the eight-blade propeller caged in wire. Above this hovers the baithouse, a two-level houseboat dragged out of the river and perched on pilings of stacked cinderblocks like some low-rent ark for the end times said to come. It's flat-bottomed and blocky, with a sitting deck at the stern. The railed roof holds an irregular flock of white plastic chairs, and a hand-painted sign hangs from the edge: WILD DILL'S BAIT 'N TACKLE.

Lawton leads them past the dock to the pale cut of the bank, and they pull themselves dripping from the water, the hull of the houseboat hovering over them like a threat. The cinderblocks are stacked unevenly, like books in a genius's office, and little mounds of powdered concrete halo their bases. The sitting deck, set like a porch at the stern, serves as the entrance, reached by a set of metal rolling stairs that once graced the tarmac of a jetport.

The yellow lights they saw from the bridge, they're bug zappers. A throng of them have been strung through the trees, hellish lanterns that snap and hiss as they work, exploding moths and mosquitos in sooty poofs.

"Jesus," whispers Hunter.

Lawton turns his eyes on him, big and glowing, and holds a finger over his mouth. He slips off his fins, dainty as bedroom slippers, and clips them to his vest. He is shirtless beneath his vest. His arms look ax-hewn, his shoulders like knotty oak. He kneels and cups his hands in the shallows, pulling his beard into a long red point. When he stands, the lights flicker evilly above him.

"How do I look?"

"Like the devil."

32

New France, March 1565

The enemy village lies in a fold of low yellow hills, the circular huts emitting thin spires of smoke. No one moves within the walls. A couple of dogs. A *barabicu* burns before the council house, a sacred fire pit. Meat lies smoking on a wooden rack above it, untended.

Le Moyne cannot tell if his weapon has grown heavy or light. His arms are shaking, as if strained, and yet he feels he could fling the instrument wheeling against the sun. He looks to the hill before him. The cold yellow grass bends in the wind. The woods are calm.

Lord d'Ottigni strides before the French ranks. The panache of his helmet waves proudly over the field, a bloodred plume. His cuirass shines like the torso of a god. His face undercuts all this, ugly and serious as an ogre's. He carries no arquebus, not since the flash-burn. He draws his sword and raises it silvering into the sun.

"En avant, marche!"

They start down the hill, arrayed like the iron tip of a spear, and all at once enemy warriors come streaking from the woods. Their teeth are so white, thinks Le Moyne, their limbs so brown and strong. They scream as they come, a shrill tenor that sounds almost girlish. Arrows scatter the sun, wiggling as they fly, and without thought Le Moyne finds himself crouching to one knee, lifting his gun. The clubmen are coming now, racing through the ranks of archers. Metal trinkets jingle about their waists and thighs, and strings of glass beads, and they hold their war clubs high over their heads as they run.

Le Moyne leans into his arquebus, aiming downhill, and pulls the trigger. The weapon leaps in his arms, belching smoke. He watches a red star erupt in the chest of the warrior before him, a bowman nocking his arrow. The man falls to the ground, flopping and clawing at his heart, a burning stone he hopes to free. Already Le Moyne is reloading as one of his comrades steps ahead of him, firing, guns booming everywhere as he works. They are moving forward almost as one, treading over the bodies of the dead and dying, a storm of powder smoke rolling down into the fold of hills, spitting bolts of flame.

The enemy is where the holy man said they would be, armed with their clubs and cords, but he was wrong in his presage of defeat. The enemy warriors shudder and crumble at every thunder of the guns, struck down as if by the sound itself. Here is a truth barked louder than words. A destiny. Utina's warriors fall screaming upon the bodies of the dying like wild dogs, dragging them into the trees. There they cut a line around the crown of the skull, winding the hair up in their fists and tearing it free, balding heads to the bloody pate.

Lord d'Ottigni waves his men on, deeper down the slope of the meadow toward the village itself. They will take what provisions they can and burn the rest, nothing save a toppled forest of charred timber left in their wake. No one will be left to bar their march into the mountains.

"En avant, marche! Ne faites pas de quartier!"

Give no quarter.

Just then a warrior comes charging out of the powder-storm, a giant of a man wreathed in smoke, trailing three striped war-tails like some new kind of beast. He charges for d'Ottigni, raising his club two-handed to brain him where he stands. Lord d'Ottigni catches the blow clanging upon his shield and runs his sword through the man's navel, planting his boot just below the wound to free the blade. The man falls squirming to the ground, clutching his belly and roaring. D'Ottigni pierces his heart, and the man thrashes like an insect as he dies. The scar-faced lord steps past him and keeps advancing down the hill, his plumed helmet gleaming in the sun, his bloodied sword urging them on.

The villagers are fleeing from their huts now, panicked like ants, and the enemy warriors are turning tail to the coming storm, the pale soles of their feet flashing as they fly for the woods. But Le Moyne sees no arrows chasing after them, no men running them down with spear and club. He turns to look over his shoulder, expecting to see Utina's great pledge of warriors swelled behind him like a tide, weapons bristling to finish what the guns have started. But the warriors are scattered, knotted around the fallen, rapt in the disassembly of bodies. They drive their wedges into the joints, breaking limb from trunk, rising triumphant with their dripping trophies, the scalped heads littering the slope like a batch of grisly half-peeled fruit.

"Attention, Le Moyne!"

He ducks. An arrow sings past his head, a man behind him screams. More of them come black-streaking through the air, like wingless birds, looking for men's hearts. Le Moyne raises his arquebus again, squinting through the storm of gunpowder that stings his eyes, searching for shadows in the fog.

33

Crooked Lake, Day 3

Lawton goes first, climbing the boarding stairs to the houseboat's porch. His bare feet clap across the deck and he pushes through the dangling plastic ribbons that cover the door.

"Evening," he says loudly.

Hunter, just behind him, sees Dillard Rollins straighten behind the counter. His eyes round large a moment before narrowing. He has graying curls piled on his shoulders, uncut for what looks a presidential term, and a giant gunfighter's mustache hides his mouth. An unlit cigarette hangs down like a walrus tooth.

Lawton looks around.

"Some place you got here."

There's a rack of tackle and another of snacks. There are coils of glistening fishing line and heavy leaders and an array of angry-looking hooks, barbed and snarled in various interpretations of the letter *J*. A few gummy worms that sparkle or shift color depending on the light. There are sunflower seeds, shelled and unshelled, and fried pig ears and corn nuts, and boxes of candy bars in dusty wrappers, waiting for their gloried future in the days post-apocalypse, when they will be treasured. There are cans of peaches and sausages and Spam. Along one wall a deep freezer freckled with rust, perfect for the storage of bodies, and along the other a fog-windowed cooler housing a range of Coca-Cola products, some of them with labels not seen in years. Next to this a screened trough for live bait. Above it all hangs a big half-acre bug zapper, chandelierlike, caging an electric-blue bulb soot-spotted with kills.

Dill leans back on his stool, his eyes flicking below the counter. His surveillance screens are down there, most likely, and who knows what else.

"Something I can help you boys with?"

Lawton thumbs the barb of a big 10/0 Kahle hook on the rack.

"I heard these Kahles are real fish-killers, bad for gut-hooking."

Dill fishes a scarred Zippo out of his shirt pocket, lighting his cigarette with a snick.

"Any cat'll swallow a hook, you don't set it quick enough." He blows the smoke from his nostrils. "'Side from the fact, killing the fish is the point."

"Sure," says Lawton. "Guess you're right in that aspect."

Dill leans forward, the feet of his stool clicking down. He shelves his arms on the counter, his cigarette smoking away. He has a long face, like an old dog, but his eyes are quick.

"I seen you didn't come in a boat."

"Good night for a swim." Lawton pats his fins.

"You swim out here to ask me 'bout catfish hooks?"

"Pardon me, I should of introduced myself." Lawton walks up to the counter. "Name's Lawton Loggins, and this here's my brother, Hunter." He pauses a moment, leaning his hands on the edge of the counter, cocking one eye at the man. "Hiram Loggins, he was our daddy."

Wild Dill doesn't blink.

"I'm real sorry to hear that," he says.

"You know anything about it?"

"'Bout what?"

"'Bout the way he went down."

Dill leans back on his stool and examines the tip of his cigarette.

"I heard it was a sturgeon got him."

"You don't think there was nothing funny about it?"

"Funny how?"

"I heard there's been something going on, on this river. Something funny. And I heard you were the man to ask about it."

Wild Dill looks over them, past them, his focus shifting across the room. Hunter notices the man's hands have crept to his sides now, below the level of the counter. Surely Lawton sees it, too. His own hands are still on the counter's edge, his heels elevated from the floor like a boxer's. He doesn't turn to look, can't, but Hunter does. He doesn't see anything at first. No one is on the porch. Then he sees what has the man's attention. A giant cockroach has fixed itself over the door, hump-winged and gleaming, its antennae dancing like tiny reeds.

"Goddamn things," says Dill. He reaches under the counter. Lawton tenses, ready to strike, but the man pays him no mind. Up comes a lever-action rifle in miniature, a Red Ryder BB gun like from *A Christmas Story*. In a single movement he has the toy gun shouldered, high-aimed, a fart noise as he pulls the trigger. The roach's wings spread wide as the BB strikes it, a whorl of black petals that falls flat on the floor, upturned, legs beating the air.

Wild Dill works the lever and sits back on his stool, the air rifle propped on his thigh.

"Nasty fuckers." His eyes are glassy, watching the stricken insect. "Got 'em so big out here they set off the goddamn mousetraps. People think people run the world. They don't. It's the goddamn bugs."

"Huh," says Lawton. "Some shot. That how you got your name, sniping roaches?"

"No," says Dill.

"You were telling us about our daddy."

Dill's focus shifts back, surprised to find the boys standing before him.

"No, I wasn't."

"But you were about to."

Dillard Rollins lays the rifle on the counter. It still has the original leather thong hanging from the lariat ring. He sucks on his cigarette, a crumbling pillar yet to be ashed even once.

"I'm real sorry your daddy got hisself killed, son, but I don't have nothing to tell you."

Something goes through Lawton's body then, like a shadow or current. The bug zapper flickers and snaps. Hunter looks up in time to see the puff.

"Don't or won't?" says Lawton.

"What's it matter?"

"Oh, it matters."

Dill leans forward, eyeing them through his hangdog face.

"I got my name about ten years ago," he says. "I was big into antler velvet then. Women'd come out here to get some for their husbands, try sprinkling it in their coffee or whiskey. See if it might wake up a sleeping cock. This boy said I was putting it to his old lady whenever she come out here for the stuff. Said I must of fucked her some kind of good on that velvet, 'cause she wasn't never the same after that. He come out here with a pistol, old cap-and-ball Colt like a cowboy or something. He come down the bridge, just like you two, and I was up there fishing largemouths in the shadow of the piers. He started shooting soon as he saw me, before he was even out the trees. I had my old Smith & Wesson .38 on me." He taps the back part of his hip. "Fired once."

"What range?"

"Seventy-five yards."

"Prone?"

"Standing."

"That's a lucky shot," says Lawton.

"Not for him."

"I want to know what happened to my daddy."

"No, you don't. You want to walk out of my place before I got to put you out." Lawton's face is bright now, wired for extra voltage.

"You're a real bad mother, ain't you? What you got under that counter, baggies of crystal and a sawed-down twelve?"

"Try me and find out."

"What happened to our daddy?"

"He was a son of a bitch, and he had him son-of-a-bitch sons."

Lawton straightens from the counter, slowly, and looks around. The muscles in his jaw work. Through the windows the bug killers spark and pop, worlds on the edge of shorting out.

"It's like you got you a complex or something, ain't it? Like you're some kind of bug murderer out here."

Wild Dill jams his cigarette in the tray.

"Kill 'em all if I could."

Lawton nods, his hands hooked in the lapels of his vest. He starts to turn away, then lurches across the counter and embraces the man in his mammoth arms, hauling him flailing and kicking from the stool and onto the floor with a crash that shakes the houseboat. Lawton kneels over him like a lover, his forehead pressed to the floor so the man can only flail vainly at the back of Lawton's head with his fists. The bug zapper is swinging over them, the room swimming with light. Lawton drives his knees under Wild Dill's armpits, forcing his arms akimbo. They flop uselessly, and Lawton sits upright on Dillard's chest, riding the man's thrashings like a bucking horse.

"Hunter, hand me that roach."

Hunter looks down at it. It's still squirming, death throes or dead nerves. He picks it wriggling from the floor and brings it to Lawton, who takes the antennae in the pincer of his thumb and forefinger. He holds the winged medallion over the man's face, swinging it like a hypnotist's watch, the barbed legs chewing for grip.

"Thing is, Dill, our daddy taught us you always eat what you kill."

Wild Dill has his mouth clamped shut, his lips tucked between his teeth. He grinds his head this way, that way. His eyes are white, unable to close. His throat rattles with terror. Lawton lowers the gruesome pendant closer to the man's face, letting it swing back and forth. Closer, closer. The legs comb through the bristles of Dillard's mustache. It's too much.

"Russians," he bursts out.

Lawton pulls the roach back from his face.

"Say what?"

"Russians. They shown up on the river a few years back. Keep to themselves, mainly, two or three motoring up and down the river in a couple old skiffs."

"How you know they're Russian?"

"Couple boys run into them said they sounded like *Rambo III.*"

Lawton rolls his eyes.

"So they're Slavic, maybe. What is it they're into?"

"Hell if I know. Poaching, maybe. Snaring whitetail or baiting alligator. There ain't nobody down in that part of the river, hardly. Could be anything."

"You got any truck with them?"

"I never hardly seen them. Could be they ain't but fishermen, working the trade same as everybody else, just in a different language. It takes all kinds, I tell you. America was built by immigrants."

"That seems a enlightened notion, coming from you."

"Fuck you, you big ginger fuck. I was smoking grass and eating pussy, you was still swimming in your daddy's balls."

Lawton lowers the roach closer to the man's mouth.

"It's a big pill to swallow, Dill. Maybe it'll help your attitude some."

"Goddammit, I told you what I know."

"Not all of it."

"Uncle King, he's the man you need to talk to. Crazy fucker knows every bend of this river. Every fathom. Knows it like the veins run down his own arms. Anybody knows what's going on, it's him. What's going on and where. Talk to him and you'll see."

"How do we find him?"

"I don't know. I swear I'd tell you if I did. No one does."

"Too bad." Lawton clamps shut the man's nose. Soon, he'll have to open his mouth to breathe. "Time to take your medicine."

34

Darien, Georgia, 1993

Hiram Loggins stands on the Darien River bridge, his hands gripping the rough surface of the concrete guardrail, his body whipped and moaning like an empty bottle in the hurricane wind. He wears a beard of vomit and his skin is burning, branded by the signs that swathe him, and he can't hardly breathe.

His boat is gone.

The riverfront docks are half a century old and they don't float. They've been swallowed up in the risen tide, and the shrimp boats heave dangerously in the water, foundering on their lines, a fleet being dragged under as if by jealous tentacles. Others are simply gone, empty spaces in the docks, busted mooring lines swirling in the current. Some of them ax-cut, surely. Boats given up to the storm, bad seasons traded for insurance checks. His had been tied abreast of two others, down past the Thompson's Seafood shack that is now just a tin-roof island. All three of them are gone. In the trees downstream he sees the upturned hull of a boat being thrust again and again into the scrub pine like an insult, leaving parts of itself high in the branches. It isn't his.

His money. All his money was in the boat.

Sixty thousand dollars.

His future.

"Why?" he croaks.

He looks at the town, the riverfront buildings standing from streets of windblown surge, their window glass rattling like teeth. Then he looks out, seaward, to the risen mountains of swell, his boat surely smashed against those granitelike faces, swallowed in the hungry valleys they make.

He should have known it would come to this. Goddammit, he should have known. A decade of working other men's decks, back bent, bowing under the hard lash of their words. Taking so much shit he could taste it in his mouth at the end of every day, all those things he wanted to say and didn't, his pride rotting inside him like a disease. For nothing. His boat lost. His dream of the future pulled under.

His *Annabelle*.

"Why?" He is speaking to the waters, he realizes. To the ghost-memories roaming the deep. "Why the *fuck* won't you let me up?"

He looks down at his hands, white-knuckling the railing as if to keep him from going over. Below that the churning waters, white-whipped, cold as slate. His skin is on fire now, his breast bubbling with spite, and he feels like a weapon against the world below his feet. He will leap in, an anchor of superheated hate, and the depths will erupt from him, sizzling and boiling, the waters destroyed in the heat of his rage.

Just then a touch, a tug. He looks down to find his two boys beside him, holding to his shirttail, their faces uglied with concentration. His eldest, six, is red-haired like Annabelle, as if from sheer ambition of his seed. Hiram raises a hand to pat him on the head, this boy, like a good father would. Like he wants to.

His fist falls like a hammer into the freckled face. The boy crumples at his feet. The younger boy falls over him, crying, then looks up, his face twisted with hate. The six-year-old pushes himself from the ground and stands as before, bloody-faced now, holding his little brother's hand. In that moment Hiram loves the two of them so much he cannot speak.

35

Fort Caroline, March 1565

Le Moyne bolts upright in bed. His chest is thundering, his face burning like a shield in the sun. He is slick with sweat, slimy as a newt, and his bedcovers lie coiled at his waist. He blinks. He was there again, high over the field of battle, watching the disassembly of bodies, the limbless torsos riven in pools of blood. He has been there again and again. In the dream he is the sun, floating in power over the land, and the feast of death is his. Trophies of limb and scalp are raised for his scrutiny. Arrows are thrust into the anuses of the dead to honor his rays. And in the dream he is well pleased at this, at the land gleaming bloodred beneath the fire of his gaze.

Across the room, La Caille rolls up on his elbow.

"Qu'est-ce qui est faux?"

"Nothing, my friend. A nightmare."

"Again? *La bataille?*"

"Oui."

Dawn is beginning to seep under the door, between the planks, like a liquid that glows.

"You should draw it."

Le Moyne thrusts off his covers and sets his feet on the earthen floor. His bones grind like stone pestles in their sockets. He is so thin.

"I have not the strength to draw, La Caille. I will eat my paper."

La Caille laughs, the hard scrape of the cynic in his throat.

"Careful, Le Moyne. It is possible that your paper will be all that is left of us one day." He lies back down. "After all, Christ himself lives in a book."

Le Moyne thinks of the archer he shot, the man clawing at his chest.

"And in the hearts of men."

"Yes," says La Caille, repositioning his covers. "And there."

They gained but little from their victory in the west. King Utina would not follow them down into the village to burn the council house and huts, nor would his warriors pursue the fleeing enemy. They cared only to return triumphant to their people, to feast their victory. He who struck first and hardest, who was fiercest of spirit on the day of battle—he was victor in the savage mind. For the accumulation of territory they cared nothing. This, Le Moyne realized, could spell their doom.

He slips on his tunic and boots and walks out into the dawn. In former days, the fort would be alive at this hour. There would be pots bubbling over cookfires, the hiss of fat, the bang and scrape of hammers and saws. Progress would sound through the place.

Few now welcome the sun. Those awake shuffle slack-faced about the fort like ruminants, hands dark-stained from grubbing in the woods for roots and berries to eat. Some are heading for the great cypresses just beyond the walls. They ascend them by rote, their handholds worn smooth by other dawns, and perch in the uppermost branches, rocking as upon topmasts at sea, watching the horizon.

The ships will come, says their commander. Any day now.

Le Moyne walks the other way, climbing a ladder to stand above the sharp teeth of the palisade, a long cadre of trees ax-hewn to vicious points. Below him the river wears a white shroud of mist, a ghostly dress that swirls. Many of the trees are still out of leaf, bony and gnarled as he and his comrades have become. Heartless and scarred. Atrocities have been committed, native homes burned, as if this might impel the victims to feed them. Now it is said you can walk three miles in any direction without glimpsing the dark face of the savage, retreated as he has from the clanging armor of the fort, the guns and torches and white cheeks caved with want. Saturiwa, king of the coast, who helped to feed them and build their walls, is but a rumor now, rarely seen or heard.

Le Moyne stares down on the river, willing his eyes to see beyond the mist, to glimpse the mysteries curling through the night-dark of the bottoms. He is looking for his creature, which not even the sun-god can see cruising through the depths. He sets his hands upon the teeth of the palisade and leans forward, the sharpened points pressing into his palms. He believes it will rise again, his monster, revealed to him like the dark flesh of a lover come in the night. It will be the greatest sight he has captured, an image that speaks to all of the mystery and savagery of this new land. His hands will unearth it from darkness. They will scrawl it like the rivers that slither from the mountains, creatures rumored to carry in their bellies such power and gold. A discovery of such magnitude will make his journey righteous. It will consecrate the blood he has spilled. It will be the sign of God to him, risen like a word from darkness.

His palms are screaming now, the bones quivering like chords under the pressure, and the tongue stone is heavy in his pocket. Blood rushes to the doors that might open in his hands, red rivers yearning to be freed. A little harder now and he will be released, delivered into the long belly of night that flows into the sea.

Just then: shouts from the treetops. Cries and yelps. He scans the river, panicked, not seeing anything. Is he missing a glimpse of his creature? His hands come away from the palisade, red-cored, and the words turn him seaward.

"*Des voiles!*" he hears. "*Des voiles!*" Like the cries of a hawk.

Sails.

36

Altamaha River, Day 3

"P oachers," says Lawton. "I don't like it."

They are standing beneath the houseboat, Lawton slipping on his fins.

"You don't know they're poachers," says Hunter.

"What else are they?"

Hunter looks at the cinderblocks pillared beside him. One good shoulder blow, like he would throw an undersized cornerback, and the whole place would come crashing down on top of them. "I don't know. They could be shad fishers."

In the spring, the shad run upstream to spawn, whole clouds of them silvering under the river's skin. Lawton stamps his fins into place. "That ain't exactly a year-round occupation, now is it?"

They hear a retch above them, and a wet comet splats on the bank, flecking their shins with bile. The pool, yellowish in the moonlight, steams. Lawton looks up at the hull of the houseboat, his teeth showing.

"Goddammit, Dillard. Don't you got a toilet for that?"

"Fuck you, Loggins, you sick son of a bitch." Another retch, strings of ropy saliva. "I'll kill you for this."

Lawton grins, speaking to the hull.

"It'll take more than that Red Ryder, you sorry fuck."

"Fuck me," says Dillard. "I can still feel it squirming in my mouth."

"Now quit your bellyaching. Them's a delicacy some places."

"Did it come out?"

Lawton steps out slightly to look at the puddle of vomit.

"Yeah." He cocks his head. "Still squirming."

Dillard exhales in triumph. A thump as he sinks to the floor.

Lawton looks out at the slough, the bridge hulking across the water like a monument.

"Uncle King." He squints, as if he might see the old man out there on the water. "Wish we would of known to ask the first time we come across him."

"I think he's gone somewhere downriver."

"What makes you think that?"

"I think I heard him go past that night we spent on the island."

Lawton turns.

"Heard? How'd you know it was him?"

"I don't know," says Hunter. "I just did."

Above them another thump, a creak of hinges. Lawton raises his eyebrows. "Time to bug out." He produces a coil of parachute cord from somewhere on his person—his vest seems to harbor an endless supply of such tackle. "Should of done this before, put us on a umbilical."

Hunter looks at the cord. "Umbilical? We're just swimming back to the bridge."

"I ain't telling Mama I lost you out here."

"Lost me? Where the fuck am I gonna go?"

Lawton is already threading the cord through the D-ring on Hunter's vest. He looks up at the houseboat again. "We got to head out, Dill. I'm sure you'll be Wild again by morning, old buddy."

The old gunfighter groans.

"Kill 'em all," he croaks.

They waddle down to the water. Above them the bug-lights flicker, a galaxy hastily wired, the stars winking in and out.

"Wait," says Hunter, tugging the cord to stay them.

"What?"

He looks down at the spew of vomit at his feet. The roach is struggling amid chunks of dinner, legs chewing air, guts seeping yellow. A seed of agony. A peach pit. Hunter's feet are bare. He clenches his teeth and steps on the insect, pressing it under the hard ball of his foot until it crackles, bursts, squirts like a ketchup packet beneath his big toe. He chokes down a wad of vomit.

Lawton looks down at Hunter's foot, his teeth showing in his beard. He looks into Hunter's face. Starts to say something, then doesn't.

"Huh," he says. "I know some bad mothers wouldn't done that."

Bile wells in Hunter's throat, his shark's tooth sharp as a dagger.

"I ain't asked your fucking opinion about it, now did I?"

Lawton lifts his hands, holdup-like, his eyes wide.

37

Fort Caroline, March 1565

The ship that appears in the river's mouth is a caravel, light and fast, lateen-rigged with triangular sails such as the Spanish prefer. A vessel not laden with the salvation they hope for—bread and wine and salt pork, countrymen and tidings from France. A ship such as this can be delivering only one cargo: death.

"Les Espagnols!"

Panic within the fort. Men slip and fall in the mud, diving for their weapons, and others come streaming from their huts wearing nothing but armor, their skinny white legs struggling to keep them upright beneath the weight of shields and helmets and breastplates. They scramble to the walls, red-faced and blowing like overworked horses, their guns bristling along the river.

At each of the embrasures, the *canonniers* work to range the vessel beneath the bronze barrels of their eight-pounders, shifting the guns on their wheeled carriages. Le Moyne thinks of running for his arquebus but can't bring himself to leave the wall. The caravel is coming fast. He imagines the river erupting in white mountains of spray, the vessel passing untouched through a hail of cannon fire to spill its load of Spanish pikemen on the beach. He and his countrymen will have time to loose but one volley into the invaders, perhaps two, and then the fighting will be hand to hand on the walls and in the mud.

"Shall we fire?" they ask.

Laudonnière stands at the parapet now, taller than the rest. He lifts his arm.

Men wipe their brows with the backs of their hands, awaiting his signal. The fort hisses with the sound of lighted tapers and fuses. Any second, their leader's hand will fall and the fort will explode in fire.

"Wait!"

The cry comes from the corner farthest downriver. It is Lord d'Ottigni. Le Moyne recognizes the plume of his helmet, the gleaming wreck of his face.

"Wait! They speak!"

Shouts from the boat travel weakly across the water.

"*Nous sommes français!*" they call. "*Nous sommes français!*"

We are French.

The ship is Spanish, or was, crewed now by men who are no strangers to the fort: the mutineers. Inside the walls, the men of La Caroline curse and spit. Their mutineers have returned home, it seems, wasted with famine and treasureless aboard a stolen ship. They anchor themselves just beyond cannon range of the fort, hoping for mercy.

Laudonnière is shouting orders, red-faced, calling for a raiding party to be formed.

La Caille watches the flurry of guns and armor. His hands are behind his back, his necklace of boar tusks draped over his chest. He leans toward his commander.

"Sir," he says, "what is to keep them from pulling anchor and fleeing the moment our boarding party pushes from shore?"

Le Moyne, standing nearby, watches Laudonnière chew the side of his mouth. His ruff collar has yellowed like a dying carnation.

"Have you a better idea, La Caille?"

La Caille has pulled his dagger from its sheath. He digs the point under one of his nails and winks at Le Moyne.

"*Bien sûr,*" he says.

Of course.

Le Moyne sits huddled beneath the canvas of the pinnace, the small-boat of the *Breton.* Around him sit twenty-four others, hunched in darkness, their arquebuses propped between their knees. The timbers of the vessel creak beneath them. The seats of their breeches are soiled with leak-water. The canvas covering, used to hold down supplies, swells enough to allow glimpses of river between the tie-downs. The mist curls from its surface in slow flames, cool and white. It is just before dawn, a day after the caravel appeared in the river, and they are headed for where it sits anchored before the fort.

La Caille is visible in the bow, along with two others. A committee that will not alarm. With the ship nearing, he whistles, and a burning taper begins being passed hand to hand. They try not to cough from the smoke. Before long the air is crackling, men's faces lumped strangely in the smoky glow, their matchlocks a finger's touch from going off. The smoke, they hope, will be lost in the mist.

They feel the boat slow. In glimpses they see the dark-wet timbers of the caravel, like a fortress wall. Outside, voices they can hardly decipher, the clatter of boots. Then a second whistle from La Caille. The canvas tarpaulin is thrown off, skirling away like a sail, and they rise in unison, a bristling of iron like a pipe organ, each weapon aimed to kill. Half of the party boards the caravel, as prescribed, while the rest provide cover. The mutineers have failed to ready their own weapons. Le Moyne, landing on the deck, watches them fall to their knees, stick-arms raised like supplicants', bony angles paling through their faces. A ship of half-ghosts floating in the dawn, men emptied by hunger, their dreams fallowed at sea.

Le Moyne wonders how little different he and his comrades must look.

Fourneaux, leader of the mutiny, is a thin man now, surely for the first time in his life. His natural pear shape has been cut by the blade of want, whittled down to a skeletal core. His breeches have been shortened for comfort, his knees knobbed like those of a shorebird, his calves and thighs wasted to bony stilts. His face is that of death, his skull pushing through the skein of life that conceals it. The feathers are missing from his hat.

Laudonnière stands before the broken men. His collar seems stiffer today, whiter, his chest more fully swelled. His face is grim, as if displeased with the return of his prodigals. As if it pains him to speak their fate.

"God," he says. He pauses at the word. "I ask you men: Who but God has elected our king, by whose pleasure we embarked upon this journey? It is His Majesty in whom the power of God resides, and we are bound by oath to spare not our lives in service to him, and to obey whomever he appoints to command in his name." He pauses again, hands clasped behind his back, chin high. He is nodding faintly, as if in agreement with some dictum whispered in his ear. "By such contract you have fed upon the king's bread and drunk his wine, you have been given safe passage across the oceans and through the storms. And yet you abandon your integrity the moment it suits you, choosing to pursue earthly gains in lieu of the duties to which you are sworn. In doing so you have disobeyed not only man but God. For just as our king has been elected to reign over us, so have I been elected to rule in his name, to carry the writ of his power in my hand. You have thought, perhaps, that in this new land you might escape the justice of man, for your king is far, your sins hidden from his sight. Perhaps you could. But no man might escape the justice of God. Whose winds but his have brought you back here, to receive the fate you have earned?"

Le Moyne, watching, can feel the swell of the men, the wet mouths and heavy breaths, like a pack of dogs. The want of bread has been forgotten, for this moment, in thirst for blood. Laudonnière looks from face to face of the returned, as if deciding each of their fates individually. He decrees that the four leaders of the sedition are to be hanged, naming them each, the nobleman Fourneaux first among them. The others will be repatriated.

Grumbles and murmurs from the crowd. Unrest. Some of the men go to speak with him. Laudonnière cocks his head, allowing their petitions. He nods and nods, as if considering mercies. A generous ruler.

Yes, he decides. Yes. They may put the condemned to the firing squad instead of the noose. Yes, they may hang their bodies high along the river's banks, a feast for the vultures and crows.

38

Altamaha River, Day 3

Hunter feels the tug of the umbilical as they swim. Lawton's long black fins cycle beneath the surface, pulling him along. He knows a flashlight would illuminate a galaxy of white-fired eyes along the banks, like monsters in the dark of a closet or under the bed. Tethered to Lawton he feels safer. Anyone would. A vessel towed in the wake of a destroyer, with no bearing of its own. No control. Without thinking, he pulls his dive-knife and cuts the line.

Lawton rolls over in the water.

"The line break?"

"Must have."

On the bank Lawton looks at the length of parachute cord, the white yarn-guts spilling out at the cut. He looks at Hunter.

"You cut it."

It's almost a question.

"I didn't like being roped in like that."

"It was for your safety."

"I don't need to be put on a leash."

"It was just a buddy-line, Hunter."

"Then why do you give a shit?"

Lawton looks down at the cord, frayed in his hand. He shakes his head, unable to understand, and Hunter feels a pang of regret for cutting it. He starts to reach out, to touch his brother's shoulder, but Lawton has already turned into the bush, disappearing into the shadow of the bridge.

They hike through the swampland dark. The concrete supports loom like monoliths, ruins of a disappeared civilization, each clasped in a dark harness of vines and roots. Moonlight falls broken through the canopy of cypress and tupelo, lying before them like shattered glass. Hunter keeps expecting it to crunch under his feet. They find an old maintenance ladder and climb back up to the long road of leaves.

Hunter's knee hardly hurts now. Sometimes the pain will rise and rise, peaking like a mountain inside him, like cold screaming stone, and then he will be outside of it, numbed, his knee pulsing like a tiny beacon at the bottom of a sea thick and dark as vein blood. In the hospital, the heavy opiates streaming through the IVs felt almost familiar, a dark tide that floated him over the pain. Sometimes, swinging the ax at practice, his shoulders will be balled with acid, his forearms corded with burning fuse, and then he will be out of himself, gone, and the block of pine will fall white-hearted at his feet like a surprise.

He watches Lawton marching down the long tunnel of trees, where railcars once screamed. His brother has made a career of pain. The men he ranks among, they are the elite, the tip of the spear. They can run and swim and climb for hours, tireless as machines, and shoot with lethal precision when they stop. They can jump from aircraft at the edge of space, the earth curved beneath them, and land in fields one-tenth the size of a city block. They can navigate underwater at night. But most of all they are the great pain-takers, their kind culled in the wake of cold and privation, endless miles of ocean swims and beach runs, scalded lungs and torn feet, vomit, bullhorns spraying abuse. Miseries of every kind, which words cannot wrangle. Pain that goes on for weeks, months, until the few who remain are scooped up like hard little stones on the Pacific beach.

Hunter thinks of asking Lawton how he copes, if it's the same for him. But you rarely talk about that kind of pain, he knows. It isn't as therapeutic as it is for other trauma. The power is in the silence, he thinks. The brotherhood of endurance.

He doesn't open his mouth.

They make camp at the end of the trestle, elevated high over the river. Across the water, the lights of Altamaha Park burn in the night, a city in miniature. Shadows move in tents and trailer windows, romances played out by lantern or flashlight. Stifled giggles, animal grunts. Now and again a broken bottle, an empty can crushed underfoot.

They have brought up their sleeping bags from the boats. They lie head to head along the old rail-bed, staring up. Lawton tugs on his beard.

"It could be they're cooking meth downriver. Back on one of them backwater sloughs."

Hunter breathes in, exhales through his teeth.

"You mean these Russians?"

"*Slavs,*" says Lawton. "We don't know they're Russian. Slavic accent, they could be Poles, Serbs, Czechs." He is counting them off on his hand. "Ukrainians, Bulgarians, Slovaks. Bosniaks."

Hunter rolls over.

"Who gives a shit what they are? There's people whose job it is to worry about it, and we aren't them."

Lawton shakes his head.

"This river ain't the same as it was, brother. I don't like it."

"Because there's Slavs on it?"

"That ain't what I mean and you damn well know it."

"Things change, Lawton. Hell, we learned in biology your skin replaces itself every twenty-seven days. You ain't even laying in the same hide you were a month ago."

Lawton touches his forearm, his thumb finding the frog.

"Something ain't right, brother. I know it."

"Ain't right about what?"

Lawton's thumb covers the tattoo, pressing it like a button.

"About Daddy's death."

Hunter glances down his body, the black bag of ashes sitting at his feet like a bag lunch.

"He's ash now, Lawton. You got to let it go. Let *him* go. That's what we came here to do."

He looks back at his brother, the top of his head as he lies in his mummy bag. He's getting a bald spot, Hunter sees. A white dime amid the stew of red. Lawton's head rotates slightly and he spits—*thwop*—a thick gobbet that arcs through the steel trusses, glistening, tail skittering like something that could grow legs and croak.

"Letting go," he says. "Never been too good at that."

Hunter wakes in the night. The rails are thundering beneath him, the bridge groaning in pain. He looks frantically for the midnight engine, the white ball of power come boring out of the darkness. Nothing. Not yet. He looks for Lawton. He is lying athwart the tracks, asleep. Hunter shakes him, pinches him. Slaps his face. His brother is dark-browed, too stubborn to wake. His body is snared in vines, Hunter sees, roots the size of man-arms or snakes. He is tied to the tracks like a damsel, a witch at the stake.

"Lawton. Lawton!"

Hunter tears at the roots; his fingers bleed. It is like great muscles clutch his brother, thousand-year arms skinned with bark. Hunter looks for his ax. There it is, leaning against the trussworks, the handle bone-colored in the darkness. He takes it up. The world flares white, and he can feel a heat rising against his back. A star, iron-tailed, is screaming down the tracks, an event that can't be stopped. An extinction. He straddles his brother and raises the ax, tears streaking his face. He is looking for the place to strike. The vines are like an armor, a history that binds him, and Hunter wonders if they will bleed. Lawton's eyes are open now, his beard a ring of fire around his face. He is grinning, his eyes full of light, as he looks at the risen ax.

"Don't," he says.

39

Fort Caroline, April 1565

The day has come. The food is gone, the storehouse empty. Le Moyne stands on his bluff over the river, pen idle. He is watching the carrion birds coil black-winged over the executed mutineers, their ruined bodies hung from a crude scaffolding erected on the riverbank. Despite himself, Le Moyne envies those birds. At least they have something to eat.

He drops his head and starts down the slope, joining the others as they work along the river. They are tearing palmetto plants from the earth, their hands red-torn from the barbed stalks. The ground lies cratered in their wake. The roots are something, anything, to boil and eat. A soldier with a pitted face, shirtless, is preaching the evils of Utina as he works. Utina the great deceiver, who has led them only upon paths of folly in the west. Utina, who has made of them his handmaidens, aiming their guns upon his own ambitions. Utina, who has brought them, finally, to this ignominious end.

"The savage cannot be trusted." The man tears a root from the ground. "They are an impish breed, in want of souls."

The others nod, grunting in agreement. Le Moyne says nothing, focusing on the work.

"They are godless," says the man. "No higher than beasts."

Yes, say the men. *Verily. In truth.*

"Liars and connivers," says the man. He casts a glance at Le Moyne, still silent. "They have hearts as black as this earth." He raises a clump in hand. "What say you, man?"

Le Moyne grips the barbed shaft of the plant before him, gritting his teeth.

"I have seen their hearts," he says. "And they are red."

"You have missed my point, sir."

Le Moyne yanks on his plant, the roots popping from their foundations.

"Perhaps."

They pick berries, tiny and dark, that upset the bowels of many. They hunt what game they have not already killed or driven from the lands about the fort. In the fields they dig for the roots of the sorrel plant. Men gather fishbones from the refuse piles and grind them into meal. Others, the entrepreneurial of the garrison, have hoarded a small store of acorns, which they grind into meal and sell at twenty sous a plate.

The second week of the famine, Le Moyne accompanies a hunting party three leagues upstream, seeking the muddy lagoon where a legion of *lagartos* congregate in the morning hours. They are arrayed like stone-carved basilisks, absorbing the heat. Lord d'Ottigni leads them down the gangplank, his wrecked face gleaming in the sun. They go barefoot, armed only with pikes and sharpened staves—their guns cannot penetrate the armored hides. They stomp ankle-deep through the mud, emboldened by hunger. The monsters come awake before them, as from dreamless stone, turning their yellow jaws toward the bare ankles of the men, the white calves. Their heavy bellies rattle with threat. Le Moyne can feel the mud quivering between his toes.

They surround a huge lizard that curls itself against them, hissing at the ring of whittled points. They are trying to mimic the native hunters, who ram pine spears into the mouths of the beasts, turning the crushing force of the jaws to their advantage. The long rows of teeth lodge in the soft wood, sealing shut the mouth, whereupon the savages overturn the beast and attack the soft belly with spears and arrows and clubs.

They move closer, closer, their weapons trembling. Le Moyne can almost taste the tender white meat of the tail, like a treasure beneath the green mountain of hide. The man beside him inches nearer, his mouth open, his tongue out. Their eyes are fixed only on the head, the eighty-some teeth snaggled like crude daggers, when the tail comes wheeling around, a giant's club that strikes with a sickening crack. The man beside Le Moyne falls screaming to the ground, his knee buckled inward.

"Attaquez-les!" cries d'Ottigni, and they rush the beast, jabbing their weapons into the armored hide. The tail reverses direction, snapping and throwing spears like so much kindling, and men fall screaming, clutching their hands and wrists. Several of the spears strike home, but now they are turned upon their masters, jutting from the monster's hide like spines or quills. Le Moyne leaps away as the haft of his own pike, wrenched free of his hands, flashes past his jaw. Men are scrambling in the muck, the beast whirling and roaring before them. Lord d'Ottigni, sneering, draws his sword with a sounding ring.

"Slut-mother of Christ!"

He leaps between the wooden spines with surprising alacrity, straddling the beast between his knees, as if he would ride its spine, and drives his sword two-handed through the base of its skull. The lizard, skewered to the earth, shivers and quakes, dying, and the men stand stunned, as if witnessing the awful work of some demon or god. The lieutenant's face is red-halved, disgusted, as he rises from the animal's back, eyeing the men.

"Espèce de couilles molles."

You of soft balls.

They cannot lift the carcass, so they rope the neck and drag it open-jawed and web-footed to the boat, cutting a bloody wake through the muck. They sail home to butcher the kill, the injured men sprawled on the deck, groaning their agonies to the sun.

Still they continue to waste, wrecked by their own bones, their skin stretched ever tighter over the joints and spurs of their underpinnings. Their faces are sunken like the revenants of old tales, sallow and cave-eyed. Their jaws hang unhinged; they mouth-breathe at even the lightest work. The Indians, seeing them, will not approach the fort. They can see the desperation in the Frenchmen's eyes, Le Moyne knows. The savage hunger. Already there have been perverse acts, natives killed, food stolen from their huts. Soldiers roving the country in starving bands, daggers winking, tapers hissing in the night.

The sun grows hotter, the world blooms green. Tools lie idle, earthworks crumble. Gaps open in the palisade. Of the Apalatci mountains there is nothing now. No one speaks the name, like that of a traitor they wish to expunge from memory, history. A collective shame best forgotten. May comes and the crops have not yet ripened in the fields. There is no corn nor beans nor acorns in the villages. The Indians sell them fish from their cypress dugouts, making the white men wade out to them, far out of sight of the fort. Their prices are extravagant. Soldiers sneak downstream to meet them, returning without boots or hats, knives or shirts. They trade their armor and swords, their trinkets from home. Le Moyne sees a man return almost naked, a single large fish clutched like a silver-skinned babe in his arms.

Still he sings his Psalms in the afternoons. His voice is shaky and weak; his own ribs seize him like talons. The words seem empty to him, said so often they are devoid of meaning. They have become but patterned mouth-sounds, no more comprehensible than the savage incantations of the *jarua*. He kneels upon the riverbank, watches the current slipping through his fingers. Only one line runs again and again through his mind, rote as a beggar's.

Give us this day our daily bread.
Give us this day our daily bread.
Give us this day our daily bread.

In the mornings he fights the temptation to climb one of the trees, to perch like some pale and wingless bird among the others, hoping dawn will reveal the fleet of ships that will save them. He is hollowed out, a vacancy full only of want. The art has fled from his hands, his heart. Meal and roots he cups to his mouth, handfuls of river. He looks at his reflection in the water. A creature unrecognizable almost, wavering like a spirit. Is this the monster he sought? The wonder at the end of the earth?

A night in May, a month after the food runs out. Le Moyne is drawn to a crowd along the northern wall, a half-circle of men huddled in all positions.

Standing, squatting, sunk down on all fours in the dirt. All of them watching. It is a gray-haired bitch brought over on one of the ships, whelping, her great body quivering as the pups come curling from her womb in their glistening cauls, furred already with their eyes mashed closed. A man with pointed mustaches presides, his beard grown scraggly down his neck. He is taking trades. Bronze and knives, tiny sacks of meal. Bundled sheaves of sorrel root, dirt still clung in the hairs. Men jab their hands toward him, showing what they have. Voices wrestle for attention. When a deal is struck, his assistant hands the whelp still dripping to the buyer, and the buyer scurries into the darkness, hunched over his prize, tearing open the caul like a gift.

That night Le Moyne lies on his bed, staring up at the thatch of palms.

"I saw a man selling a litter of puppies tonight."

La Caille places his hands behind his head.

"Pour manger?"

"Oui." Le Moyne breathes in. "I did not know whether to cut the man down, or check my own purse for fifty sous."

"You would not have done such a thing, Le Moyne. I know you."

"No, my friend. But I fear the day I will."

40

Altamaha River, Day 4

They leave Altamaha Park at dawn. The old trestles crouch above the mist, the graffiti on the swing span barely visible. There are the names of lovers and boys' clubs, a cross-eyed smiley face, an RIP for this person and that. The location itself is an honor, like a highway overpass. The risk and trouble involved.

The water has a new urge to it, grumbling against the stone piers of the bridge. A new force. It is ridged like bark. They let it carry them on, the stamp of civilization soon swallowed in the trees behind them. The RVs disappear, the tents and trucks. No mark of man, nothing to tell them they are above the river's power. The mist glows white-gold as the sun strikes it, prettiest as it burns away. Lawton has his sunglasses on.

"You really think it was Uncle King you heard the other night?"

"I do."

"You just knew it was him, huh? Sure you weren't dreaming?"

"What if I was? Paddling upstream won't get us real far."

Lawton squints, tugging on his beard.

"That time we went to Disney World, didn't you have some dream the week before?"

Hunter draws his paddle from the water.

"All I remember is Cinderella's Castle all covered in snow, like a giant iceberg."

"Then that white hurricane come through, took Daddy's boat."

Hunter nods.

"Yeah, I guess so. I don't know, probably just a coincidence."

Lawton is quiet a moment. His face looks soft, young. He hooks a finger in his beard, opens his mouth twice before any words come out.

"Tell me something. You feel anything when he died? Like before you knew?"

Hunter dips his paddle back in the water, the current curling around the blade.

"Daddy? Not that I remember. Why, did you?"

Lawton shakes his head.

"I don't know," he says. "Maybe. We'd been operating up near the Pakistani border, going after an HVT—High Value Target—this Taliban bigwig liked to carve people up. Real piece of shit. We spent three days watching the hut of this widow he liked to bend over the well. Well, he never showed, so we footed it out to the extraction point. On the bird, everybody was nodding off. We hadn't hardly slept for seventy-two hours." Lawton's cheek bulges. He toys with the tobacco pouched under his gum. "Out of nowhere I got this burning in my arm, like from the ink, like that frog was gonna leap from my skin, and I had this sudden feeling I'd been hit. Like a cold arrow right through my chest." He palms his heart, as if to show the entry wound. "I turned around, checked to make sure a stray round hadn't come through the fuselage, some goatherder's AK. My heart was going a million miles an hour, right up in my throat. I couldn't hardly breathe. Thought I was having a heart attack or something. The guys saw me pawing myself like a crazy person. I told 'em it was a cramp, too much heavy benching the week before. Told myself the same. The next week, I got back from another long-range patrol to find out Daddy had been killed. I looked back at the operational records. It was the same day I'd had that . . . attack."

"They say it's sometimes like that."

"They say a lot of shit. Still, it kinda makes me think of that Shakespeare quote you said. 'There's more in the world' and all that."

"You think you were close enough to the old man to feel him go?"

"I don't know, brother." Lawton looks at his boat. "If fucking somebody makes you close to them, what does beating them do?"

Hunter thinks of the big knuckles of his father's hands. His eyes sting.

"This Taliban piece of shit, you ever get him?"

Lawton inhales, his chest swelling with pressure.

"We got him. Too late we did. Somebody had found our tracks near that widow's hut. He thought she'd dropped the dime on him."

"What did he do?"

"The red tulip."

"Which is what?"

"I'd rather not talk about it, brother. Suffice to say she saw a lot of her own meat, her own insides, before she died."

"That's some evil shit, man."

"That's just some."

Hunter shakes his head.

"I don't care what they say, there's people that deserve a bullet."

Lawton picks up his paddle.

"Easy to say," he says. "Harder to do."

The river is nearly straight here, broad and strong. The mist is gone; the surface burns like hammered tin. Hunter thinks of Uncle King out there, seeking something people have glimpsed a thousand years and never caught. The river winds and Lawton points to a creek mouth on the right bank.

"Alligator Congress. Good place to look."

Hunter feels a prick of fear in his belly, like a tiny knife, but paddles on. They enter the mouth of the creek, and soon the narrow banks widen into a backwater lagoon, an expanse of shallows and mudflats and half-submerged trees. Their father took them here once when they were little, just before dawn. He shined a flashlight across the flats, igniting a whole universe of red eyes, floating like planets before a man-made sun.

"Indians used to hunt gators here," he told them. "With nothing but spears and clubs and balls that drug the ground like Santa sacks."

"Nuh uh."

"Yes huh," said their father. "Why you think they wore them loincloths? Them Indian balls wouldn't fit in no tighty-whities, I can tell you that."

Boy-Lawton stared at the red galaxy of eyes, silent. Entranced. In his mind, Hunter knew, he was clad only in animal skins, plunging the cold stone of a spear into an alligator's heart. Not a one of those eyes deigned to blink or look away, and now it was the old man who seemed rapt by their gaze.

"Confident fuckers," he said. "Cain't blame them, though. They been here longer'n us. Any luck, we won't take them with us when we go."

"We're going away?"

The old man spat.

"Sure. What don't? Hell, this river used to be lined with trees twice this tall, stalked by dinosaurs the size of school buses. Some say that's what the Altamaha-ha is. A dinosaur slipped through the cracks of time."

"Will we slip through the cracks?"

Hunter remembers his father looking a long time at them, searching their eyes for signs.

"You two might. Me, I'm pretty sure I'm fucked."

The water here is shallow. Hunter poles his paddle to the bottom, testing the depth. In the big river you know alligators might be down there, many leagues below. Here they are likely just a few feet below the surface, lying still as old cypress logs, some as big as your boat. Lawton points them around a grove of cypress and tupelo, and the mudflats shine before them like something polished, an ancient nation presenting itself to the morning sun. On them lie a few reptiles, heavy-bellied and somnolent, positioned like a museum exhibit. Just the right amount of randomness, of specimens large and small facing this way and that. These remnants of what once ruled the earth. Hunter imagines his own species after some similar fate, tiny pink pygmies made to live at the mercy of saurian gods.

Lawton sets his paddle across his lap and leans on it, elbows out. He squints at the biggest gator on the bank, staring it down. The big reptile's mouth is open, as if smiling.

"You're a ugly fucker, ain't you?"

The alligator is motionless, flies jeweling its back. It might be molded from rubber like the ones from the tourist shops.

"If you're looking for a fight," says Hunter, "that one's too big."

"I ain't looking to wrestle him, brother. I just wanted to see what was in those eyes."

"What do you see?"

Lawton straightens, relaxing his stare.

"Nothing, brother. A stone killer, like the rest."

The alligators watch them pass, their eyes so like alien worlds. Their teeth are visible outside their jaws, like they're grinning every second.

"Lazy mothers," says Hunter.

"It warms up, they'll go to work," says Lawton. He looks around, scanning the flats and shallows. "I figure old Altie must be a loner. But if he's got any friends, these would be them."

"He's not feeling social today, I guess."

"Nope, his hunter neither."

"Maybe we ought to just find your film crew buddies again, see if they might know where he's at."

"Shit, them fuckers couldn't find their assholes with a garden hose."

They paddle out of the lagoon and back into the big river, brown and swollen under the climbing sun. Hunter looks back. The alligators are still fixed in place, heads up, worshiping the sun. He looks at Lawton.

"How you think old Dill hauled that boat of his up out of the slough?"

"I was wondering the same myself. I figure he must of built the pilings first, then floated it in during the spring flood. Either that or he brought a crane in there on a barge, but I don't see how they'd get it under the bridge."

"You ever seen that German movie with the steamship in the jungle?"

"What do you think?"

"This rubber baron—in Peru, I think—he wants to build an opera house in the Amazon."

Lawton grunts.

"Well, he finds a parcel that'll make him rich. Only problem is, it's on a river that's blocked by impassable rapids. But there's a second river that flows parallel, and the two rivers get within a few hundred yards of each other at one point. So he goes out there to haul this three-hundred-ton, three-story steamer from one river to the next, over this big fucking hill in the jungle. Forty-degree grade. Crazy thing is, they really did it for the movie."

Lawton straightens. Now this is interesting.

"Some portage. How they do it?"

"They build capstans on terraces cut up and down the hill, manned by an army of natives, and just drag the motherfucker with all these hawsers. Plus they rig pulleys to the steamer's paddle gears somehow."

"So this dude builds his opera house?"

"Not exactly. Indian chief thinks they've angered the river gods, defying nature and that. He cuts the ship loose from its mooring while everybody's asleep, and it goes running the rapids anyway, sliding sideways, smashing into walls and rocks. The ship survives, though, all battered and listing, and the baron makes enough to hire a traveling opera troupe to play on the deck."

"Made out better than Daddy, I guess." Lawton sniffs and wipes his nose with the back of his hand. "I guess we should of asked old Dill how he done it, there after he got so talkative."

Hunter shrugs, watching his paddle.

"By that point, I think he would of told us he used a herd of woolly mammoths to haul it out."

Lawton frowns.

"What, you think he was bullshitting us?"

"I think he was trying to keep from eating a cockroach."

Lawton huffs, his muscles rumbling under his vest.

"See how that helped him."

Hunter doesn't say anything. Doesn't want to fight. Instead he leans back in the cockpit, lifts his face to the sun. He lets it bore through his skin, warm his blood like one of the reptiles on the banks. A creature of old time. When he opens his eyes, Lawton has his head turned over his shoulder, and he's grinning big. Past him a johnboat floats along the bank, full of men in khaki shirts wielding sound-booms and cameras like clumsy weapons.

"Lookee-who," says Lawton.

41

Hiram Loggins motors upstream in the battered johnboat lent him some decade and a half ago. Given him, more like, by Annabelle. Not the first of her gifts in the dark hours of that night, memories that ring inside him still. He is hollow but for that, her name banging around inside him like a pocket-gun left in the dryer. It bangs on his heart, his ribs, the floor of his gut. Sometimes it goes off. His fists shoot through the smoky bars, the riverfront docks, the midnight decks of other men's ships. The county jail where he's in and out.

His boat is gone. It was never found, nor the two tied alongside it during the storm. The lockbox he kept hidden behind the bulkhead—lost too. His life savings sunk like a treasure in the coastal waters, unsalvageable. The paper surely sogged away into a kind of ash, bitten and spit out by wads of baitfish. When the floodwaters receded, he went down to the docks and found the mooring lines still tied to the cleats, the ropes clean-cut, as by knife or ax. He had insurance—the bank required it—but the payout was insufficient. He found himself hugely upside down because of the interest, with no cash to pay the balance.

A month after the storm, he came across the owners of the two other lost boats in the cut-and-shoot bar off Highway 99. They were laughing together over puddles of spilled beer, temples of downturned shot glasses. He ignored them, went straight to the bar for a tallboy and shot of rye. Still he could hear them whispering behind him, snickering. They were big men, sun-spotted and scarred, with iron-gray beards and muddy tattoos. Men who hadn't had his luck in seasons past. Who had been waiting for such a storm, perhaps, their insurance pumped up to snuff.

"Hey, Loggins," said one. "Sit for a drink."

Hiram didn't turn around, leaning on his elbows as he waited for his drinks. He needed that streak of oaken fire, that frosty gold to put it out. He looked at them in the mirror over the bar.

"No thanks, I feel like standing tonight."

"Ain't you been standing all day? On what, old Mackey's boat?"

The other man sniggered.

The bartender set down the tallboy, ice-cold, and began pouring the shot.

"Two more," Hiram told him.

"Man's got to insure his assets, this day and age," one of the men started telling the other. "It don't pay to do one of them high innerest deals."

Hiram took a long pull of his tallboy, then set it back on its napkin. He took the three shots of rye in the triangle of his hands, like pool balls before the break, and walked to the table where the two men were sitting.

"What's this?" said one.

Hiram set the shots on the table.

"I just wanted to thank you," he said. "For everything you done for me."

The two men eyed one another. The neat little shooters quivered on the table, asking to be drunk.

"Well now," said one, licking his lips, "I can't say we done much."

"More than you know," said Hiram. "Listen, I want to make a toast."

He took up his whiskey and propped his elbow on the table, holding the shot glass in the setting of his fingers like an amber crystal. He watched the men's hands crawl across the table, taking up the whiskeys despite themselves. He looked them in the eye, one after the next, serious as Sunday school.

"To clean slates," he said.

The men clinked their glasses against his own.

"Clean slates," they said.

They threw back their heads to shoot the rye. Hiram set down his own shooter, undrunk, and drove the glasses into their teeth with his fists. The men fell gagging from their chairs, rolling on the beery floor, wailing through broken mouths. He watched one of them spit up his front teeth like breakfast cereal, glopped in milky blood. He took up his shooter and threw it back, a long rail of fire down his throat.

The Sheriff gave him three weeks in county for that. He didn't make it official. Everybody knew what the insurance companies didn't. Still, it didn't help for long. Hiram was never a brittle man. His insides had always been good. But something went out of him with that boat. His dreams left him. He could no longer see his future. He thought a vision would come to him. A path. He hunted for it in evenings along the river, among the great old trees, the virgin cypress centuries old. He waited for his skin to burn, the signs that clad him. Nothing. He saw Annabelle on the moonless nights. He slunk across the marshes like the dirty thing he was, hating himself, only to grasp her cool white legs. It didn't help. She would never be his. Nor did the whiskey help, the fights, the two little boys growing up loyal and strong.

It has been three years now, and he is headed upstream. It's Sunday morning. In the bottom of the boat sits a cement block, a pile of heavy anchor chain.

All his life. All his life he has felt the blackness lapping at him, hungry. All his life he has been trying to rise, thrashing and tearing for light, for escape. He is so tired now. Below him lie the sunken boats and drowned dreams, the ghosts who walk the river's bottom—one of which he helped to put there. Lately the memory comes rising unbidden, and he feels the fingers of that day sliding through his hair, twisting, forcing him down, down, down. Into blackness.

He rounds a bend and there stands the railroad bridge at Everett City, a behemoth of iron and stone over which the great smokeless engines still cross like toys. The trusses shine under the morning sun, a skeleton-work of iron, and below them something he never expected: a maze of white pleasure boats anchored at every angle, silent, gathered like a flock of birds come down on the river. People are sitting on their bows, feet dangling in the water, looking up. Hiram looks, too: a white man stands on the bridge itself, high over the water, his cassock-draped arms held out like wings. A little coal-black child stands on either side of him, clinging to his vestments. His adopted children. His voice booms across the water:

"'I will say of the Lord, he is my refuge and my fortress. My God, in him will I trust.'"

"Shit," says Hiram. The boats stretch from one side of the river to the other.

"'He shall cover thee with his feathers, and under his wings shalt thou trust. His truth shall be thy shield and buckler.'"

Hiram starts threading his way through the boats, maneuvering around anchor-ropes and silver pontoons. "Goddamned menace to navigation." The people smile at him, whole families with eyes like dope-smokers and dressed for church. He frowns at them.

"'Thou shalt not be afraid for the terror by night, nor for the arrow that flieth by day.'"

Before him a deckboat of people in their Sunday best, swaying like cattails in the wind.

"'A thousand shall fall at thy side, and ten thousand at thy right hand. But it shall not come nigh thee.'"

Yes, say the deckboaters. *Yes.*

"Goddammit," says Hiram. He has seen plenty *come nigh,* no shield nor feathers in sight. He revs the little outboard, going around the deckboat in a snarl of whitewater.

"'Thou shalt tread upon the lion and adder. The young lion and the dragon shalt thou trample under feet.'"

Hiram can feel the words coming down on him, heavy and sure, trying to push their way through his skin. Words of power and might, which have done shit-all for him so far. Maybe in a world of dragons and lions, of make-believe. He spits.

"'He shall call upon me, and I will answer him. I will be with him in trouble. I will deliver him and—'"

Hiram kinks his away around the last of the boats and cranks open the throttle, an angry wail beneath the hollows of the span. He flees it all. The man, the bridge, the secret stored in the white belly of scar on his palm.

He is a mile upriver when he cuts the engine. He's heard something, inside him or out, like a gnashing of iron teeth.

A train is coming down the line.

"Oh God," he says. "The bridge."

He rips the motor to life and tears a circle in the river, racing back the way he came.

42

Fort Caroline, May 1565

Le Moyne inhales, trying to still his hand. The stylus is trembling, as if he were about to do evil with it. He is only trying to draw the scenes he witnessed in the west. The shaman writhing upon the shield, the battle on the hill, the corpses dismembered by cleaver and knife. The events, chained with all those others before them, that brought them to this extremity. Alone and friendless, unable to feed themselves, the green enormity of the land all about them like a sea. They have driven away the Indians who might help them and failed to provision themselves against such want. They have waited for ships to come that never did.

"Hunger is a wound," La Caille tells him one night. "But it does not bleed. Rather it swallows up everything in itself. Compassion, decency. Even God. You must retain your purpose, Le Moyne, or you will become like those dogs out there. And die like one." He throws his hand toward the dark of the fort, the boar tusks rattling at his throat.

"Draw," he commands.

Le Moyne works his stylus across the paper, bleeding his memories onto the page. He works to recall every detail, every tendon that rippled beneath the shaman's skin, every stripe of muscle that clad the three-tailed giant that Lord d'Ottigni killed, every speck that bloodied the cleaver used to part limb from trunk in the wake of battle. He leaves these images like a gift upon the paper, a story perhaps to caution those who come after, who might find these pages leather-bound in the hall of whichever Indian king scavenges them first. He feels himself in a race to finish. The others watch him with slackened jaws, confused. This man who draws as if his life depended on it. They come to watch.

That night, Le Moyne lies on his bed looking at his own hand. Every vein is visible, blue as rivers in a desert of thinnest white flesh, of bony ridge and knuckled hill, a whole country on the back side of his hand—this strange device that pours out new lands still.

"Tell me, La Caille, what is your own purpose in all this?"

La Caille has his dagger out. He is cleaning his fingernails, spreading his hand wide to critique his work. Now he curls his fingers beneath his eyes, rubbing his thumb across the nails to test their sharpness.

"I may yet get us out of this mess."

Laudonnière stands on the parade ground before his men. His cheeks look stove-in, his eyes tiny in their hollows, twitching like prey animals afraid of the light. The slack of his tunic belt is long as a tail. Lately he has been sick, confined to bed.

He rises only for his chambermaid, say the men.

Yea, that she may have something hard on which to sit.

He is standing slightly canted, a post set errantly in the ground. Only his chest looks full, swelled by breath or bombast. La Caille steps forward from the audience.

"Sir, you know that we honor your judgment as our commander, a position well merited, as evidenced by your conduct through our many travails—"

"There is no need for preamble, Captain La Caille. You may state yourself plainly."

La Caille nods.

"Sir, I fear we are falling victim to the fate of previous expeditions, believing ships will come that never do. Perhaps there is another war at home, or a storm has beset the fleet. Whatever the reason, we must work toward our own salvation now instead of waiting for it to arrive by sea. If we do not, we will perish within these walls before the year is out. This is not only my belief, but the belief of your men."

Laudonnière exhales, his chest falling. He frowns at his boots, nodding as if to a pipe melody. Such a strange sight, thinks Le Moyne, to see him so unhackled. Amenable. A humility found, perhaps, at the pointy ends of his bones. Finally he raises his head.

"I must cling yet to the faith that our ships will come. To do any less would be to doubt our very destiny in this land, in the will of God to spread his name upon our lips." He sighs, a scraping of stones in the throat. "But I believe we are prudent in preparing for ourselves some other means of returning home."

There are nods from the crowd, grunts of agreement.

"But what would you propose, La Caille? The *Breton* cannot carry us all."

"No, sir. But if the shipwrights were to add two additional decks, I have done the figures and it would be close. Plus we have the caravel now. Between the two vessels, there should be space for all."

La Caille does not add what he's confided in Le Moyne. He estimates the space sufficient only after their number has dwindled in the coming weeks. For men are beginning to die now, the first found unwaking in his bed three days ago, mouth frozen in final gasp, skin stretched like a death shroud over a weeks-old cadaver. Then another two this morning, lost to the eternal slumber. Already there are whispers over the bodies, what should become of them.

What sustenance they might provide. Does life not spring from death? Is this not the order of the world?

The seller of whelps: "Tell me, Le Moyne, do the Spanish not eat the flesh of Christ?"

"Ask again, man, and I will drain the wine from your throat."

"And would you not thirst to drink it?"

Laudonnière looks out across the assembled men, his head tilted as if making calculations. Perhaps he knows the secret of La Caille's mathematics. Finally he nods.

"It is a good proposal, La Caille. I will call together our artificers and shipwrights to draw up plans. We will begin work on the *Breton* immediately."

Le Moyne can feel the men come alive at this. A future. A hope. But La Caille raises his hands, settling them, his face cast grim.

"Thank you, sir. But let us not forget that it will take weeks to ready the ships. We must secure sufficient provisions to stead us not only through the work, but the voyage that follows."

Before Laudonnière can reply, Lord d'Ottigni steps from a group of officers. His half-face gleams like newly hardened wax.

"Sir, the savages extort us, prey upon us in our time of weakness. They treat us as if we are not but savages ourselves. Give me fifty able men and I shall bring them to heel. The steel at their throat, they will grant us whatever provisions we require."

There are murmurs of assent from the crowd, the rattling of swords.

Laudonnière straightens, his eyes no longer shy in their wells. They glare.

"We will resort to no such means. If we sour our relations with the natives, we abandon our duty to France. We swore each of us, gladly, to imperil ourselves in service to our king. We will not break that oath at any cost. Frankly, I am surprised you would even suggest it."

Lord d'Ottigni retreats back into the officers' ranks. His scarred face is frozen, unblushed. A stormlike darkness settles into its features. Laudonnière clasps his hands behind his back. He is taller now, in command. His doublet rounds across the chest.

"I will lead a foraging party up the coast myself, commanding one of the barques." He looks from man to man. "Place your faith in me, you men. I will secure the provisions we need. And recall your oaths. We are sons of France, the legacy of our nation in this land. We are to comport ourselves as such, leaving the name of our king untarnished should our very lives be forfeit. But know this: my own gut will wither before I let starve the men under my command."

It is a good speech. The men give *aye*s and happy grunts. They stamp the earth with their dirty, boot-shorn feet. Their commander will place his own life before them. He will undertake the most perilous and vital of all enterprises. He will fill their hurting bellies himself.

Le Moyne looks closely at the man, trying to discern whether the glow of success is upon him in this venture, the favor of God. If it is not, they will soon be but a nation of ghost and bone, the dream of a king buried in alien ground.

43

Altamaha River, Day 4

The producer man has on his floppy hat, the strap cinched tight under his chin. His cheeks bloom fat and red, as if by garrote, his jaw bulged fat with a jawbreaker or gumball. He is jabbing his finger at a log drifting downstream. The tumorous end vees snoutlike as it comes.

"That one, that's the one! Fucking Christ, it's perfect."

The cameramen are fumbling with their devices, twisting off lenses and flipping switches, their hands trembling as they try to capture the shot in time. The producer makes a camera frame of his fingers, the L-shape of one hand inverted over the other. He squints one eye through the rectangular portal, tracking the log.

"Yes, that's it. Perfect for a commercial break. The Zeigarnik effect. Keep them enticed. Is this the glimpse we await?"

They are floating in the shadow of an overarching cypress, lying in ambush for whatever suspicious piece of driftwood or debris comes floating downriver. Above them rises the pale shoulder of Clark's Bluff, the high woods groomed here or there for the sometime placement of tents and campfires.

Lawton raises a hand to hail them.

"Ahoy there!" He has a double-stacked grin on his face, big as a truck.

Four faces turn to look, long-jawed. The cameras drop slightly, and the log slips past unfilmed. The producer man looks at Lawton, at the passing log, then back at Lawton. He is trembling, reddening like he might burst. He jabs his finger at the log, jabs and jabs.

"Keep filming, goddammit! If you miss this shot so help me God, I will rip off your heads and shit Butterfingers down your necks."

The crew, hunched beneath his words, swing their cameras toward the fleeing length of oak, but it's too late.

The producer man stomps the deck.

"God damn me. God damn me to hell!"

Lawton slides in alongside the johnboat. He watches squinty-eyed as the log drifts away, whistles.

"Shame. Damn shame. You really could of fooled some them reality TV fools with that one."

The producer man has his hands on his hips. An apron of sweat darkens his shirt.

"You son of a bitch, I'll have you know I called the sheriff's department on you."

"So they told me," says Lawton. He yawns into the sun.

The man's face swells an ever darker red. Hunter feels the instinct to look away, like he would from an overinflated balloon.

"I'll be pressing charges through the appropriate channels as soon as we're done filming."

"Oh come now, wasn't nothing but a love-tap."

"It was *assault.*"

"No." Lawton rests a hand on the gunwale of the johnboat. "*That* wasn't assault."

The man takes a deep breath and looks up at the trees, revealing three brown lines of grime lodged in the fatty folds of his neck. After a moment his chest clucks, in laugh or growl. He looks down again, and his face is changed. Lighter, somehow.

"I'm beginning to think you are something sent by my enemies. A redhaired android programmed to fuck my ass."

Lawton grins. Now they are talking.

"That sounds about right."

The man pushes his floppy hat off the back of his head.

"Not if you're me, son—" He catches himself at the word, but Lawton only smiles.

"Listen." He taps the gunwale of the boat. "Unless your enemy is Admiral of the Pacific Fleet, I don't think we got a problem. All I'm looking for is a little information."

The man palms the balding dome of his head, strangely pale and tender over the red-weathered rest of him.

"Information about what?"

"About your boy Uncle King that's hunting the Altamaha-ha."

"Ah," says the man. "Him."

"We need to talk to him."

"So do I, Christ knows. So do I."

"You know where to find him?"

"If I did, do you think we'd be filming shots of driftwood at the spot of a forty-year-old sighting of this goddamn monster he's after?"

Hunter speaks up. "People saw the Altamaha-ha here?"

The producer nods. "That's correct, in 1970. Two brothers were fishing from a houseboat, using a mixture of oatmeal and Red Man baking soda on a three-pronged hook. They reported hooking a creature the size of a small tree, gunmetal colored with a gatorlike snout. They said it made a wake like a power-boat, broke their forty-pound test line like *that*." He snaps his fingers.

Hunter looks across the water. It seems so calm, benevolent, not hiding a whole universe in darkness.

Lawton grunts. "How come the old man's hunting it?"

The producer shrugs. "That's a large part of what we're trying to uncover in filming. He has some end-time ideas, certainly. Poles melting, waters rising. But it probably goes deeper, given his history."

"History?"

The producer man thumbs the strap at his neck and cocks his head upriver.

"They closed the bridge because of him. His two children drowned. Surely a man doesn't emerge sane from that, not fully."

"Wait," says Hunter. "That was him?"

"That's right. It's not a secret, is it?"

Hunter looks at Lawton, who squeezes his beard in his fist. They were schoolboys when it happened, the names long lost, first to go in the wake of tragedy.

"Jesus," says Hunter. "We didn't know."

They are all silent a moment, listening for the far-off whistle of a train. Hunter squints an eye.

"Hey, tell me something. How come y'all were filming that monster cypress up Miller Lake? Just for extra footage or what?"

"We thought we might find him up in there. Those old trees, he likes to talk to them."

"Talk to them?"

Hunter and Lawton look at each other. They know where to find the old man.

They paddle on, saying nothing to the film crew of where they are headed. Some three miles downriver is Lewis Island, a long tract of tidewater swamp that runs alongside the river. A wild place, undeveloped, its very shape fluid, shrinking and swelling based on tide and season and weather. Much of the year the few trails that lace it are underwater, the floor of the island concealed in flood. At its heart, hidden, stands an ancient grove of cypress and tupelo gum, thousand-year trees saved from the logging crews by their seclusion, their mysterious ability to remain unfound. Their father took them there as boys. He was one of the few who could find the place, marching them through the soupy earth, along paths cut by wild pigs and deer, until they stood among the old giants. Totems, they looked, of a disappeared civilization. Columns holding up the roof of a world so much older and larger than the one they knew. Hunter had never understood why their father, hard and hard-fisted as he was, would go out of his way to show them such places, with so little flourish or explanation. He would place the two of them before such a site like offerings almost, and Hunter would feel something was expected of them. What exactly, he was never sure.

"All the trees on the river used to be like this," their father told them. "Virgin forest, untouched since before time. Then we came and cut them all." He stared at the trees, hands on his hips, then spat in the grass. "See if they might tell you something. They used to mean something to me, but I don't know."

Afterward he marched them out, driving them through whining clouds of mosquitos and grasses that trembled with lizards and snakes. He warned them away from the place in the spring of the year. When the river was high, the wild pigs and cottonmouths retreated to what scarce clusters of dry ground remained, islands in miniature themselves, each become a savage congress of everything toothed and tusked and fanged. Everything that could kill you and would.

They paddle for the island, the swollen river gurgling at its banks.

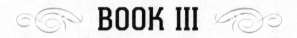

BOOK III

The old man is bent over the iron barb of his harpoon, sharpening. In his hand is a golden ingot, his whetstone. It gleams with oil. It is yellow coticule, a quartzite born in the bowels of mountains, heated and compressed into strata so hard only the most prized jewels can scratch it: ruby and sapphire, topaz and diamond. It is quarried from the Ardennes, famed for honing the swords of Roman phalanxes, the razors of Venetian barbers. He is trying to shave the thinnest layers from the yellow stone, like eons of old time. But it is the iron that yields. The edge of the flue whitens with malice, a sharpened rictus that will slide gleaming into the hearts of beasts and men.

The old man lifts his head. Is that thunder he hears? There is a storm coming, after all. This he knows. Far over the horizon, clouds assemble heavy and dark as ships, an armada bellied with fire and flood. The waters will rise, their secrets laid bare, and new kings will reveal themselves, swelled with faith in their gods. The old man lifts the barb to his mouth and blows away the swarf, a silvery puff. Is it sharp enough yet? It must be as sharp as the spear of Longinus, the Holy Lance. It must be sharp enough to pierce the flesh of God.

44

"What are you doing, monk?"

Le Moyne looks up from his drawing, the paper secured to a wooden board seated on his knees. It is one of the carpenters speaking to him. The man is straddling the ship's rail.

"I'm working."

"Is that what you call it?" The carpenter thumps his hammer against his thigh, revealing a cadaverous grin. "I call it the work of a sodomite."

Le Moyne shakes his head, smiling.

"No, my friend, you are mistaken. That is you stabbing your hut-mate in *le cul* every night."

The carpenter laughs, a dead man's croak.

"When I come off this ship, see that I don't stab this hammer in your ass."

"Make sure to use the big end," says Le Moyne. "I do not wish to be disappointed."

The *Breton* is anchored before the fort, moored to the palisade by several long hawsers. Men climb about its decks, hammering and sawing, the ship itself emitting what sounds a constant groan of pain. The weathered timbers, so strong and sea-rimed, have been set upon by saw and ax, a mania of pale-cut wounds, the decks laid open as if for surgery. The men themselves join in the chorus of agonies. They are so weak now. Their bodies seem something of terrible study, lessons in anatomy more grotesque even than the cadavers of executed criminals in the medical halls of Europe, set to with scalpel and forceps. Only the damned are chosen for dissection, of course, so that on the day of Rapture, no member of the elect will find himself unable to rise upon his ruined, excavated body.

Such worlds Le Moyne is seeing beneath the skin, rivers forked blue and red, in spidery webs and lightning jags, storms of bruise and lands of fissured striation, bony outcrops like strange and secret formations of stone. A terrible knowledge, rarely glimpsed, for even the hanged and beheaded have their final meal. Le Moyne knows this is not the record of new and terrible worlds his king sought of him. Still, he will not shy away from recording what he sees. There is reason to believe he will never again see France, perhaps not even the close of the year. He will leave what truth he can upon the page.

Today he has taken a break from the shipwork to sketch out the murder of Gambie, a member of the expedition who struck out alone the previous fall to build his fortune, trading in cheap Parisian trinkets with the Indians. Glass beads and blades of worthless alloy, scarves dyed garish hues. He ensconced himself on a midriver island the shape of a ship and took the daughter of a local chief as his wife.

In Le Moyne's sketch, the man kneels in the center of a cypress dugout, blowing into the glowing roots of a meager cookfire, the smoke balling up before his face. In the front of the canoe, a native stands paddling. He is looking back at the Frenchman, a sad cast to his face. Behind Gambie crouches a second native, bent nearly double, a hand-ax held high over his head, the blade poised to descend into the white man's skull. His eyes are round, almost sad. His muscles ornate.

The men of Fort Caroline found the boat tangled along the riverbank, the Frenchman's head cleaved nearly in two, his brains spilled out like curdled cheese. The story emerged only later. It turns out Gambie had become like a king among the island natives, a harsh ruler who lashed his subjects with fire-hardened canes for the smallest of transgressions. At the time of his murder he was on his way to visit his old friends at La Caroline. In his possession were all of the riches he had so far accrued. He was going to leave them at the fort for safekeeping. Perhaps he knew the Indians had come to hate him. Even his paddlers were men he had beaten. One of them, recalling his mistreatment, fell upon the Frenchman with his ax, offering repayment for months of abuse.

Le Moyne, sketching, senses someone over his shoulder and looks up. The scarred face of Lord d'Ottigni, iced in sneer. His hand falls large on Le Moyne's shoulder.

"Yes, Le Moyne. That's it. Capture the savages in their murderous nature."

"That is not my intention, seigneur. I hope it to serve only as a warning that we not mistreat the natives of this land. A message to those who come after."

"Mistreat them, eh? I would treat them to the edge of my sword, the blackguards, and happily." He spits. "I am beginning to wonder which side you are on, Le Moyne."

"I did not know there were sides to take."

"Ah, then you are not as smart as I thought."

Laudonnière is a fortnight on his foraging mission, long enough to travel some forty to fifty leagues. May turns to June, the sun buzzing hotter in its arc. The very land steams. It is a diaphanous heat, impossible to escape. Men grow ill. Work on the *Breton* slows. Any day Laudonnière will arrive, and they will feast and return to their labor. Meanwhile they grind roots in stone mortars meant for mixing gunpowder, making meal of whatever they can.

In the afternoons Le Moyne takes up his arquebus and sets upon the footpaths and game trails he knows so well, hunting the great shorebirds in their rookeries, long-beaked and highborn atop their leafy towers. Mostly he misses, their great wings unfolding against the sky. In the lesser branches perch clouds of birds with spoon-shaped bills, their wings faintly pink, their necks kinked like the letter *S*. When he nears, they turn of a one, their long spatulate bills swinging like ship's oars. Other birds, black as night, stand spread-winged and haughty on slanted limbs, as if posing for shield crests. Sometimes an iron-gray heron will haunt the shallows, lean as a wizard.

Once he watches a raptor tear a fish from the river, a blade of living silver caught wriggling in its talons. The bird is darkest brown with a white head, like a mountain peaked in snow. It lands on the riverbank nearby, gutting the fish with its yellow hook of bill. Le Moyne hits the bird from a distance of eighty king's feet, a lucky shot, then plucks and roasts it out of sight of the fort, not wanting to draw men slavering and desperate to his cookfire. For this they might kill. He eats half the bird himself, his fingers flecked and gleaming with shards of meat. The rest he disburses in secret among his closest companions, thighs and wings wrapped in green folds of leaves.

He sketches whenever he can, his only reprieve from hunger. He lives in the minutest detail. The striations of a native's chest, the upturn of a soldier's mustaches, the feathers of a bird in their tufted ranks. The hunger if anything makes his eye keener, his lines sharper. There is strength, he learns, in knowing you may not live long enough to complete the work of your hand.

He is on a bluff he knows, working on the raised head of the ax that murdered his countryman, when he hears shouts of excitement, the blow of a trumpet. He hurries down the trail, breaking from the trees just above the fort. Laudonnière has returned. Men are splashing into the waters before his barque, their bodies haloed in white ruffles of current, their arms outstretched like those of street-beggars. They cling to the sides of the vessel, open-mouthed, as if they might be fed. But even from this distance Le Moyne can see the length of the commander's face, the long-jawed hollowness. It turns first one way, then another.

Nothing.

45

Altamaha River, 1996

It is nearly dark now and still they work, a motley fleet of government and civilian boats dragging the river for bodies. The ballasted hooks and drags arc across the water, hand-thrown again and again, their ropes unfurling after them, the surface geysered with their splashes. The ropes float wormlike on the surface until the descending irons draw them down, the hooks hand-dragged along the black bottoms until they snag. They bring up crumpled lawn chairs and shed cypress limbs, beer and soda cans faded logoless with old-time tabs, a fishing pole with a live river cat still hooked on the line. They bring up mud-wrestling Barbie dolls and condoms luminescent as jellyfish, an old television set shot full of holes.

"Somebody ain't like *Andy Griffith*," says Hiram's helper, a chuckling old drunk.

Hiram remembers hearing of Old Man Gillis pumping three rounds into his TV after the finale of *St. Elsewhere*, maddened at the revelation that the whole show was cooked up in the mind of an autistic child. The old man lived up Penholoway Creek, with a TV aerial raised high over his floathouse like a metal bird, and Hiram pictures the blasted television set tumbling downriver year after year, a few feet or inches at a time, until it arrives beneath their hook.

If it can make it this far downriver, he worries what else? What other secrets might they bring up?

He squeezes the rope hard in his right hand and pulls up his hook, empty this time, and throws it again. The sheriff's department has only a couple of special body drags. At the call for help, the rivermen showed up in droves. Sheepishly they pulled their neatly coiled snagging hooks from this hidey-hole or that. After all, snag-fishing is illegal in the state. The bridge stands unfazed before them, throwing its great skeletal shadow downriver by the last light of the descended sun. White pleasure boats line the river at anchor, the banks jumbled with pale-shirted intercessors, black-skinned and white, kneeling in prayer or hand-chained in song. Their voices drift across the river, punctuated by the crashing of hooks.

That morning, Hiram had rounded the bend upstream of the bridge too late, the unscheduled freight train just bursting from the trees, whistle scream-ing, and before it the robed mania of Uncle King, skirts flying, crucifix bounc-ing against his chest, his children clutched each to a hand, the three of them unable to outrun what was coming. At the last moment the holy man turned and hurled the two children out of harm's way, free of the bridge, and turned toward the driving engine, disappearing in a scream of iron.

The train skidded down the rails, raining sparks. The people shrieked. The two children whirled like rag dolls from the span and crashed into the river, a fifty-foot drop, and didn't come up. The worshipers began shedding their Sun-day shirts. They dove and dove again from their boats, searching. Hiram, too, thrusting himself as far down as he could go, touching the blind world of the bottom before he had to explode for the surface. Once, coming up, he saw the face of one of the children break the surface just downstream of him, long enough to loose a gurgled scream before she disappeared again, pulled under by the current or something else.

Then more shrieks from the crowd, and Hiram turned to see Uncle King rise soot-faced from the rails like a resurrected corpse, called up as if by the screams of his daughter. He shed his robes and dove from the bridge himself, a white spear of flesh. He was under a minute, two. An eternity. He surfaced empty-handed. He and the others dove again and again, hour after hour, until it had been so long they brought out the hooks.

Hiram hauls his in again. It has triple flukes like a grappling hook, the shank lead-weighted to sink. It looks like something from a medieval armory, a device for scaling castle walls or dragging men screaming from their trenches or foxholes. He touches one of the barbs with his thumb. He thinks of the pale flesh of his two little boys, so easily broken. A motor is coming upriver and he turns to look. A sheriff's boat idles through the line of draggers. In its bow stands Uncle King, shirtless and erect. His old boxer's body glows like white marble in the failing light, fleshed in the hard angles of the flyweight, the geometric planes scratched here or there with tattoos. The sheriff's boat slides right past Hiram's own, and Uncle King looks directly into Hiram's eyes as he floats past. Hiram is prepared to acknowledge him now—blood brother—and yet the old man's eyes register nothing as they pass, no recognition. They are gone to worlds their own, planets of hurt and loss you only go alone.

Hiram thinks the man is being allowed again to dive for his children, returned to the place of loss like the holy thing he is. A candle-white form on the river. But as the boat passes, Hiram sees his hands are not clasped behind his back but cuffed, and he sees the worm of scar crossing the heart-line of the man's palm. Hiram touches his own matching scar, brought back to the boyhood day they drew the shoddy lockblade across their hands, holding them clasped like arm wrestlers until their blood fully mixed. He thinks back to what came before, the secret they meant to seal in the meat of their palms, the hurt they sank to the river's bottom.

He looks down at the hook, knowing what terrible secrets it might find.

He throws it again.

46

Altamaha River, Day 4

The sun roars at noon height, birthing thousands of stars across the river's surface. Hunter has his sunglasses on, and the explosion of light is still hard to bear. It makes him think of the day of his father's funeral, a day so bright it looked washed-out, a scene from one of the seventies cop shows on daytime TV. *CHiPs* or *Dragnet*, one of the reruns his father could stare at while slurping a can of beer, sunk in something between boredom and zen. The service itself was in their mother's church, the Baptist stronghold the old man would never step foot in. Lawton wasn't there. Their mother had requested emergency leave through the Red Cross, but his command denied the request, responding that he was on a long-range patrol, beyond the scope of safe extraction.

Hunter was left to do the eulogy on his own. He struggled to find the seams of strength in the old man's faults, the deposits of power and lore that men might admire. His hands shook on the lectern. His voice was strange.

"Our father, he was a hard man. He wasn't partial to hugs or hand-holding, to displays of affection. He didn't speak his love. But there were things he did hold close. There was the river, for one, more a father to him than any flesh and blood. On his days off, he'd take us upstream, have us sitting scrubbed and solemn in the bow like we were going to church. Maybe we were. His church.

A swampland cathedral, roofed in leaves and plumbed with creeks, columned with cypress and gum. We knew its sights and secrets, its hidden sloughs. In showing us the river—his river—I believe he let us into his heart, at least some part of it. And that's how I knew we were loved."

Hunter went on to talk of how the old man had never given up despite the years of setbacks, the lost boats and empty nets. He didn't speak of the knottiness of the old man's fists, oak-solid, nor his love of whiskey. He didn't mention the stormy air of discontent that hovered always about him, ready to crack thunder. He let these remain unspoken, the shadow of the words he spoke.

"He was a man who fought every day of his life. He didn't always fight the right things, or for the right reasons, or in ways that fell within the laws of man or God or even, I suspect, his own heart. I can't say that I understood him. I'm not even sure I really knew him. But I knew he'd never give up his dreams. I knew he'd die with his teeth in their throat."

Hunter looked across the church as he spoke, surprised at the turnout, the pews filled with people he hardly knew. Sun-spotted old men with faces like hammered leather, clumped in twos and threes, and blacks in their own rows of pews who worked the docks or decks or shelled shrimp in the ankle-deep ice of the processing houses. There were several men with stars over their hearts, their radio mikes draped over their shoulders, the cords braided like service distinctions. A few women suspiciously attractive, one with flame-colored curls and nails painted the bloodiest red, her eyes hotly welled, the tears trembling as if in fear of the blue worlds that sprang them.

Hunter is reexamining these pews of memory, searching for anyone with a look of triumph on his face, a killer's pride, when Lawton's voice cuts in.

"Hey."

Hunter looks up.

"What?"

Lawton is pointing to a creek mouth on the left shore.

"Hornsby Creek over there. Good place to look, long as we're going past."

They paddle diagonally for the creek. Near its mouth a slanted water oak, bowled over by the flood, flounders in the current. The naked crown, half-submerged, is stretched downstream, as if river, not sun, demands such upreach. The water churns through the skeleton branches, darkly riffled, and the tree trembles and trembles; it won't be long. The creek itself is narrow, no more than twenty yards wide, and tunneled in cypress and gum. Sunlight shafts through the stained glass of just-budding leaves, speckling the surface yellow and gold—perfect camouflage for moccasins scrolling across the surface.

Before them a deadfall of timber lies nearly flat across the creek, a two-trunked oak gapped and bowed like the doubled bones of a man's shin. There doesn't look to be space enough to slip beneath them, but Lawton leans far forward in the cockpit, and under he goes. Hunter follows, using his deck rigging to pull himself flat, hoping the bag of ashes behind him won't snag. They enter a hall of cascading light, the new leaves slightly translucent, glowing. They purr as the wind sifts through them. A log juts diagonally from the water, wet-dark, upon which a line of turtles has assembled like friendly tumors, their heads extended into the shafts of sunlight.

They round a bend in the creek to find a boat hoven up against the bank, a twenty-foot cabin cruiser of 1970s vintage. It's canted on the bank, abandoned. The cabin glass is cloudy but intact, the hull a matte green, sanded over for paint that never came. The aft deck sits partly sunken in the creek, a pool of black water where the engine would be. The craft is losing the mark of being man-made. The hard lines of logic are softening, surrendering to age and growth, the colors melding with the surrounding flora. It might be the shell of some once-living creature, left now for who-knows-what species of jellied inhabitants.

Lawton paddles up to it. He wipes the cabin window and tunnels his hands to peer inside.

"Can't see nothing."

His knees come up out of the cockpit and he pulls his boat onto the bank alongside the wreck. He climbs onto the bow and squats on the balls of his feet, the deck canted at a hard angle from level. The bow hatch gapes open beneath him, black as a mouth. He pulls the dive-knife from the scabbard over his heart.

"Lawton—"

Too late. He grins and drops through the hatch.

"Crazy son of a bitch."

Hunter runs his bow into the bank and steps out, the mud blurting under his feet. He can hear rustling in the hull of the cruiser, a hollow thump. Someone groans. Hunter jumps onto the bow, ax in hand, and makes ready to drop through the hatch, but Lawton's head rears out of the darkness, looking up. His face is covered in blood, a river delta spread from a gash in his forehead. Streams zigzag around his nose and down his cheeks, running red into his beard. He's grinning.

"Jackpot," he says.

He holds up a cardboard flap, like the sign of a homeless man. In ballpoint pen, someone has drawn what looks like a seaborne dinosaur: fins like a sea turtle, four of them jutting oarlike from the pear-shaped body, and a long tail, an S-curved neck atop which sits a dragon's head, long-snouted with big round eyes and a mouthful of daggered teeth.

"Altie," says Lawton. "I'd say we're on the right track."

"What happened to your head?"

Lawton's eyes turn up, as if he can see the gash in his brow.

"Oh. Bumped it."

Hunter looks past him, into the hold, just to be sure.

47

New France, June 1565

Six leagues. The distance from the barques to the village of Utina, king in the west. A march that will take them six hours to complete. Before Le Moyne is a forest of arquebuses, iron barrels set in walnut and fruitwood. They sway over the shoulders of their bearers, pricking the sky. Despite the length of the march, each soldier has his taper already burning, ready to light the fuse of his matchlock. This visit is not to be a friendly one.

Le Moyne had seen this coming, had known something wicked would follow in the wake of their commander's failed foraging mission. Work on the *Breton* had all but halted, the men too weak. Desperate, Laudonnière appealed to his ally in the west, Utina. The chief could offer but scarce rations, he said. What corn he had he needed for seed. But send him a company of men to quell a disobedient vassal of his kingdom, and there would be plenty of corn and acorns to be seized.

A week ago, Le Moyne watched the war party stumble nearly dead down the gangplank of their barque, returning from Utina's western lands. They looked half-ghosted, skull-faced and hollow-eyed, paling already into the next world. Utina had used them to advance not upon a vassal of his kingdom but an enemy, one whose village offered nothing in the way of food for seizure.

The men called for an audience with Laudonnière. They chose Lord d'Ottigni this time to speak for them.

"Deceivers," he told the assembled crowd. "*Trompeurs.* Serpents, like that of the Garden. They have made of us their handservants."

Oui.

"The savage has betrayed us at every opportunity. Cheated us. Has even in his boldness murdered one of our countrymen."

Absolument.

"They would let us to die in the land of their bounty, we who might offer them the word of salvation, the truth of Christ. We who have shed our blood and the blood of our foemen in their name." He thumped his chest.

Quels ingrats.

"It is time, then, that we turn sword upon the serpent. That we force him to our will. I say that we seize the man himself. Utina. Mark me, friends: I will make him to share his bounty, or else his bowels will steam at my feet."

Men clapped and stomped the earth. They rattled their swords in their scabbards.

Bravo! they said. *Saisissez-le!*

Seize him.

Le Moyne, watching from the crowd, looked to Laudonnière. He had been forgoing his collar of late because of the heat. His doublet was soiled, his neck a shrunken vine, a red warp of apple at the throat. He swallowed hard.

"We have to consider the consequences of committing such an act."

Lord d'Ottigni spat, his face scar-white in the sun.

"Aye," he said. "And those of committing it not."

Again the cheers, the clang of steel and thump of flesh.

Laudonnière's eyes retreated into their hollows. He looked down at his boots, a scarecrow-man in overlarge rags. He said nothing.

They march straight to the great house of the king, seizing him without so much as a shot. Cries of alarm bound through the countryside—too late. Utina's warriors are scattered, unprepared to retort with arrow or club.

Le Moyne and his comrades are two days back at the boats, a company fifty-strong, waiting for the king's ransom to be paid. On the first night, the women of the village appear on the river path, armed only with wails and moans. But their eyes, Le Moyne sees, jet here and there, recording the river landing, the heavy-timbered barques, the bristling of guns from the decks. They see their king chained to the mast.

The next day a mass of archers appears on the path.

"Come," they say. "Come. Our enemies from the foothills have burned our village in absence of our king. You must help us."

Laudonnière looks to Lord d'Ottigni, who sniffs.

"Tell them there is no smoke," he says. He juts his chin upstream. The forest there quivers, wind-moved or something else. "And tell them we see the clubmen hiding in the wood, *en embuscade.* Tell them they would be wise not to think us fools."

The natives look surprised at this. Quickly they bring forward a basket of fish and another of acorns, as if in penance. It is scarcely enough to feed the fifty men of the guard, let alone the rest of the fort. At the end of two days, they have failed to purchase the freedom of their king. Laudonnière is ill with frustration. D'Ottigni watches the woods over the barrel of his weapon, then looks back at the king chained to the mast.

"They believe we will put him to death whether they pay the ransom or not," he says. "That is their own custom, and they judge us by it."

Utina holds out his manacled hands, his palms paler than the rest of him, as if to offer apology.

"We go," says Laudonnière, motioning to the men. "He comes back with us to the fort. They will learn we mean to keep our word."

As the men make ready to sail, Le Moyne scans the forest a last time, knowing it full of watching eyes.

What folly they must see.

48

Altamaha River, 1996

Nearly midnight. Blue light splashes through the trees, silent, followed by red. It paints the walls of the park's store and bathhouse, the fishing pier, the RVs parked like a herd in the trees. Hiram Loggins is breathing hard. In one hand he holds a pair of heavy pliers from the boat, a cutting blade set deep in the jaw. In his other hand a twelve-gauge flare gun, blaze orange. He is standing in the shadow thrown by the camp store, open late to feed and provision the searchers and grievers and police.

His boat is tied up at an old dock floating downstream of the park. On the water he can hear the crash of hooks, the songs of mourners. They are singing of swinging low and flying away, of going over Jordan. Nothing has been found, no bodies. Just more of the wreckage that litters the river bottom, a whole broken city of objects cast off or sunk or simply lost. There are appliances murdered, microwaves and boomboxes bludgeoned or shot full of holes, and toys and tackle from every era, and deadheads of virgin pine whipsawed from the forest a century ago.

Hiram peeks his head around the corner of the building. A patrol car sits in front of the store, lightbar cascading blue to red, blue to red. Soundless. A deputy leans against the driver's door, arms crossed, watching the river. In the backseat, sitting upright behind the Plexiglas divider, a pale javelin of flesh. Uncle King. A man who saved Hiram once, more surely than any lost soul.

Hiram is going to return the favor.

He flattens himself to the wall of the store and his mind fumbles over shields and bucklers, feathers and wing-shadows of scripture. Anything that might help him now. Then he fills his lungs with air and steps from under the gutters and raises his flare gun to the moon. The round tears into the sky, sizzling upon its braided tail of smoke, and already he is disappearing behind the store. The flare casts its hellish light on the river, lighting it like a sluice of molten ore. He knows the sight, so much like the muddy waters of the Cua Lon River, when he raked the jungle with tracer fire. Every face is turned up to look, open-mouthed with awe. The deputy comes round one side of the building, curious, as Hiram comes round the other, crouched low, heading for the cruiser.

He pulls the handle and the door pops, opening, and then he is face-to-face with Uncle King. The man's hair looks grayer than earlier today, almost white.

"Give me your hands," says Hiram. He has the pliers out.

Uncle King doesn't move. His eyes are wide, floating hazily in his skull.

"Brother," he says.

"Gimme them hands," says Hiram. He reaches behind the man and pulls his hands toward him, the metal bracelets gleaming red under the flare. He sets the chain in the cutting jaw of the pliers and squeezes both-handed, veins spilling out of his arms.

Uncle King watches him.

"Hell's done took my children, brother."

Hiram looks up, squeezing with all his might. Wetness trembles in the man's eyes.

"It ain't either," says Hiram. "We'll find them."

"Same's it took Old Hallam, the yellow-face, he that sleeps yet in the pit."

Hiram's blood jumps at the name; the chain pops.

"That son-bitch is doing more than sleep." He points out into the dark. "Now run."

Uncle King doesn't move.

"What's ate them, then, they ain't come up?"

Panic is rising in Hiram, his skin on fire. The deputy will be back any second.

"Nothing's damn ate them. Listen, man, you got to run."

When he doesn't move, Hiram grabs him by the upper arm and pulls him from the car. They fall together in the dust. The flare is flickering now, dying out, the darkness swarming in like a flood.

"Goddammit."

Hiram hooks Uncle King under the arms, struggling to his knees, heaving the man up.

"We got to go," he says. "Come on."

"They say it's my fault, brother."

The flare goes out, the night suddenly darker, stunned blue and red. King puts his hand around Hiram, ready to be led, and just then Hiram hears the metallic click of a hammer being cocked. He turns, slowly, to see the deputy there behind him, a big nickel-plated revolver gripped in both hands. It isn't a professional's gun. It's a fancy kind of pistol carried by someone who might like to use it. There is a lopsided grin on the man's face.

"You dumb sons of bitches," he says.

Hiram tenses, ready to spring, but King seizes his hand, right to right, like men shaking. Their scars touch.

"Find them, brother."

49

Altamaha River, Day 4

They float down the big river. The sun has tipped westward, beginning its long roll from the sky, and a swallow-tailed kite wheels and dashes overhead, trailing her long fork of a tail, black as a serpent's tongue.

"What else you find back there?"

Lawton scratches at the gash in his forehead, inspects his thumb for blood.

"Nothing much. Few cans of beans stacked real neat. Roll of TP. Milk jug full of drinking water. Seems Uncle King has him a hideout in that old wreck."

"Maybe we should of stayed there to wait on him."

Lawton isn't listening. He has the cardboard flap out, studying it over the paddle in his lap. One hand rises to tug on the end of his beard.

"Looks like one of those what-you-call-'ems. Like a brontosaurus that swims."

"Plesiosaur?"

"Yeah," says Lawton. "One of them. Like the one in Loch Ness."

He cocks the paper one way, his head another, as if this will give him the angle he needs.

Hunter rubs his nose. "You know when they first started digging up fossils, Darwin hadn't come along yet. People didn't know how the creatures fit with scripture, being pre-human and all. They figured them from a world before Adam, full of sea dragons and eternal night. Called them pre-Adamites."

"Huh." Lawton is still intent on the sketch. "Thing is, I can't see just one of a thing surviving. There's got to be least two, male and female, and young'uns. They ain't trees, living a thousand years. They got to breed. There'd have to be a pod of them. Nothing survives on its own."

"We even having this conversation, Lawton?"

"The old man always thought there was something to it. The Altamaha-ha."

"That's right. And this is the same man said G.I. Joes were dolls and dolls would make us queer. Said Hillary Clinton had a foot-long dick and wore a set of jelly-packed tits for show. Remember he'd be out on the water on the moonless nights, saying the pitch dark kept his senses sharp?"

Lawton sets down the paper.

"You just can't believe in nothing he did, can you?"

"It ain't that."

"The fuck it isn't."

"I can see his flaws."

"You see what you wanna see, Hunter. Always have."

"That's rich coming from you."

"Always picking everything apart. It's a pain in the ass is what it is."

"You're a real dick sometimes, you know that?"

"That don't make me wrong."

Midafternoon they turn into Stud Horse Creek, a mile-long stretch that winds like a racetrack through the cypress. Hunter watches a swallow chase a fly across the creek, the insect darting erratically over the water, like an uncoiling string, until the swallow clips it from the air. They are nearing the delta, where the river will fork and fork again, fanning seaward through the marshes, and the ruins of rice plantations and shell-rung villages and perhaps even an ancient fort might be found.

Hunter hears a motor through the trees, closing fast, and he watches a wood stork unfold its great black-edged wings, fleeing in slow motion across the creek. The steel hull of a skiff flashes from the bend in front of them, cutting high and hard, skidding across the water. A boy stands shirtless at the helm, white and lean with a white-blond scraggle of beard. A rifle is strapped across his back. A small doe lies in the stern of the boat, curled in blood, a red hole in her side. The skiff roars past them, never slowing, and Hunter sees a wicked gleam in the boy's eyes, like the slashed blade of a knife. Then he is gone, around the next bend, and Hunter is left thinking of the boy Andino mentioned, the one who slung live cats over powerlines.

"Mother*fucker*!" Lawton holds his paddle level as his kayak hops up and down on the chop. "I was swimming this river when that little son of a bitch was still sucking titty-milk."

Hunter watches the heavy wake of the boat thump the creek bank.

"I don't think it's deer season."

"If it was asshole season, I'd be tying that little motherfucker on the hood of my truck."

Stud Horse Creek dead-ends into a smaller creek, like a T-junction in the swamp, and they paddle to the right. The sun is still white in the west, half-fallen from its noon zenith. This new creek kinks and curls even more sharply than the first, reversing whole directions, sawing itself ever deeper into the swamp. A flight of cormorants skims low over the water, feathers a glossy black, like birds risen from an oil slick. Around the next bend a group of roseate spoonbills sits in the branches of a big cypress, white-necked with pink wings. They are friendly birds, and sort of sad, too, with their goofy bills. They look like wooden spoons, the kind used to slurp spaghetti sauce and spank the bare asses of unruly boys.

"It's the crawdads they eat," says Hunter. "Makes their wings turn pink."

Lawton spits. "That's funny. I don't remember giving a fuck."

They nearly miss the canal. The mouth is crisscrossed with leafy overgrowth, concealed like a secret door in the wild. The canals were dug by logging crews in the sixties, the dredge burden used to build roads that bore men and equipment over the soupy earth, reaching the virgin cypress at the island's heart. They pass one canal and paddle into the second, pushing their way through clutches of vines and branches, the shielding fronds of palmettos. The canal is narrow, perhaps ten feet wide, a sword of water piercing the undergrowth, with the old causeway running along its shoulder. They paddle until the snags and deadfalls grow too thick, then shore their boats, tying them to a water tupelo grown straight up in the middle of the road.

The sun itself is hidden by the trees. Light slants in through the branches and leaves, crudely jeweling the ground. Lawton looks at his wristwatch.

"Best get to it. I don't want to sleep out here."

Hunter looks around. The old road is hardly worthy of the name, a feeble causeway among the explosive green on every side. He gets his hand-ax from the boat, Lawton his machete. They take a drawstring nylon bag with water bottles, matches, waterproof jackets stuffed in sacks. A couple of energy bars and emergency blankets folded the size of card decks. They start to walk. The palmettos push in on every side, spiky and green, woody vines snarled about them like ship's rigging. A surge of tide has come and gone, the muddy ground covered in shallow pools, tea-dark, which linger at the feet of endless cypress and tupelo gum. The great trunks are everywhere, stone-gray and tusk-scarred, their branches bearded with moss. Every direction the same, a swampy maze.

Hunter's feet make prints in the earth, and he knows they should be wearing boots for the snakes. It is a hike of some half mile to the island's interior, and soon his knee has begun its throb. Around him the world is turning cooler, darker. Older. He hears snaps in the brush, the crackle of leaves, beasts rifling through the maze. Birds screech from treetops. The cicadas roar as one, in siren or song. A big vein stands out on one of Lawton's calves, zigging like a river on a map. He slashes and chops at the vines and brush that bar their path, the machete secured to his wrist with a loop. Hunter's hand-ax has a leather thong at the end of the handle. He's secured this to a carabiner on his vest. The tool bobs along at his side, its edge muzzled in leather.

At flood stage, men and women hunt the hogs of the island with assault rifles, the wild hulks driven to what high ground remains and killed in droves, bristled mounds of hide bleeding into the mud. Some years ago a man from town, hunting alone, was shot in the head. The man who mistook him for a hog was his boss at the hardware store, neither knowing the other had taken the day to hunt. The shot man made a full recovery, despite the bullet passing partly through his brain.

Hunter rehearses the steps it would take to bring his hand-ax to bear, unclipping the carabiner and unsheathing the bit. Long seconds, he knows, when bad things happen quick.

They have been hiking nearly an hour when they come upon a giant iron chassis, brown with rust. It's a donkey engine, or was, a diesel winch once used to drag whole trees through the swamp. It sits on a massive sled, a contrivance of drums and pulleys and gears, the braided steel cable frozen on its enormous spool.

"Somebody left in a hurry." Lawton juts his chin. A felled cypress lies some twenty yards away, still bound in the cable's choker. It was dragged only partway back to the machine and left there, a carcass half-sunk in decades of moss and muck.

Hunter reaches out to touch the winch. It is of a color, the red-brown of old train rails, its pistons and gears seized by age and rust. More monument now than machine. The spool at its center is the size of a whiskey barrel, sized like a reel for dragging leviathans from the deep, and a dizzy of levers and controls juts from one side. He sees the finned rectangle of a detached radiator lying in the mud nearby.

"Let's keep on," says Lawton. "Find them trees."

Soon the road ends and they are directionless in the swamp, trudging over the sodden earth, watching for old-growth survivors to shoot skyward from the muck. The way is thick with bright shoots of grass and palmetto, endless groves of new-growth cypress and tupelo. There are pools left by the tide's retreat, vast purgatories where armies of crawdads lie trapped, their oversize claws working in slow motion. They crawl over one another, looking for answers.

Hunter and Lawton walk and walk, hacking their way through the undergrowth, breathing hard. Another hour. Longer. The handful of anti-inflammatories Hunter swallowed with lunch is wearing off.

Lawton stops, hands on his hips, his chest heaving.

"Where are they?"

"It's so thick you got to walk right up on them."

"No shit, Hunter. I just thought we would of done it by now."

"No need to be a dick about it. I been nothing but a good sport about this shit."

Lawton looks at him, his mouth set tight in his beard.

"The fuck does that mean? I'm just trying to figure out what happened to Daddy."

Hunter looks about. Dark is coming early through the leafy canopy, the light flattening in its slant. The world turning, and Hunter feels a tug inside him. A limit. He's let this go on long enough.

"Thing is, Lawton, we already know what happened to him. You got to accept that at some point."

Lawton spits and wipes his mouth. One eye rises cold over the back of his hand.

"You don't tell me what I got to accept, Hunter. You don't tell me shit."

"It's time somebody does. It ain't healthy, Lawton."

"*Healthy*?" Lawton seems to swell between the trees, his shoulders rising like a yoke. "It's about time you step out of the sheep-world you're living in, Hunter. Your cute little college bubble. The world ain't a healthy place. It's full of sick people doing sick things—rabid as wolves—and the only reason they ain't infected your cute little world is because there's people out there willing to put them down."

"This ain't some Third World war zone, Lawton. Daddy's dead and there ain't a thing we can do about it."

Lawton steps toward him, quick, his finger flicking like a switchblade in Hunter's face.

"You know what, Hunter? Sometimes I think you just don't give a fuck."

Hunter feels his body grow taller, swelling with rage.

"You really are the high and mighty, aren't you? The son he really wanted, loyal as a fucking dog."

Lawton's eyes blaze, set alight.

"You ungrateful little prick. I lost my chance to play for Navy because of you."

"Don't put that shit on me. That was your fuckup. Always got to prove you're swinging the biggest dick in the room, don't you? Show everybody how them big balls of yours just drag the ground."

"Least I ain't a half-cripple with a pile of books for a crutch."

Hunter's eyes burn. He is seven feet tall, built of brick.

"That panic attack of yours on the chopper, too bad it *wasn't* a fucking bullet."

Lawton lunges at him, arms out.

A bluff.

"Pussy," he says.

Hunter hits him in the mouth with a straight right, his knuckles cracking on jawbone, and then they are on the ground, thundering in the mud. Lawton is bigger, stronger, but Hunter is fiended with rage, wild-struck, his knuckles and elbows edged for blood. He wants to beat it out of his brother, the dumb worship, the stupid duty locked in his mind. He wants to break him, to spill the softness he keeps hidden inside. The tender blood. He wants to roll in it, to scream and cry. He rises atop the fury of limbs and lands a blow on Lawton's forehead, busting open the scab. Blood flees over his brother's face, zigzagging in gleaming creeks and forks.

"Is this what you want, you son of a bitch?"

Lawton's mouth is closed, his nostrils flaring. His blue eyes, surprised at first, burn coldly through the blood. He works his arms in and out of Hunter's blows, maneuvers his feet. He is trying to grab hold of one of Hunter's wrists. Hunter lands blow after blow, fists and elbows, but the flesh is obstinate beneath him, clad with muscle. It's like hitting a sack of feed. It maddens him, and he strikes harder, faster. Lawton gets hold of his wrist and pulls the arm straight down to him, clasping Hunter's hand over his heart, and then his leg comes sweeping over Hunter's head, hooking his neck, and Hunter is thrust to the ground, his arm locked across Lawton's body.

Arm-bar.

Lawton bridges his belly, bowing Hunter's elbow the wrong way.

"Submit."

Hunter, locked like a man on the rack, says nothing. His body rages in place, quivering against the pressure.

"Submit," says Lawton. "Say 'uncle.'" He bridges himself yet higher, threatening the joint. "Tap out, goddammit. So help me God, I'll break your fucking arm in half."

Hunter's elbow is going the way it shouldn't. He can feel the tendons straining, the searing jets of pain. The first rips in the cords that bind him.

A pain he knows.

"Fuck you." His neck is jammed in the crook of Lawton's leg. His words strangled, unbeaten. "Break it, motherfucker."

Lawton roars, releasing his arm. He kicks himself away and stands red-faced over Hunter, panting like a beaten man.

"Pussy," he says.

A flung little stone, weak now. Defeated.

Lawton turns and storms off into the swamp. The last Hunter sees is the flash of a hand, a middle finger raised high and crooked, like for those two little boys spitting from the bridge.

50

Fort Caroline, July 1565

A black tower of smoke leans against the western sky. A wildfire, perhaps. From this distance it looks motionless, charcoaled. Le Moyne, sitting on his bluff, returns to the new piece he has been working on. In the foreground of the page, six naked Indians hold a tree trunk, three a side, ramming it into the mouth of an alligator. This is the hunting scene he has witnessed several times. The scene he and his compatriots tried to replicate with such calamity.

But to his surprise, the creature begins to swell beneath his hand, to transform, the tail lengthening into a mammoth *S,* the snout sharpening into a beaklike point, the eyes retreating into hollow orbits of skull. The arms grow muscled, with sharp elbows and knuckled claws. He can almost hear the anatomy of the creature snapping and groaning under the force of his will, the mountains of armor surfacing along the spine, the ribs curving out like those of a ship's hull, the heart inflating to the size of a man's head. The page seems almost to tremble, a guttural bellow such as the beast might make, and the lives of the six hunters fall into question.

Le Moyne sits back from the work, breathing hard, his forearm burning from exertion, the tongue stone heavy in his pocket. The lines are steady and sharp. Inspired. He gets up to fetch La Caille.

———

They approach the room where Utina is being held, Le Moyne going first. Guards are posted on either side of the door. They cross their halberds before him, barring entry until he shows them the note of permission he carries, signed by Laudonnière. They uncross their weapons but slowly, eyes narrow with suspicion. The men of the fort are furious with the captive chief. Since he was taken hostage, his people have tried again and again to deceive them. Some of the men have clamored for the chief's life. *Hang him, quarter him, shoot him against the wall.* The guards are posted as much to protect Utina as to prevent his escape.

The Indian king is squatting on his heels in one corner, refusing chair and bed, his ink-scrawled body covered in a white linen shirt that fits him like a sail. His brow is gathered, his hands working carefully with a pair of reeds, twisting and folding them one upon the other, the chain of his irons scraping the earthen floor. He looks up.

"*Olata,*" says Le Moyne. The word for chief. He gestures toward the chair. "May I?"

Utina shrugs, looks down again at his work.

Le Moyne sits.

"What are you making?"

The chief mumbles something, and Le Moyne looks to his friend.

"Man," says La Caille. He leans against the wall.

Le Moyne removes the roll of paper from his pocket, the sketch. He sets it on the floor and pushes it across to Utina.

"Do you know this thing?" he asks.

Utina looks over the top of the reeds a moment, then casts his eyes toward the door and speaks. La Caille translates.

"He wants to know if Saturiwa, king of the coast, has come for his head."

Le Moyne leans back in the chair.

"Tell him yes, his enemy has come, but our commander denied him."

Utina sniffs at this, then looks again at the paper on the floor, speaking.

"He says he knows this thing," says La Caille. "Though he finds it a poor likeness. The claws are not like this. The neck is too short."

Utina casts his sharp-nailed hands at the drawing, chattering. La Caille grins.

"He has many grievances with your picture, it seems."

Le Moyne smiles and interlaces his fingers against his chest.

"Well, tell him I spent too much of my talent on La Caille's mother."

"Bastard," says La Caille, grinning despite. He translates for Utina.

The war-chief looks from one of them to the other, slyly. An amused show of teeth.

"He says it is the great water-serpent," says La Caille. "That which hisses and bellows."

Le Moyne leans forward, clasping his hands between his knees.

"Ask him where I may find it."

"He says he thought it was corn we sought."

"Tell him I only wish to see it."

Utina makes a noise in his throat.

"He says you cannot even see your own god."

"That isn't true," says Le Moyne. He taps his chest. "We see him here."

Utina keeps speaking, jutting his chin upward.

"He says every eye wishes to see the serpent, as every belly wishes bread. He says his own god has ripened the crop. He says to tell our commander that his people will now deliver all the corn we may desire."

"Tell him I did not come to speak of corn."

Utina holds open his palm. There stands a doll of corn husks, arms outstretched.

"He says you should have."

"*Merde*," says Le Moyne.

As they step out the door, he hears a crackle of husks, the doll crushed in the man's hand.

That afternoon, Le Moyne returns to his bluff over the fort. More dark pillars hang over the river now, a forest of smoke. The sun is descending, an angry red eye that burns through the haze. Le Moyne squints as if he might see the roots of the fire. It is too far upstream. He is laying out his materials, brushes and vellum and gouache, when cries rise from the fort.

"Ils sont de retour! Ils sont de retour!"

They are back.

He looks up to see a barque rounding the bend, returning from a foraging expedition upstream. The crew lines the rails, dancing, prizes of corn held aloft while men crash into the shallows beneath them, fighting one another for alms. Le Moyne leaves his brushes and paints; he is running toward the riverbank, hot springs bubbling under his tongue.

He wades into the shallows. Around him, men are shoveling the corn ears into their gnashing teeth, husk and all. They huddle waist-deep in the river, shoulders rounded over their boons.

"Have you any more?" he cries.

The crewmen shake their heads.

"No, man, you are too late. We took all the corn we could find."

"But take comfort," says another. "We have avenged our countryman Gambie, so despicably murdered. We have burned his island village to the ground."

"Yea," says another. "Like a ship burned to keel."

By nightfall the fort is alive with moans. Men writhe in their beds, unable to belly such glut. Their stomachs are shrunken to tiny fists, confounded by even a single ear of corn. Their bodies are too weak. When they struggle outside their huts to vomit, others are waiting with spoons. Le Moyne watches through a chink in the wall of his hut. Shame, it seems, learned first in the Garden, is first to go, men so quick to crawl on their bellies, to grovel in the dirt like swine. He closes his eyes. He thinks how Utina was right: he has never even seen his own God. How easy it must be to have one that arrives each day at dawn, rising as surely as anything in the world, and what strength it must give you and what joy. Never has he wanted so badly to see his own God, who plies the heavens, a Spirit sliding unseen through the world of men. A God of mystery, armored in shadow, who so rarely shows his face. Le Moyne turns over in bed, away from the wall, trying not to think of his spoon.

Mid-July, they return to the western lands with their hostage, hoping the people will ransom their king. They leave their barques at the river, then march the long leagues to Utina's village, the manacled chief paraded before them like an honoree. Every soldier, Le Moyne included, wishes to believe the man is speaking the truth. That his fields are ripe, his people prepared to pay his ransom from their harvest. Utina says he has sown whole fields for the French. Never again shall they hunger.

Instead his people parley.

"Our king must be free," they say, "or we will not give up our grain."

"If we pay his ransom," they say, "what is to keep you from killing him?"

"Release him," they say, "and we will pay."

The French confer.

"Yet another ploy," says Lord d'Ottigni. "We must not let him go."

Laudonnière gazes at the thick forest that swaddles the village, roaring with insects and birds. His cheeks are splotchy and red, as if someone has slapped him repeatedly with a glove.

"Give me the key," he says.

D'Ottigni stands back.

"Sir."

"La clé, seigneur!"

D'Ottigni's face darkens. He reels in the key he has taken to wearing like a necklace beneath his tunic. Laudonnière takes it and turns to the interpreter.

"Tell them I want two hostages in return," he says. He looks at the villagers, holding up two fingers. *"Deux otages."* He speaks slowly, as if speaking to children or idiots.

Le Moyne looks at the natives. They nod eagerly at the interpreter's words, and soon two young men are brought forth from the crowd to be set in irons. Laudonnière begins to unshackle Utina.

"Ten days." He speaks for all to hear, but his gaze remains locked on Utina's face. "In ten days we will return to collect what is owed. If we are refused again, we will cut the throats of our hostages and set fire to your lands. Your enemies will tread upon your graves."

The irons fall at Utina's feet.

"Ten days," Laudonnière repeats. "Our final visit to your lands."

Le Moyne looks at his countrymen. Surely there is some better way of putting it than that.

51

Lewis Island, Day 4

Hunter slogs through the brush and mud, looking for his brother. The world is dimming, twilit, the green blades of sea oats sprung like glowsticks from the muck. There is no road, and his legs are black to the knees. The mud makes wet sucking sounds beneath him, almost sexual, and more than once he stubs his toe on the spiked point of a cypress knee. They are everywhere, thrust like rotten canine teeth from the earth. He crosses a creek, balancing on wet roots that straddle the flow, and pushes through saloon doors of palmettos, his legs sinking thigh-deep in a muddy flat. It is cold down there, far from the sun, and his foot touches something strange. He yanks it free and peers into the hole he stove. He reaches down and up comes a man's tennis shoe, black-caked, heavy and limp as something dead. He tosses it into a nearby pool for the crawdads to study.

He fights his way across the mud, swinging his arms parallel to the earth, his body tottering like that of a man in cement boots. Halfway across, his shin strikes something and he trips. His outthrust arms plunge into the swampy earth, and mud slaps his face. He rises, blinking the cake from his eyes, and finds a braided steel cable buried like a tripwire in the mud. He begins following it, pulling the line foot by foot from the muck. It runs on into the trees, slithering over roots and through pools, crossing game trails churned over by paws and hooves. Mosquitos sing in his ears. He slaps them from his face and neck, his head bent to the ground, eyes tracing the iron seam weaving before his feet. The ground begins firming, rising, and he pushes through a thicket of palmetto, his arms red-scratched and stinging, and there before him stands the massive trunk of an ancient cypress, like a stone tower from the earth. The cable belts it, the choker set with a giant steel knuckle rusted brown.

His eyes begin the long trek up the trunk, seeking its heights, when he hears a rustling in the palmettos on the far side of the tree. The fronds are batting one another, gossiping. He steps in their direction.

"Lawton?"

A feral hog shoulders from the thicket and freezes, balanced atop a set of tiny hooves. It is black-bristled and round as a barrel keg, the yellow-white tusks bent upward from its jaws like the wickedest grin. The beast twitches and lowers its head, its spine razored in hackles, and Hunter shoots out his hand, palm-first, like a crossing guard. The animal seems to gather into itself, bunched like a giant black knot, and Hunter roars from the floor of his gut, as if that might stop what's coming. A bolt of light slashes across his vision, called up as if by his own voice, and there is a liquid crack, like from a beer can opening. The boar rolls onto its side, screaming, a long wooden pole shuddering upright from its shoulder, the iron point buried deep in the mountain of flesh. The stubby legs kick and kick, the animal turning a circle in the dirt, unable to right itself, its tufted tail slapping the ground as it screams.

A heavy rope falls down the tree, bouncing and straightening, and a shirtless man comes climbing down. His narrow back is burled and knotted with muscle, his great shock of hair nearly white. He turns from the tree and Hunter sees it is Uncle King himself, lean as a blade, like some creature that only hardens with age. He nods to Hunter, then pulls a long pig-sticker from a sheath on his belt, holding the blade low to one side as he approaches the dying boar. It has slowed its thrashing, its hooves casting drunkenly at the air, the panic spent in red gushes from its heart. The haft of the harpoon ticks gently now, in time to its breath or heart. Uncle King walks behind the animal. It can hardly lift its head to watch, a small black pig's eye following the wink of blade. Uncle King kneels and draws the knife across its throat with an underhand cut. The blood comes bubbling out, foaming in the gathering dark.

The old man looks at Hunter.

"Firewood," he says.

Only then does Hunter realize his ax is in his hand, white-knuckled, the edge-muzzle cast off. He looks a long moment at the weapon he holds, then up.

"Thank you."

The old man doesn't seem to hear him.

When he returns with an armload of shed limbs and kindling, Uncle King has the animal hung from a low branch, its ankle tendons pierced by a crude iron gambrel. He has already skinned it, the pale muscles glowing in the near-dark, a ghostly twin of the black creature it was. Nearby sits a large white ice chest, scraped and stained, that he must have dragged from a nearby creek. A four-pound box of Morton Salt sits on top.

Hunter says nothing. He's covered in mud and the temperature is dropping with dark. He bends himself to the fire, building his teepee of kindling. The old man hands him an ancient Zippo without asking if he's brought a lighter himself.

He hasn't.

Soon the fire is going strong, an arrowpoint of flame bouncing against the dark. They wait for it to burn down to coals. The creature hangs legless now, gutted, a long dark vent in the belly. The organs have been cast into the woods, the hunks of meat salted and set in the cooler. The old man cuts the loin into medallions and pierces them on a long whittled stick, balancing the spit across a pair of Y-shaped branches driven on either side of the pit.

Hunter sits on the ground, rubbing and scratching at his shins. Already the skin is rising in red little hills that itch. The old man looks at him, his eyes very open. They look stunned or dazed, like the eyes of men huddled under bridges or cardboard boxes.

"Chiggers," says the old man.

Hunter nods. "Yes, sir. Hopefully they aren't the real ambitious kind. Boy Scout camp once, I got them way up where you don't want them, if you know what I mean."

"Aye." The old man nods deeply, discussing a weighty matter indeed. "A devilment of the tallywacker, rival to the child-pox. I know it well."

Hunter sculpts his shins from the knees down, as if he could keep the bites from climbing any higher. He thinks back to his red-welted organ, meanly colonized by the chiggers of Camp Tolochee. Camp Torture-Me, they called the place.

"It was a devilment, all right."

Uncle King squats on his heels before the fire, turning the crude rotisserie. Fat drips into the coals, hissing, and Hunter's mouth waters.

"You got to get ye-self accustomed to such. Flood-times is nigh, all the world shall be again as ye see here." His hand swings in a half-circle, as if pushing open a door. "What scarce land remains made swampy and tidal, stomped soft underfoot, a savage ark of everything doomed."

"Flood-times?"

"Aye. Already the hellfire of our long making melts the great ice upon the poles. The waters are rising, and with them the beasts that ruled in the times before. They shall rise in unison, survivors freed of their lochs and inland seas, given to procreate in the black bellies of the earth, the eternal depths. We shall be fed upon by old evils, a hell of our own making."

Hunter looks at his hands, the nails dark-grimed like those of a mechanic. When he pushes his fingers into the dirt, he can almost feel the cold of the river.

"Sounds a little out there, if you ask me. No disrespect."

The old man holds his hand open before the fire.

"Has God not given us ample time to prove ourselves worthy of dominion? Of the image in which we are made? What god, I ask you, would find us not lacking? A creation with which he was well pleased?"

"I don't know," says Hunter. "Guess I hadn't really thought of it that way."

The old man keeps working the rotisserie, the tattoos crawling over his skin.

"Maybe you ought, son. Maybe you ought."

Hunter eyes the tattoo over the man's heart, the serpent trampled by a woman's foot.

THE DRAGON SHALT THOU TRAMPLE UNDER FEET.

"So you believe you been set here to kill the beast? Keep it down?"

Uncle King stops turning the meat.

"Why else were my children took down?"

"I'm very sorry for your loss, sir. I remember it from when I was little."

The man's eyes go wider yet, gazing beyond the firelight.

"Don't be sorry, son. It gave me my faith."

"I thought you were a priest before."

The old man shakes his head.

"Nay, I was a quoter of words. A mindless servant. Will-less. Now I understand that new creatures, more worthy than us, will be given rise. Chosen. And I intend to stop them." He looks at Hunter. "I am at war with God."

Hunter scratches his chin.

"That doesn't sound like the smartest fight to pick."

"Would you not be tired of the rote-believers, the deniers and hypocrites? The dismal forms of these your children? Perhaps he wants someone to fight him, to challenge his will."

"I don't remember anything about that in Sunday school."

The old man leans toward him, the fire throbbing in his eyes.

"There are future testaments to be written. They are being made even as we speak."

Hunter looks away. The medallions, thick-cut like giant marshmallows, hang over the coals. He is feeding words into this fire, sure as tinder, but he can't seem to help himself.

"My—our—daddy, he always did believe in it, the Altamaha-ha."

"And you, do you believe?"

Hunter looks into the fire, hands cupped over his knees.

"I don't know." He bites the side of his mouth, narrows his eyes. "Most I could say is, I'd like to. I'd like to believe my father was right for once. That something such as that could exist."

The old man sits straighter on his heels.

"An honest man," he says. "Tell me, what was your father's name?"

Just then Lawton steps from the woods, crashing through a palmetto thicket. His arms are latticed with scratches and cuts; twigs and leaves dangle from his beard. A headlamp glares from his forehead like the eye of a cyclops. He takes in the scene, the pork roasting over the fire, and grins.

"Y'all sons of bitches feasting without me or what?" He claps a hand to his mouth. "Oh, sorry, Father."

Uncle King brushes away the offense.

"Come," he says, "join this party of sinners."

"You don't got to ask me twice," says Lawton. He sits down heavily next to Hunter, clapping a hand on his shoulder. He squeezes once—in apology, perhaps—then rubs his hands together.

"So who killed the fucker?"

After dinner they follow Uncle King up the tree. The rope is knotted for grip, and they climb some twenty-five feet from the ground, reaching a plywood landing built over a heavy limb. Here they find a rope ladder, and up they climb, like men scaling a castle tower. It is dark, the moon skeltering strangely through the canopy, and the ladder twists and strains. Hunter's arms feel willowy, too light to hold him aloft, and yet they've never been so strong. He is next after the old man, Lawton below.

"Careful you don't fall," says Lawton. "I don't wanna die with your ass in my face."

"Careful I don't pinch one off on your head."

But when Hunter holds his breath, he can hear even Lawton breathing hard, fear or something like it pumping from his lungs. The fire coals are a red dot far below. He looks up and sees the pale soles of the old man's feet, surprisingly clean despite all that time on the ground. Above him floats a darkness, faintly geometric, like an alien craft hovering over the trees. Then the man disappears, leaving a square of moonlight glowing in the belly of the shape. Hunter keeps climbing, and soon he is through the portal, emerging onto a wooden platform set high over the forest like a widow's watch.

He crawls to the edge, and the canopy of lesser forest swirls beneath them, a sea of branches and leaves that murmurs in the wind. Here or there other old-growth survivors tower over the forest like points of overwatch. In the distance, cell towers blink their ruby lights against the horizon, and he can see the flare of this town or that over the far pine barrens, like treasures hidden in the trees. Lawton climbs up through the hole in the floor and rolls onto his back, his chest lumping like a boated fish's.

"Christ," he says.

Hunter rolls onto his back beside his brother. Above them the wash of stars, so close. Hunter watches them. He knows this space map is eons out of date, twinkling with the ghosts of suns long dead, their light still shooting the endless years through space. He knows new stars have been born, and he wonders what manner of creature will look upon them ages hence, huddled atop a world flooded blue as a marble or rimed white with ice. Will they have the slit pupils of serpents, as the old man believes, or will the earth stare blindly back, an orb of lifeless ocean and stone, storm-ridden, as before the coming of God or light?

Lawton rolls his head toward the old man, who is sitting cross-legged on an unfurled bedroll at the other end of the platform. Around him are his necessities, food cans and jugged water and coils of rope.

"You build this?"

The old man shakes his head.

"Not me," he says. "Tree-climbers. They come from all over the world for trees like this." He reaches out and pats one of the crown limbs that cradles the platform.

"I don't doubt it," says Lawton. Hunter is enjoying him there, shoulder to shoulder, the two of them breathing hard. But Lawton sits up and slaps his hands on his knees. "Okay, what you know about Hiram Loggins?"

52

Altamaha River, 2001

Hiram cuts the motor of the johnboat in the shadow of the railroad bridge. The sun is melting across the western horizon, pouring a milky red light onto the river, and the great skeleton trestles, quiet now, stand hulking and backlit against the sky like a word. Something that means not only sadness, but the surviving of it. A structure stubborn, unbroken, like the kind of old man Hiram hopes to one day be. He reaches under the aft thwart and hefts his snag-hook and coil of rope. It is a Sunday evening, his hour of keeping the promise he made to his once-brother before a deputy kicked them to the ground.

Find them.

He slings the hook over the river, the rope uncoiling like a tail. It crashes into the current and he waits as the iron prongs sink their way to the bottom, drawing out line. He thinks of this bridge in the long ago. More and more the memories of his boyhood rise unbidden. The spring day he and Uncle King—both eleven years old—completed their log-raft, built in the tradition of the sharpshooters of the timber days. Theirs was much smaller, of course, constructed in secret in the woods above Snakebelly Creek. They hewed pine saplings roughly square with a stolen broadax and laid the timbers out shoulder to shoulder, fastening them with cross-binders, ashwood poles spiked across the pines. Two shoot logs formed a pointed bow that would glance off the river's bars and bights, and they had two ammo boxes for dry storage and a cast-iron pot filled with sand to serve as their firebox.

This boy-made vessel would deliver them from the worlds they knew, the shouting voices and hard fists that filled both of their homes, the shrieks of pain that pierced the thin shantyboat walls. They launched their raft without ceremony, their provisions stolen from cupboards and drawers and tied down with careful knots. Their only companion was a feisty terrier mix named Fight, a dog they both owned, having found him barking on the roof of a swamped houseboat floating downriver two summers before. They had long poles, such as the rafthands once preferred, and paddles, too, taken from neighbors' canoes left vine-covered in the woods.

They spoke of what they would do in the port city of Darien, some thirty miles downstream at the river's mouth. They would be deckhands on shrimp or crab boats, working the inland waters day and night. They would shell shrimp from coolers if they had to, or be errand boys at the mills, or sell peanuts and peaches at the roadside stands to Yankees chasing the sun. They knew they could live off of almost nothing, because they already had. But they would live fearless now, among men without the sire's right to slap and beat them, to make their mamas spew blood and spittle, blubbering for mercy at day's end. They would be free.

The river was in flood, fast-moving from storms in the west, and they made good time through the many bights and rounds. They had left, as planned, on the day a new run of Old Man Gillis's white whiskey spread along the river in hundreds of mismatched jugs and jars. It would be at least two days before they were missed. They spent the first night on the bluffs of Sansavilla Landing, sleeping under a tarp they'd strung between two trees, their raft tied off to a big water oak. They were on the river again by first light, floating through the ghost world of dawn, when a lumped shape appeared from the mist off their starboard bow. It was a man floating belly-up, his arms stretched out like a starfish's, his torso covered in a rancid orange life jacket. His face was yellow, his eyes closed in death or sleep. A plastic jug of water or whiskey floated alongside him, attached to his wrist with a makeshift leash.

They pulled the raft in close.

"Mister?" said Hiram. "You alive?"

No answer.

Uncle was calm, his eyes hard.

"See what Fight thinks," he said.

The bearded little terrier, triple their age in dog years, had shown himself a good judge of character in times past. He balanced on the outermost log and lowered his head to sniff. His body went suddenly rigid, scruff hackling, and before they could push away, the man's eyes snapped open and he reached and grabbed hold of the raft. He nearly swamped it climbing aboard. Fight leapt back, planting his paws, barking murder, and the boys pushed their oars before them, holding the man at bay. He squatted at the far end of the raft with a lopsided grin, a sallow face. Riverwater streamed from a dozen places in his body, as if he'd been shot full of holes. He held out a hand, friendly-like, for the dog to sniff.

"Come on, buddy-pup. Name's Hallam. Skelt Hallam. I ain't gonna hurt ye."

Fight ventured one step closer, then two. He looked over his shoulder at them. Hiram nodded. The dog probed his nose toward the outstretched hand, one paw lifted, and Hiram saw what was coming too late: the man's other hand swung in a roundhouse from the dog's blindside, slapping it rolling and tumbling across the deck with a yelp.

"Fight!"

The dog hit the water on its back, bobbing up like a cork.

The boys lunged at the man with their paddles, stopped dead at the barrel of the snub-nose revolver suddenly in his hand, drawn from somewhere beneath the life jacket.

"Not so fast, you little fucks."

The hammer was already cocked. Behind the man Fight was churning water, trying to keep up. He barked, barked again, a high note of panic in his throat.

"Please, mister," said Hiram. "Let us get our dog."

The man reeled in his jug and popped off the top for a long, double-gulped swill. He wiped his mouth with the back of his hand, then eyed the dog over his shoulder. It barked again. Hiram made for the edge of the raft.

"That pistol ain't gonna shoot," he said. "The shells are too wet."

The man raised the pistol, quick, and fired twice. Fight screamed, his gut ripped open like a sack. A red mania of thrashing limbs, his yelps high and terrible, his snout bobbing for life. Then the staccato cough, his throat gargled with river or blood.

Hiram lunged but Uncle grabbed his wrist.

The wicked man smiled, tracking Hiram with the gun. There was grime creased in his yellow face.

"Best keep you boyfriend there on a leash," he said. "I can put 'em down all day."

Fight went under. Gone. A red eddy on the water, flecked with fur and meat.

Hiram was trembling. He didn't know whether to fight or cry. Uncle held him fast. A calmness had fallen over the boy. Uncle's eyes were glassy, his hand strong. He licked his lips.

"Some shooting," he said. His voice was flat.

"Korea," said Hallam. "Slants." He had another pull from the jug. "Mowed them down like yard grass."

"Is that what's wrong with your face?"

The man looked confused.

"My face? Naw, that's just my got-damn liver. It's about give out on me."

"Oh," said Uncle. He paused, his eyes gone far away. "I thought maybe it was all them yella men full up in your blood."

The jug stopped halfway to Hallam's mouth. His lips hung open a moment, then slowly warped into that crooked grin. He lowered the jug and leaned toward them.

"Tell you what," he said. "Big ole riverboat like this, I expect me some entertainments. Y'all got some entertainments for me?"

"Can't say as we do," said Hiram, shaking. "I expect we're plumb out."

"Naw," said the man, pushing his tongue through a missing tooth. "Don't you go selling yourself short now." He pointed the gun from one of them to the other. "I expect y'all got some *natural* entertainments I might could enjoy."

"Natural entertainments?"

"How 'bout you two little queers kiss for me?"

Hiram reared. "How 'bout you go *fuck yourself*—"

The barrel exploded and Hiram felt the round snap past his ear.

"I ain't asking twice, cocksucker."

Hiram's heart was thumping brutally, like a fist against his chest. Hiram looked at Uncle, then at the man, who cocked the hammer back. Uncle grabbed him by the back of the neck, two-handed, and planted a kiss on his lips.

"Tongue!" roared the man. "I want to see some tongue!"

They started to pull apart. *Pow!* Another shot. Two left.

Uncle's tongue speared its way into Hiram's mouth. It wriggled in there like something on the end of a bait-hook. Hiram's face was burning, scalded with shame. He opened an eye and saw the man had his fly open, his thing out. He was bent forward, coaxing and tugging it, that bubble of tongue poking through his missing tooth. His face even yellower now, the very color of sick.

"You." He pointed to Hiram. "Come over here." He pointed the gun between his legs. "I got just the thing for that mouth."

Hiram looked around for help. Nothing, just fog in every direction. Nothing real but this. He was crying, he realized. The sobs racking him. He thought of diving for freedom but remembered Fight, his blood unraveling in the current.

Pop!

"Best get to it, boy, less it's a bullet you want in that mouth."

Hiram started across the raft. The man's organ ticked through his fly, a foul growth Hiram would have kicked and trampled coming across it in the woods. He knelt, slowly, and wiped his mouth on the back of his sleeve. He bent toward it, and the man's hand found his head, fisting his hair, twisting it into a knot. Down he went, the salty-sweet bulb sliding past his teeth, toward the back of his throat. He coughed, choking, and the thing came spit-strung from his mouth.

"Let me do it," said Uncle.

Hiram turned and there was Uncle beside him, standing. Face quiet, chin set. Hiram hardly knew him, a boy seen from a distance.

"You'll get your turn," said the man. "Don't you worry 'bout that."

"I ain't got a gag reflex," said Uncle.

"Bullshit."

He knelt and shouldered Hiram out of the way, and Hiram watched in horror as Uncle took the thing in his hand and slid his mouth right over it. His head sank, then rose, and the man let slip a groan, his eyes rolling back in his head. Hiram knotted up his shirt in his fists and bent double, trying not to wail against the backs of his teeth. When he opened his eyes he saw Uncle's free hand coming out of his rubber boot, folding knife in tow, his head still bobbing. He opened the blade against his leg, so quiet, and Hiram, in abetment, did not scream as Uncle pulled the organ from his mouth and wrenched it sideways, cutting it free of the man in a long drive of blade that ended deep in the man's inner thigh. Blood burst from the stump, spewing like a hose, and the man stood roaring from the ammo box, ramming the pistol in Uncle's face. It clicked—a dud, the powder wet—and the man sank, clamping his hand over the leaks. Blood sprang between his fingers, spurting this way and that. When he looked up his face was white, unyellowed. He looked half a ghost.

"Got into the artery," said Uncle. "You ain't got long. Repent for what you done."

"Fuck you," said the man. He tried to raise the pistol, but it weighed too much.

"Repent," said Uncle. "Save yourself from hell."

The man's eyes were closing, his head lolling like a fading drunk's.

"I been." He panted. "I been there already."

Uncle opened his hand. The severed organ lay there, and the man dropped the pistol and took it. He held it down to himself, like he might reattach it, and soon he slumped forward, head between his knees, as if to examine the work more closely. The wounds kept pumping, covering his face, a planet aswim in blood.

When it was done, Uncle stabbed him several times on either side of the backbone, gill-like wounds to free the air from his lungs. They rolled him over and sat the heavy anchor on his chest and lashed him to the iron weight, coiling the rope under his arms again and again, using their hardest knots. They were just rounding the bend upstream of the bridge, the trestles shadowlike in the fog, when they rolled him over the side. He floated there a minute, face-down, and then he began to sink.

Hiram feels his hook reach bottom. He begins dragging the prongs along the riverbed, inch by inch. The evening sun has been swallowed in the trees, the sky blistered red. He feels a slight pressure on the hook and yanks, setting the flukes in another lawn chair or milk crate or busted television set. To his surprise, the line jerks in his hands, nearly ripping him from the boat. He crashes to his knees, rope burning through his scarred palm. He envisions a monster on the end of the line, yellow-faced and bloated, a man grown gills and fins and sharp yellow teeth.

"Hallam, is that you?"

Hiram Loggins sets his white rubber boots against the inner curve of the hull and rises, his whole body going taut. He begins to fight.

53

Fort Caroline, July 1565

Le Moyne, abed a bloody pallet, roars against the pine branch set between his teeth. The arrow shaft stands throbbing from the flesh of his thigh, the skin puckered and stormy at the root. Above him the surgeon, bone-saw in hand. Le Moyne roars again, trying to rise, but men kneel on his every limb, holding him in place.

Someone touches his forehead. He hears the voice of La Caille.

"He's only going to cut off the fletching, my friend. That we might remove the shaft."

Le Moyne rolls his head and sees, across the room, a pot of oil bubbling on the fire. They have cut away his breeches. His body is a waste, his legs the girth and pallor of bleached bone. They quiver beyond his control. His friend places both hands around the arrow's shaft, steadying it, the boar-tusk necklace rattling at his throat. The surgeon begins to saw.

Le Moyne's screams throttle the bit, the pinewood singing between his teeth. He can feel every evil bite of the saw, the arrowhead rocking in the meat of him like an anchor, a stony root. They might be cutting through his very bone. The fletching comes free and they roll him onto his side without saying why. When they hammer the arrow through the back of his leg, freeing the dart, his bowels break loose. A foul stench blooms in the room.

"*Je suis désolé,*" he croaks. "*Je suis désolé.*"

La Caille places a hand on his sweat-blistered forehead.

"No, my friend. I am the one who's sorry."

They pour the oil boiling into the wound. The pain screams through him, bright as the sun, loud as God. He did not know he could hurt so bad. He lifts from the floor, peeling from his own flesh, as if his spirit will out. Then darkness.

They should have known. The signs were everywhere. Three days ago, they marched into the western lands, the kingdom of Utina, to collect the ransom they were owed. All along the way, arrows were staked in the ground, scalps dangling from their nocks. Ominous banners planted all through the land, haunting their every step. The men cast sidelong glances at one another.

"What can it mean?"

"Perhaps they wish to honor us."

"For what? Seizing their king and demanding ransom?"

"More than a few of these trophies were won by our own guns."

"And what a lot of good that has done us."

They were three days in the village, waiting while the ransom was assembled at their feet. Sacks of corn and grain, one for every man, that would be clumsy to carry. Utina, their once-hostage, was nowhere to be found. Finally they discovered him hiding in a den on the outskirts of the village, and he told them the meaning of the staked arrows: war.

The chief held up his hands. He could do nothing, he said. His people would not listen. It was Lord d'Ottigni they hated, he of the ruined face. They had pledged to bald the white-faces, every one, and lift their fragmented bodies high against the sun.

Lord d'Ottigni, in command, growled.

"Your sun will see his children rot."

He ordered each man to take up his sack of grain. They must move quickly now, before the savages could act. Le Moyne was chosen as part of the vanguard, eight men strong, to move ahead of the formation. Before them lay the wide path out of the village, drowned in shadow, set like a canyon through walls of towering pines. The company moved out, the grain heavy on their backs, their bodies stilted beneath the weight. A company of men starving, staggering into a trap sure to come.

Six leagues, Le Moyne thought. More than half a day's hard march, and an attack could come at any step. Death was everywhere, it seemed. In his stomach, the hollow place that could swallow him up. In the woods, the spears and arrows sharpened for blood. In the river itself, swimming with teeth, with drowning currents and hidden shoals. In France, it never seemed so hard simply to survive. There was disease, war, the threat of Catholic swords. But it was not a constant siege, as here. Here the land was unbroken. In this country so green and rich, thousands would die, he realized. They would die in the pines and on the rivers, in the mountains his countrymen never reached but someday would. They would die by cold and hunger, by arrow and club and claw. By their own ropes and daggers and guns, their own hands and visions and dreams. This land was savage at its heart, an ocean of wildest green that would wreck whole nations of men, the virgin roots catching their blood.

The first scream was almost a relief. The man ahead of Le Moyne crumpled, grasping a shaft newly sprouted from his belly. Now more arrows, like sudden weather, whistling as they passed. Le Moyne dropped his sack and crouched behind its bulk. An arrow struck it, a puff of chaff, and he raised his weapon, firing into the throng of archers streaming from the woods. A man fell, squirting and flapping on the ground, and Le Moyne began to reload. His comrades were firing at will, an angry sea of powder smoke tumbling and churning over the road. Natives jerked and twisted, their naked bodies cracked open in pink bursts of spray.

Arrows mobbed the sky, quick as hornets, and he heard the wet crack of them striking bone, the concomitant screams. When the main column caught the vanguard, a second legion of archers attacked from the rear. Men yelped, back-shot, as missiles crisscrossed the air, leaping from the smoke.

Hours, it went. The Indians would not approach too closely the mouths of the guns. Le Moyne knew they feared French steel, the blades that hacked so cleanly through clubs and limbs. Instead, groups of archers would scamper forward, shrieking, and loose their arrows in unison, a swarm of them rattling against the sky, and then dart back into the woods. The ground bristled with arrows, shafts canted like strange crops of weeds. The men themselves looked little different, their flesh sprouted with quills. Still they fought. The Indians began rushing in, in groups of twos and threes, grasping their loose arrows from the ground.

D'Ottigni stood in the middle of the road, arrows singing past him.

"*Les flèches!*" he yelled. "*Cassez-les en deux!*"

Le Moyne grabbed the arrow nearest him and broke it in two, as instructed. Others were doing the same, snapping them over their knees or stomping them into the ground. Nearby, a small grove of arrows stood random-struck, knee tall. Le Moyne kicked and trampled them, the shafts snapping like bird bones beneath his feet. When he looked up a lone arrow was bearing down, meant just for him. It buried itself in his thigh, and he fell seated on the ground, staring wide-eyed at the wound. A man stepped alongside him, firing on the archer as he fled. The warrior fell, wounded in his lower spine. The bottom half of him lay still, the top half of him struggling to drag his dead legs across the ground.

Le Moyne felt the shooter's shadow cross him. He looked up: Lord d'Ottigni. Le Moyne had never seen him use a gun.

"*Levez-vous, Le Moyne! Battez-vous!*"

Le Moyne nodded. He got up to fight.

It was dark when they reached the river. Nearly half of them pierced, bleeding, staggering up the gangplanks into the barques. Le Moyne had been dragged on a hastily assembled travois, same as the others who couldn't walk. The moon throbbed over him, watching him gasp and cringe as the sled hit bump after bump. The Indians had begun melting away once their arrows were spent, but a few fought on, loosing single arrows out of the dark. In the wake of the march lay the sacks of grain, discarded, bleeding their ransom in the road.

54

Altamaha River, Day 5

Hunter hears a faint scraping and opens one eye. On the low edge of the platform a robin perches, watching the dark world before dawn. It has gray wings, its chest a ball of fiery orange, like some herald of the coming sun. It hasn't yet sung. Hunter closes his eyes, remembering the boyhood story of how the robin got its breast. A father and his son, in the cruel wilds for the night, took turns to keep a fire going on frozen ground. The boy was tired, his eyelids heavy. His father was already asleep. In the shadows beyond the fire, a wolf in wait. A tiny robin, gray as the wood, swooped down to fan the flames with his wings, keeping the fire alive through the night, so long his breast burned red.

Hunter opens his eyes again. The robin is watching him. A single eye, black and tiny as a bead. Hunter waits for the bird to sing its morning song—*cheerily, cheer-up*—but no. Its wings flicker and it drops over the edge of the platform, gone.

Hunter looks around. Lawton is curled on his side beneath a blanket, his head pillowed on a straightened arm. His hand is slightly open, like he just dropped something. Uncle King is gone. His pallet is neatly rolled, his cans and jugs arranged in soldierly rows. Hunter closes his eyes, trying to remember last night. He was so tired once they reached the top. The hike, the fight, the boar, the climb—he could let all of it go at last. Exhaustion hit him like a drug, an opiate in the blood, and the heavy blanket felt so soft on the planked floor of the platform, high over the concerns of the world. The night a starry dome, so dark and cool. His body seemed almost to melt. He could remember dozing in and out, catching only scraps of conversation. Lawton and the old man talked long into the night, it seemed. The two of them shadowy in his mind, voices alone, melding with his dreams.

"If it really exists, how come you're wanting to kill it? Hell, if the thing's time has come, so be it. You're the one was saying man's had long enough to prove himself. I ain't disagreeing. I seen a lot of this world from forty thousand feet up, and we look like some kind of disease on the land, black-topping forests and blasting mountaintops, draining marshes and building our houses and condos on top. On the ground it's worse. I seen women with their noses cut off, their ears. I seen little boys castrated for talking to us. I seen a woman once, she was hung by her hands, her skin cut under the armpits and peeled down to her waist. Drugged so she'd come awake hanging there bared to the meat, folds of outturned skin hanging down like flower petals. *The red tulip*. It's a thing. It's named. I put a round of five-five-six in the brain of the man that done it, and at the time I wanted to do the same to his whole fucking family. His mother, his dog.

"What I'm saying is there isn't much to recommend us as a species. Not many of us, at least. Me included. But my daddy believed in that creature down there, and he wouldn't of wanted it dead. Just the opposite. He'd of wanted to know that big-toothed son of a bitch was still down there, a thing man hadn't yet killed. A great fucking spite."

Hunter, hearing this, felt a part of himself swell toward his brother. He wanted to reach out, to touch him on the arm. To let him know. But his limbs were too heavy, weighted by sleep. They would not move. He could feel himself falling deeper, as if into a welcoming cave. He wanted to bring Lawton and the old man with him, into this good place, but they would not be moved.

"Get up and piss, boy. The world's on fire."

Hunter blinks open his eyes. A big toe is prodding his shoulder. Lawton's.

"College making you a damn layabout or what?"

Hunter sits up and rubs the sleep from his eyes. The sun is breaking ground, a red bubble flushing the sky.

Red sky at morning, sailors take warning.

"Fuck you, I was up half an hour ago. You were so conked out there wasn't nothing to do but go back to sleep. I don't know how you can do what you do for a living and sleep like that."

Lawton grimaces.

"Yeah, the boys might of put a bullhorn in my ear once or twice."

"I hope you pissed yourself."

Lawton tugs on his beard.

"No comment."

Hunter crawls to the edge of the platform. Mist rises from a vent in the trees, the river sliding unseen beneath them. A flight of white ibises skims in chevron over the cypress, glazed red. Hunter does not see his robin. A bright stream zags across his vision, falling against the trees. It's Lawton, hands on his hips, shins against the railing, pissing. Hunter thinks of those boys on the bridge, that first day, watching their spit sail south. He stands next to his brother and wrangles his thing from his shorts, flying a bright banner over the trees. He squints at the dawn.

"You weren't kidding."

"About pissing myself?"

"About the world being on fire."

Afterward, Lawton sets to work on a can of beans the old man left out for them, working the rim with the prong of his Swiss Army knife. His brow is dark, his tongue lumping his cheek like a dip. Hunter watches him.

"What you find out last night?"

Lawton shrugs, intent on the can.

"Nothing. Old man wouldn't tell me shit."

"About Daddy?"

"About anything."

"What y'all talk about, then?"

"Nothing, really. Went to sleep right after you."

"Bullshit you did. I heard y'all talking. Must of been a good hour you were at it."

Lawton's knife slips, gouging the web of his thumb.

"Fuck." He holds the bloody place to his lips and sucks.

"Lawton."

Lawton lowers his hand from his mouth, examining the wound.

"I don't know what to tell you, brother. You must of been dreaming again."

Hunter grabs the can from Lawton's hand and chucks it over the railing.

Lawton watches it tumble down toward the canopy, his jaw open.

"Hey, I wanted to eat that."

"Then you shouldn't be such a dick."

Lawton holds him in his blue eyes; they almost dance. Now he smiles, starts down the ladder.

The tide has come and gone in the night, the coals of the cookfire sogged. The trees wear high-water marks on their feet. Uncle King's iron gambrel still hangs from the tree branch, but the guts and castoffs are gone. A few bones scattered this way or that, a mess of earth churned over by hoof and claw, like a battle in the dark.

They look around, Lawton tugging on the end of his beard.

"All that not-talking last night," says Hunter, "you least could of asked him how to get out of this fucking place."

Lawton squints at the sun coming sideways through the trees.

"We follow the way the shadows point. West. We'll hit the creek we come in on and find our boats."

He leads the way, cutting a path with short, precise slashes of the machete. Woody vines and palmetto fronds, sliced, hang in place a beat before they fall. Hunter trails in his wake, ducking under branches and stepping over shallow creeks slippery with roots. They are black to the knees, their exposed skin angered with bites and scratches. The swamp is alive around them, choral, full of beasts unseen. Feral hogs on their own trajectories, like something slashed on a chalkboard, and songbirds that drape themselves tree to tree. Men as well, with minds fixed like stone, who make jagged lines across the world, unbending from one decision to the next. And below them all a creature that moves in silence, big as myth.

The light streams red at their backs. Hunter watches Lawton thumb the tattoo on his arm between slashes of the machete, and he touches his shark's tooth on its length of string, fingering the barb.

55

Fort Caroline, August 1565

A volley of gunfire shakes the air, and Le Moyne comes fast awake. Now a second volley, more distant, in echo of the first. He rolls himself from his hammock—prescribed by the surgeon to keep the insects from his wound—and takes up his crutch. He hobbles from the hut in his bedclothes, making for the wall, following the planks set like bridges across the muck. Yesterday at noon, alien sails sprang along the horizon, and Laudonnière ordered the men to their stations. They donned their breastplates and helmets, took up their halberds and spades and guns, and readied themselves along the wall. Even Le Moyne. He stayed awake long into the night, his arquebus laid across his lap, waiting for what enemies might come. Spaniards, probably. Catholics who loved blood. But late in the night his chin began to drop. Again, again. It bounced from his chest. Men were snoring along the walls, too tired to fear their deaths. Too hungry. Le Moyne's hammock called to him, his waiting cocoon.

Now it is morning, and men stand all along the palisade in defensive position, their armor gleaming, their weapons booming fire. Powder smoke curls over their heads, wind-churned, and Le Moyne throws down his crutch and climbs the wall, his wound protesting every rung. He sees a fleet of seven ships arranged in battle formation, big as islands in the river, their gunwales lined with armored men. Their weapons are aimed heavenward, iron stalks belching fire and smoke, and Le Moyne realizes the men along the wall are cheering. The soldier nearest him grabs his shoulder and shakes him, his face huge with glee.

"Ribault!" he cries. "It is Captain Ribault! We are saved!"

It is the twenty-eighth of August, 1565. The resupply ships have arrived.

Earlier that month, Le Moyne began venturing forth from his hut. His wound was a puckered mouth, messy as a babe's at table, but there was no rot. Several of the wounded were not so lucky. They lay abed, their bodies stormed black with decay, death slowly chewing them from the world. Meanwhile the sun glared down, angry, so hot the very air faltered and swayed, heat-stricken, and the river steamed like bathwater. The men of the fort staggered beneath the heat, covered in a slime of sweat and mud. Many now slept in their filth, surrendered to it, and they made but little progress in shipbuilding. The weather seemed only against them, lashing them again and again with afternoon squalls that made soup of the fort. The spirits of the men seemed worn, dwindled like unstoked flames. Their heads bobbed stupidly on their necks, their faces blank. Two of the garrison's best carpenters were killed stealing Indian corn. The master shipwright concluded the *Breton*—their way home—would not be ready for sail as soon as hoped. The men wanted him shot.

Le Moyne spent his days of convalescence on a stool set next to the door of his hut, taking the sun, sketching, or fiddling with the tongue stone in his pocket. The men who passed him were mostly shoeless, their clothes in rancid tatters, their bodies red-burned and flaking, welted with bites and sores. They scratched and dug at their bodily nooks. Bits of food clung in their beards. One day he watched a hook-nosed tailor named Grandchemin—his neighbor—root through the crotch of his pants with one hand, stepping into the light to examine what curiosity he'd found. Whatever it was, he crushed it between his fingers and went back inside his hut.

A voice behind him:

"Ah, the glory of France."

Le Moyne turned, startled, to find La Caille at his side. His friend was grinning, his black beard dagger-sharp as ever.

"*New* France," Le Moyne reminded him.

La Caille gazed about them.

"Is it so different, my friend?"

"I should say."

La Caille squatted down to Le Moyne's level, the necklace of boar tusks rattling at his throat.

"And when, my friend, were you last in the lesser *quartiers de Paris*?"

Le Moyne frowned. "Still, I never thought I would die in a mud street like this."

La Caille clapped a hand on his shoulder, waving his hand toward the anchored hulk of the *Breton*.

"Confidence, man, you could still die at sea."

Ribault. The man who commanded the Charlesfort expedition in '62, erecting markers of French dominion along the coast. He comes ashore beneath the blaring of trumpets, the salute of guns. A man who cuts the air as he walks, his nose sharp as something hewn from marble, his beard a fiery red. His face freckled, flecked as if with some lesser's blood. Rugged men flank him on every side, armed for war.

"They say he is the greatest seaman in all of Christendom," whispers the soldier next to Le Moyne. "Look at him. Can you not believe it?"

He can. Surely the man has been sent to relieve Laudonnière of his command. There are rumors that the admiralty is displeased. Le Moyne doesn't care. That night they slaughter a pig from Ribault's stock and roast it whole on the spit, and wine spills among them like so much blood. The laughs of the men are softer, less wicked and sharp, and they huddle long into the night, tale-bearing about their cookfires. In the morning they rise crimson-tongued, full of piss and hope, and stagger down the riverbank to bathe, emerging white-scrubbed from the river like new men.

56

Altamaha River, Day 5

Y ou're shitting me."

Lawton is staring at Hunter's boat, canted among the ferns of the logging road. Their father's ashes are missing. The bag was riding just aft of the cockpit, secured beneath the crisscrossed diamonds of black elastic cords.

"You sure they were here when we left?" asks Lawton.

"I'm sure. I even thought of bringing them."

Lawton turns an eye on him.

"Well, why didn't you?"

"I been carrying them the whole damn trip. Why not you?"

Lawton growls and squats. The tide came in the night and shifted the boats. They are still tied to the tupelo, but the bushes in a small radius have been smashed, flattened by swinging hulls.

"You sure you had them secured good?"

"You know I did," says Hunter. "You been bird-dogging my ass the whole time."

He kneels beside the boat and palms the deck behind the seat, there where his father's ashes had been, as if he could read their whereabouts by touch. There are slight scratches in the plastic hull. Absently he traces them, feeling his brother's anger throb in the air. Lawton is squatting on his haunches, beard in fist, eyeing the forest like something he will burn to the ground. Just then, an answer rises through Hunter's fingers—a logic—and he looks more closely at the deck.

"Lawton, look here."

Lawton comes near, looking over his shoulder. On the deck, knife-scratched like a glyph, is a single word: UP. They look, and there above them hangs the black bag of ashes, dangling from a tree limb like a sack of food in bear country.

"Hell," says Lawton.

The rope crosses the limb and slants through the trees, anchored to a sapling. Hunter slips the knot, dropping the sack into Lawton's waiting arms. He walks up to him.

"Funny the old man knew what was in the bag, you not talking to him and all."

Lawton looks at the bag in his hands, like something he's just discovered. He seems almost to jerk, shoving the bag toward Hunter.

"Probably thought it was lunch is all. Didn't want them hogs to get at it."

Hunter takes the bag. It's dry, untouched by the tide. He leans into Lawton's face, squints.

"Better check them eyes of yours, big boy. I think they're turning brown."

They break from the creek, sliding back into the big river. The sun is climbing, the water gleaming like polished brass. Hunter looks over his shoulder, trying to see the high platform where they spent the night. He can't. The cypress grows too deep in the island's heart, far from the winches and saws of old, hidden by an army of second-growth timber. Already it seems a dream.

Cottonbox Island appears, a green fin of pine that splits the river. In high school they would anchor here, drinking beer and throwing footballs in the waist-deep shallows. Lawton would have the floating cooler tied to his belt, the big cube tumbling and crashing whenever he surged and dove for misthrown balls. He said it was better than parachute sprints.

He dips his paddle in the water and broadsides his boat, looking at Hunter.

"Let's lunch here. Somebody threw my breakfast in the woods."

He grips the sides of his cockpit and lifts himself from the seat, the hull quivering beneath his balanced hands, his legs unfolding from the boat's hollows. He slides feet-first into the river, bouncing as he touches bottom. He looks up, teeth clenched in grin.

"It ain't a hot shower."

Hunter gasps as the water swims up his shorts. It seems so much colder than two nights ago on the bridge, as if the river is skipping seasons, sliding straight into fall. He starts to say something, but Lawton has already shrugged out of his vest and ducked under the water, a ball of white flesh hovering beneath the river. He breaks the surface roaring, the angular slabs of his body flushed pink, his veins glowing a cold blue. The water blades from him, clear and bright, and his shoulders look geologic, like formations of freckled stone. He wades back to his boat and peels up one of the deck hatches, rummaging.

"You gonna fix us lunch?" asks Hunter.

Lawton tosses him an MRE in a desert-tan pouch.

"Meal, Rarely Edible," he says. "Compliments of Uncle Sam."

Hunter tears it open with his teeth. Inside he finds a pouch of marinara sauce with meatballs, a packet of raspberry drink mix, a bag of cookies dotted with pan-coated chocolate discs—generic M&Ms.

"Yum, yum, yum."

Lawton pulls his smartphone from a clear plastic dry bag.

"Best try it before you pop a woody." He holds the phone aloft like some instrument from the days of sail. Hunter tears the white plastic spork from its cellophane wrapper.

"You got any signal out here?"

Lawton doesn't answer. He has his own MRE hanging from his teeth now, his thumbs tapping away at the phone. The device looks tiny in his overlarge hands, out of place.

"Weren't you seeing some Air Force girl last Easter?" asks Hunter. "Chopper pilot?"

"Helo."

"What?"

"Helo. We don't call 'em choppers."

"That's funny, Lawton. I don't remember giving a fuck."

Lawton grins.

"I'm just checking in. Work stuff."

Hunter tears open the pouch of meatballs and sauce. It looks like someone threw up a nice Italian meal in an airsickness bag. He sporks the red gruel and shakes the raspberry drink mix in his water bottle, a milky pink foam. Soon his belly is full, his head dreamy with influx. Sugar and sodium, fat and protein and electrolytes. He burps. He holds the bowline of his boat and kneels, letting the river swim over his shoulders, whispering its power. He's been in so long he's numbing to the cold.

Lawton has put away his phone. He stands waist-deep in the river, shoveling his rations into his mouth. His beard has dried into its old wild form, fire-orange, and the muscles of his temples and cheeks pulse darkly as he chews. His freckle-dusted body is trembling slightly, his nipples dark as stone. Beneath him the river looks almost burnished, a brassy hue. It breaks at his waist, curling downriver in long snakes and folds. Hunter lies back, letting the river lift him, shoulder his weight. He closes his eyes. His limbs feel lengthened, drawn out in the current's will. His blood swims with the tide. The sun rises, high as a god, as it has again and again through a thousand histories, and for a moment he is legion, inseparable from all those who lift their faces at noon, who have and who will. So many believe a kingdom will come that makes light of every day, gold of every hour. A world of future myth, tinted gold, in which the rivers will be stilled, and nothing will be lost, and no secrets will lurk in the bottoms. But the kingdom is here, he knows. Now. Ten thousand fortresses risen and dashed, and the rains fall yet in the mountains, and the river moves.

The day goes sudden dark, like a hood coming down, and he opens his eyes. The river is black, the sun lost behind a gray whale of cloud. Lawton looks small and far away, his body shockingly white, as if the blood runs cold beneath his skin. He is talking but Hunter cannot hear him, the voice heavy and muffled. He lifts his ears from the water.

"What?"

"You awake?"

"I'm talking, aren't I?"

"You could of been dreaming."

"So what if I was?"

"You eat a good solid meal?"

"Enough. Why?"

"Good," says Lawton. He turns and starts readying his boat.

By noon a cloudbank, heavy and dark, is crowding the western horizon, and they are under way. A cold wind rises behind them, riffling the surface, a shiver across the river's back.

57

Fort Caroline, September 1565

The shadows are long, the day ending, when shouts rise along the ramparts. Six vessels of unknown origin, sighted off the coast. They are sailing right for Ribault's resupply ships, now anchored at the river's mouth. Le Moyne, newly free of his crutch, hobbles toward his bluff above the fort. Others are already gathered, breathless as they watch. Some have shimmied into the trees. All look across the delta, the vast expanse of brown marsh where the tide flows in and out. The alien fleet drops anchor across from the resupply ships. Le Moyne and his companions can hear the bleat of trumpets, the vessels hailing one another over the water.

"*Les Anglais?*" says someone.

"Let us hope."

Below them the fort is still, all work ceased as men stand poised on high vantages, stretching to see. The shadows lengthen, lancing toward the scene at the river mouth. It has been hardly a week since Ribault arrived to take command, but the days have been long and full, new colonists and old working side by side to rebuild the earthworks and palisades. Foodstuffs have been brought ashore from Ribault's ships, the bakery chimney emitting a constant chuff of smoke. The world seemingly returned to form, as if destiny shines newly upon their work.

The two lines of ships hover in opposition, motionless, like pieces upon a chessboard. Perhaps they await some cue, an opening dictated from a throne across the ocean. These chessmen of kings. Without warning the foreign ships erupt, their sides flashing in unison, long shoots of flame leaping from their guns. The hull timbers of the French ships splinter and quake, receiving the blow, and the sound of cannon fire comes rolling inland, tumbling over the river and marsh and slamming into the men on the bluff.

"Spaniards," says one. "God help us all."

The French ships cut their anchors and flee. Well into the night, fire pops and cracks along the horizon, a storm rolling low against the sea.

Noon of the following day the French ships heave into view, their masts stabbing the sky, their hulls topping the horizon like a wave. The wind is ripping, the water capping at the river's mouth. The small fleet crashes up and down just off the coast, toyed by the heavy surf. A messenger posted down on the seashore comes running into the encampment, breathless with news. Le Moyne and others climb down from the walls to hear.

"The wind keeps them offshore," says the messenger. "They signal us to come to them."

Laudonnière, deposed, has taken to bed. A fever, some say, spurred by his fall from grace. The men look to Ribault. The great sea captain runs his fingers through his red beard. He shakes his head.

"No. The Spanish may have captured the vessels in the night. It could be a trap." He looks from man to man. "We wait."

Later that day, a tiny shape appears inshore of the ships, thrashing through the breakers. A swimmer. He is brought into the fort on the back of a mule, swaddled still dripping in a large blanket, almost dead from the feat, like the long-runner of Marathon. He brings a message from the captain of *le Trinité*, lead ship of Ribault's fleet. The Spanish force is under the command of Pedro Menéndez de Aviles, who says he is under order of his king to hang and behead all Lutherans in this land and upon its seas. He pursued the French ships long into the night, his guns never silencing, but the French were able to outpace his fleet. At daybreak, the Spaniards anchored far down the coast, putting ashore a large company of negroes armed with spades and mattocks.

At this news, Ribault shows his teeth, unsmiling.

The next day a party of friendly natives arrives from the south, bearing further news of the place. They say the Spanish are entrenching themselves, working their slaves day and night. Ramparts are being erected, trenches dug. Earthworks raised from the ground. They say the Spanish are calling the place San Agustín.

Ribault calls a council of war, to which Le Moyne finds himself invited. In the room stand the chief military officers of the fort—more than thirty of them—and civilians of certain status. Ribault sits at one end of the long table, Laudonnière the other, a phalanx of captains between them. Laudonnière stands first to speak. He has dressed to receive them, his red doublet now ragged and overlarge, creases of pain writ in his face. His hand trembles slightly on the back of his chair.

"I—like the rest of you—would like nothing more than to strike the Spanish at first opportunity. But I must counsel prudence. Such a course should not be taken rashly. Seigneur Ribault, I propose that you and your men remain here to fortify our defenses against a seaborne attack. My men and I, who know the country well, will travel overland to settle this matter with the Spanish."

The first settlers—Le Moyne included—murmur their assent.

Agreed.

Our commander has spoken well.

We should hold the ground we stand.

Yea, protect the walls we have built.

Ribault leans back in his chair, his great hands laced across his chest. When they finish, his chair rocks back to earth. He rises, enormous, setting his fists upon the table. His eyes blaze.

"Before sailing from France, I received word from the Admiralty that this Spaniard Menéndez meant to attack us, and I was told we were to yield nothing to the man. We are to drive him from this land or else bury him in it. If we march overland against the Spanish—to this San Agustín—we may very well lose the opportunity of destroying his force. They could simply retreat to their ships. The better plan, I believe, is that we sail against them, now, with every available man and ship, and seize their vessels at anchor. They will have no refuge save the works their slaves are building. They will be trapped."

He looks from one face to another, eyes yet blazing, as if he could sway each man with a look. Le Moyne watches the officers shift beneath his gaze, scratching their chins or rubbing their hands, and he realizes that the man is truly possessed of such power. Laudonnière, alone, stands against him. He is trembling visibly now, but his spine and jaw are set.

"Seigneur Ribault, we must remember it is *la saison de l'ouragan*. A whirlwind could land upon us at any time. To sail now, we endanger our entire fleet upon a single venture, while imperiling those who remain."

Ribault sits back. His blue eyes flood the room with contempt. Coldly they rove the first settlers, seeing their sunken cheeks and blistered skin, their humbled hearts. His gaze falls upon Le Moyne. Le Moyne sees the cold sea in those eyes, the unbanished pride. He knows what the man will say even before he does, dismissing the old commander's concerns with a wave of his hand.

"The Spanish sail in this season, do they not?"

Laudonnière remains standing. His eyes are pleading now, almost wet. They crawl from face to face, but the officers look at the table, the sergeants their boots. He looks to Ribault.

"Please, sir, I beg you to hear my advice."

"I have heard it, sir. And I have made my decision. We sail at once."

Le Moyne stands straight-backed on the main deck of the warship. His arms at his sides, his chest pushed out, his leg yet lame. He can feel his blood beating against the welted flesh, the pain tolling through him like a bell. Ribault has commandeered Laudonnière's men as well as his own, and every soldier well enough to stand has made ready to sail. For three days the wind has blown against them, keeping them at anchor among the islands of the river's mouth.

It blew hard out of the south, the very direction of this Saint Augustine. Finally the conditions have righted, and Ribault has ordered a final inspection of the men before pulling anchor.

Lord d'Ottigni paces slowly down the line, his eye appraising each man through the frozen half-mask of his face. He carries his sword in hand, sheathed, using the blunt point of the scabbard to prod and inspect his soldiers. He pokes them here or there, as if testing their joints or muscles. He lifts loose garments to see what disease or contraband they might be hiding. He dresses them down for ill-sharpened blades, unclean barrels. For smelling like goats or pigs or the cunts of whores.

"These Spaniards fashion themselves conquerors—*conquistadors*—and like all Catholics, they have a great thirst for blood. We will give them plenty this day. We will make them to lap like dogs in the pools they shed."

The men stamp their feet, thundering the deck.

Yea! Hurrah! Slaughter them whole!

Lord d'Ottigni stands before Le Moyne.

"*L'artiste*," he says. "I am glad you have come." There is no mocking in his voice, not since the battle in the west, when Le Moyne stood to fight despite his wound. "How fares the leg? It has healed so quickly?"

"*Oui, seigneur.*"

"You are sure?"

"*Oui.*"

D'Ottigni nods, then jabs the metal tip of the scabbard into Le Moyne's thigh at the very spot of the wound. Le Moyne gasps as if skewered, the leg buckling beneath him.

D'Ottigni turns to his sergeant.

"This man is unfit for service. Have him remanded to the shore boat."

"*Seigneur, s'il vous plaît!* I can fight!"

D'Ottigni turns and clasps his shoulder. "I know you can fight." Now he leans close, the dead ridges of his face scraping across Le Moyne's cheek. His voice is a whisper: "But someone must live to tell the world of our great *glory* in this land, yes?"

Le Moyne opens his mouth to protest, but d'Ottigni is already gone. The sergeant points Le Moyne down the line, one hand palming the pommel of his sword.

On the shore boat, Le Moyne finds himself next to his neighbor, the tailor Grandchemin. The man is sulking, hands clapped on either side of his head.

"What have they sent you back for?" asks Le Moyne.

The man shakes his head.

"I am to repair some garments for Lord d'Ottigni, for his return to France. He says he does not wish his family to know how poorly he has been living here." The man shrugs. "He says it is work he wishes completed at once."

Le Moyne feels a tightness in his throat. He can see it clearly: the lone trunk delivered home from a foreign shore, the garments clutched to a grieving woman's chest. She holds a shirt to her nose, trying to remember his scent.

D'Ottigni does not believe he will live.

Le Moyne calls to the men aboard the ship. He asks them to send for his friend La Caille. But it is too late. The anchors are already being pulled from the water, the sails swelling with power. The great wall of the ship moves away from their boat, a moat of sea dividing them. La Caille appears finally at the rail, waving with both hands, but their cries to each other are lost, scattered by the wind. Le Moyne sends his love across the water, thumping his chest, and he thinks he sees La Caille, tiny now, do the same. His heart feels huge, balled like a giant's fist, and he wants only to open it, to reach his friend.

O Lord protect my brother aboard that great lumbering ship and return him safely to my arms. Bless my countrymen every one Father God that their swords and spades and shot may find Spanish hearts—every last one of them, if that is what it takes.

The fleet has hardly crossed the horizon when thunder cracks overhead, so loud men cower and duck, and Le Moyne falls to his knees, clutching the tongue stone to his breast.

58

The river is black beneath them, the sky pale. The wind cold, born in mountains far out of sight. Hunter looks over the side of his boat, his reflection gliding alongside him. It wavers and shudders, shadow-dark, like some spirit in the water. He looks away. On the right bank lies Cambers Island, the site of a rice plantation in antebellum times. The field hands fled the place after the Civil War, when the overseer proved ignorant of their freedom. The place is nothing but trees now, scarce hint of those who lived there before. Hunter stares on into the maze of trunks and vines, into the shadowy vents, unsure what he expects to see. Ghosts, perhaps.

From the air, or satellite, other signs can be seen. The geometric grid of dikes and canals cut into the swampy earth, still visible, like signs for the gods. The rice fields were flooded and drained by a system of locks, the slaves toiling daylong in the ankle-deep muck. A third of them died in the first year of work. But here, from this level, nothing but trees and marsh and swamp.

Hunter looks ahead. Lawton sits very erect in his boat, his paddle wheeling side to side, steady as a clock. They will be down into the lower delta soon, the river branching, birthing the fan of child rivers that reach wildly for the sea. The cypress and tupelo will grow sparser, leaner, giving way to the brown expanses of salt marsh that border the coast. At last the line of sea islands will rise against the ocean, an armada humpbacked and green, their seaward edges paled with fine quartz sands. There is Wolf Island, a refuge for migratory birds since the 1930s, and Sapelo Island, where the Gullah people live, descendants of fugitive slaves who still speak their creole tongue. Below that is Saint Simons Island, a moss-haunted realm of golf courses and beach resorts, and all of the lesser-known islands between, rumored stomping grounds of pirates and Confederates. And so many people believe the state is landlocked. In the men's room of a bar in Darien, a sticker has been pasted on the mirror: GEORGIA HAS A COAST?

They are close now. Perhaps five miles to the interstate bridge, another ten to the ocean. They will cast their father's ashes into the black waters of the marshes, where the river flows both ways, in and out.

They have been under way less than an hour when Lawton pulls his phone from the pocket of his vest, squints at the screen, then tucks it away. He looks over his shoulder.

"I got to take a leak."

"You serious?"

Lawton is of that special breed who refuses to stop on a road trip for anything as insignificant as a piss. Same as their father. On road trips the old man made them piss in mason jars he brought for the purpose, and this with contempt.

"Serious," says Lawton. "Must be getting old or something. All these muscles shrinking more than my dick." He jabs his thumb ahead. "This bend ought to do me."

They shore their boats at a small bluff of orange silt, concave beneath a green lip of turf, and Lawton starts up the bank. Hunter follows him, realizing he, too, could use a pit stop. Maybe it was something in the powdered drink mix—

He stops cold, a thrill risen in his gut. At the crest of the bluff, where a line of water oaks stands at attention, there is a break in the understory. A path, too high to be seen from the water. A secret door. He thinks of how Uncle King knows every inch of the river, its secrets and ghosts. The locations of sea monsters, shipwrecks, perhaps even an old French fort.

"That's what he told you, isn't it—"

Lawton wheels and glares at him, one finger to his lips: *silence*. Then he turns and starts down the path, moving in a half-crouch. Slowly, slowly. Stepping here and there to avoid sticks and leaves, his bare feet soundless on the trampled turf. Deft for so big a man. Practiced. Hunter follows, a little behind, careful of his own feet, the sound they make. The wind rises, swirling through the trees, leaves humming on every side. They are fifty yards down the path when they cross a small creek and find an alligator gar lying across the trail, gutted. It is four feet long, a torpedo of a fish with hard, enameled scales and outsized teeth. A living fossil, dead. A warning. A black vent has been sliced in the yellow belly, the innards scooped out and left to rot in a ropy pile. Maggots glisten in the cavity. Flies abound, ticking like tiny robots across the exposed viscera. It smells like it looks.

Lawton lowers himself to one knee and cocks his head, examining the work. Hunter starts to say something, but Lawton's blue eyes cut toward him, killing the words in his chest. Now Lawton rises, and on they move. The path winds deeper into the woods, zagging around deadfalls of old timber, crossing shallow streams where Lawton kneels for prints. Hunter is breathing hard now, like he would after a standing block chop. He looks down and finds the hand-ax at his side. He doesn't even remember taking it from the boat.

Another hundred yards on and both of them stop.

Before them two saplings stand arched over the road, their upper reaches lashed to form a makeshift arbor. The skulls of small animals and fish dangle from the branches on lengths of fishing line, a crop of cruel ornaments trembling in the breeze. Their hollow sockets sway this way, that way, guarding the path before them. Hunter reaches up to touch one—a raccoon's skull, maybe, or a large gray squirrel's—then doesn't. When he looks down again, Lawton has a gun.

"You fucking liar."

It isn't a fort. It is a tar-paper shack, built narrow and long like a shotgun house, dirt floored with papered windows. A lank square of burlap covers the front door. Hunter's voice is low, edged between them like a knife.

"What did that old man tell you last night?"

Lawton glances at him, then reverts his eyes to the shed. His brow is dark. The pistol is small, chunky and modern and black. Another thing kept hiding in that vest.

"He said it was a place we ought to see."

"What kind of a place?"

"A place that holds answers."

"To what, exactly?"

Lawton watches the place, cataloging corners and exits, fields of fire.

"That wasn't exactly clear."

"Here I was thinking he told you the location of the old French fort, and you were holding out to surprise me."

"It's probably nothing. A hunting camp. Maybe those poachers . . ."

"You're just a goddamn broken record, huh?"

Lawton turns, eyes blazing.

"There's something evil on this river, Hunter, whether you want to believe it or not. Maybe it had to do with Daddy's death, maybe not. But he ain't the first turned up dead or not at all, and the Sheriff's been doing shit-all. Somebody's got to get to the bottom of it. I didn't come halfway around the world just to sprinkle them ashes like a bunch of pixie dust. I'll know the reason why."

Before Hunter can reply, Lawton jams his phone in his hands.

"Shit goes south, you hit number one on speed-dial and run your ass for the boats."

"What's on speed-dial, a goddamn drone strike?"

"Friends. There's people know I'm here." He edges back the slide, the brass glint of a shell in the chamber. "Sit tight, I'm just gonna clear the place."

"Not by yourself you're not."

"Oh yes I am. This is my decision. I'm not putting you at risk."

"It doesn't work like that, Lawton. You doing this touches us both."

Lawton puts a hand on his shoulder.

"You're a good brother, Hunter. And I'm proud of you. I have zero doubt you could of made a frogman." His big hand squeezes. "But I'm the one trained for this. You follow me, I will beat the ever-loving shit out of you."

Hunter grabs for his vest too late. Lawton is already breaking across the clearing, crouched low, making for the corner of the shed. He pauses there, setting his shoulders behind the weapon, and starts across the front of the building. His upper body is locked in firing position, his feet moving trimly below his fixed hips. "God damn you." Hunter breaks from the bushes, scampering toward the shed. Lawton has stacked himself against the doorframe, his pistol angled low, his chest moving up and down. Hunter comes up behind him, his heart whirling like a siren, and starts to grab for his brother's shoulder.

"Lawton—"

It's like touching a trigger. Lawton's body explodes. In a single motion he whips wide the burlap flap and sweeps into the darkness.

"On the ground! Everybody on the ground!"

There is commotion, the crash of a table or chair.

"Hands! I wanna see your hands!"

Hunter ducks through the flap.

"I said *on the ground*, motherfucker!"

Lawton brings the butt of the pistol down hard on a man's face. He falls to the ground, blood springing from his nose.

Hunter stares.

There are two of them, rough men in tan overalls blotched with oil or blood. They lie facedown, asses clenched, fingers laced behind their heads. The windows are papered over, discolored shafts of light slanting down on the prone men, churning with angry mobs of dust. The rest of the place is jumbled in darkness, a mystery until their eyes can adjust. Lawton glances at Hunter. His blue eyes are bold in the dark.

"I'll deal with you later." His voice is calm. Angerless. He turns back to the men, stepping among their bodies. "Now which of you motherfuckers is gonna tell me what happened to Hiram Loggins?"

The nearest man turns his head to the side, one eye round as a fish's.

"We don't know this man."

The words are clumsy in his mouth. Accented.

Lawton kneels and pushes the pistol into the base of the man's skull.

"The fuck you don't."

59

McIntosh County, 2001

Annabelle Mackintosh sits on her porch smoking another cigarette. It is moonless tonight, and the crumpled pack sits nearly empty on the side table, like smashed origami. He isn't going to come, she thinks. Hiram. She blows the smoke through her teeth. It isn't him that maddens her on nights like these. It's her own self. That here she sits in her crumbling tower, a single story barely afloat of the muck, waiting for a man that isn't hers. That never will be.

She sees his wife sometimes in the grocery in town. She turns her cart down the aisle and there the woman stands, steel-haired and strong-jawed, examining cans of soup or beans. Her boys trail behind her, sprinkled with acne, shoving and making faces when she isn't looking. The older one has red hair, the sight of which burns like fire in her chest. Annabelle wheels her cart from the scene, as if she's turned down the wrong aisle, before any of them can see the hot flare of shame on her face.

She lights her last cigarette from the burning nubbin of her old one. There are cool blue veins on the backs of her hands now, like streams pouring from the hills of her knuckles, and her hair is beginning to lose its flame. She will have to start dyeing it soon. She holds the smoke a long time in her chest before letting it out, surveying her realm. There is the uncut grass, the imploding boat shed, the muscle car dying slowly in the yard. The tires are dry-rotted and nearly flat, the red paint bubbling along the fender wells. Her husband is north of three hundred pounds now, bloated on Popeye's and bourbon-Cokes, an oily mass that jiggles and farts when it moves. The doctor says his heart won't take much more abuse. He tried putting it in terms Barlow would understand:

"It's like trying to run a tractor trailer on a little Honda engine. Something is going to go boom."

"Doc, you ain't just compared my heart to some Jap-built piece of shit, did you?"

She has tried making him boiled chicken, skinless, and steamed vegetables like the doctor prescribed. Salads with translucent dressing and bowls of nutty brown rice. He won't eat it. When she put the FryDaddy in the attic, he called her a good-for-nothing bitch. When she said she wasn't going to make any more of the food that was killing him, he said good thing the trash out by the interstate would. Her long hate of him—of what he had made of himself and the life he promised her—has turned somehow to pity, even compassion.

Hate was so much easier.

Her cigarette is nearly out. She sucks it right down to the filter, feeling the heat build in her lungs. She tries not to think of what might be keeping Hiram tonight. Of that good woman at home, those two boys growing up straight and strong. She stubs the cigarette into the ashtray and slips out of the bloodred high heels he likes, not wanting to wake up Barlow when she stilts back into the house. She stands, trying not to look at the blue veins running down the tops of her feet.

"Pssst."

She jumps.

There's Hiram at the corner of the porch, a big shit-eating grin on his face.

"Thought I wasn't coming, huh?"

Annabelle bites down on the corners of her mouth, trying to fetter her smile. She leans back, allegedly yawning, letting her body express itself against the dress.

"Oh Hiram," she says. "You're too late. I'm so tired."

He grins wider, coming around to the door.

"Bull-fucking-shit," he says. "You ain't been tired of me a day in your life."

He's right.

She comes to the door. He won't touch it. Never would. It is always her who must open the door to their sin. He stands a little below her on the stoop, shirtless, sheened in sweat, and she sees that angry new burns rope his forearms. His fingers are covered in white tape, tattered with blood, and blood vessels have burst beneath his eyes, like doubled shiners. She opens the door.

"Jesus, Hiram. You get jumped by a she-gator on the way here?"

"Don't go getting jealous on me, woman." He winks and takes her hand. "Come on now, I got something I want to show you."

She resists.

"I'm getting old, Hiram. You know I like a little foreplay first."

"Not that, girl. Something else." He tugs gently on her hand. Once, twice. He's smiling big, like he rarely does. Like a little boy.

"Come on, come on."

She gives, letting him pull her across the yard, the ground soggy between her toes. They leave the triangular flood of the porch light, stepping into the outer night. The marsh lies spiked against the sky, whispering. He leads her down to the little mudbank where he always shores his boat. All but the pilot's seat has been covered in a gray wool blanket, rumpled and creased like a tiny range of mountains in the night. Like the Appalachians, far over the horizon.

"You better not have a damn body under there, Hiram."

"Faith, woman." He winks, whipping free the blanket with a flourish, like a magician wielding his cape. She looks at the thing.

"What is it?"

"Our future."

"It's a big dead fish, Hiram. It ain't the Altamaha-ha."

"No, it's better." He pulls a hookbill knife from his back pocket and makes a long cut down the belly, prying open the cavity with both hands. Annabelle peers into the great fish he's gutted, and Hiram slides his chin over her shoulder. His words tickle her ear.

"Black gold."

She steps back and looks at him.

"Is it legal?"

"Legal." He squints one eye. "Well."

"Well, what?"

"It used to be."

"Used to be? So did wife-beating, Hiram. And lynching people."

"This ain't the same."

"It ain't straight."

"Straight? The world's a crooked fucking place, honey. Crooked as the river I pulled this from. There ain't a straight line in all of creation, except what we put there. And what have them lines ever pointed to but money, honey. Every last one. I thought I was pulling something evil from that river, something I never had the strength to bring up. And it's given me this. It's a sign is what it is. See?"

"I see a big gutted fish, Hiram, that never hurt nobody. I see a man used to talk like those waters were something holy, something we ain't completely fucked up."

His eyes narrow. He is no longer the boy of a minute before.

"No, people been fucking up this river for ages. Cutting the trees, building their plants and mills. Sucking the tit of the river and shitting on its back. I loved it my whole goddamn life, treated it right. It's time it loved me back. Anybody deserves to pull something good from them waters, it's me. I paid in full, like you don't know. And this? I got just the men to help. It ain't straight, honey. It's full circle."

Annabelle steps back.

"I don't like it, Hiram. Whatever money you make from this, you think it's gonna win me somehow, but it ain't. It's too late. What we have is what it is and it's only ever gonna be that. You ought to know that by now. This? I don't like it at all."

His face hardened as she spoke. She could almost see her words glancing off his cheeks and forehead, the stubborn shield of his face.

"You think you don't like it, but you will."

"I won't, Hiram."

"All them fancies you grown up with gonna be eating out my hand. You watch."

"I won't like it."

"You will."

His eyes are far off, seeing the day she would.

"I won't, Hiram. *Ever*."

His eyes come racing back, so fast she feels struck. He points in her face, his ravaged finger trembling.

"You will, god damn you."

He settles the blanket back over his prize, tucking the corners down good. There is a gentleness to his movements, a care. He might be tucking in one of his boys, if that is something he does. She doesn't even know. He steps knee-deep into the water.

"Hiram. Don't go."

He says nothing, sliding the boat down the bank.

"I should of left him a long time ago," she says. "Barlow. When I could."

Now he looks at her, his teeth glowing in something like disgust.

"Yeah. You should of."

"You leave now, like this, you best not come back."

He goes rigid, waist-deep in the water, and her heart sings.

"Sorry, baby. I'm already gone."

He steps back, fading shadowlike against the greater dark, eyes twinkling like hard little coins. His boat slides from shore, whispering through the reeds, swallowed in the night. A little later, the cough of his outboard firing up. Annabelle's legs give out. She sinks on the bank, wailing into the crook of her arm.

60

Altamaha River, Day 5

Their eyes slowly make light of the place. There is a long metal trough running down one wall, irrigated by a garden hose, and a strange assortment of cutting blades dangling from a wire of hooks above. There are mini-fridges like students have in their dorms, three of them standing shoulder to shoulder against the back wall, and coils of rope and long nets strung along the walls. Bottled water and boxes of energy bars and noodles sit in pallets in one corner, and army-type cots line another wall, only two of them made. Two naked bulbs hang from the rafters, doused, and a braid of extension cords slithers along the floor and under the blanket draped over the back door. The place smells about like the gar in the woods.

"It is fish camp." The man's eye twitches over Lawton's pistol. "What it looks?"

Blood bubbles from one nostril as he speaks. He has a stiff beard, wide and gray. He is huge and blocky beneath his overalls, but gentle somehow, like an old bear. Lawton leans closer, sniffs.

"I can smell the shit on your breath, motherfucker."

"I tell you truth."

Lawton's eyes come up, checking the room.

"Where is it you're from?"

"Ukraine."

Lawton cocks his head toward the other man facedown in the dirt.

"Him, too?"

"My son."

"What y'all doing in this neck of the woods?"

"Fish."

"Yeah," says Lawton. "You keep saying that."

The boy on the floor shifts like he might rise. His father barks at him, the words foreign and harsh. The boy freezes.

"That's right," says Lawton. "Daddy knows best."

The big man hardens at this. He has his hands laced behind his head, the fingers huge and squared-off, the nails framed in grime. He is missing the last two fingers of one hand. He looks up at Lawton, and there is blood in his teeth.

"You think this is first time I have gun at me?"

"It ain't the first time that matters, big man. Only the last time counts."

"In Afghanistan I fought *dukhi*. More scary than you."

Lawton nods.

"The *dukhi*," he says. "The ghosts."

The man's eyes go wide, and Lawton's teeth show.

"Me and my boys fought some of those mountain ghosts our own selves." He leans close. "You'd be surprised how scary I am."

Hunter looks at the burlap that covers the back door. The wind tugs at the flap, winking light, and before he knows it he is moving that way, drawn.

"Be right back," he says. "Gonna check out back."

Lawton looks up.

"The hell you are. There could be somebody out there."

"There's only two cots made up."

"We can't assume, Hunter. Like Daddy used to say: Assumption is the mother of—"

Hunter is already through the flap. It's like stepping from a cave. A cold wind sways the trees, the sky gray and low over their upstretched branches. He can hear the rumble of thunder in the distance, like a train coming, and the muted holler of his name. Lawton can't leave two men sprawled on the floor, and Hunter can't help himself. The shark's tooth itches his neck. There is something he has to see.

More boxes of supplies are stacked against the back wall of the shed, including two fifty-five-gallon drums with FLAMMABLE stenciled on the side. The power cords are zip-tied into a bundle that disappears into the mouth of a ribbed plastic sheath skating down a path into the woods. He follows it. It is trampled flatter than the path from the river, double-cut from the passage of an ATV or side-by-side. Twenty yards down the trail, the ribbed tube snakes into a little clearing where two gasoline generators sit under a fly of camouflage netting. They are Hondas, whisper-quiet and expensive, chugging loyally under the trees. Beside them a half-horsepower, shallow-well water pump sits atop a tubular storage tank.

"Some fish camp."

He keeps on down the trail, the hand-ax held at the neck, the haft bobbing against the belly of his forearm. He knows he should not venture this far alone but cannot seem to stop himself. There is a scent curling through the trees, like the gar but stronger. The trail breaks from cover, running into the straight-cut canal of an old rice field, one of the many that grid the delta. Below the raised impoundment floats a steel-hulled skiff with a Yamaha outboard bolted to the transom, the cowling pulled off for maintenance. On the bank, a homebuilt trailer is hitched to a four-wheeler, the pair parked jackknife in a turnaround spot. To one side, he sees what he smelled: a giant pit of rot.

Sturgeon. Fish endangered, protected since before he can remember. At least thirty of them lie strewn in the grave, as if machine-gunned, some the size of torpedoes. No meanness to them, these bottom-feeders, their toothless mouths gaped in death, their white whiskers—barbels—curved like cartoon mustaches. Their bodies clad in prehistoric armor, in long chains of hardened scutes, ridged like mountains of bone.

A jerry can sits at the edge of the pit, a box of matches on top.

These fish who swam among the dinosaurs. They will burn.

He whirls to go, to tell his brother what he's found, and a boy is standing on the path where it breaks from the trees. The boy from Stud Horse Creek. His jaw is covered in a blond beard nearly white, his green eyes buzzing serpentlike in his skulled face. He wears a pair of brown duck-bib overalls, like a starved version of the big man in the shed, his arms wiry and blue-veined where they sprout from his chest. In his hands he holds a carbine, a semiautomatic hunting rifle with a banana clip, and Hunter feels his world change in an instant, warping and righting as if struck. It is suddenly colder, more finely wrought. He sees a lone redbird chittering on a limb, bright as blood. He feels the whisper of grass against his shins.

A smile rips the boy's face.

"This?" He nods toward the pit. "Very bad luck."

"Is that right?"

"*Da.* You see once?" The boy sucks his teeth. "You see *bolshe nichevo.* Nothing else."

Hunter thinks of the two researchers gone missing, the cats flung over high-voltage line. He thinks of the fishes in their mass grave, gape-mouthed, and his father's broken heart. Death smiling white-faced over it all, like the coldest sun. The shark tooth throbs.

"I'm not a regular fish."

A blue vein webs the boy's forehead.

"Not yet."

The boy's shoulder leaps against its skin, spidering with sinew, the gun swinging up, and Hunter springs into the space between them, ax in hand, the head sliding long from his arm like a tomahawk. The barrel shortens as it rises, turning into an evil little mouth, and Hunter has halved the distance when he realizes he isn't going to make it in time. He hurls the ax. It cartwheels through the air, iron-wheeled, and the boy ducks. The butt clatters off the tree behind him as Hunter lowers his head into the boy's chest, driving him against the tree.

Now they both have hold of the gun, yanking and shoving like schoolboys, and Hunter pulls his arms and rams the point of his knee between the boy's legs. His face greens but he doesn't let go of the rifle. Instead he lowers his chin and too late Hunter sees the crest of the boy's forehead driving for his face. His world explodes in light, blood searing through the channels of his nose, tears like acid down his cheeks. He wants to let go but doesn't, holding to the weapon like some holy staff that will part seas and swallow serpents whole. To hold it is everything. He steps backward in the muddy earth, twisting to wrench it free, and his knee cuts screaming from under him. Now he is on his back in the mud, empty-handed, and the barrel is coming for him, pointing him into the earth. His heart feels enormous, leaping against the cage of his ribs, and his hand finds the ax. He will cut through the white tree of this boy, down to the bloody stump. He will cut through a whole forest of these boys to reach his brother. The barrel closes over him, and he raises the ax.

A whip of flesh from the woods, flashing the space between them, and Hunter looks wide-eyed to see Uncle King crouched beside him like a fighter, a sea monster inked rampant on his shoulder blade. The boy wheels, aiming, and the old man slips to the outside of the barrel, his head tucked between his balled fists, and rises swiveling on his front foot, delivering a left hook to the point of the boy's jaw. The boy spins and jams the barrel into the ground at a diagonal, hunched over the butt like a man skewered, and Uncle King yells at Hunter over his shoulder.

"Go now, boy! Find your brother!"

He dances to the side, fists up, his head bobbing and ducking like a snake from a basket. The boy rises smiling before him, blood in his teeth, the rifle stuck in the mud at his feet.

"Go!" The old man's eyes are wild. "The kingdom is upon us!"

Hunter rises and runs hobbled and skipping for the shed, the trail zigzagging before him. He comes tearing through the burlap flap, heaving, and he is dizzied in the sudden dark, his vision flecked and starred. He sees only murky dark shapes, as in deep water.

"Lawton?"

A white palm swims out of the dark, silencing him. Dimly he sees the two men sitting along the wall, their hands zip-tied in their laps, and his brother leaning before them.

"You telling me a single big female could be worth as much as a car?"

"*Da*. Very nice car. BMW."

"Lawton," says Hunter. "We have to go."

His brother, rising out of the dark, does not seem to hear him.

"So my daddy stumbled onto your little racket up here? Threatened to out you and you killed him, that it?"

The old soldier looks stunned.

"*Kill* him? Mr. Loggins, I was his friend. I work here for him."

Lawton steps back as if punched.

"Bullshit you did."

The man raises his hands and points to the four corners of the shed.

"He build this house. Hiram's house. We worked for *him*."

The big poacher looks at the two brothers, his beard long and jagged, his face pleading.

"You look." He nods toward the central framing post. "You look."

Even Hunter bends toward the post. There, carved in a nearly circular knot of wood, is a down-struck trident. Mark of the Delta Devils, terrors of the Mekong, kings of the brown water.

"His sign," says the man. "Hiram's sign."

"No," says Lawton.

The big poacher holds his bound hands against his chest, as if praying.

"You tell police, you burn his name." He looks from one of them to the other, pleading. "You burn his *dream*."

Hunter watches his brother's shoulders sag. The faith hissing from his chest, the ghost he kept so close to his heart. Hunter grabs his arm.

"Lawton, we have to go. There's a third one out there and he had a gun."

The big poacher blanches.

"Yuri! He is back? You must go! He is *psikh*. Psycho. My brother's son. Someone get hurt!"

Lawton doesn't seem to hear. He looks at Hunter, wide-eyed.

"Caviar," he says.

———

When they step again into the light, the storm is close. Big clouds the color of bruise hang just over the trees, like an invasion, and the world has taken on a certain violet clarity, as if charged. The first streaks of rain slant down through the sky, striking the roof of the shed with hollow claps. They start down the path to the river.

"I checked the refrigerators after you left. They got it packed in tins like shoe polish. Caviar, man. Fucking sturgeon roe. They catch them with trammel nets, tow them up the canal to process."

Hunter puts a hand at the small of his brother's back to speed him up. They left the two men bound against the wall, but they aren't the ones he's worried about.

"Him," says Lawton. "Him of all men."

He shakes his head, cursing their old man under his breath. Raging. And Hunter knows why. Their father was a hard man, yes. Even cruel. But he was a man of the river, they thought. A keeper of it. Hunter, pushing his brother along, can feel the power quaking beneath his hand, and he knows Lawton can't hardly stand it. He is not made for this. His world is too sharp-cut and sure, its shape honed and set. And for a moment Hunter wishes he were that way, too. That hard and unbending, like something made with a knife. But he isn't, and he is afraid what his brother might do.

They reach the river and slide down the embankment to their boats. Lawton stands over Hunter's kayak in the spitting rain, looking down at the bag of ashes, addressing it.

"Guess you got what was coming." His leg whips back. "You dead son of bitch!"

His foot wheels and snaps, kicking the bag free of its rigging. It flies across the beach, lands in a dark dent of sand at water's edge. Hunter limps across and picks it up. He turns and holds it out to his brother.

"We've got to move. You're taking this on your boat."

Lawton looks away.

"I don't want to."

Hunter steps forward and rams the ashes into his brother's chest.

"I ain't asking."

Lawton cradles the bag against his breast.

"Those French you were talking about. What happened to them?"

"What do you think?"

61

Fort Caroline, September 1565

Le Moyne looks out upon the great bend of river where his monster might live, the belly of water rain-cratered and capping in the wind, and he prays and prays for his brothers at sea. The great cypress trees along the banks are swirling and crashing against one another, like an ocean themselves, and a dark line of siege towers threatens the coast, storm clouds dropping wet panes of glass that shimmer and crack with jags of light. Le Moyne prays to God and to the river itself. He prays to the beasts that swim in the slumberous peace of the depths, hardly cognizant of the soundings and wreckage of the upper world. He prays for salvation.

Laudonnière was right: *un ouragan* is upon them.

A hurricane.

A week ago, in the wake of the fleet's departure, the sky darkened, like night come early, and the rain began to fall. It has not let up. Day and night it lashes them, slung sideways by torrents of wind. Huts blow down. Thatch roofs tumble away in the gale. The fort turns to slop, knee-deep, and men huddle shivering in their blankets. They totter about like lepers, back-bent with faces cloaked. A horse slips and breaks a leg, drowning in the muck. They eat it. Rain gushes down even the chimneys, snuffing any effort at warmth. The river rises maddened before them, foaming between its banks, and the sun remains unseen. Le Moyne must wonder if a second flood is upon them, if they have triggered the wrath of God in this new land. Or perhaps it is the sun-god against them, turning his white eye blind to their peril, letting the violence of the earth run unchecked.

There are no more than 150 people left at the fort. They are the sick and wounded, the servants and couriers, the men who cannot even load an arquebus, and they are the women and children, too. Ribault has left behind but twenty good men who can fight. Le Moyne is on the wall day and night. There are hardly enough men to rotate the watch.

Dawn of the eleventh day, and no one has been seen in the lands about the fort. The word comes down the line: the officer of the guard has taken pity. They are to retire to their quarters for three hours' rest. Le Moyne comes down from where he was praying on the wall. He staggers gratefully to his hut, setting his arquebus against the inside of the door, rolling himself clothed and booted into his hammock. He closes his eyes, listening to the rain drum on the thatches.

In his dream they break like a river from the trees, iron-scaled, their breastplates clattering over their hearts, their crested helmets cutting the air like so many fins. Their faces are long and dark, daggered by black spade beards, their eyes white and round with hate. They carry swords and spades and poleaxes, the edges honed bright, and they spread as they come, overrunning the meager defenses on the fort's landward side, scattering the white flesh of its inhabitants like game. The people scream as they are cut down, churned under the armored flood.

Le Moyne's eyes snap open, awake, and then he is out of his hammock, shooting between two conquistadors who stand very real at the threshold of his hut. He passes between them untouched, as if he were for a moment but the dream of himself, and it's like they never see him. Like a spirit passing. All around him now is the wreckage of bodies, bright-slaughtered against the black earth, and the mother-wails of the stricken, the undead, and he knows this is no dream. Limbs lie strewn in the mud, fingers and toes yet twitching, and severed heads stare open-mouthed in lasting wonder. There the headless torso of a child, chest-down, like a broken doll in the muck.

He runs stiff-legged for the nearest embrasure, where he must scramble over the broken bodies of men who rushed to the wall, a mound of them oozed and tangled beneath his boots. He steps on their faces, their necks and backs, climbing through the notch and leaping into the moat on the other side. Then he is out of it, black-slopped, scurrying across the open ground and into the woods.

"Let us wait until morning," says one of the men. "Surely the fury of the Spanish will abate. Then we will surrender ourselves to their mercy."

"Mercy?" says one of the others. "Do they know the word? We would be better off fleeing into the wilds, taking up with the savages until God shows us some path."

They are huddled in a small clearing in the woods, Le Moyne and four others who have escaped the fort. They are quivering from cold and fear, clutching themselves.

"There is another way," says Le Moyne. "We make for the coast and find one of the small ships used to offload the provisions from France."

The men shake their heads.

"It is too far, Le Moyne."

"I know these paths. I can guide us."

"Suppose we cannot find one of the boats?"

Le Moyne looks from one of them to the next.

"We must have faith."

Again they shake their heads.

"Go chase your boats, Le Moyne. I would rather try my luck with the savages."

The rest of them nod in agreement.

They each clasp arms with Le Moyne, bidding him farewell, and then they are gone. Le Moyne stands a long minute beneath the dripping woods, alone, and then he turns for the sea.

"Le Moyne, up here!"

It is Grandchemin, the tailor, wedged in the crook of a tree, wearing only his nightshirt. He glances at the woods about him, then slides down the trunk, his toes probing the ground.

"Have you seen any others?"

Le Moyne nods.

"Four. An hour ago."

"Where are they now?"

Le Moyne shakes his head.

"They decided to try their luck with the savages."

"And you?"

"I'm trying for the coast. I could not convince them to come."

Grandchemin looks this way, that way, as if a Spaniard might leap from a bush, poleax in hand. His Adam's apple quivers in his throat.

"By God, you've convinced me."

They are all day on trails known only by the deer and the Indians and Le Moyne in his afternoon walks with sketchbook and arquebus. Faint corridors through the forest, deserted now, as if some plague has emptied the land. The trees crash overhead, their branches tangling. The earth sucks at their feet. They cross risen creeks that tumble and swirl through the sodden earth, smashing against their thighs. The rain spats their faces and eyes, and they trudge with their hands held before them, trying not to trip on cypress roots thrust like spikes from the ground. The leaves seem only to taunt them, so bright and slick, like little shields bouncing in the rain.

They come finally to the land's edge. The expanse of salt marsh lies before them, brown-gold under an iron sky. The day is darkening, the sun descending unseen. Night is moving in from the sea, shooting dark rifts between the clouds. They are miles yet from the green humps of the seaward islands where the boats might be at anchor.

Grandchemin holds his elbows in his hands, as if to sheathe their bony points. He looks back at the woods out of which they came.

"What now?"

In answer, Le Moyne steps down into the marsh, his boots swallowed up to the knee. They fight on through the falling dark, thrashing through the chin-high reeds, jerking their feet in and out of the muck. Again and again they fall, leaving their blood in the grass, and they have not even considered the tide. It rises belly-deep in the night, and cold, and they have no rest. They can but kneel in the flooded plain of grasses, the tide lapping at their throats and chins, the rain beating down on their heads. Two strange polyps on the water, ghost-white, calling out to their god. Dawn breaks colorless over the land, and they see no boats.

"Le Moyne, I cannot go on."

Grandchemin is standing knee-deep in the water now. His nightshirt clings to him like a second skin, the hair-patches at his chest and nethers darkly evident through the soiled cloth. His face is nicked red, bleeding. His Adam's apple like something gone rotten on the vine.

"You can, Grandchemin, and you will."

"Let us go back and surrender. We are men of value, Le Moyne. We have skills. Surely they will take us in."

"They will kill us, man, like all the others."

Grandchemin looks down at himself.

"Would it not be a better death than this?"

They squat in a thicket, watching the fort. Spanish sentinels are visible on the walls, their polished helmets ridged like the skulls of brutes. Now and again cries of laughter lift from the place. They sound black-throated to Le Moyne. Wicked.

"I pray you, man, do not go. God will open some path for us yet."

Grandchemin shakes his head, his eyes fixed upon the fort.

"I have made my decision. If I am treated kindly, you may follow."

"We will go together."

"No, man. This is my path to walk. I will not have your fate tied to my own." He turns to Le Moyne. "Farewell, my friend."

They embrace.

"*Je vous recommande à Dieu*," says Le Moyne. I commend you to God.

The old seamster begins threading his way out of the woods, and Le Moyne creeps up to his bluff overlooking the fort, where he used to sketch and paint. Grandchemin emerges from the trees, hook-nosed and bony as a crane, hobbling in his once-white nightclothes across the open ground. The men upon the wall spot him, calling to others below. The gates open and out steps a party of three armored men, their bodies clanging as they stride to receive him, their palms set casually on the pommels of their swords. Heads appear all along the wall behind them, watching.

Grandchemin falls upon his knees as they near, his arms flung wide, the oversized nightshirt hanging upon his thin-whittled frame like the sail of a ravaged ship. The sleeves catch the wind, fluttering, and his long button-sewing fingers are spread wide, as if he would embrace these men who now encircle him.

"*Merci*," he beseeches.

A metallic flash, quick as thought, and his right arm lies severed on the earth, writhing like a giant worm. He screams, the stump spurting red into the grayed-over world, and a second sword flashes, taking his remaining arm. He falls upon the ground, his armless trunk flopping in a ragged aura of blood, and the men along the walls roar with pleasure. The third soldier sweeps his sword and takes the man's head. They bend and quarter him, then raise the bloody fragments of his body upon the tips of their steel.

All along the wall, cheers and applause.

62

Thunder cracks like a shot, like the sky has broken, and the rain comes hissing down in angry streaks. They are pulling into the current, the river quickened with storm, and Hunter is leading them now. Something is driving him, like fear but stronger, surer, spreading through his whole body. It is something he knows. That they need to distance themselves. That they are in danger. That Lawton is.

He doesn't have Lawton's strength, his muscle, but he is light and fast in a boat. His keel cuts cleanly through the roughened current, and he pushes hard, setting pace. He looks back at Lawton, and his brother is digging, his shoulders balled beneath his shirt, his beard dark and pointed beneath his chin. A flash of lightning, the dimmed world made white, and Hunter thinks he sees tears streaking his brother's face. Maybe the rain.

His shoulders are burning, his lungs, his breath coming ragged through an open jaw. His heart booms inside him like an alarm. He uses the paddle like he would an ax, driving the blade flat and deep with every stroke, his cadence machinelike. Relentless. This engine that runs on pain. He knows he has to stay ahead of Lawton. He has to lead them now. Somehow he knows. His brother will follow if led.

They are less than a mile downriver when he first hears the engine, the high wail of an unmuffled outboard. It is coming from upriver, the way they've come. He looks back. Nothing, not yet. It's still in the creeks that feed the river. He looks around. The banks are dense, overgrown, guarded by half-submerged trees rocking in the current. He knows they are a good five miles from the nearest marina, and the town of Darien is nearly as far. Unless—

He looks back at Lawton.

"Rifle Cut."

A shortcut, a narrow canal straight-cut by slaves in the 1820s for boats bringing timber, tobacco, turpentine, into the Darien docks. Overgrown now—only paddlers negotiate it.

Lawton shakes his head.

"We still have to scatter his ashes."

"We're taking the cut," says Hunter.

The storm worsens, the river crumpling in dark swales and whitened caps. The world gone twilight, strange and dim, then exploding in absolute nakedness, too bright to see. The wail of the outboard flutters in and out of their hearing, closer and farther as it negotiates the serpentine kinks of the creeks. But getting ever louder. Gaining.

They enter the cut. A strange thing, this man-made geometry in a world of spiraling creeks and black mud, where wildness rules. A brutal thing. Black men sunk to the knees, the waist, hacking away with sharp implements. A world cut straight, at the behest of distant masters.

They can hear the wail of the boat rising behind them, nearing.

They paddle harder, deeper into the canal. Their mouths are open, their shoulders burning. Digging, digging. Trying to outrun what's coming.

Too late.

The wail peaks, and they can only turn to watch it come, watch the steel bow burst into the canal, fill it completely, a bullet in the throat of a gun. No way out.

It doesn't. The skiff flashes past the mouth of the canal, never slowing, the men aboard staring straight ahead. Hunter looks at his brother, his mouth open.

"They didn't see us."

Thunder cracks overhead and Lawton straightens, looking up, like someone has called his name. When he looks down again, his eyes are the wildest blue.

"Blast caps. I saw blast caps in the shed."

"What?"

Lawton is already wheeling his boat in the canal. His face a grimace, little time to explain.

"It ain't us they're after. The thunder, it's *cover*."

He digs his paddle deep into the current, nearly vertical, his back spreading like a shield. The blade flashes this side, that side, his boat making a zigged white wake, accelerating.

"Goddamn them," says Lawton. "God *damn* them."

Hunter scrambles to turn his boat around, to keep up.

"Lawton!" he cries. "Lawton!"

Hunter can't catch him. His arms and shoulders are screaming, his lungs searing. His heart hammering. One mile, two. The pain howling through him, saying, *I am here I am here I am here*, and Hunter going outside of himself, his mind fixed only on his brother. And still he cannot catch him. Lawton is slamming his paddle into the waves, ripping speed from the water, his boat slithering with power. Not leading them now, no. Fleeing. Outrunning the little brother who would only slow him, who would try and stop him.

Hunter is ten yards behind when they shoot into the broad bend of river, where it carves hard against a wedge of high ground, and the poachers' skiff chugs midstream in the current, high over the ninety-foot sturgeon hole said to lie like a mineshaft in the riverbed, the great fishes stacked like cordwood in the darkness.

The white-bearded boy is standing in the bow of the boat, the carbine strapped over his shoulder, one eye purpled in bruise. He is holding a stick of something. He brings a thin flame to it, and it begins sparkling in his hand. A fuse. He smiles, sharp tongues of light licking his face. The sky flares, the trees along the bank whitening like a wall, a ghost fortress rearing pale and huge from the earth, and Hunter knows this is the place where hundreds died.

Where hundreds will.

Lawton unzips his vest, drawing the pistol as if from his breast. He cups it close with both hands, like a dark little bird, then pushes it straight toward his target. Hunter thinks of the ravaged fish in the pit, soon to burn, and an old man perhaps among them, his mouth gaped to the sky. He thinks of saying nothing.

"No!" he cries.

The boy looks up, startled, and sees the gun.

The sky crashes in thunder and light, and it sounds like a shot.

The boy drops the dynamite.

It bounces on the gunwale, and Hunter sees what will happen before it does: the stick tumbling over the side, the waterproof fuse hissing into the depths. The muffled thunder of the blast, the white geyser of spray. The corpses drifting to the surface, slowly, like so many souls. The river blistered with their white bellies, dozens of them, giants black-mouthed and round-eyed. Awestruck. A kingdom raptured, risen in night. The great myth of the river rising among them, a dark monster coiled and kinked like a diseased organ. Inanimate now. A creature made hoax, composed solely of retreads and twine. Returned only to this.

Hunter sees it all happen.

But it doesn't.

The dynamite twirls in the air, sparkling.

It bounces back into the boat.

The boy lurches after it; so do the others. They struggle and scream on their hands and knees, clawing and kicking, fighting like dogs in a pit.

Too late.

The hull channels the blast. It blows straight up, a bulb of white light that lifts them ragged over the water, jointless and piecemeal, like broken dolls. The wreckage floats down, gently almost, and the bodies crash.

Quiet, all sound stolen from the air. The hull smolders, a blackened shell canted strangely on the water, surrounded by debris of every kind. Metal and netting and meat. A slick of oil has caught fire. It burns low on the water, a twist of smoke. Hunter looks at Lawton. He is still holding the gun. Staring at the wreckage. His eyes wide now, and soft.

Hunter swallows, licks his lips.

"You didn't—you didn't shoot, did you?"

Lawton blinks, as if coming awake. He leans over the water and spits. A thick little island of white. He looks up again, and the softness is gone from his eyes. They are hard, hard as Hunter has ever seen them.

"Blast-fishing accident," he says. "Happens all the time."

63

New France, September 1565

Three of them, he sees, reeling like a single drunk beast through the woods. Survivors. They crash through brambles and thickets, nearly naked, their bodies torn ragged and bloody by the forest's jags. He steps out of the bush where he has been hiding, waiting to see if they are Spanish or French.

"Le Moyne!"

It is a man called La Crete, of Rouen, and a Belgian Le Moyne doesn't know. Staggering between the two of them, her arms hooked in theirs, is Laudonnière's chambermaid, so long rumored to be overzealous in service of her master. She wears a red wound on her breast, the mark of a Spanish sword, but her eyes are fierce, undefeated. Le Moyne feels a sting for having thought ill of her in the past.

They all of them embrace, brother creatures in an alien world. Le Moyne, so cold and alone, feels his heart flare like a blown ember in his chest.

"Where are you headed?"

"The seashore."

"Come," he says. "I know a path."

They are perhaps a mile farther along when they come across Laudonnière himself, their old commander, dressed yet in his ragged red doublet. He is tending to a man with a sword-gash in his neck. They say they escaped through a breach in the wall when the Spaniards entangled themselves in the ropes of the courtyard tent, bringing it down upon themselves like a great bedsheet, their pikes piercing the fabric like mad little quills. Laudonnière is knotting a stocking about the wounded man's neck. Le Moyne squats down beside him.

"Can you walk?" he asks.

"*Oui. Toute la journée.*" All day.

Le Moyne smiles and claps the man on the shoulder.

"Good," he says. "You will have to."

They are fifteen by the time they reach the marshlands, picking up other survivors along the way. The sky is low, dark-bellied, spitting rain. The golden plain of reeds spreads before them like a meadow.

"It doesn't look so bad," says Laudonnière.

Le Moyne reaches out, letting the first line of swordlike reeds tickle his palm.

"How it looks is not the problem, I'm afraid."

They are all night slogging through the wetlands, the tide running up to their navels, their wounds stinging from the salt. The edges of the grasses burn against their skin, and they leave a trampled corridor of bent and bloodied reeds in their wake. Surely, thinks Le Moyne, unknowing men would think it the work of some crazed creature of the forest, gut-shot, dragging itself to the sea to die.

He is colder and hungrier with every step, his feet numb, so sogged he fears them inseparable now from the cured skin of his boots. In the night his thoughts turn again and again to thin-limbed Grandchemin, hacked to pieces for the amusement of those upon the wall. A gentle man, with no drop of meanness in his marrow. And again and again Le Moyne envisions his monster rising vengeful from the darkness, curling high over the fort, its tail cracking like the whip of God. He envisions it smiting the Spanish barbarians for their sins, lashing them from the walls, red-flooding the river for leagues. The animals stricken before they can take root in the land.

But this is fantasy, he knows. Such violence will be the task of men.

Dawn breaks a steely gray before them, dark silhouettes floundering against the impending light. They stumble upon another group of survivors, a flock of them squatting wrecked and motley in the reeds. Roars go up on both sides. They embrace, their bodies quivering with cold and joy. An hour later they find a small island in the marsh, no more than a grove of pines, and two of their band shimmy up into the trees. They begin to shout and swing their arms from the upper reaches, their cheeks flushed with color as they descend.

"There is a ship!"

"It is anchored at the river's mouth!"

They cross two wide creeks that day, using long poles to which they cling two or three a side, thrashing to keep their heads above water. Miraculously, no one is lost. They are another long night in the half-drowned reeds, the rain beating down on their heads, and when the wind cuts hard across the shelterless plain they hook themselves arm in arm so as not to be driven down into the muck. Their tattered vestments snap in the gusts, blown sideways, and Le Moyne holds the maidservant by her wrists, looking away as she squats to relieve herself in the wind-bent reeds.

In the morning they can see a ship mast in the distance, a dark cruciform planted at the river's mouth, and by noon they can see the ship itself rocking on the inshore swells. They cross another wide river, again using poles cut by a carpenter of their company, and on the far bank they stagger on through the reeds, veering drunkenly, their legs buckling now and again so that men fall to kneeling as if so inspired. Le Moyne finds himself at the head of this procession, pushed on by those behind. They are like a current at his back. He cannot collapse, he knows, or they would follow him down. They are of a will now, their bodies wrecked and failing, a single long train of flesh delivering itself to the sea.

Sometime later he trips, lurching forward through the reeds, and splashes headfirst into a wide arm of water. He thrashes in the darkness, upturned, trying to right himself, until strong hands hook him beneath the arms. He is lifted choking from the water and hauled over the side of an open boat, landed like something caught on a line. Men pound his back, slapping the water from his lungs. He blinks the salt from his eyes, staring up in wonder.

"Christ," he says softly.

The sailors above him smile.

"*Pas encore*," they say.

Not yet.

They sit huddled on the main deck of the *Levrier*, the ship they saw anchored at the river's mouth. They are cloaked in the crew's own shirts, passing a flagon of brandy from one to another. Small boats are still coming in, picking up other survivors from the marshes. The sky is beginning to darken, the world deepening from gray to blue. Le Moyne has a sip of the brandy, letting it burn down his throat, then hands it along. He stands and walks to the rear of the ship, stepping up onto the quarterdeck at the stern. He looks west, inland. There in the distance he can see the dark hulk of the fort, set amid the wilds like a giant foundered ark. In two days they will sail for France. He, Jacques Le Moyne de Morgue, has come across oceans and through storms and famine and war. A flower painter. He has come to record the savage beasts that reside at the reaches of the earth, those perhaps of long teeth and armored scales, and found numbered among them the gods and kings of men. He looks a last time upon the ridged flesh of the water, waiting for something newly awful to rise from its belly. He sees nothing save the river itself, and his own reflection fluttering upon it.

A ghost.

He opens his hand. In it sits the tongue stone. It seems dulled from the wear of his pocket, the rub of his thumb. The edges slightly rounded, like a heart hewn from rock. He hurls it far across the water, watching it plop back into the river. Perhaps the tide will drive it upstream, home. For another hand or foot to find.

He leaves the rail, stepping down again onto the main deck, into the company of men.

64

Altamaha River, Day 5

The interstate bridge rises in the distance, a lithic gray hulk presiding over the swamp. It wheels with jeweled lights, red and yellow and white. The drivers pass high over the land, dazed by the hum of their machines, the sanctums of metal and glass that protect them from the wastes of swamp, the nameless creeks and rivers and shoals. The history they will never know.

Hunter looks back a last time. The fire has burned itself out, and the skiff sits awkwardly on the water, tiny now, haloed in wreckage. Someone will find it, eventually, and the sheriffs will be called out. They will fish in the bodies, the limbs and boots tangled in the reeds, and they will tow away the foundering skiff. It will be filed an accident. They will never know of the kayaks that passed the tragedy—their hulls leave no tracks. The mouths that could speak will not. It will be years before anyone finds the shed, if they ever do. The hogs will discover it first, rooting through the packaged food, shitting plastic wrappers through the woods. Creeper vines will climb the walls, and the weather-treated boards will warp, the tar paper curling with age. Birds will brain themselves against the window glass. Floods will come and go, the walls tattooed with waterlines. Perhaps one will sweep the place away.

Hunter, if he is lucky, will grow old and gray, a stone tooth hanging from his neck, grasped in some golden instant by the tiny hand of a babe. The trees will keep watch along the bluff, tall and stoic as a wall. The sturgeon will hover fat as cannon in the river dark. Gentle as sheep.

Safe.

The river turns. The bridge rises slowly against the sky, like a gateway of some kind, and soon they are sliding beneath its shadow, listening to the rhythmic pounding of traffic on the joints. Hunter swallows.

"That one in the bow," he says. "With the rifle. I think he might of got Uncle King back at the camp."

Lawton's shoulders rise, fall.

"I thought the old man might show."

"He saved me," says Hunter. "Twice."

Lawton nods. There is a heaviness emanating from him. A coldness, as from stone.

"Probably he saved us both."

Hunter feels the urge to reach out, to touch his brother on the shoulder or arm. To bring warmth back into him. Blood. He clears his throat.

"They got what was coming," he says. "Them in the boat."

Lawton is silent a long time.

"Sure they did."

Miles on they pass beneath the old coastal highway, silent at this hour, and a marina swings into view, lit like a floating city. A motley flotilla of cabin cruisers and pontoon boats, fishing skiffs, speedboats raked low on the water. A line of identical twenty-eight-foot offshore boats, battleship-gray with badges emblazoned on the hulls. The restaurant at Mudcat Charlie's presides over the docks, a haven of college football and horse racing and everything fried. The rain has quit, the sky still bruised and quaking. The sun is nearly down. The restaurant windows burn gold over the boats. People laugh silently behind the glass, sipping sweet tea with crumbled ice.

Hunter thinks of his father speeding along this water in the last light of day, his chest bare, his chin high. A man certain of his dominion. Then a sturgeon lifts like a god from the river, armored and sun-blazed, and Hunter wonders if anger clutches the old man's heart in that final instant, a bloody fist shattered at last against the world. Or does he stare slack-jawed at the creature instead, this ancient fish that stands with the cypress and the serpent and the river of old, and is his heart full of wonder?

Hunter closes his eyes, opens them.

The marina slides past. They paddle on through a small cut, following the river until it widens, opening its mouth toward the sea. Lawton removes the dry bag from his boat's rigging and sets it on the deck in front of him. He opens the top and looks at Hunter, who nods. Lawton pours the contents over the side, their once-father dusting the current like a fall of dirty snow. Hunter watches the ashes darken on top, then cloud palely beneath the surface, curling seaward like spirit or smoke. The same path the sturgeon will take in the fall of the year, an unseen fleet of them lumbering blindly, together, into the ocean's deep. They will return in the spring, like they always do. They know. Just as Hunter does, seeing the pale mask of his brother's face, set now like a shield of bone. He knows he will never be back.

They turn their boats homeward, parallel, brothers against the falling dark.

Epilogue

The old man stands tall upon his boat in the failing light, the barb of his harpoon catching the last of the sun. The wound in his side blazes like a cardinal. Below him the river moves, alive, a great form sliding below the surface, ridged like the river itself. The creature he has hunted so long, passing like the shadow of God beneath his feet. He will make it to bleed. He raises his weapon yet higher, poised in power over the water, and he does not hurtle it into the river's heart. He sits, slowly, and lays the weapon across his lap. He closes his eyes, listening to the flood of the river against its banks, waiting for the world that comes.

✎ AUTHOR'S NOTE ✎

The events at Fort Caroline—the first European fort in what would become the United States—are touched by mystery, gleaned as they are from the written narratives of those here involved, the facts of which are perplexing, even contradictory. The exact location remains unknown. For years, it was thought to have been on the banks of the St. Johns River in Florida. Now many scholars believe the fort was located on the Altamaha. Though I have endeavored to stay true to historical record when possible, I have taken much license, making the historical figures and settings my own. I would be remiss not to mention some of the contemporary sources and modern scholars who have aided me in this process: Jacques Le Moyne de Morgue, *Narrative of Le Moyne* (J. R. Osgood and Co., 1875); René Laudonnière, *Three Voyages* (The University of Alabama Press, 2001); Charles E. Bennett, *Laudonnière & Fort Caroline: History and Documents* (The University of Alabama Press, 2001); Miles Harvey, *Painter in a Savage Land: The Strange Saga of the First European Artist in North America* (Random House, 2001). This last book I highly recommend for readers who would like to learn more about the French experience at Fort Caroline. I am greatly indebted to Scott Juall, Ph.D., who has worked extensively on the French voyages here described, and who allowed me to lean on his expertise in this area, as well as the language of the period.

❦ ACKNOWLEDGMENTS ❦

To my parents, who always believed I could walk the paths I chose, even when it must have scared the hell out of them, and who have been there to listen during the darker hours of this journey. God does not make better parents.

To Heather, big sister, who is hero and mentor, noble and strong, unafraid of the true word or hard road. We are there for each other, always, and it is one of the greatest blessings in my life. And to Rick, who believed in a young English major—thank you, brother.

To Christopher Rhodes, who is not only the best agent in the whole world, but a fine man and an incredible friend.

To Whit Dawson and Ben Galland, who are my brothers, deeper than any blood. You have been my anchors, my rocks, and taught me so much. I love you both. Here's to many more "research trips" on the river.

To Jason Frye, who has always blessed me with a bent ear and steady editorial hand. I am so grateful for you. You writers, I cannot recommend Jason's editing enough. Run to him, now.

To Majsan Böstrom, who believed in this story early, with faith and fire—who just seemed to know. Thank you. I'm very lucky the world made us friends.

To George Witte and Sara Thwaite and Jessica Lawrence of St. Martin's Press, who are the stuff of dreams for a young writer—brilliant and giving and wise, with big muscle and bigger hearts. Thank you for your faith in me. I'm honored, every day, to work with you, and I hope to do you proud.

To Wiley Cash, whose advice and wisdom have been invaluable. Rarely do your heroes turn out to be such fine people. I'm speechless with gratitude. Just . . . thank you. A thousand times.

To Peter Maguire, who has been so generous in sharing his experiences, his wisdom, and his kitchen. You took me seriously long before there was any reason to, and I will always be grateful for that.

To Scott Juall, Ph.D., for lending his overwhelming expertise on the subject of Fort Caroline, sixteenth-century French, and the most creative of French insults. Truly, it felt something like destiny when we connected, and I am so incredibly grateful. It has been an honor and a pleasure, my friend.

To Brad Williams, formerly of the Georgia Department of Natural Resources, for the gift of your stories, and to Howell Boone, captain of *Miss Bertha*, for the gift of yours. It is people like you, willing to give a young writer your time and words, who make a book like this possible.

To Chelsea Hopkins and Tara Muenz, for your kindness and cartographic assistance, and to the Georgia Department of Natural Resources and Georgia Environmental Protection Division for providing the underlying maps of the river—and everything else you do. Thank you.

To Kristen and Waylon, I have not forgotten your faith. Though you are far, I thump my heart now and again, thanking the universe for the influence you had on my life. I am a better man for it.

To Emily Smith and Beth Staples, who have been so welcoming and kind with me—I'm honored to call you my friends.

To Steph Post and Leah Angstman and Ashley Warlick, for your unbelievable kindness and support over the years. I can't thank you enough. And to my soul-brother, Kent Wascom, and his wife, Alise—I wanted to write books so I could know people like you.

To everyone at the Southern Independent Booksellers Alliance, and all the indie booksellers across the nation whom I've had the honor and pleasure of meeting—thank you, all of you, for putting books and readers together, and making dreams like mine a reality.

1. The Altamaha River, also known as Georgia's "Little Amazon," plays as an important role as the setting of the book. What do you think the river represents to the two brothers, Hunter and Lawton?

2. In the first chapter, Hunter and Lawton paddle beneath two boys sitting on the Altamaha Bridge, playing hooky. Each brother reacts differently to the boys—how are their reactions indicative of their different characters and personalities?

3. The novel is full of the illustrations of Jacques Le Moyne, the first European artist to capture the flora and fauna of the New World. How do these illustrations shape the reader's sense of Le Moyne as a man, as well as the French culture he represents?

4. Uncle King is one of the more mysterious characters in the novel. What significance might his name hold? (Hint: check the Hebrew word for "uncle.")

5. Jacques Le Moyne finds a glossopetra, or tongue stone, in the shallows of the river. How is this talisman illustrative of certain themes of the novel?

6. Hunter wears the tooth of a prehistoric shark— Megalodon—around his neck. How might this pendant relate to Le Moyne's tongue stone?

7. The search for a legendary river monster, Altamaha-ha, is central to the novel. Why do you think humans are so fascinated by cryptids—creatures of cryptozoology? What does it say about the nature of faith, myth, and story?

8. Do you believe the Altamaha-ha "exists"?

St. Martin's Griffin

9. Hunter and Lawton's father, Hiram Loggins, is engaged in an affair with Annabelle Mackintosh for most of his adult life. Beyond physical and romantic companionship, what do the two represent to each other?

10. Hiram Loggins is an abusive father. How does this shape each of his sons in different ways?

11. Tattoos are an important motif throughout the book. Explain how they help define certain characters—Hiram, Lawton, Uncle King, Saturiwa—and what symbolic meanings they might hold.

12. How might the world be different if the French foothold at Fort Caroline had survived? If the French Huguenots, as portrayed in the novel, had become a larger cultural influence in this part of the New World?

13. Le Moyne arrives in the New World as a conservative flower painter. How does he evolve throughout the novel? How is he a different man by the time he reaches the deck of the *Levrier*, the ship that will sail him home to France?

14. The novel is composed of alternating story lines, both contemporary and historical. How do these story lines echo and speak to each other? How does the Altamaha River help both to link and differentiate the experiences of the French colonists and modern Americans?

15. There is a varying level of friction between brothers Hunter and Lawton throughout the book. What do you believe are the roots of this tension? How does the altercation on Lewis Island, as well as the later discovery of their father's poaching business, help to redefine and recalibrate the brothers' relationship?